For my friend F. H.

Kevin

M. J. Mollenhour

ARCTURUS

A Jack McDonald Novel
About Soldiers, Spies, Pirates, and Terrorists with
Romantic and Historical Twists

Learn more at:
www.MJMollenhour.com

For information about special discounts for bulk purchases, please contact Talavera Media at: bulkpurchase@talaveramedia.com

First Edition

ISBN 13: 978-0-9799672-0-7
ISBN 10: 0-9799672-0-1
Library of Congress Control Number: 2007907331

Layout by J. L. Saloff, Saloff Enterprises
Cover design by Cory Mollenhour, art@talaveramedia.com
Author photograph by Kelly Rogers Photography

Fonts: Bell MT, Geometric 231 BT, Trajan Pro

Printed in the United States of America on acid free paper.

1.02

ACKNOWLEDGMENTS

Reader, you might find these "thank you notes" interesting.

Thanks to the men who are the unsung, never-taught-in-schools, Congressional Medal of Honor winners Jack McDonald talks about. You might review their stories at: www.themedal.com.

Thanks to Captain (in 1974, anyway) Mike Byington, commanding Charlie Company, 1st Battalion of the 506th Infantry, honored here by promoting young Jack to Captain and making him the CO. Thanks for putting up with me as a young Platoon Leader. Likewise, thanks to another fine East Tennessean, General _____. You have had an interesting 35 year career. You might recognize yourself as the inspiration for General Ortega.

Linda, thank you for setting me up with Tom Bird's course. Otherwise, I wouldn't even yet be finished with Arcturus. Dustin, thanks for your excitement over the novel finally making it to print. Jordan, thanks for encouraging dreams and success. Cory—great graphics, man. Lane, thanks for your tips on how to get past "writer's block" and for never missing an opportunity to promote the book. John Dupree and James Wagner, thanks for advice on the plot and the operation of the M-1. Kevin, that was great detail on the Coast Guard.

For specific, contemporary, weapon-handling techniques and colorful inspiration, thanks to Pat Rogers of EAG Tactical, www.EAGTactical.com and David Blinder of Personal Defense Training, Inc., www.PersonalDefenseTraining.com. These guys are great trainers and shooters, as well as serious, committed, patriotic Americans.

Lastly, thanks for the inspiration you are, my unnamed, anonymous Iranian friends, living now under the oppression of your government. May The Lord protect and keep you from the Sayadar until we meet again.

This book is dedicated to
the memory of Martin Burnham,
deceased June 7, 2002
and to the soldiers who fought to free him
and his wife, Gracia,
from the Islamic terrorists who kidnapped them.

Aboard the Arcturus
Atlantic Ocean, 125 miles northeast
of Miami, Florida
Approaching the Abacos chain,
in the Bahamas' "Out Islands,"
Early July 2007

Jack slid his hand onto the back-strap of the .45 automatic holstered on his belt, barely concealed underneath his lightweight, buttonup, "I'm on vacation" shirt. He formed his fingers into the precise grip Jack had practiced so many times. The cold, serrated-metal friend filled his hand and answered back. Reassured, Jack stretched over the rail again.

Waves lapped against the *Arcturus*, beating out a certain rhythm, like the thrumming, chugging of an old, reliable engine. Jack eyed the placid Atlantic below suspiciously. Sure, it would grace with its fresh, quickening, salt smell, cooling spray, stunning beauty and pleasures, bestowed on the wicked and the good alike, regardless of their intent—but it might just destroy either, mindlessly, in a heartbeat. *Lap!*

Lapped, Jack said in his thoughts. This ocean *laps* at boats and men. Yet, here he sailed, as so many before, taking his chances with this paradoxically, simultaneously, alien-natural power.

One or two laps from you too hard and people vanish! Jack accused. Been going on for centuries: that hungry ocean and those luckless people, sucked down in a heartbeat, with the ocean closing over them and lapping, lapping, lapping not even leaving a hole or a mark. Vanished.

As if to affirm Jack's accusation, the Atlantic impertinently licked again at the boat, smacking the hull to scorn it like a splinter in its finger and warning over and over, endlessly, that the sea might munch the *Arcturus* anytime it pleased.

Simple. Jack McDonald—ex-infantry—didn't trust the sea. Knew it was fickle, knew it was coldly neutral, like a sociopath. So immensely powerful, like God, only His soulless, material creation with no heart. Unfathomable power without innate mercy: what a monstrous combination!

Jack resigned in disgust from the Army in March, shook hands with his Lieutenants and his own Battalion Commander and friend, drove past the golf course and the old Officer's Club where he had unwound with comrades, out Gate 1, down Highway 41A, and away from Fort Campbell, Kentucky and the 101st Airborne Division (Air Assault). Yes, resigning relieved him of the military's hovering, career "ticket-punching" tedium, but now, like never before, an odd feeling called "strangely out of place" possessed him immediately outside the post. He missed the men of the 1st of the 506th "Currahee" Air Assault Infantry Battalion already. Well, he had his reasons for resigning and it was done. What now?

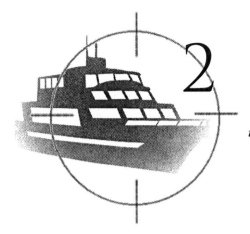

Aboard the Corsican Sun
Perdido Cay,
the Abacos chain,
in the Bahamas' "Out Islands"

The Atlantic's cold, gray waves piled up first against the bay's shallowing entrance. Here, they surrendered most of their strength, and rolled more tamely toward the tiny cove on the bay's far south side. The cove's crystal-clear, blue-green shimmer proclaimed "Pure Caribbean!" even in the pre-dawn dark.

Palms lined the cove's shore. White sand glistened in the moonlight. Yellowtail snapper trolled the 8' depths, sheltering from the Atlantic's power and predators.

The rocket-propelled grenade's explosion shattered this pristine peace, sending the dead and stunned fish floating to the surface. Raucous laughter erupted on the *Corsican Sun.* Cuban-accented Spanish voices cheered and cursed.

"See, I told you," the rocketeer boasted to his three mates, reliving his glory by—once again—pointing the now-empty RPG-7 tube up and out, filling in with his own shouted "Boom!"

They all knew wasting the RPG round on fishing would also net them trouble but they could not argue with the result. As one man swiveled the searchlight across the still-reverberating cove surface, their next meals arose. To Hell with sitting with a pole in your hand.

The Cubans, ages 18 through 41, had been to sea a full week. They'd sat in this same cove for the last three days. Give any men boats, guns, and "toys"; then play "boredom" with their brains, and bizarre behavior begins. Add some meanness and the bizarre twists from benign toward the malevolent.

"Sierra four, Sierra four, over."

The "fisherman" turned to face the now-crackling radio. "Get that, Hermon," he commanded, savoring his assumed, temporary celebrity.

"This is Sierra four, over," Hermon answered his leader, Revaca, on the radio aloft in the nearby helicopter. He'd heard the chopper fly out northwestward earlier and knew Revaca was patrolling.

"We're up here at 2,000 feet and show a radar contact 80 miles from you, heading generally this way," his leader, Revaca, advised.

"Do you want us to go check it out?" Hermon suggested.

Silence. *Idiots!* thought Revaca, holding the microphone but shaking his head. *Why me?* After forcing his own bored impatience back under constraint, Revaca delivered his instructions—his reminder.

"No, (*fool,*) our job is to secure the cove and fasten the—objects— in place as we were ordered, no more, no less. How could we do that with you chasing around in the ocean?" he could not resist chiding.

"*Si,* what then?"

"Sit where you are. If anything changes, I will let you know. Resume your work when the sun permits, finish up and—let's all get done and get the Hell out of here. Oh, and remember your radio language! Out."

"Roger," Hermon agreed. He turned to address the other three hands who had also heard the good news. "Well, we've sat, and smoked, and shit, and even slept all we can; let's get a fire going on the beach and grill some fish."

Two men leapt overboard into the shallows and waded, using

lines to gently pull the *Sun* closer to the beach, while the other two collected firewood. Nights creep by so slowly when you're bored and dawn remains four hours away.

3

It's "Tommy this!" and
"Tommy that!" and
"Chuck him out, the brute!"
But it's "Savior of his country"
When the guns begin to shoot.

—*Rudyard Kipling's "Tommy"*

As a 28-year old Army Captain, combat and leadership pressure had strung Jack McDonald pretty tightly. He emerged from a world of rough, physical training, punctuated by snap, life-or-death decisions, amidst an atmosphere of competitive, even partly-crazy, young men, required to so-carefully control, but suddenly to kill. But for the Infantry Officer's Advanced Course interlude at Fort Benning, Georgia, just after he put in four years and made Captain, and other than advanced training—Ranger, Airborne, Jungle Warfare, and Tracking School—the Army had assigned Jack to serial "shooting deployments" in the Philippines, Iraq, and Columbia. (Oh, yes, and then there was that *last* assignment as a Company Commander at Fort Campbell, Kentucky, home to the 101st.)

Jack thrived on his seven Army years spent learning specialized, military skills and facing raw challenge hunting the enemies of the United States of America—a challenge he would now have to find some substitute for. He might hunt, or hike, or get back into soccer as off-work pastimes. It was *that other thing* he wondered if he could replace. Jack had driven off and left *it* behind.

Jack could not quite identify *it*. He found himself reverting to this ever-so-military word: *mission.*

In the Army, despite all of the Green Machine's insanity and

6

self-destructive masochism, he possessed *mission*. No, *mission* possessed him. The *mission* pervaded all and overshadowed the bureaucratic politics. Now, that *mission* belonged to others—those who remained in the service. Jack strove to establish his new *mission* but the endeavor continued to fail him, even though hours in the truck during March and April, watching highway roll beneath him, carved aside the time for him to plan this new phase of his life. Jack, of course, made a plan.

Indeed, his plan seemed good. It probably *was* a good plan. Trouble is, the hours of solitary reflection lured him toward, and finally slammed him against a rock wall of insight: his good plan belonged to somebody else. Leaving the Army might have been right—he'd hardly had a choice—but his newly selected direction was another's place, context and life—not his.

The spring and newness of civilian life had dulled the stalking reality. Summer travels were OK, catching up with old friends. Jack saw a few places he hadn't seen before. Terrain in the Rockies was cool, but, he knew, beginning in the fall, it would be "Get up in the same place every day, at the same time, go to the same buildings, listen to professors wax on about the arcane aspects of management psychology," while he built a resume' toward a career.

And then what? What *mission* demanded Jack's new education, his *new* skills? What would compel the new Jack forward? He could lead, but to *what* would he lead the people under his responsibility? (Jack simply assumed that, regardless of the direction he picked, he would be leading others.)

Arcturus had bailed him out. He'd lined up a graduate school slot in an excellent program that offered promise, planning to start in the fall, just driving around the country to kill time and "transition." He would warm in the summer sun, acclimating to civilian life as his hair grew a bit. In the meantime, Jack planned to camp, live out of the back of his truck, and sometimes stop in on friends across the country. He would roll his sleeping bag out within sight and sound of the cold water flowing over the stones at Pacific Creek in the Tetons where an old college buddy worked. While his friend guided tourists over the mountain trails, Jack would stalk moose from this base camp and dodge grizzly bears.

Jack hit the "start" button to replay the mental lecture to himself on his duty to get responsible again somehow-sometime, but it all seemed so—what? He knew it must be all right; just about everyone else did it, and even seemed enthusiastic about it. It just seemed so—*civilian*. Yeah! That was it! The plan exuded an undefined "otherness" about it that emphasized his uniformed career's utter distinction from the non-military world he had now chosen, or had been compelled into.

Logic either blessed or cursed Jack. Gradually, to the duet performed by the music of rubber-on-the-road accompanying radio, Jack worked out his dilemma, reaching some conclusion somewhere between Abilene and Tacoma. Whether he had grasped it before or not, Jack was military in his *soul*—whatever that meant—only not on the payroll any longer. No longer on the roll call, Jack remained on the "soul call." He was like the ghost of a dead Captain vainly trying to materialize in front of his unit standing in formation, but unable to descend to plant his feet in front of his troops, always hovering, shifting, and utterly unable to comprehend its ethereal detachment.

The spectral vision haunted his thoughts. From a sleeping bag in the desert just outside Phoenix, he stirred, suspended between sleep and wakefulness, and recognized his own face on the ghost Captain. With his hand on the grip-throttle of the Mercury outboard propelling him past alligators lounging in Georgia's

ARCTURUS

Okeefenokee Swamp in late May, Jack comprehended his gift, and his conflict congealed. Hanging up the BDUs and turning in the ID card transformed only his appearance and legal status; however, Jack remained a *soldier*, lost from his unit, and assigned no mission, with no hope of re-joining his own unit (since he had none) or even sidling up to another unit. He was, Jack pondered, *out*. This frightened him. *Out!*

Soldiers—particularly infantry—across the continuum of time and place, share in common with each other alienation from their own society. Kipling's terse, gritty poetry sums up Tommy Atkins' pathetic crack at fitting into the society that had been his home. *Tommy*, Kipling's fictional, despised, hero-representative for all British soldiers, and—by extension—for all G.I.s too, discovered to his annoyance, that the bartenders ("publicans") who used to welcome him as a jovial, paying customer now held him in nothing but disdain. The culture flatly did not know what to *do* with him. Some not only failed to understand that he represented *them*, and that he fought for *them*, but they also turned on him like mean dogs:

> It's "Tommy this!" and "Tommy that!" and
> "Chuck him out, the brute!"
> But it's "Savior of his country"
> When the guns begin to shoot.

"Ground Pounders." "Grunts." "Snuffy." "Snuffy Smith." "Troop." "Gyrene" (for the "Jarhead" Marines). "Ragbag." "Maggot." Call him what you like. In an earlier war, "Stars and Stripes" correspondent Bill Mauldin drew his beloved characters, Willie and Joe, to personify the exhausted infantrymen slugging it out in Europe. These dirty, sad-eyed, ordinary, extraordinary, but never-beaten men endeared themselves to millions back home.

"So, where is Bill Mauldin today?" Jack had often asked.

Jack scorned those reporters from today's news networks who, by staying aloof, betrayed their utter ignorance about the military every time they opened their so-smug mouths. To the soldier watching the news, the reporters might as well have sounded a loud siren and preluded their newscasts with

> I'm going to act like I know what's going on over here, but I never got off my duff (duffle bag) and mixed with the troops. I never bothered to learn the first thing about soldiering. I am not Ernie Pyle or Bill Mauldin, and I lack their courage. I will never be found on my belly with troops under fire except by major mistake.

They would, no doubt, work from "fact"-sheet briefs. These identified the soldier's unit by the curious military number and letter mixture that only military people bother to learn to decipher. Proud units like the 1st Battalion of the 327th Infantry (Regiment) write the unit designation as 1-327 Infantry. The news-dogs breathlessly stand before a camera on the nightly news, telecasting to millions, dressed in some form of khaki from the TravelSmith catalog, assume serious, knowing, insider looks, and satellite their cowardice and ignorance to the entire world by announcing that the "one-three-two-seven Infantry" had done this or that. No, dolt! The "first of the three-two-seventh" went out there today, killed some of your sworn enemies to protect your sorry ass, and stopped bullets for you! C/1-506 is not "C slash one-five-oh-six"; it tells the soldier immediately that Charlie Company, 1st Battalion of the 506th Infantry is around. That's 506th Infantry *Regiment.* That soldier is assigned to the "1st of the 506th." These are proud units of heritage and deserve better.

ARCTURUS

The mark of the reporter who forayed out of the protected enclave and got with troops was easy to spot. Snuffy took care of him as a comrade, correcting his off-target jargon in a flash. Maybe Snuffy, in his disgust at seeing himself betrayed by the newscast slant night after night, kept Newsdog coolly repulsed, ignoring him or maybe even tricking him by withholding jargon lessons, permitting him to reveal his naked banality. All they had to do was listen to Ollie North's broadcasts, but apparently, they were too busy sipping wine back at the hotel and eyeing up the news-babes to listen to real, dirty, tired, military men and women. Bitterness swept Jack's feelings as he remembered his platoon's combat and recon patrols in Iraq and the Vietnamesque betrayal the Army endured at the hands of their own countrymen.

Those reporters epitomized to Jack the chasm between civilians and those who put on the uniform and saluted. "Respect for and basic knowledge of the American armed forces should be a part of high school civics classes," Jack, the education expert, theorized. How many kids could tell you the difference between a Sergeant Major and a Major? How many knew what "all of those stripes on the sleeve" stood for? How many could identify the Combat Infantryman's Badge? He supposed kids were too busy learning about the plight of the polar bear to learn respect for the people in uniform who secured their liberty for the last 300 years (Jack counted the French and Indian wars.) As a result of this intentional education deficit, America feigned affection for its troops, but fawned over civilian entertainment idols, Jack carped. Hell, they'd all know television's idol *de jour* caught on camera by name, face, and nipple-imprints on the wet T-shirt, but how many could name even one Congressional Medal of Honor winner—from any war? Just one?

Civilians! *Well, now I am one!*

4

I never worry about hurting the feelings of the good officers when I draw officer cartoons. I build a shoe, and if somebody wants to put it on and loudly announce that it fits, that's his own affair.

—Bill Mauldin, "Up Front"

One of Ernie Pyle's sayings scared the Hell out of Jack: "I'd quit it and come home for good except I don't suppose I could live with myself if I did, and would gradually go nuts."

Would Jackie-boy go nuts? Would he find himself incessantly typing out "All work and no play makes Jack a dull boy"? He hadn't *quit*, but he was—*out!* And—of all things—during *training! Training!* He'd committed the unpardonable sin during *training*.

Maybe he should have kept his mouth shut when that asinine bird-Colonel alighted from the chopper in the middle of the night with his dogs, relieved Jack's platoon leaders from command right in front of a Platoon Sergeant and his Squad Leaders, and started cursing Jack in front of his troops when he'd intervened.

Maybe he should have exercised calculated restraint. Maybe he should have summoned up the more diplomatic Jack. Maybe he should have gauged that he was about to make a "career decision." Maybe he should have consoled his fired Platoon Leaders later, offering nice reference letters for their civilian job applications. Maybe he should have saved himself by staying out of it. Naaaaaah!

They were good boys, those fresh 2nd Louies. They needed experience, and he was by God the one the Army chose to give them just that. Second Lieutenant Platoon Leaders come in a staggering variety of sizes, shapes, colors, endurance levels and combat competence. The Company Commander in a light infantry rifle battalion gets three of them.

These three had it together as well as any he'd seen. They exuded motivation all over the place, together with that irreplaceable natural sense of "What's going on where?" He had them for *such* a short time, too. They'd move on and be re-assigned before the year passed and Jack had experienced so much he wanted them to know about. Jack's Battalion Commander was the same kind of man: every minute counted because soon, those troop-leaders with the green felt "tabs" on their epaulets would move on and into darkened houses, teeming streets, and trackless jungles where death glared.

Then, bedlam struck from the sky. The Division Chief of Staff just had to get off his duff, commandeer some chopper, and go "to the field." Apparently, that meant chewing out the first officers he found once he and his mutts un-assed the bird. In an insane, fateful confluence of time, place, and the Peter Principle, Jack's three Platoon Leaders were the first.

During a company-sized helicopter insertion and raid exercise on a mock terrorist supply and explosives manufacture warehouse, Jack had stopped the problem, told everybody to "take five," and gotten with his lieutenants. The 2nd Platoon leader spotted something Jack hadn't thought about—something that made Lieutenant Hudson look hard and suspect that they had found much more than just ammo and explosives. He was right too. He'd radioed it in. Jack was impressed. However, knowing this was "just training," Lieutenant Hudson was about to shelve his insight, pick up, and continue the mission handed to him, ignoring the unexpected lead to the terrorists' cell leader.

Jack radioed all of them on the "company net," had them get their Platoon Sergeants to get their men "down-and-out" to secure the area, and called his Platoon Leaders to the "Company CP" (command post) to brainstorm the problem and squeeze every lesson they could from it. He was thinking about how to phrase his compliment to Hudson without causing it to go to his already charged-up head when the COS (POS) strode up with his pair of tethered, pampered, Irish Setters and laid into Jack's lieutenants for "standing around chattering like grannies at a quilting bee while their men took the war seriously."

The 1st Platoon leader tried to explain and "got relieved" of his command. Now on a drooling roll, the mad Colonel relieved the other two for good measure. That pretty much terminated the three, young 2LTs' careers. That Officer Efficiency Report might lurk like a cancer for a few years in their files, but it would metastasize and eventually mark them for career destruction. Jack overheard the Colonel shouting as he walked up to what he had thought was going to be his lesson in intelligence-gathering opportunities.

Jack, as a combat-hardened, Silver Starred, three-campaign, seven-year veteran Captain—a United States Army Infantry, 101st Airborne Division (Air Assault), Company Commander—had gotten in The Screaming Eagle's Chief of Staff's face—out of earshot from the troops—and let him have it.

Maybe the divorce, foisted on Jack during his shooting war in the Philippines, pressed Jack just enough against the edge that he could not tolerate the pompous, absurd, caricature-of-an-officer alighting by his own personal Little Bird chopper at 3:10 in the a.m.—with those dogs! Damn that woman! Can't blame her, though. Not for that.

ARCTURUS

The Colonel had deserved it. He had breached the chain of command, bypassing not only Jack, but also Jack's beloved Battalion Commander and his respected, but more distant, Brigade Commander as well. That might have been something the officers could all have worked out later over drinks, but Jack could not forgive the man's reckless wrecking of three, fine, young Lieutenants' careers needed so badly by America.

Now, his Lieutenants' former CO, his own career marred by the Colonel's ordering him relieved of command too, would pay the price. Letters in your file at Infantry Branch, Department of the Army and even mediocre Officer Efficiency Reports eventually caught up with you. Jack had written the proverbial "handwriting on the wall" personally, by choice. Jack wrinkled his brow, smiling at the framed vision of the look on the man's face and basked in a bit of pride at having done the right thing.

It cost him his rank, his career, his uniform, and the identity he had always held dear: a United States Army infantryman. To Jack, there was no higher aspiration. Now, all lay shattered.

Well, that was fine! All was *never* shattered. He would thrive. He would "continue the mission" only in a different way. He would leave the Army behind and embrace civilian life, which, Jack decided was probably *normal.*

The percentages said so: most people built things, administered stuff, sold goods or did whatever civilians do during the day and then went home at night to a *life.* That had to be *normal,* didn't it? Killing evil people and constantly training to learn more and improved methods to kill more evil people was *abnormal.* Right? Had to be. Necessary, but not *normal.*

Jack had often reflected at zero-dark-thirty, while stumbling one leaden foot in front of another, bruising his shins on fallen limbs, clawing up and falling down ditches, and on and on into the bleary-eyed dawn, wondering what in the world he was doing out here in one of the world's forgotten corners while everyone else was home in bed, snug and warm, sidled up to the warm wife? Now, he had his chance. He would *re-train*—make that return to college for a Master's degree, or a Ph.D.—and launch a new *career*, working regularly during the day and getting a *life* after the workday was done.

After service, Snuffies fit back in, get jobs, start businesses, and thrive in general. Most never forget who they were and are; they just add the cumulative experience to their inventory of memories and grow new interests.

Some few, however, never make the transition. Sure, they look all right; they dress in civvies, earn paychecks, get promoted, drop all but a reminiscence of the military jargon, slump a little, add inches to the waistline, and succeed, but these never see themselves as civilians. They live more like unassigned *soldiers*, lacking a mission, and on a long, long leave. For that group, civilian life is like a poorly-patterned-and-cut pair of cheap blue jeans; you can put 'em on and wear 'em out, but they will look lumpy and sag around your butt, and feel weird.

That was Jack's analogy and he worried that he belonged to the group that would never fit in. He would wander the earth like Jacob Marley's ghost: suspended between two worlds and alive in neither. The specter of the disembodied Captain floated back into Jack's mind. This time, Captain Specter wore jeans sagging around his butt.

So, when his friend and mentor, Major Cantrell, phone-bombed him in late July from the TOC (Tactical Operations Center) at the

Arcturus

75th Ranger Regiment headquarters at Fort Beginning School for Boys (officially known as "Fort Benning, Georgia"), and pushed him toward this job opportunity that led him aboard the *Arcturus*, Jack didn't ponder more than a minute whether to chuck the whole start-graduate-school-in-the-fall scenario, and sign on. He was genuinely grateful to Cantrell for the opportunity. (That means he promised Cantrell a beer.) The money was good, too. That wouldn't hurt. The duty was easy. Easy? Hell, it was even pleasant. Hardly a tough mission, at least as long as all went as expected. Just a sea cruise with this decent-seeming group. Jack suggested Shanghaiing Jack's former Executive Officer (XO), also recent from the uniform, and Jack and Cantrell IM'd Bobby together to harangue him to climb on board. Cantrell signed off, asking Jack if he was getting pudgy already. Real funny.

On board, they were—literally. Both young men vaguely expected to return to "the plan" after this mission, this gig, this "patrol." They viewed the *Arcturus* mission as a patrol: of limited duration and specific purpose. Cantrell interjected the boat trip as a nice diversion, from the boys' perspective, a Caribbean interlude between the Army and the seemingly inevitable working their way back into civilian life. Jack cajoled Bobby into joining, selling him on the legendary "cream job" neither had ever landed (nor sought) in the Army. Jack sailed his new boat down to Miami, docked it at a marina in Biscayne Bay, linking up with Bobby there and sharing the slip fee, eager to see what lay in store. Now, they were at sea, and in the Bahamas, no less. Jack and Bobby clinked their mugs and concurred: "For a couple of Tennessee boys from Podunk, it don't get no better than this!"

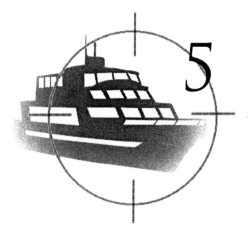

Perdido Cay,
the Abacos chain,
in the Bahamas' "Out Islands"

"Sierra four, Sierra four, over."

The Fisherman, having assumed custody of the radio as a trapping of leadership, responded, acknowledging: "Sierra four, *mi amigo*, over."

"Sierra four, the radar contact continues to approach, now about 30 miles out. What is your status?"

Fisherman looked around at his three *compadres* and regretted seizing the chance to become "The Man."

"Waiting for dawn. All quiet," he answered, mostly truthfully.

"Prepare to leave the cove and go to the mouth of the bay. I don't want you drawing attention to the cove. Just station yourselves there and wait.

The men scooped wet sand over the embers, waded the short distance back to the *Sun* and started its engine. At least they were moving!

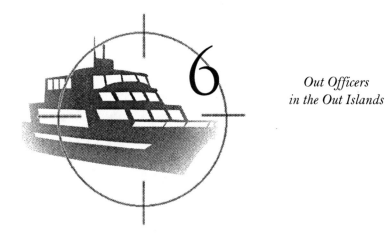

6

Out Officers
in the Out Islands

J ack stood and embraced the horizon luxuriously, elbows out in front propped over the rail, conditioning his rippling neck and shoulder muscles, hands clasped together, bent at the waist, relaxed, enjoying the ember tendrils of the dawn creeping across sea and sky, dissolving away the black, then the gray. Somewhere from just under the deck, a low voice murmured, announcing a passenger's stirring. He glanced to identify the early riser (and, without thinking, to assure no threat), and to scan the deck once again.

Who was up? The young woman usually rose early for some reason. Wonder if that's her.

Had to admit. Getting up was never that easy for him. Preferred to stay in the rack awhile, whether between the sheets or on the ground, under the poncho. Rarely got to though. That was OK. Too much life going on out there to miss it by staying in the rack.

The cook started the coffee early, just like a proper ship's cook should and that first cup drew him out of bed like a Sirens' call.

Another sea-related danger! The Sirens! Damn. Just one more way the sea was out to get you, to draw you out, suck you in and down and cold and dead.

There were so many ways! And you couldn't see them until they were upon you. What about those British tourists just about capsized by a whale exploding from the deep, suddenly, to leap onto their boat. He guessed whales could *leap*. He didn't know what else to call it. He recalled the news article. Everyone lived, so *sure*, they all guffawed about it afterward to the reporter, showing off the expected, classic degree of British, understated cheek, and, no doubt, being bought brews with one of those crazy British names all over England's southern port towns just to tell the tale, but he figured it had been no joke at the time. The whale had meant no harm apparently. One of the Brits fiddling with a waterproof, digital camera shot pix of it swimming around and away.

Nevertheless, after "Jaws," everyone with any sense knew that all manner of voracious sea critters lurked beneath the glassy sur-face, picking their own time to pierce your world in full, mindless attack. That must fit under the "Environmental Hazards" portion of the Patrol Order briefing.

He laughed—again, in his mind. His face betrayed only a spar-kle in the eye, if anyone had seen it. Jack looked down again at the sea, lapping at *Arcturus*.

Lap—lap. Onomatopoeia: words that sound like what they are, what they do. Man, how it was weird that he could still hear his old high school English teacher speaking the long, rhythmic word.

Lap, lap, lap. Jack swept his eyes down over the *Arcturus's* shin-ing hull, cooling his face with light salt spray, warily watching the saltwater buffet the hull. Maybe the sea actually tasted the yacht, testing it like a spoonful of hot chili to see if it wanted to swallow it whole, like just an insignificant bite. The ocean could do that. He shuddered, and felt the fear course through his body—controlled, but there—zinging through like one of those invisible, theoretical, sub-atomic particles with quarkish names. As far as he was con-cerned, he sensed the fear for a good reason.

As if to mock Jack, for the time though, the surface swayed the boat, floating it gently like a cork. He glanced up, raised the binoculars hanging from a strap around his neck, and scanned, spying nothing in sight but more water, and, beyond that, more water. Cottony clouds hung from the orange-streaked, dawning sky like the bolls he used to see back home, only suspended like ghosts on strings dangling from the roof of this world of shimmering, restless, powerful potential-energy. Maybe that was an island way off ahead and to the right. Jack felt that the northwestern Bahamas reached out to wave and welcome him. He'd welcome them back as friends.

He missed trees in every one of their twisted shapes: leaning out over mossy ditches, shallow and steep; clumps of brush hugging pine-needled forest floor; fallen, rotted timbers and other cover; even the webs strung across the trails by the spiders afresh every evening. The sea forced a feeling of alert-but-exposed, with line of sight 360 degrees all the way out to the far horizon. He even missed poison ivy briefly. Briefly. Let's not get too carried away with this revulsion to all things maritime; let's not venerate landsman status too much. *This is definitely not infantry environment*, he groused to himself.

Yet, despite Jack's wired sense of impending, wet doom, nothing at all threatened while the low chop lapped, lapped, lapped against the hull. Just like for thousands of years. The sameness and beat thrummed, inducing his mind to wander, a bit theatrically, he critiqued. That's what minds do when they wander, don't they? Why not? Unlike a night ambush position where every shadow seemed to twitch during the witching hours, any affront to the endless water would stick out like a sore thumb. He shrugged his shoulders and indulged the fantasies from the Romantic Age.

What brash quests had been launched, what desperate, booming battles had been fought, what hopes beckoned from across the expanse? What treachery stretched its grim, icy fingers from beneath, all while the surface danced with those pretty waves, mindlessly lapping against the hulls of heroes', villains', geniuses', and idiots' ships? A guy could not operate much on this environment, could not use it much, could not change it and control it. That, coupled with his own admitted ignorance of sailing and all things naval, he decided, gnawed at his gut and made him a confirmed landlubber from Tennessee where waves of densely-forested hills and valleys rolled solidly before travelers like a leafy sea.

Jack turned his head to scan the waves near the boat, and then outward in sweeps. Nothing.

The voice again. Turning more slowly back, he spied her emerging from the passageway leading up from the cabins where the clients and crew quartered.

God, what a gorgeous girl you created! Bronze, supple, always on the verge of a laugh. Nice, actually. Strong, even muscular in a carved, female-shaped sort of way, but kind. Where did such girls come from? They, along with the power and beauty of the sea, chocolate, orange juice, strawberries, and other wild, natural wonders, proved the Creator, he supposed. How else could you explain it? And beer. Don't forget beer. Beer proved the existence of God too, he mused. Something Ben Franklin said that he saw on the front of some T-shirt. Jack wondered if Franklin really said that. Probably did. If he didn't, he should have: "Beer is proof that God is good, and loves us." Roger that.

All of the passengers were courteous enough, not pretentious, not people to put on airs, although Bobby and Jack kept a professionally courteous distance; this was, after all, a *mission*. They were not aboard as guests or anyone's *compadres*. Their calling—as that of all American soldiers and others charged with protecting lives—

was higher, they proclaimed from the cabin of Jack's 28 foot sail-boat-home, rocking by the quay in Biscayne Bay, south of downtown Miami, as they planned out the clients' protection over steaks and clinked their frozen beer steins together to confirm their lofty purpose: Brothers of the Grail, or the Ring, or the Beer Mug or … something like that anyway. These people hired them on as on-boat bodyguards and they would get more than their money's worth. Just like America got from its soldiers. They were, after all, soldiers-turned-executive-protection.

Granted, the Operations Order for this one had been unique to their experience, a twist on their past life, but their training had at least given them a format for planning such missions, and taught them to exercise their creativity in filling in the details. There surely were guys tougher, more experienced in what they were about to do, but no bodyguard could have more steeled himself to *the mission*— when *the mission* was thought or voiced, the word was reverenced and measures from imaginary Bach played solemnly in the background.

One night, as Jack swayed in his hammock in his sailboat's cabin, he sat up, smacked his palm beside his head and shook Bobby.

"Hey, ragbag!"

"What!"

"You have grossly overlooked the obvious: the piece of equipment our lives depend on." Jack accused his friend, glaring at him and sticking his finger in his face.

"You're crazy!" Bobby retorted. Then, after a pause: "What are you going on about? Rifles?"

"What about the *Arcturus*, Bobby? As infantry, (Jack did not say "former infantry") we know nothing about ships other than LBRBs. Or is the *Arcturus* a boat? Ship? Boat? I don't even know *that?* It's like not knowing the maximum effective range of a 105." Jack referred to both "little bitty rubber boats" and the 105mm artillery piece as he demanded his friend's attention to their oversight.

"We have almost screwed up here," Jack continued, the apparent learning-gap widening. "Bobby, we have got to at least get familiar with navigation, and I'm not talking about land nav either."

They set about studying the boat, ascertained its performance capabilities, and cross-examined its mechanic—its *engineer*, to employ nautical parlance—who gruffly surrendered to their good-natured, but relentless insistence on personal, hands-on instruction.

As good landsmen and ground-pounders would, they bought the maps, which the swabbies called *charts* they discovered after being the butt of laughter in the marina shop, checking and re-checking the route. They failed to escape in time and asked about the Bahamian Cays, drawing more guffaws when they pronounced the odd word like "Bays" instead of "Keys." The good-natured men, nonetheless, flooded them with information, opinions and lore. Back in the sailboat's cramped galley, charts to the "Cays" spread out before them, the fact that the "terrain" was flat, wet, and formlessly level stayed them not one bit in the least from plotting azimuths, checking for islands, and measuring distances. Lacking hilltops, valleys, interrupting rivers and lakes, and other distinct terrain features to plan around, they memorized the names of the major islands within 100 miles of their plotted route, and quizzed each other while running the beach back and forth from South Beach

Park to keep in shape. Back in the cabin, they laid the islands out from memory, using coins, and joking about "pieces of eight."

Jack and Bobby came to understand that the depth measurements on the "charts" were the elevation contours that depicted the terrain on the topographic maps with which they were so practiced. They studied radar capability and radio, listing frequencies and phone numbers for weather, emergency, government and other possible communications needs.

Next, they camped in the main library on Flagler Street, studying marine navigation, keeping the *Bowditch* treatise off the shelf for three days. When the time came for their interview, they had peppered the taken-aback interviewer, admonishing him to hold an operational security meeting with all hands immediately. Bobby warned that they would brook no treacherous Long John Silver aboard the *Arcturus*, using the grizzled pirate leader character from *Treasure Island* to jam the betrayal point home. That, together with their presentation of the Operations Order probably got them the job, Jack proclaimed, toasting Bobby.

Later, Gordon told them that no other applicants had even offered a plan, other than to bring guns, swagger, spew "tactical" jargon, drop names, wear cool sunglasses, and show bulging muscles. Gordon had laughed to tears when he recounted the tale, but his eyes had razor-engaged theirs in a conspiratorial sort of fashion, and they knew he was dead-damn serious. Gordon complimented the young men on their Operations Order, which they wrote following the Army's well-known outline used universally by soldier-leaders planning operations, and remarked that he noticed their adaptations to make the Order fit naval operations. He enjoyed their joke when they included sharks under the "Enemy

Situation" portion of the Order. There was something about Gordon.

Jack grinned. They had, indeed, gone the extra mile, whether nautical or otherwise. Jack had bought the sailboat with his saved-up leave money after taking the job. They would get some nautical experience and a portable place to live at the same time. Then, at Gordon's instruction, Jack drove from Miami to Tampa where their clients headquartered for their personal interview and presentation.

Their own plan included carefully-chosen weapons and staying in top shape too, but presenting the Operations Order for guarding the *Arcturus*, its crew, hosts and guests had taken the better part of an hour. He and Bobby had traded off portions of it so that the interviewer learned them both. No big deal. They had merely used the specialized Operations Order in the Patrol Order format Ranger School had so generously shared with them, and these people ate it up. They Power Pointed it, complete with diagrams, pictures, lists, call signs, and ambush drills. They finished with the requirement that, if hired, Jack and Bobby interview each passenger and crew-member to determine their own level of training and combat response, and to assure that each was briefed on OPSEC. These boys were taking this *seriously*.

Once hired, Gordon permitted them to brief the crew, maybe just for the entertainment value the boys figured. All were, of course, impressed. Jack affirmed in his mind, it was a sound plan, at least within the confines of their knowledge and experience about seagoing operations that, Jack admitted, was woefully scant.

They got the job though. Great job it was too. Ten thousand in advance as a retainer, ten apiece at launch, and ten at the end, for six weeks of cruising the Caribbean! He'd take that kind of job any-time. Graduate school was still out there, but now a lot more tolerable with cash in the bank. They were honest-to-God naval infantry now! Hilarious. They were *Gy-reens!* They'd demanded that they be able to search the ship to assure no illegal drugs or other anti-American contraband fouled the hold, and then approved the launch as legal and worthy of patriots.

Jack e-mailed his brother that he would be gone for awhile. He squared away his bill paying, and linked up again with the *Arcturus* and its crew in Tampa, where Gordon had arranged a place for Jack to leave his truck. After one last fried-oyster platter at the Rusty Pelican, they motored away from Tampa, clearing Passage Key on an idyllic day, waving at the lounging locals. Then, they passed through the breakers and were in the Gulf of Mexico, white sand and tall condominiums fading behind, while striking a course south and later south-southeast, as the guys confirmed by their landlubberly, infantry-grunt, hand-held, orienteering compasses. No sense assuming these people actually headed the right direction, after they and their men had been dropped off so many times by the helicopter jocks at the wrong DZ (drop zone). You are responsible for where you end up. *Check it yourself or slog through the extra miles of mud to get to where you were supposed to be.* (That's going to be an extra challenge out here.) It was just plain hard not to hoot with delight.

Lark or not, they mentally squared their jaws. Only a few months before their resignations from the service, a newspaper story popped up about private yachts and small craft seized and scuttled after their owners and crews were butchered and tossed overboard. Jack knew that more horror and rape than that must have haunted those black-and-white fact descriptions but the nature of the crime was such that the killers left few details. "Drugs" everyone agreed. Probably true.

Pick off a known boat, legally registered to a law-abiding citizen, board it, enjoy the women and then kill everyone on board, "disposing" of the bodies. Then, run the drugs with the boat, slipping in "under the radar" of the Coast Guard and the DEA as just another cute boat name and legal number that no one would suspect. (How might *Lucky Break II* be for irony or *Miss Fortune*? Where did these guys come up with these boat names?) Once delivered, take the boat back out, link up with your pickup, scuttle the hapless craft, and leave literally no trace of your black deeds.

Piracy. 21st century style. Pretty slick. Pure evil. Jack had dug into this and found to his surprise that pirates boarded boats to rob, rape, and kill more frequently than the public knew. German shopowners would finally sell the business and launch their dream-of-a-lifetime cruise, crossing the Atlantic to lounge around in the Caribbean, unarmed and naively unaware of pockets of pirates plaguing blue water cruisers. The lucky ones told their stories to Klaus Hympendahl and made it into print in his book *Pirates Aboard!* The unlucky ones never made it to the interview because neither Klaus nor anyone else could find them. Jack studied the accounts and marveled that the survivors debated whether they should have carried guns! He wondered what position the dead cruisers would argue were they still alive.

Bobby had made them an appointment with the DEA office boys in Miami, picking their brains about drug smuggling. The disgusted DEA contact from Georgia displayed obvious disdain, making it oh-so-plain he had been *stuck* with them. To say he was "guarded at first" understates his revulsion.

However, he must have confirmed who the men were, and then,

seeing their serious intent to approach this job as professionals, he opened up, appearing to take them on in true confederate fashion, as allies in a lost cause. Even bought them drinks. He converted from stiff govo-jerk into a fount of information, delivering a professorial lecture on the economics and tactics of the drug traders. He exacted a promise from them to turn in any field intel they came across to him on return, and scrawled the name and number of a Coast Guard contact who he urged them to call on as a man of like vision, warning them first that this Coast Guard Lieutenant was crazy.

They left their meeting stunned at the depths of human depravity, puzzled over the insatiable appetites that churned up unbelievable underground violence in their country, and much less naïve about the raw power of cash. Marx was right, Jack thought: *Capital is a social power.* Lots of money compounds the force of the Devil geometrically. Hmm. This fit squarely under the "Enemy Situation" portion of the Patrol Order. The enemy was without mercy. Without it. No joke. Not just saying it. Satanic, he figured, considering the torture stories the finally eager DEA guy had told them about. Must have been a cathartic experience for him. He seemed to almost squeal with enjoyment as he watched their eyes get big. Perverse.

So, the probability of an attack on those in his charge was minimal, but the consequences were unthinkably horrible if pirates attacked and succeeded. They would, therefore, by God, not board the *Arcturus. Currahee,* he thought, swearing by the 506th Infantry's battle cry, motto and all-purpose exclamation.

Gordon and his cohorts must have considered the same grave consequences, and reached the same conclusions, resulting in Gordon having called his old friend, Cantrell who passed on the lead to Jack. Cantrell was a wiry, tough man, quick of wit, not a *prima donna*, and thought well of Jack from their days in the Philippines tracking and killing the Abu Sayyaf. They appreciated the tip. With his feet propped up on an austere desk at Harmony Church in the pines where he was hanging out and checking out the most recent crop of Ranger School graduates, Cantrell immediately told Gordon to hire Jack and Bobby.

At first, it seemed too much a lark. Bobby had plans to start school in New England, aiming for an MBA in management. Jack smiled at his own arrangements to get an MBA in industrial psychology. What had he been thinking? "Management consulting," he had reasoned, not knowing what it entailed, what opportunities it offered, or how to break into it once supposedly educated and turned loose on corporate America's manufacturing giants. He could always gear it up again. The brick buildings on The Hill at the University of Tennessee were not going away. Plenty of time for higher education and civilian careers.

The combination of cash, camaraderie, and Caribbean cruise just—well, you see, don't you? What adventurer, if free to do as he might please, could turn it down? The element of risk mixed in with the exotic (and money) made it absolutely intoxicating, and there they were.

The more Jack thought about it, the more satisfied he was with the whole deal. His unlikely presence, acting like a jarhead, infantry-on-deck Marine, he thought, made eminently good sense after all. He laughed at the logical absurdity of it all, and soaked in the smell of the salt spray and the warming, spreading sunshine on his arms. Thanks, Colonel Dipshit!

Cruising smoothly down the Gulf of Mexico for 250 miles brought them to the southern tip of Florida, where *Arcturus* turned eastward, threaded through the Keys, completed rounding the Florida Cape, and then ran north up the coast. After a good meal in Fort Lauderdale, the *Arcturus* crew motored northeast, headed toward the extreme northeastern banks of the Bahamas, still another 200 miles away, where she would turn southward, staying in the Atlantic, off the eastern side of the islands.

Few Americans realize the wild maze of sparsely inhabited islands and "cays" lying only a stone's throw from Florida's Gold Coast. Maybe people think of the Bahamas as two or three islands. Fact: the Bahamas number in the hundreds, with some islands as of yet not even named, much less occupied. Lacking rich resources or fertile soil, the most obscure remain almost as they were 1,000 years ago. Their waters range from surprisingly shallow, often no more than 10 or 20 feet deep, and less, to the mile-deep chasm pointed at centrally-located Andros Island known as the Tongue of the Ocean.

Collectively, The Bahamas fashion a mesh of channels, shallows, passes, "sand-flats," islands, and holes that feed sharks and delight exploring boaters, but also screen desperate drug couriers. It is simply impossible for the Royal Bahamian Defense Force (the BDF) to defend the integrity of this porous nation of theirs, stretching 500 miles north-to-south, much less patrol its labyrinth.

These particular, extreme-northern, neglected, dots ahead of *Arcturus* line up loosely north of Grand Bahama Island, and stand less than 100 miles due east of the Florida beaches and coastal inlets at sophisticated Boca Raton. The American public presumes its government to exercise omniscience over traffic through the Caribbean, and over the slightest movement through the close-by

Bahamas in particular. The DEA and the Coast Guard know better.

Perdido Key is one of the tiny flecks of terra lying like skin on the body of the Caribbean nations and islands, stuck into the face of the North Atlantic with the gentler Caribbean Sea miles to its leeward, south side. Part of the Bahamas' "Out Islands," these islands grasp onto their parent, watery nation almost as a forgotten corner, aspiring in vain to join the commerce, but too remote from the busy tourism of Nassau and Freeport. Neither part of Grand Bahama Island, nor the popular Abacos group of islands just nearby, the unnamed extension of ocean floor perched on the edge of the continental shelf is so oddly isolated that the risk of interdiction is slim indeed.

By the time Jack spotted the first tiny island that marked the break between the Caribbean Sea and the open Atlantic Ocean, routines had been set, adjusted, improved, and all worked like clockwork.

Shunning complacency, they randomized the otherwise too predictable patterns wherever randomization worked. Jack and Bobby met each night on the deck to probe the plan, test its details, plug its holes, account for the unforeseen, and to write annexes for additional contingencies. In the quieter hours when the guests were below in their own meetings about—whatever (they had a lot of these), they rehearsed contingencies: loss of communications, fire, explosion, and mechanical failure. While unlikely, they included worked-out drills for "actions on contact": attempted boarding by an attacking vessel, being hailed and halted by an apparently government-operated patrol boat, approach by "fishermen," and other worrisome possibilities their minds dreamed up that might look like an attack. They considered the possibility of a traitor on board just for extra swashbuckling intrigue effect, and casually interrogated each person on board. They played a game between themselves based on identifying the spy, pretending it was first this one and then that one. They laughed, but the game was serious and it kept them on alert to the possibility.

They even had a plan for carrying out all of this combat capability in civilian guise and in what they assumed to be the party atmosphere of this cruise. Shunning military-looking clothes, they chose functional khaki pants or cargo shorts and lightweight shirts suitable for any port or casual-dress restaurant. A close observer would have seen that the beach-motif shirts nonetheless sported patterns and colors that blended into land and vegetation, such as green and brown bamboo-cane prints.

No long guns slung over the back. These, they mounted in custom-made covered cupboards they had insisted be installed, with Gordon's reluctant permission, at select handy locations. The only visible signs of the young bodyguards' purpose were the alert countenances both wore, the unshakable just-out-of-the-military look complete with still short, but inching outward hair, and—of course, the .45 automatics holstered at their sides, visible under loose-fitting, button-up shirts. They found no way to conceal a full-sized Model 1911 under shorts and tropical-weight shirts, and they wanted the guns absolutely available at all times. They had debated this over Jack's table, as his boat-home rocked by the bay next to the quay, and agreed that the pistols would separate them from the crew and remind everyone concerned of their business purpose. So, the steel spirits of John Browning and Colonel Colt stalked the deck as silent partners.

Not that they disliked their *charges*, as they came to call them; indeed, the clients all were uniformly pleasant, sincere, clean, intelligent, and altogether the kind of people you would want as neighbors and friends. He was even a little jealous of their obvious affection for each other, and the ease of their manner during their meetings and meals. The girl was alluring and, under different circumstances….

But, Bobby and Jack were not the boat's owners or crew; neither were they part of the sponsoring organization, *Cuban Quest*; they were—literally—hired guns, with the single purpose of protecting these people. Period. They were worker bees; no, soldiers. Tools, really and voluntarily. They had, as the Brits they had soldiered with might say, "taken the King's shilling," together with all that it implied.

So, the former infantry Company Commander and his former second-in-command XO (Executive Officer) rose to the sense of duty and mission (that they both needed at a deep down, intrinsic level, whether they comprehended that need or not), even a *civilian* (read that with some derision here) mission, and consecrated themselves to the job at hand over handshakes, grilled T-bones and ice-cold beer. They would prowl the decks like watchmen on the wall: intelligent, alert, with carefully-selected and oiled firepower, ever on guard over their charges, but unobtrusive, clandestine insofar as possible, like a skilled but deadly waiter, hovering in the background, ever watchful to rise to the need of the moment, but hardly seen. They liked it that way, and figured that was about as covert as a couple of ex-Rangers could be in the circumstance.

Therefore, the M-1's stood, oiled daily, with an 8-round "clip" loaded, one round in the chamber, racked like a pair of unflinching tin soldiers, poised behind their doors, ready for action, in case the enemy needed long-range killing. The M-1's fired effectively out to about 500 yards, sold commonly for not a wad of money and were good enough for those men wading ashore at Normandy,

Their companions racked next to them, the Remington 870 pump shotguns, awaited the desperate hour of close-combat scum-clearing, buckshot in the tube, slings attached in a most non bird-hunting fashion, needing only a single firm pump to make them ready. Those, they had considered sending off for conversion by a specialty scattergun company. In the end, they left the shotguns as bought, with the single exception that Jack installed a *flexitab* anti-jam device. Jack considered the pay for this job, and the prospect of a next, similar mission, and shelved the idea of synthetic stocks, extended magazines, and ghost-ring sights as capital improvements after this job. In the meantime, these weapons stood deadly enough and graduate school seemed to fade away.

The M-1's were considered antiques from the World War II era in the U.S., but were standard issue for some of the Caribbean area forces. Sure, a compact, select fire would have been nice, like an M-16 or an M-4 carbine, but neither man had the U.S. license for full automatics and neither wanted to go to jail anywhere, much less in some equatorial Hell-hole. Both young ex-officers owned their own semi-automatic AR-15 civilian versions of the M-4 carbine: short-barreled, collapsible stock, customized versions jokingly called "M-4-geries" but they reluctantly stored them away, leaving the carbines in Tampa with Gordon's friend. To the uninitiated, those pieces looked black and ugly, terroristic in psychosis, criminal in intent, and more dangerous: more likely to result in jail. Plus, out of the woods, and off the mud-colored streets where action tended to pack in closer, and at open sea, they conceded they needed the extra bullet-weight of the bigger round. They might have gone for an M-1A, the semi-automatic version of the 1960's M-14 rifle, but, those cost about $1,000 each, neither man owned one, and, again, the powerful rifles spoke just a bit too loudly of something other than just a "boat gun" on board for sharks.

Unspoken, but independently in the back of both of the young men's minds, was the scene from *Jaws* with crusty, maybe even insane Quint, with his old M-1 on board the *Orca*. Good all around rifle, less likely to attract attention, and adequate for even large sharks they subliminally assessed. (The Bahamas teem with sharks, you know.)

They considered leaving the Colts behind, the need for handguns seeming so remote, but in the end, well, it just didn't feel right to walk about without any weapon within an arm's reach. Therefore, handguns designed in World War I, in continuous faithful service over the century, and now resurrected in snazzy, heavily customized form for the Marine Corps' Special Operations Capable forces (MEUSOC), remained on the list, like a workman's hammer or measuring tape, on the belt, the right tool for the right time.

Jack's older Colt Model 1911 Government .45's were centerfire, large frame handguns, utterly reliable, balanced, proven manstoppers for pistols, and Jack already owned two of them, making them the obvious handgun of choice. These, they carried "cocked and locked," round in the chamber, hammer back and cocked, thumb safety on. Unlike the M-1's, these were new guns, identical to the old service models, but newly manufactured. The .45 had made a comeback from never really going away, despite the Army's adoption of the Beretta 9mm. The Marines just would not give up the .45, and small contingents covertly clung to them. Men who knew guns swore by its short trigger-press accuracy and undisputed, heavy-bullet, impact energy.

The newest evolution of the .45, now about 100 years old, exhibited all of the customized improvements the usually austere Marines had dreamed about, making a truly fine piece. Jack, however, didn't own one. He did own his two, solid, government-model pistols. Nothing exotic by the day's standards, but these known, reliable choices rounded out the weapons with immediately available defense. If, for some reason, they bumped up against some third-world government, these familiar and older weapons would, perhaps, get them all in less trouble.

Besides, the openly-carried pistols, and physical weight and pressure of the cold automatics reminded both guardian and guarded why the men were on board, like a constant call to duty, whispering also to others: "Don't be fooled; these are dangerous young men, just as willing to kill as to laugh." The holstered autos broadcast the message, healthful for all: "Keep your distance." Jack unthinkingly rehearsed his grip again on the back of the Colt, sliding the thumb above the safety, and indexing his trigger finger along the side of the Kydex-shielded trigger guard, extended forward, poised to press the trigger when on-target, as a soft voice from behind him teased.

If I can just see the European war out, I think I might feel justified in quitting the war.

—*Ernie Pyle*

Donna luxuriated in the boat's gentle rocking, smelling salt sea and hearing the whisper-like wave-tip caresses against the hull below her cabin. Checking the porthole revealed her suspicion: dawn. The day, the boat, and the mission—all underway. This thought immediately flashed the reminder of her purpose for this cruise, quickening her awakening responses, and stirring Donna to her feet. A swipe with the still damp and now cool bath cloth, a few brush strokes of her hair, a quick selection of shorts and tee-shirt, and she turned to climb the short steps to the deck to meet this day in earnest. She paused at the first step up, listening for the boat's early stretching sounds and heard no one else stirring.

Donna turned instead toward the coffee maker setup in the galley between her own berth and the steps. She sniffed the ground roast, scooped in what looked like enough, and started the promising process, retiring to her own room once again while the pot filled. Donna gave thanks for the day and its promises.

While she tidied her room and donned jeans instead of shorts to ward off the yet cool morning, she considered the young man Gordon had joined to the crew. Gordon had eyed his niece with bemusement when she asked him about Jack, and she had blushed at his obvious teasing. Nevertheless, she had learned what Gordon

38

had to tell her, or at least what Gordon *would* tell her. Jack—and Bobby—were like so many young fellows in so many ways: healthy, quick, alert, laughing, and handsome—yes, they were cute. She had been wary, but had grown to appreciate that neither Jack nor Bobby flounced around with the arrogant bravado she had just *known* they would exhibit. No, both were approachable enough to a point, but distant, not from haughty self-aggrandizement, but from something else. They were not unfriendly, but not part of the gang, either.

Jack seemed so—*distantly deep* was the best way she knew how to put it. Businesslike, oh, yes. All business. Yet, this simple guard-duty seemed only to scratch the surface of Jack's mind, his heart, his intensity. In some ways, he and his friend were both hired hands, no more. Yet, Gordon had carefully selected these young men, and she knew enough about Gordon's depth to know that he picked these two for more than just filling two slots for bodyguards on board.

So, what moved Gordon to call Jack? Why Jack? Why not a dozen other still youngish, cropped hair, fresh-faced, muscle-guys-with-guns? She had watched enough of them wend their way through her Uncle Gordon's screening and had met enough at Destin, Florida, where Donna came of age. Bigger applicants than Jack and his friend Bobby had approached Gordon—and her—although she knew from Gordon that Jack had led Rangers in at least somewhere in South America, somewhere in the Far East, and in Iraq, and had seen a "lot of combat." Donna could only guess as to what that entailed. Gordon refused more information. She would demand more of Gordon—after the mission was complete. She wanted to know what Gordon saw that she only barely caught hints of and—she was curious. Yes, "curious" would be the word for it.

Donna understood "restless" if that discontented spirit bothered Jack who, like her, probably ought to be pursuing something more stable than the *Arcturus* cruise. Donna answered to her own reasons for being on board, but many young men Jack's age held steady positions, owned homes, and had children running to greet them at the workday's end. Gordon had explained Jack's—and Bobby's—cause for "changing circumstances" but, still…. Was Jack one of these unsettled men never content?

Donna had turned down two marriage proposals already. She had also rejected an attractive offer from an Orlando firm, choosing instead to board *Arcturus*. Yes, serious matters moved her to call Gordon but, in all fairness to Jack, "restless" explained why she approached her uncle in the first place. Were it not for her, *Arcturus* would be pleasure-cruising without higher aim or purpose. Recently out of law school, she should be impressing her firm's managing partners with her grasp of securities regulation law. Instead, the lithe, strong, green-eyed, 25-year-old, someday-a-lawyer rocked with the *Arcturus's* gentle sway, gathered her shapely sea-legs, and daydreamed over the man on guard above.

Why was she thinking of Jack, and Gordon's sizing Jack up, and Jack's controlled violence.

She recoiled. Was that it? Was the unseen current *violence?* She hoped not, and then grimaced, knowing that Gordon would never have hired men were they not instantly capable of violence. *Let's be fair:* she wanted them ready for violence, but in a controlled, focused—*right* way. Was that too much to ask? Why was she asking for *anything?*

This is impossible! Check the coffee!

Donna idly perused the copy of Jack's security plan posted in the galley as she prepared the coffee paraphernalia. Jack would be atop the boat right now, somewhere on deck, watching. Donna finger-looped another mug from the cabinet, choosing a solid, thick-handled mug boasting the royal crest of Spain, no doubt a keepsake from one of Gordon's adventures. She filled it with the fresh, steaming coffee, poured some cream into it, and, with both mugs in hand, negotiated the steps, the occupied hands and thoughts testing her balance.

Donna spied Jack's six-foot-one, lean figure to her left, leaning across the bow, peering out to sea. She smiled, deciding to show him that she, too, could be stealthy when she wanted. Her rubber-soled shoes stifled all sound of her approach. *Hmmm. Better not get too close and startle him while I'm holding two mugs of hot coffee.* Worse could happen, she thought, as she saw Jack's right hand move slowly to the gun on his belt. Had he sensed her noiseless approach? No, his hand just rested atop the gun, but he continued staring straight out to sea. Yes, some quieter announcement was called for with this young man, in this setting, rather than a practical joke "Boo!" Bad idea!

"What are you about to do, Jack? Shoot some albatross for breakfast? If you've read *Rime of the Ancient Mariner*, do you know what that would do to us all?" She opted for the soft-voice, light-tease approach, instead, and smiled in anticipation of his response.

Jack jolted at her voice. He couldn't help it. He breathed intentionally slowly, removed his hand self-consciously from the weapon, turned and beamed his best smile on the beautiful girl greeting him, looking like she was laughing at him, but only as a tease, an ice-breaker without condescension or airs, he surmised. She probably knew the reaction she caused (How could she not?), but she was so kind, she just ignored it. Maybe she really didn't realize it.

With an exaggerated bow, he greeted her: "Good morning, Lady Donna. I see you're up bright and early. What a delightful start to a sunny, clear day." *Dumb thing to stammer!* She was so smooth it didn't matter and she covered for his overt discomfort.

"Yes, Mr. Soldier-turned-sailor, I do love the sea and the day is already a thing of wonder," she affirmed, and smiled full into his gaze. Then, with a sense of mission-concern: "Is everything all right?" she inquired.

"Oh, quite peaceful," he was quick to reassure. Returning to business mode, he continued reporting: "All was fine last night as well. We have a radar signal approaching from ahead, he indicated cocking his head seaward, but I see no sign of trouble. Bobby will be getting up soon and I'll get a little rest," he added a bit lamely and for no particular reason that he could think of.

She eyed him quizzically. "Well, maybe I'll stand watch with you for just a minute then, if that's OK?"

"Sure." He made it a point to add emphasis.

Well, maybe it was OK. Of course he *wanted* her to. But, it just didn't seem like he could be doing his job standing next to her. Distracting, to say the least! Not that there was anything to be distracted from. Of course, that's when they always hit. Whoever *they* were. Shut up and bask in her presence for a few pre-breakfast minutes, and let Bobby worry about the day shift. Passing time in the presence of a friendly, beautiful maiden, followed by bacon, eggs and coffee, all at sea, in the balmy Bahamian sun east of Florida— Jack added it to his list of "it don't get any better than this" scenarios.

She must have read his mind. Donna broke into a huge smile. Melted him. Without a word, she offered the stout, Spanish mug of steaming coffee he somehow had failed to spot. He hadn't even noticed it or the aroma. She truly was precious.

"Thanks, you read my mind," he burbled, reaching out to take the offer, their eyes locking briefly. More quizzical smile.

"I'm good at that."

"Coffee?"

"No, mind reading."

They laughed, for the moment, a young man and a young woman enjoying each other's company, away from the busy press of the churning mainland occupations so many were right now fumbling toward. The glorious dawn grew somehow more wondrous on this perfect day. (Well, *not perfect* a voice rasped in some professional corner of Jack's consciousness; great evil lurked.) Yeah, maybe, but evil always lurked since the fall of man and was at least lackadaisical enough to lurk out of range at the moment. *Thank you, oh despicable Evil One, for this brief break, but don't for a single second think you are going to lull me into ambush.*

They turned together toward the horizon and side by side, both leaned out over the bow rail, relaxed, embracing the sea's morning nod to the fullest. As they leaned into the rail, her arm brushed his. She turned casually toward him, not willing to squander the moment, and locked his eyes.

"Why are you here, Jack McDonald?" She asked softly, but clearly, as if this were a mere question about his favorite movie, or whether he liked popcorn.

She held his gaze. He had to respect the concise courage and maturity she showed by driving straight to the salient, utterly sweeping around small-talk like Patton blazed past a stronghold. His mind rebelled though, grimaced, and felt *bothered*, as if she had flung a piece of sawdust into his eye while cutting wood. This probing personal question was a bit unfair, he thought.

The answer was obvious and enigmatic, mundane and cosmic,

capitalistic and utterly Romantic, in an eighteenth-century sort of way. She must know that. Why ask?

He was a little irritated. Were Bobby and he not somewhat secretive, shadowy? (They tried to be.) They were not the kind of men to talk freely about such things. To each other, maybe, but not.... He shifted uncomfortably, subtly signaling his unwilling-ness to so engage, but she did not back or look away and the question hung. *Off base!*

All right. What was he supposed to say? Why am I here? Was he supposed to tell this gentle girl: *To kill cruel summbitches if called on to protect good, innocent people? To put my own life between yours and death so that you might live? For good money? For the sheer love of waking up doing something weirdly different, physically dangerous, and all while making money at it? To share another adventure with my com-rade, Bobby and see if we both live through it? To scratch the itch in my trigger finger in a socially acceptable, sublimated sort of Freudian way? To honor those gone before me who did not stay their hand when the times called out for men of courage?*

Why was he *here* and not doing something similar elsewhere, for someone else, maybe even for the bad guys? It struck him, as moments hung, as their eyes locked and as she peered into his soul, that he didn't *know* for sure why he had boarded *Arcturus*. Then, the sudden realization that she already knew that *he* didn't know, jolted Jack again.

Oh, sure, all those good reasons were part of it, but he could have been in the Army still or could just get a job and go skydiving on the weekends. He considered the bolt-from-the-blue revelation smacking him "up side the head" that he *needed* to protect her and these other people on board the *Arcturus*.

He narrowed his eyes as he drifted this distance away, consider-ing the profound ramifications of this new revelation about himself and, looking through her maybe a bit too hard, noticed her eyes widen and her body move back almost imperceptibly, probably in fear. He softened. The last thing he wanted to do was push her away. He moved almost unnoticeably toward her, past the "casual," invisible space boundary.

"I'm here so that you will live," he murmured simply, softly, almost without thinking about it, sounding clumsy and melodramatic even as he said it.

Nevertheless, it was true, he immediately reflected. It was true even though this anachronistic truth reached back into another time, drawing from the best of history and chivalry. It was not only true; it was a pretty good, concise summary, he decided. Jack looked Donna in the eye. She stared up at him and caught her breath.

"Well, getting to be a busy intersection out here," piped Jack's former Executive Office, now joint venturer, dissipating the moment's spell, but tactfully as if the world had not stopped, as if time itself had not stalled for these two. "Who do you think might be paying us a visit at this hour? Is that the 'newsie' delivery? Jack, ole boy, I say, shall we ask them to join us for tea or shall we keel-haul their mizzenmasts?"

Jack could not help but burst out laughing and started to join in the rollicking good fun Bobby was so adept at sparking. Bobby's countenance always broadcasted "I'm up to something!" even during those interludes when he was innocent, if he were, indeed, ever innocent. Jack loved this about Bobby: mischief—hovering. But, he saw that Bobby's face did not match his comic tone and turned to follow his gaze.

There it was: barely perceptible, but there, sure enough. They had company. The radar contact had arrived. The *Arcturus* was not the only boat to ply these waters.

8

*Aboard the Queen Indiaman
October 20th, 1814*

The Sussex Weekly Advertiser of 20th October, 1814 carried the story, mixing local interest with Indies exotica:

Miss Lucy (Lewes) Rand, of our own Sussex, together with 4 other ladies, was a passenger on the *Queen Indiaman*, en route from Torquay to Madras, when on July 9th, 1814 the vessel was attacked and burned out at a small island in the Caribbean Sea. Miss Rand was one of five ladies on board who lost all their clothes except what they wore. Their journey from their home in South Devon did continue, only briefly interrupted, on a companion ship. Unfortunately, the piracy of Napoleon's ship Captains will continue to require caution and extra distance added to already arduous journeys between the Mother country and India. Where is the Admiralty? Can our brave sailors not hunt down the beasts who now range so far as the Americas?

Miss Rand, we pray to our Lord, is now safely with those who love her in Calcutta, where she intends to wed Mr. John Shoolbred. The *Advertiser* toasts the couple, cheering them to long life and good fortune, and invites their return to our fair shores.

The erroneous piece's typical British hopefulness could not begin to convey the sweaty desperation of the *Queen Indiaman's* crew as they strove to save the lives of the passengers, not knowing the outcome.

Lucy turned to survey the scene orchestrated behind her by the obnoxious Mr. McBan. Sailing from her home in Devon had been quite pleasant so far, but for McBan's ways. She disliked the man intensely. She turned her back to the sea, spied a group of sailors sneering, but cowering and avoiding McBan's eyes, and she gawked in disgust as McBan berated the men in his snide, presumptive tone. Her heart groaned for the sailors, although her face portrayed nothing. The Captain or the Mate would approach, she was sure, and intervene, establishing once again that McBan did not captain the ship, regardless of his ambition and authority, whatever its source. She briefly mused over the imaginary sight of seeing McBan being cast overboard, and blushed with shame at the surprising direction her feelings swept her thoughts. *McBan the Jonah. Jonah McBan. Ban the Jonah.* She turned the words over in her mind and toyed with the murder fantasy, giving way to it.

McBan had boarded after setting sail, not until the *Queen Indiaman*, almost clearing the south tip of England, made an unannounced and odd stop at Hugh Town in the Isles of Scilly. McBan strode aboard at night with an air of position, presented himself and a leather pouch of orders to the frowning Captain and later supervised the stevedores personally, cursing them continually as they wrestled large wooden crates marked only "Hemp" (but with the royal seal on each) through the hatches and down deep into the hull. Lucy's curiosity prompted her to take the direct approach and ask McBan why hemp was so important that it demanded the personal attention of so important an officiary, but he had deftly fielded her prying sarcasm, snarled contemptuously, and dodged the question completely, admonishing her condescendingly that "Proper young British ladies should mind their place and business." Lucy seized the opportunity to ask the more approachable ship's surgeon about the goods later, but he had only shrugged as if to say, "I don't want to know and neither do you." She dismissed the newly sawn wood crates from her concerns and turned her thoughts to travel and to India, and, of course, to John and their soon-to-be wedding.

So, they had sailed without further incident, entering the trade winds and running with full sails all the way across the Atlantic, avoiding the French Navy as they wound their way far away to India—at least, without further incident of note, because "McBan's company is definitely not of note," she spoke to the wind, and felt like she had taken him down a notch by the mere observation and relegation of the man to lesser status. Dinners had strained her good manners, with McBan's bragging and loudness dominating each occasion. She tried to be charitable at first, as the Scriptures would admonish her to do, but soon gave in to simply despising the man.

For indeed, John McBan strained the ability of even the charitable to tolerate a boor. He held a Navy commission as Lieutenant but flaunted special orders from Horse Guards—from King George III, essentially, although, in practical reality, from the plotters and powers behind the wars and the King. McBan exhibited talent for getting things done and simultaneously advancing his own standing. He commanded connections across the continent, stretching even into hostile America. He concocted a plan and advanced it to the Foreign Office: "The McBan Plan" his jealous detractors derisively labeled it, muttering among themselves.

Britain was not only fending off Napoleon, but was also in the midst of a rather successful adventure across the Atlantic, essentially resuming putting down the rebellion in the American colonies, although few perceived the Crown's (McBan's) grander design.

The War of 1812, as the Americans called it, was a mere sideshow for the British, but in its backdrop, defeating Napoleon created opportunity, and McBan knew how to strike at opportunity.

McBan's plan was simple. He played on his understanding of human motivation, of human prejudice and hate, mixed together with solid practical economics. McBan learned from British sympathizers in America that some of the Indian tribes had organized under Tecumseh of the Shawnee, and Menawa of the Creeks to resist the United States in its seemingly unstoppable ambition to spread west. At this point, the Mississippi River marked their incursions, but no one expected them to halt at the river and the Creeks and Shawnee east of the Mississippi saw their land, their way of life, and their own sovereignty melting away.

At least, they glumly watched in resignation until America boldly stepped into the face of the Union Jack and ordered it to stop kidnapping American citizens at sea, declaring impudent war as the only way to effectively communicate, once again, to the King. Almost immediately though, the faltering nation took hard punches, threatening its very existence. Washington literally burned as Redcoats stalked its deserted streets. Her enemies savored the aroma of the smoke and warmed in the glow of the flames, gloating in her misfortune and spawning more plots to work her undoing.

After defeating the French combined fleet at Trafalgar, men in London's muffled, walnut-paneled, carpeted clubs and offices quietly began to speculate over fine whiskey on whether the upstarts had let their guard down too much. A supreme British Navy, now in control of the seas and with Napoleon surely almost out of the way, had time to turn its full power westward and reclaim America. After all, only a few short years had passed since 1789, and the

British saw no reason to consider American nationhood sacrosanct.

Indeed, almost ten years after Nelson drove the French from the seas, and with Napoleon receding from the Iberian Peninsula on land under Wellington's pummeling, why not re-take the former colony and undo the aberration? "The World Turned Upside Down" indeed! Time for a new song for the Redcoats to pipe. Just as Britain would frustrate rebellion and revolution that had threatened to intoxicate and inflame Europe, the Empire would reach far across the Atlantic, slap its former colony, and re-establish the monarchy, order, and commerce-under-control. A most natural extension of *pax* Britannia! Why, "America" as a nation was nothing more than a crude interlude, a mutinous, country-bumpkin frolic that was now to be put down, and McBan would be the siege's architect.

And oh, what a plan! Hit America with far more than the regiments soon to be freed up in Europe. Multiply the forces by buying Mexican alliance with Spanish gold stolen by the French, and by arming the red men with French muskets, all confiscated from Wellington's loot taken from Napoleon at Vitoria! Out of convolution, McBan would incite revolution!

McBan's own, close trade-interests with the New England states were not unlike those bonds of commerce other English merchants enjoyed, and England would not want to leave relations with the states so bitterly strained as to impede the flow of profits. The New Englanders were largely against the current war anyway. What irony if the land of Paul Revere himself were to nudge closer to the Mother Country just enough to edge the McBan Plan toward success! McBan would enjoy power, position, and—if he worked the invisible details of the McBan Plan to conclusion—a fortune outside the grasp of Parliament's hated income tax.

All depended on retaking the colonies by proxy. Let the Indians wreak havoc; encourage the Mexicans to sortie across their own northern border, drawing off American troops to the Southwest. Indeed, he foresaw a stunning alliance with the whipped French, appeasing them and leaving them Mexico in return for rattling sabers against the Americans. He knew they wanted Mexico, having assumed ownership briefly while Napoleon occupied and controlled Spain. The Mexicans won independence in 1810, but McBan read the French ambitions correctly when he secretly offered them the chance for at least some residual empire.

McBan laughed aloud, drawing the bemused looks of his club members as they puffed their cigars and wondered what Mr. Ambition plotted now. It had really been so simple. The entire campaign was surely already won over Port and roast venison in London even before McBan presented himself to Wellington in Spain. The timing was perfect. McBan had stood before the soon-to-be Duke, delighted to watch the puffed up field soldier's face grow dark with restrained rage.

All Europe knew that the French in full retreat from Spain were pulling their wagon trains *en masse*, and the raided wealth of Spain with them. Treasure on the move! Even the French soldiers who dared were picking at it, on pain of death of course. Wellington designed to finance the final push of the war (and his career of course, thought McBan) with the gold Wellington's (and McBan's) spies reported to be concentrated with the retreating French in sleepy Vitoria. Wellington's regiments had topped the ridge above Vitoria, broken through Napoleon's artillery rain, and routed the French, sparking chaos as men from both armies scooped up what wealth they could purloin. Napoleon's entire raided fortune—the collected gold, art, jewels and other treasures of conquered Spain— lay there for the taking! McBan simply must have a part of it!

51

The King concurred. Not with McBan purloining the war chest, of course: the King acceded to McBan's purring design to scoop up the thousands of French muskets and accoutrements, along with the Spanish gold in Napoleon's wagons. McBan tantalized the King with his plan to win back the American colony. McBan savored the irony of Aztec gold, seized by the Spaniards, then from the Spaniards by Napoleon, and, only in part, returned to the New World to aid in what McBan proposed would be French-dominated Mexico's renewed ascendancy! The King went along with it. McBan laughed aloud, and excoriated the stevedores, earning the scowl of their crew chief.

And so, in the middle of the night, south of England, tackle creaked. Sweating stevedores swung mysterious crates aboard the *Queen Indiaman.* For his covert preparations, McBan chose the sleepy Hugh Town port out of the way of French and perhaps even American agents who were, no doubt, drinking, whoring, sub-verting and buying information in the busier ports miles away in Poole, Portsmouth, Plymouth, and Bournemouth on England's South coast. Thus, as the *Queen Indiaman* slipped out of Hugh Town in pre-dawn hours, and worked its way to the Bahamas, men who were supposed to be keeping an eye on British machinations spent their youth and their governments' money on—distractions.

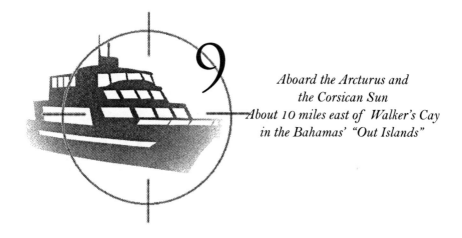

Aboard the Arcturus and
the Corsican Sun
About 10 miles east of Walker's Cay
in the Bahamas' "Out Islands"

inocs up. Still only a speck. Dawn's early light glimmered not quite enough yet to illuminate the white, fishing-charter-looking boat approaching *Arcturus*. What were they going to do anyway, broadcast Captain Kidd-like intentions? This was the Atlantic ocean, with the Bahamas off to starboard, and there *were* a couple of other boats out there. Some people just fished. It's not as though he'd spot the *Jolly Roger* flying from her mast, even if the unknown crew were a drug-running, murdering collection of snakes.

This vessel's course pointed steadily in their direction, though. Longer than the usual fishing charter boat. No sails, so this contact was no European blue water cruiser. High mast. That didn't mean anything, necessarily, but the high mast improved communications. Jack had picked it up on the *Arcturus's* own Furuno 48-inch radar an hour before dawn. Nearing the end of his watch, the radar's alert tone suddenly squawked, starting Jack from the pre-daylight quiet. The blip first appeared off Perdido Cay and hovered there, but now moved on a line intersecting *Arcturus's* own course. Efforts to hail its captain met with ambiguous silence. *Not good.* Intersection time came sooner than Jack had expected.

"What do you think?"

"Nothing to think, yet."

"Yeah."

"Bobby, let's run the drill. Agreed?"

"Yeppers and gippers, skipper," Bobby concurred and saluted.

The bodyguards notched this scenario high on the list of probable responses: "Approach by unknown threat vessel" they had called it in the "Actions on Contact" annex to their OpOrder. Their plan called for simple, progressively-heightened measures that eventually included aroused, armed passengers. The men were to position near the rifle locker with each man poised to hit the horn switches they had ordered installed as part of the boat's outfitting. (Got to be able to shoot, move and communicate; they did the shooting, the boat did the moving, and the horns were part of the overall combat commo plan.)

They had debated whether to make their armed presence obvious, warning away some enemy, but also alerting an attacker to the armed defense. They had decided to take the Ranger way: deny the enemy the intelligence about his own "enemy situation" and go on "stand to," keeping a clear field of fire at the approaching vessel, but with weapons staying hidden. If the approach were from one direction only, then the plan was sound. If from multiple directions, then they would call up additional crew to stand by and take up other OPs (observation posts). Otherwise, Gordon from higher up on the boat could cover 360 degrees.

The approaching boat remained on course to intersect *Arcturus*.

Probably just a friendly, vacationing couple feeling comradeship with fellow, lighthearted blue water sailors and saying "hello," perhaps with radio trouble. Not likely; modern radios perform reliably. Maybe they have older models. They might need medical care, or some supplies, or need a weather report, but no one appeared in the binocular field of vision waving or signaling for help. The boat closed at a moderate to lazy speed, nothing about its deck telegraphing danger.

Jack didn't like it. He watched it grow bigger in the binoculars. It came within a mile and Jack retrieved the rifles, handing one to his friend, according to their plan. Still, on it came. The solid M-1s remained out of sight, resting butt-down on the deck, each shooter keeping the rifle low but ready.

Then, at about 300 yards, everything changed. A man appeared at the bow with a tube, rested it on the bow rail, which now looked fatter than just a rail—maybe widened with sandbags. Jack gasped as he saw the man deliberately point the tube at the *Arcturus*.

"Missile!" Jack boomed out to Bobby. "Jolly Roger" he next called out, giving their sign for an attack by an approaching vessel verified as some murderous enemy. They had enjoyed choosing "Jolly Roger" as the signal for some sort of pirate attack, laughing and singing lines from Hans Zimmer's rollicking composition, *When You're a Professional Pirate*, right out of *The Muppet Treasure Island* but it did not seem so funny now.

Bobby was now to hit the horn button and join Jack, rifle in hand, hopefully before the missile launched. Studying the Somalia-coast attacks, the possibility of some sort of missile attack had occurred to them, but they measured it as remote, and just plain outside of the realm of threats that they could prepare to fend off with certainty.

Jack calculated that the tube, that he now saw had a swelling at the business end, was probably one of the ubiquitous RPG's.

"Shooter!" he called out to Bobby, who leveled his own much smaller, missile-launching M-1 across the bow to attack the grenadier. "Engage RPG ASAP!" Jack urged, hearing Bobby's M-1 boom before his own voice died away, but seeing a flash and a bluish-white puff from the attacking boat at the same time.

"Incoming!" Jack yelled to all, without time to hit the horn, as he dropped to one knee, braced his own M-1 on a life-ring hung on the rail, and began firing at the grenade launcher pirate, for he knew now the nature of the threat. He did not know the motive, nor did he need to know just now what drove this maniac, but plainly the attack was to destroy, not to seize the boat. They had run afoul of somebody's plans and were to be "disappeared." A chilling thought. This was "life or death on a lee shore," his mind absurdly describing their dire situation drawing from the expression growled by Long John Silver even as he re-acquired his sight picture.

The signature RPG smoke-trail snaked to the boat, whooshing overhead by a scant, few feet. The grenadier was either not practiced, or he was just a little excited, or perhaps he jerked at the unexpected, almost simultaneous return fire. Fool. Made a bad assumption. He should have waited until they were only maybe 100 yards out, but had probably worried about the exploding boat exacting its final revenge with its death throe fragments. His mistake. Jack grimly grinned.

Jack's rational surmises about pirate tactics failed to account for the human factor. The men on board the *Corsican Sun* had grown bored. Posted simply to guard a tiny anchorage on the precipice of the Caribbean basin, they played Texas Hold-'em and fished until tiring of those pursuits and running out of cigarettes.

Guard against what? What would they do if someone showed up? They assumed authority to harass away any curious divers or other fishermen from the cove, but had not made plans beyond those incursions. Their commander staged another poaching episode far to the south, always sure to draw the ire and attention of the Royal Bahamian Defense Force whose first and only combat was against Cuba over just such an episode. Their boss would apologize later. It was all a mistake. With the BDF on full alert 250 miles away, the men aboard the *Sun* might as well have been off the breakers of a far-flung South Pacific island.

Their own radar screen fascinated them as the blips showed the mystery boat approaching ever closer. Like a soccer goalie tiring of the opposite-field play, the screen action induced the Cuban RPG fisherman out of his "guard the anchorage" job and no sailor protested as they disobediently steamed out toward the *Arcturus* on intercept course instead of cutting the engine and drifting at the mouth of the bay, as ordered by Revaca.

At first, they approached *Arcturus* moved by no more motive than curiosity. The Fisherman—ever dominating the forefront—spy-glassed the luxury yacht and hooted to the rest when he saw Donna on the deck. On impulse, he proposed, and the crew acceded, that they approach with the RPG up as if to fire a "warning shot" across the bow (as they had seen done in movies). They would bully their way aboard the *Arcturus*, have some fun, and perhaps exact a bribe or just steal what they wanted, before departing to resume their numbingly dull duty.

In truth, unspoken to his cohorts, The Fisherman fancied himself as the first aboard where he would immediately check out the girl and maybe take advantage of her unprotected status, with armed men backing him up. If the men on board gave him any trouble, well, they would not be the first to disappear out here on the frontier between the quieter Caribbean Sea and the turbulent Atlantic. Not really sure of just what he intended, he committed a grave error. He seized the RPG and propped the tube over the bow, bringing his eye to the aiming scope just to look serious and get a better look at the girl.

Peering through the RPG's scope for the greater detail offered by the optical sight's 2.7x magnification, the clear image of two men with large rifles aiming straight at him shocked The Fisherman. He had not intended matters to go this far, but, rather than lowering the RPG and waving a sign of benign intent, the man—still ego-bloated in his own bluster—snapped out a bad decision. His hand and body flinched just as the boat struck a wave, and the tube elevated and swayed to the right, just as he hastily fired the rocket toward *Arcturus*.

The first M-1 shot achieved hilarious drama on board the Jolly Roger. These pirates had expected easy pickings. The RPG-shooting, ambitious Fisherman pitched backward, slammed by two .30 caliber slugs at almost the same time. The spotter-loader behind him suffered from the scorching, surprise RPG back-blast. Jack and Bobby shifted fire to the roasted, stunned spotter-loader, who had apparently been on deck to enjoy the show and help reload if necessary. The burned spotter did not remain tortured by his burns long.

Jack wondered why the spotter had remained behind the rocketeer, off slightly to the side but not far enough to avoid the edge of the back blast cone. His legs first seared by the hot gasses escaping the back of the tube, that pirate, too, then died in disbelief, shot in the stomach and chest with the waiting, next RPG round in his hands, "pipe" end turned toward the tube, ready for loading.

The deck erupted with two more men, one of whom presented a second RPG launcher, dropped to a knee, propped it over the rail, with all of this occurring now only 250 yards away since the pirate ship had continued its steady approach as if all were calm.

Jack responded to the "ching" sound of the empty, eight-round, M-1 clip ejecting by jamming a fresh eight rounds into "Old Reliable." Dropping behind concealment, Jack twisted slightly to reach his bandoleer pouch for the ammunition. From the corner of his eye, Jack spotted a sleek, black shape above and in the distance: a chopper! Was this a coordinated attack? What other resources did the enemy have? Another boat? Rocket launchers on the chopper? Surely not! Jack knew that a chopper so-armed meant their death. They would join the throngs of the deep! Nevertheless, the chopper stood off, hanging back, just watching.

Centering the tip of the front sight in the rear aperture, Jack concentrated on a high-chest shot on the remaining two men. The *Arcturus* rolled, but Jack and Bobby held steady and let the sight picture lower and cross the bodies of the targets. Both Jack and Bobby fired and the two pirates dropped—or dove for cover—Jack could not tell which.

However, one hard-case must have low-crawled up to the bow with an RPG, playing it safe until ready. The surviving gunner popped up, leveled off with the tube, and stuck it out while Bobby shifted fire onto him. The gunner let fly with the missile from about 150 yards now, probably feeling some satisfaction, just before he felt Bobby reach out and touch him with a shot that exploded his jaw, impaling his brain with his own bone.

Jack watched in spellbound horror as the missile seemed to

hone in with a mind of its own. He saw its engine kick in a few yards out of the tube. Then, he was thrown off his feet as the rocket-propelled, oversized grenade exploded at the bow of the *Arcturus*. Hot shards of sheared, aluminum hull sang by his head. Jack's ankle cracked against the boat's nearby storage locker. The *Arcturus* shuddered.

Jack leapt painfully to his feet, aimed toward the Jolly Roger deck, saw no targets, and poured steady shots into the pilot house until that clip, too "ker-chunged" up and away. He reloaded and scanned for more, thought he saw movement in the pilothouse of the now very close pirate ship, and poured four more slugs into the boat, two through the windows, two lower—low enough to get a crouching killer if the copper-jacketed bullets penetrated.

Crazily, the *Corsican Sun*, the name he now read from its name boards, continued on its course as if powered by spirits. He saw no sign of life on board. Casting a wary glance upward, he worried that just maybe it was piloted by ghosts in a high tech, electronic, radio-controlled manner of sorts.

Bobby raced to the bow, stopped short, turned and reported back: "The tip of the front (Momentarily forgetting his so carefully-practiced nautical terminology was forgiven under the circumstance.) is punctured and peeled back."

"Anyone hurt?" Jack called as he did a "tactical reload," ejecting the partially-spent clip in favor of one fat and full with fresh rounds.

He meant to catch the remaining three rounds popping out of the magazine well, but in the excitement, missed. The ejected clip hit the deck with the leftover, loose rounds spilling and rolling. Jack figured he could be falling all over the place like one of those cartoon characters trying to stay up with feet flying over rolling marbles. No more "tactical reloads" on ship. He had executed the tactical reload, done during a lull to assure ample ammo for the next confrontation, acting from training and he made a mental note to adjust tactics for Gy-reen type operations with the vintage rifle whose ammunition was not contained in a detachable box magazine.

It was almost funny that he was imagining Bobby and him down below fine-tuning their tactics, while still recovering from having been almost been blown out of the water. They would have been shark bait! *Damn, that ankle was on fire.*

"Don't see any wounded. First Aid?" Jack asked around.

The two crewmen emerged from below, one reporting that no one below was injured.

"Check around for wounded," Bobby directed him.

"No one's hurt," came the welcomed response moments later.

"How bad's the boat?" Jack worried, now that casualties were off the immediate concern list. He remained at high ready with the M-1, safety off and finger just outside the trigger guard, watching the pirate vessel bob in the water, still approaching, but no attacker presented himself. He believed they had killed all, pouring U.S., caliber .30, M-1 rifle, aimed fire onto the boat at fairly close range, making sure that the helm area got doused with lead. Obviously, these stupid *criminal-animalians* had made the fatal mistake of assuming unarmed victims. Wrong.

But, the *Arcturus* was in trouble, and the ominous helicopter circled in the distance. The *Corsican Sun* idled up laconically, as if nothing at all had happened, on a course to pass within fifty yards and then, apparently, thrum weirdly on out to sea. Instead, it lapsed into a circular path.

A theory sprang to mind. Jack elevated the M-1, aimed low to compensate for the lack of time for the bullet to rise to line-of-sight within such a short range, and poured fire onto the electronics

61

sprouting from atop the pilot house, reloading and discharging eight more shots in quick succession. Bobby saw what he was doing and joined in. Together, they put on quite a show, a veritable "mad minute," turning as the *Sun* showed its stern, keeping it up until the *Sun's* engine slowed and died, it's electronics interrupted, and it was dead in the water, ready for boarding. The boys had taken a prize! Aaarrrgh! Besides, they so did love to shoot.

10

The Wreck of
the Queen Indiaman

Horatio Lord Nelson's 1804 victory made the British sea captains complacent and so, upon spying a vessel far behind, but approaching, the Captain of the *Queen Indiaman* perked to attention, but not to alarm. They were in the trade winds and could hardly expect to plough the seas alone. Still, no one in the Admiralty had told him of another British vessel in these seas and the Americans' privateers had grown increasingly and disconcertingly pesky. A few French captains still raided the Caribbean too.

After two days, it became plain they were pursued, and that the chase was not going well. The *Queen* had been chosen specifically by McBan for her speed and the damned McBan had held forth conspiratorially about secrecy and speed being security enough for the voyage, as if he had years at sea! Slamming his orders from London down onto the Captain's desk like a headsman's axe on the chopping block (thought the Captain), McBan insisted that the Captain not delay to permit their three slower escort frigates time to keep up. *Damn the man! Frigates! I told them we needed frigates to fight off the wolves!* Such elementary seamanship! Why was he ignored?

Now the approaching raider sorely tested the *Queen's* speed and the voyage hardly seemed secret. Every time the Captain attempted to shift course southward, the predator shifted as if to steer the Captain back onto some designed course.

On the sixth day of the chase, while nervously telescoping the privateer, the *Queen Indiaman* ran aground, ripping her hull on a hidden reef, such as those that claimed many lives in the Americas. Lacking the guns to repulse attack, she was boarded by the privateer's leering crew, and all were murdered. The *Queen Indiaman* was torched. The poor Captain had expected gracious capture and gallant delivery to the closest British possession. His death grimace was a mixture of terror and disbelief, watching the crew break out the hellish skull-and-bones black banner as a cutlass spilled his entrails. He faintly notioned the cruel fate of his passengers and crew before closing his eyes to slip overboard to join in death the sea on which he had made his life.

All crew and male passengers were similarly dispatched, but for one. McBan shook the hand of the privateer commander, and the two retired to the Captain's cabin to celebrate with French wine, and to plot the course south, toward Venezuela and then Jamaica, to the shrieks and laughter above where the crew enjoyed the women. Lucy would never marry John, and the *Advertiser's* thoughtful concern for her, and its good-cheer wishes availed her no help. Sussex would never know its daughter's grim fate.

Alas, McBan had no reason to complain when his ship met its ironic, similarly black fate two days later. McBan's new crew fought off boarding, beat back the attacking rival American vessel, shattering its masts, and limped away, but they were forced to shelter in a nearby bay for repairs. There, in a shallow cove, with the Atlantic beating angrily just outside the bay, the traitor's pirate ship spun in one of the wild Atlantic's unpredictable currents and hit rock, trapping its already cannon-shattered hulk.

Broken oak seemed to mock "Marooned!" Plainly, they would not leave this island without another ship. More likely, they would prolong their deaths before discovery by the next interloping opportunists spied them and landed armed shore parties to gain from their misfortune. They unloaded tools and cargo, and sawed up lumber for use ashore, abandoning the ship, forlornly watching its remains grinding to pieces on the reef.

The Captain put half of the men to making shelters while the other half hauled McBan's cargo uphill to their chosen cache. Exhausted, and growing hungry, the men stewed in bitter bloodlust, maddened by the wealth paradoxically buried at their fingertips, but a galaxy away. The privateer, McBan and the entire body of castaways eventually fell out fighting over their secreted cargo, the remaining women, and the scant food salvaged, and with poetic justice rarely seen in this life, perished to the last man in the violent orgy. Some died quickly, others bled out slowly, with the wounded survivors dying the tortured death of the starving.

The mocking ship remains finally broke up like so many other wrecked hulks in the treacherous waters of that part of the world. The club men inquired of McBan less and less, and always with detached, disinterested, and somewhat smug curiosity. The successful American privateer sank off the coast of North Carolina in a storm before its Captain could report his victory and prize-taking and the *Indiaman's* shipwreck.

The British Admiralty investigation started from its headquarters across from The Red Lion pub in London but, upstaged by intensifying American seamanship and success and pressured to pull up short of discovering scandal and trickery, the investigation fizzled and faded. The few plan's promoters perceived that their pockets had probably been picked by McBan and hushed any talk of it. The plan had been so successfully secret. Besides, King George III slipped into another of his bouts with insanity and the mad King forgot his *Queen Indiaman's* cargo, his plan to re-gain the American colonies, and the plan's bombastic author.

11 *Remembering the Alamo*

Before setting sail, Jack and Bobby had insisted on seeing the *Arcturus's* specs, and on personally inspecting the craft, as if they knew what they were looking at. They suspected that Gordon strained to conceal his bemusement and played along. Indeed, they barely canned their own laughter when handed the boat's specifications, solemnly thanking Gordon, and bursting into fits of hilarity the second they achieved discretion distance.

"Burger Flush Deck!" hooted Bobby. "What the Hell is a Burger Flush Deck?"

"Maybe it was won at cards with a matching hand of hamburgers," Jack lamely suggested.

Bobby gawked at Jack, pausing for effect and rolling his eyes before berating Jack for such a stupid conjecture, offering up one no better, centered on toilets and German mayors.

In truth, the two could claim little appreciation of even luxury seagoing vessels. They had canoed, rafted, fished, water-skied, and even paddled rubber boats down swamp rivers and onto beaches. True, Jack had bought his sailboat to train and live on, and they had successfully managed it down the southern coast. However, other than this short course in sailing, their maritime experience consisted of slipping up rivers and sleeping on the decks of cutters carrying them into the attack. Their experience going *off* the deck, over the side, clamoring down cargo nets to assault some more sand far exceeded their experience *on deck* handling a boat.

The two land warriors grew to appreciate the 1971, recently re-fitted, technologically up-to-date Burger Flush Deck cruiser. Unimpressed at first, they nevertheless studied it carefully, asked Gordon endless questions, and memorized its most important characteristics, as they might memorize the maximum effective range of the Army's mortars and artillery pieces. They insisted on trying each of its radios, and practiced the nautical way of radio talk, almost eradicating the landlubberly, military manner of radio chatter. This boat was nice, they concluded in growing admiration! They saw it as confirming their theory that Gordon was a rich corporate type, plying the warm seas on a lark.

Gordon, in contrast, chose the boat for a number of other sound reasons. *Arcturus* stretched eighty-one feet, swelling to nineteen feet in the beam. She carried almost 5,000 gallons of diesel fuel and the yacht could cross the Atlantic, as she had proven under the command of her last owner. Gordon turbo-charged her two 500-horsepower General Motors engines at a shop he knew, gaining three more knots of boosted speed. He had her hull re-painted a bluish hue that blended better with the ocean without displaying overt camouflage. The *Arcturus's* five, watertight compartments struck Gordon as a particularly good idea, right at the moment.

The luxurious cruise-yacht was well-suited for its mission, appearing to admiring eyes as just another of many rich-man-toys lolling about the off-Florida Caribbean. Not so. She would not win serious races, but she could continue to open sea and beyond where lesser vessels would suffer, and wise captains would turn back. *Arcturus* carried her passengers to their objective covertly and, it is fair to say, in well-appointed, teakish comfort and safety.

Gordon eyed the Avon six-person life raft locker on the way to the bow.

At first, Jack and Bobby inspected the damage, but, as Gordon and the crew collected at the bow to peer at the hole left by the exploding RPG round, the bodyguards took up positions at the gunwales, roaming up and down the deck scanning for the next threat.

Sharp aluminum peeled back from a three-foot yawning hole at the nose of the boat's bow, perilously low. Had the attack launched an hour later, the built-in foredeck settee would no doubt have hosted several loungers enjoying yogurt and granola in the morning spray.

Each bouncing swell sloshed saltwater into the breached hull. Jack saw no choice but to nurse the cruiser ashore and patch. They carried rivets, caulk, some coil aluminum, and fiberglass to effect the temporary repairs. Fixing the boat would not require long delay. Regardless, they might not have even the brief required time for the patch.

Jack feared the chopper and the even greater danger it heralded. Pirates with the money for a chopper-coordinated raid! Jack should assume that their enemy's hand fondled the trigger of greater weapons and resources than those already shown. Quickly now. Time to act. Jack assumed authority and called a planning conference in the pilothouse—more to give orders than to plan.

"Let's get to the island," Bobby summarized, more as a statement of the tactical situation than as a request or suggestion. Jack and Gordon nodded their concurrence.

"We'll shelter there," Gordon responded, pointing to the hazily visible shore in the distance.

"What's *there*?" the two bodyguards chorused. The three looked at each other and laughed nervously, still coming down from the adrenaline.

"A small cove, exposed beach backed by moderately thick stands of trees, fresh water pools, some man-made structures, and a single rise of high ground, at least high for around here," Gordon specified.

Jack eyed Gordon hard. Gordon pretended to be gazing at the shoreline. Jack grasped Gordon's terrain analysis immediately, and it flashed through his mind that Gordon's fast summation of the critical elements of an evolving operations plan spoke of experience and deserved respect—later when they had time. *Who was this guy?* Now, though, action was required.

"Map?" Jack asked, always the infantryman.

Always the infantryman, Bobby thought. Bobby addressed Gordon, who apparently already knew what was ashore: "Sir, I will stay up here and keep watch and listen to your plan. Please brief Jack on the terrain as soon as you can." And with that, he patrolled as Gordon and Jack pulled a chart from the brass and teak chart drawers in the pilothouse. Gordon weighted down the chart with empty coffee mugs decorated with sailfish and tarpon. He wasted no time.

"Jack, look right here," Gordon jabbed with a pencil. He paused, giving Jack time to analyze the contour lines and other features indicated on the chart. The island was about five miles long east to west, and only about two miles north to south, but those were rough dimensions. Its irregular perimeter sported rocky extensions, short stretches of open beach, and coves, both deeply penetrating the land mass, and some mere shallow dips into the irregular coastline. The largest of these lay before them where Gordon had pointed earlier, Jack grasped, and the depths promised by the chart permitted the six-foot draft *Arcturus* to slip in and out, although if she took on water, they would need the spare depth the chart said they had. He hoped so; he did not relish being beached.

"Sir, I suggest we make for shore now, tow the *Sun*, leave a small team there to search it and confiscate additional weapons and tools we might use, and start repairing the *Arcturus*. I will take whatever crew you don't need to patch the boat up to the building on this hilltop, and prepare defensive positions. We have to assume we will be attacked again and prepare our own attack for that contingency. You can radio us if you need us at the beach, or if you have to abandon the boat and get to the fort."

Jack's plan sounded desperate, but he realistically assessed their exposure to air attack. He assumed that the chopper pilot would have blown them away if he had the capability; Jack wondered where he might go to arm up. Perhaps he did not need to return to a populated port, but had staged from another of the many, nearby islands, almost as secluded as they had been when Columbus landed at San Salvador, not far to the south. If so, the chopper might pick up more goons and renew the attack by landing an assault force. Jack assumed these capabilities and was not pleased.

"Oh, and I'm calling a mayday," Jack concluded.

"Do it, according to your plan," Gordon assented, and the men got busy.

Bobby radioed Chris. Thank God they had taken the time to look up the local Coast Guard presence in Miami. And thank God doubly he had been friendly. The bored receptionist had dismissively waved them to bland chairs for what looked like a long, fruitless wait.

However, a cheerful, sharp-eyed, scrubbed, STRAC looking officer exploded out of an office, grabbed their hands, shooed them to the coffee room (the "galley" he had called it) and ushered them into a cheap, but soft cushioned lounge, repaired with matching-color duct tape where required.

After his to-the-point "Who are you, whatta-you-want, what are you up to," peppering, introductory inquiry, Jack explained their purpose. The officer had apparently liked the fact that Jack's sail-boat was tied up at Dinner Key, only five miles down Biscayne Bay from the Coast Guard Station.

Chris had rocked back, slapped his hands on his desktop, star-tling Jack and Bobby, and proclaimed, "By Neptune's balls, you mercenaries got guts!"

The boys failed to fight the impulse to glance at one another, and caught each other's raised eyebrow looks, sharing a telepathic agreement: *Plainly, this swabbie is crazy!*

The USCG Lieutenant howled with laughter, stood up, and shouted to the receptionist: "We're going to lunch!"

Trapped by their tactical exigency to coordinate with support elements, the boys permitted themselves to be captured. Chris drove them off the Coast Guard's island-like facility in the bay, headed west toward lunch and pointed out Star Island's luxury homes, indicating Al Capone's mansion and Rosie O'Donnell's.

"I can tell by looking at the two of you that you are big Rosie O'Donnell fans, right? I'm sure you and Rosie are hand-in-hand on the gun-control issue!"

By two in the afternoon, all three had sore jaws from laughing. Jack and Bobby had not only coordinated for military support; they had made a friend.

ARCTURUS

Chris had grown up in Tampa, spending all spare time either in the swamps, or in the Gulf, or working on Gulf-related projects patching boats, mending nets, pouring over charts, swimming, diving, and generally expressing his love of the warm, Florida waters. After an initial anomalous tour at Bayfield, Wisconsin, perched like a hanging icicle on the sub-Arctic edge of the United States, seeming to be more a part of frigid Lake Superior than the country below it, Chris worked his way back to his home state, married, settled down, and was busy raising two tikes when not hunting drug runners and seagoing criminals. The small station at Bayfield had failed to drive him off and he had embraced the cold, the alternate universe frontier atmosphere, and the charming tourist ambiance, but had chafed to return to the ocean.

Chris was a natural for the "additional duty" of public liaison officer. The receptionist had efficiently claimed her discretionary authority to sort the boys' business, stuffing it into that category, congratulating herself for steering them to Chris and getting them out of her own way so quickly. Little did she know what confederacy she had birthed.

Chris took down their registration number and the *Arcturus's* description, burned a copy of their proposed route, noting the proximity of their destination off the Cuban coast, and marked their route on it. Then, he spent the remainder of the long southern summer afternoon briefing them on the incident log in their area. Around five, he glanced at the clock on the wall and announced the briefing over, proclaiming his need to get home and check in with his wife and two young children.

Chris seemed impossibly insane and maturely responsible at the same time. They invited him to beer. He declined, but they could see they had appealed to a part of the man he was deciding to put away for the time being. They shook hands.

In the parking lot, Chris admonished them: "Look, between the drug runners, the Communists, and the pirates of general category, there's enough out there for you to watch out for, not to even mention the weather. I don't know what you two ne'er-do-wells are up to, but you are sailing in the vicinity of some troubled waters. The Cubans avoid provoking trouble they can't handle, but they do not permit Americans to waltz around off their coast either. So don't think you are going on an illegal vacation to Havana, or that you are going to become cigar smugglers or something." He smiled while issuing this warning, and they knew he trusted them or he would not have helped.

"The USCG is not the USN and our resources are limited. Plus, the Caribbean is bigger than you think. We can pull you out of a bad storm, but we can't mount an amphibious assault on the local dictatorship to extract your sorry asses from a bad toehold on a beach. That's been tried, if you remember," Chris reminded them, obliquely referring to the Bay of Pigs invasion. They had climbed into their pickup truck with a sheaf of frequencies, call signs, and nautical protocol radio lingo tucked under their arms.

Bobby now hailed the Coast Guard, reaching a businesslike dispatcher who took the report and promised to report the incident, marshal help, and contact them. Boat trouble was one thing; an RPG attack was another. The dispatcher suspected that Bobby and his gang were up to no good, but he could sort that all out later; for now, they had some kind of maniac hit squadron running around off the coast, supported by rotary wing for God's sake! Who else might already be pirated and dead? The dispatcher thought that the attack was probably an armed robbery, Somalia coast style.

The Officer of the Day alerted the Sector Commander, and the Sector Commander called the Chief, Response Operations. This little international incident was going to call for more than just sending out a search and rescue boat. It would also take time. Dispatch reasoned, incorrectly, that the *Arcturus* folks would keep for awhile, having made it ashore and that the greater threat was now a raid on some other frolicking yachters or fishermen. His brother-in-law ran a charter out of Fort Lauderdale and might just be out that way.

His reasoning was sound, if a bit biased, concluding that the higher priority was patterned patrolling for the attackers and picking up the victims later, but he was wrong. The Cutter *Chandeleur* would stand down for now for a rescue operation, and go on patrol to the north.

12

Perdido Cay
Life or Death on
a Lee Shore

So far, so good, considering. As Jack and Bobby cleared the area near the surf, Gordon supervised beaching *Arcturus* in the clear, shallow water, in a way that was not permanent, supporting the bow on driftwood, and got the repair underway, inspecting for further damage. One crewman anchored the *Corsican Sun* a short distance away, to be inspected once the repair team started work.

Gordon left the repairs in capable hands and boarded the *Corsican Sun* while Jack and Bobby attended to tactical matters. Ten minutes later, Gordon emerged, asked for some extra hands, and ducked back down a hatch to continue his search of the *Sun*. Finishing, Gordon and the search crew returned to the *Arcturus* with an armful of what appeared to be blankets. They went below. Gordon returned to deck and radioed Jack to join him at the beach.

Gordon watched approvingly as Jack distributed weapons, including those taken undamaged from the *Corsican Sun*, issuing the shotguns to two men who stood guard by the beach. No unfired RPGs remained. Interestingly, in the pithy whole-group briefing on the beach, two other weapons turned up. An amused Jack reckoned later that they should not have been so surprised. The crowd that foresaw the need to hire two young ex-fighters to ride shotgun obviously foresaw the need to go to sea armed. And just look at what emerged!

Two crew produced a bolt action, scoped hunting rifle and a military surplus 1903A3 Springfield rifle of World War I vintage, both solid, accurate weapons shooting—coincidentally?—the same ammunition as the M-1's: the commercially common, affordable, venerable "thirty-ought six" caliber (.30-06). Not that unusual, really. Very popular caliber, widely available. Plenty of knock-down power. Cheaper than some of the newer, "hotter" calibers since the .30-06 remained in such wide use. Lots of deer rifles shot it and you could pick it up at any gun shop or department store with a decent sporting goods section.

The men explained that, at the last minute, they had loaded their personal arms, Jack's and Bobby's preparations having inspired their own. The boys were not happy about being kept in the dark, since they had required knowing the boat's full complement of weapons for their own planning purposes, but, secretly, they thanked the men. What troubled them was that they felt left out of a secret, that they were the only ones who did not know what was really going on. Jack marked down another question for Gordon, at the right time.

The boys welcomed the weapons and their owners affirmed that they knew how to shoot. Shrugging at the development, seeing no constructive purpose in berating the men, and given the lack of opportunity to test the shooters' claimed skills and the weapons' zeroes, Jack and Bobby next trooped to the high ground shown on the map, locating it easily through ¼ mile of low jungle, without use of a compass.

They planned as they reconnoitered, and wondered aloud how much there was to this cruise other than what Gordon had told them. Not every sunny sailing adventure included RPG attack, chopper harassment, and an amphibious assault against boaters armed to the teeth. Hmmm: questions of Gordon later.

Sparse, tropical vegetation clumped beneath the ragged palm and pine forest, painting an exotic scene not unlike the forest chase scene in the original "Star Wars," thought Jack, only with much lower trees.

Jack patrolled away from the beach and up a shallow incline. Behind him, toward the beach, a variety of bushes clung together tightly to give concealment, thinning gradually as the land gently rose, transitioning to palmetto underneath the trees, tied together in random spots by tangles of vines. Perfect. Two shallow creeks snaked their way downhill to the lagoon. These were two-edged swords. Yes, these ditches helped conceal a man working his way to and from their positions on the high ground above, but they had to be covered as likely sneaky approach routes by the enemy, too. In the classic defense, infantrymen might plant the ditches with Claymore mines and plan pre-plotted artillery targets on them to block enemy use of this concealment, but such exploding counter-measures were unavailable to the two ex-soldiers.

Linking up, Jack beckoned to Bobby, and the two left sight of the ship, meaning, tactically, that they could not support or help the crew by rifle fire from the ground above, once about 50 yards into the scrubby forest. Quick, concealed routes back and forth and radio communication became vital. A radio check confirmed commo with Gordon, and being able to talk and plan beat being able to see each other: they could extend the range of their observation and defense. They turned their attention to the terrain and their defensive position.

Here, on what passed for a hilltop, they were in better-than-expected shape. As they broke out of the low, sandy jungle, they were surprised to discover that an abandoned mission topped the small knoll. This lightly-jungled knoll culminated after the steady, but easy rise from the open beach. Jack could hear muffled sounds of the men laboring on the ship, a scant 500 yards away and about 80 feet lower, although the vegetation hid them.

The structure manifested its original purpose from the crumbling oak benches that must have faced an alter, adorned by a long-removed crucifix. Fixed interior carvings further proclaimed the church's original function. While the map showed a generic black square to illustrate the building's site, the map legend's simple symbol could not express what they found.

They found an ancient, weathered, but substantial stone-and-stucco Spanish mission compound, surrounded by a low wall with a front gate opening, and thoroughly overgrown with palm both low and high, all woven together with the expected assortment of tropical vines. They stood back in awe for a moment.

With little time to act the tourist, they circled the mission, looking for strengths and weaknesses, and then patrolled around the low and open tropical growth surrounding the mission, returning to the mission gate opening to compare notes and develop a defensive plan.

The low perimeter wall was a bonus. About four feet tall, and a foot thick, it would stop small arms fire despite a couple centuries' wear and tear. The wall would also detonate RPG rounds, and maybe stop blast and fragments depending on the type round the enemy was using. They did not know how many RPG's they might face, but they assumed there were more. They were concerned that the wall would obliterate into secondary missile fragments when struck, and looked to the church interior as the more likely last line of defense. The more they eyed the wall, the more they envisioned it becoming a spray of rock, once hit by an RPG. They turned to examine the building's interior.

Inside the mission church, they found a spacious, timber-framed chapel with little blocking a fighter from running back and forth. This would be their real fort, even if they skirmished with the attackers at the wall first. The RPG's could fire into the church, but the shooters could not be sure they were hitting people. Sooner or later, the pirates had to assault the building, and that attack would initiate the real fun.

Jack set about hastily piling rubble into firing positions, while Bobby scanned forward to recon more precisely for the most likely enemy approaches. While Bobby roamed around in the woods, so to speak, Jack explored the church's layout, smaller rooms, and contents. Jack touched a cool, rough stone and could not help but wonder at the hands that carved it. It looked like all had been moved out or raided. The mission was multi-level, with a tiny dungeon-like basement carved out of what he presumed to be rock. The basement included diminutive rooms for lodging and storage. Maybe it was a wine cellar. All in all, the mission's countenance conveyed humble might. Spaniards probably built it in the mid-1600s Jack speculated.

The mission reminded him—somewhat disconcertingly—of the Alamo, which he had reverently visited during a brief trip to San Antonio, and Jack so dubbed the mission after the famous last stand. Jack hoped that this memory did not foreshadow their own fate on the island. He would learn from the Alamo defenders: do not close off options other than fighting it out to the last man. Remain mobile, even while choosing to make a stand. For now, he kept the comparison and the nickname to himself.

Unfortunately, this diminutive island came bounded by its own natural, watery barrier to maneuver and flight. Planning secondary fighting positions and escaping from the static mission defense was just fine, but the island hardly offered a wide variety of other tactical maneuver plans; its size severely limited their preparing an escape. For lack of a good escape from "The Alamo," Jack determined not to just wait for an assault. While they would plan and prepare exits, and attempt to spring ambushes both within and without the compound, Jack planned to break up the attack by finding a way to assault their attackers first.

Trouble was, they probably had little time to prepare. What disadvantages did they face? That damned chopper might be the enemy ace-in-the-hole. The Texans and their volunteer allies had faced massed artillery; Jack did not think RPG's rose to that level. Instead, Jack planned to turn the mission into an attacker's grave. Still, the similarities between the two scenarios haunted him. There would be no reinforcements. If the unknown pirates overran their Alamo, there would be no legend, no movie, and no History Channel reenactment.

Scanning the back side of the hill confirmed Jack's fears. Yes, a door opened to the hilltop, but leading to the same open, low palm and palmetto, and then leading further to—nowhere for all tactical purposes.

So the defense plan that emerged was simple. Ambush the attackers. Kill!

Jack told Bobby his plan. Bobby approved of the audacity (and secretly wondered if it was really stupidity) and trusted his "CO's" judgment and specific tactics: identify the most likely approach routes from the beach to the compound and cover them with sudden rifle fire as soon as the advancing pirates left jungle cover. This required rifle fire first from concealment forward of the mission, then from behind the low perimeter wall.

To keep from peering over the wall's top, making their heads obvious targets, they kicked portions of the wall into rubble, and battered it with stones where they needed firing positions. They stacked debris to obscure the attacker's view, maximizing both cover (protects from sight and impacting rounds) and concealment (screens from view but won't stop bullets).

That was about the best they could do. They all stood back, puffing and sweating, thirsting for a drink of water, and considered where each person would be placed, when they heard the faint unmistakable sound of a chopper approaching.

The approaching helicopter circled the island from about 1,000 feet, and then turned straight for the beach where *Arcturus* lay beached. Could it be one of the Coast Guard's 'copters? No, it was too soon. Logically, who had a helicopter in this remote part of the Caribbean? Well, they knew of one for certain.

Jack radioed to Gordon, who had already hailed the USCG dispatcher, who confirmed that their rescue chopper was not yet under way. Radar confirmed the approach, although that hardly helped; they knew it was inbound and knew who it was.

The questions then were: "Was this just a recon; how many men rode the chopper and how were they armed; was this the assault?" They could not know this until the attack came. All abandoned the *Arcturus* and moved inward toward the mission. Under the watchful eye of the chopper, the rest of the party prepared the mission for attack.

13

*I wish it to be remembered that
I was the last man of
my tribe to surrender my rifle.*

—*Sitting Bull*

Jack chose his opportunity to slip through the building, and out a window backed up to thick brush, all while hearing the chopper on the opposite side. Both the sun-bleached mission and the close but low jungle screened Jack from the chopper's view. He got prone in one of the shallow creeks and slithered downhill toward the beach, standing only when shielded from above by thicker forest.

The plan included his hiding in an OP (observation post). He would be the eyes of the *Arcturus* crew, watching and learning as much as possible about whatever attacking force might land. Armed with his M-1, he intended to meet the attack before it started, but would melt away to report back if they were too numerous and too well armed for one quick-firing rifleman to eliminate.

More importantly, he expected the chopper to land troops at the beach and Jack planned their ambush. If he could kill the pilot on his approach, well so much the better. Let the laws of physics take over from there. There were numerous places on beaches and even inland where the chopper could land, but he had hoped that the beached ship would attract the chopper pilot's curious attention and that they would land there first to check the boat. Jack could not cover all possible landing zones. He had to take the chance. Making the beach look abandoned should deceive the pilot into thinking that no defender covered the beach by fire. Between the activity on the hilltop and the beached *Sun* Jack hoped the chopper pilot would opt for the obvious LZ on the beach. It looked like he had guessed right.

The chopper approached straight in from the sea. Within about 600 meters of the beach, the pilot throttled back and dropped as if on "short final" to land, and then flared and hovered, appearing to watch the boat with its bug eyes.

Jack considered shooting, but a shot with an M-1, at 600 yards with iron sights, into the cockpit of a wavering chopper presented a literal long shot, so he held fire. Jack began to breathe in and out again, intentionally, regularly, preparing to instantly resume the trigger press sequence: breathe in, breathe out and relax, hold, take up the slack or "first stage," freeze the "receiver" sights on the target, press the trigger until firing.

When done right, the rifleman's concentration blanks out anticipating the cartridge's explosion, and achieves the complex combination of holding the aligned sights on the target, while smoothly moving the trigger mechanism to the point it "breaks." A rare few marksmen, with the right rifle, with ammunition precisely manufactured or hand-loaded, and under the right conditions, could hit targets out to 1,000 yards consistently, but these shooters (both men and women) are rare, existing mostly in special operations pulp fiction and movies. Skilled shooters do consistently hit targets out to 300 or 400 yards. Expert shooters work on a couple hundred yards more range of consistent kills. Beyond about that range, shooting gets dicey. Jack never missed head-shots at 300 yards with his M-4, but he didn't have his M-4.

Jack held in his hands the revered M-1, but it was not a custom-outfitted sniper rifle. His ammo was mass-produced military surplus, not hand-loaded by a perfectionist metering out the exact weight of propellant poured into each cartridge case. The combination of rifle and ammunition was fine enough out to maybe 400 yards, but Jack figured he could not reliably place the 180-grain bullets on the moving target beyond that. He needed them in closer.

The pilot refused to cooperate. Perhaps sensing the ambush, he rotored off to his left, setting down on a beach opening out of sight a couple of hundred meters away from the boat's resting place. Jack reflected on this development. No doubt, the chopper was disgorging troops at the smaller LZ Jack had noted during his reconnaissance. The others would hear the chopper land and know that it had touched down. It was too far for Jack to race there in time to hit the chopper before landing, when he had hoped to send pilot and passengers all to a fiery impact death. Time to scat and rejoin the others? No action here.

Yet, there beckoned the *Corsican Sun*, tied in the cove to Jack's front like a duck decoy. Yeah, that was it!

Without intending it, *Arcturus* had set a trap. The airborne pirate commander probably had stuff on board the *Sun* that he either wanted back or destroyed. Jack settled low, eased the M-1 out under green cover, slowly pulled palm fronds over his back, smeared earth on his face, forearms and the tops of his hands, flicked aside a centipede and waited. The sandy leaf and twig litter found its way into his pants, behind his belt, and scratched his belly. He ignored it.

The chopper pilot, having disgorged his second troop load, lifted off as Jack hunkered down. The craft headed to sea, but then dropped just above the waves and approached the beach.

"Come to me, Baby," Jack coaxed aloud.

The pilot took the bait, and assumed that the busy work on the hilltop at the mission garnered all hands. He had not correctly assessed even yet just what he had encountered here, first out on the open sea where he had lost a boat and crew, and now on this island. Well, he was about to get schooled.

The chopper advanced as its pilot scanned for a place to set the bird down. Either they planned to board the boat and remove what evidence might incriminate them, or maybe they intended to plant charges and blow the boat, Jack reasoned. He adjusted his position to line up the rifle with the incoming helicopter, got the sight picture he wanted, and shifted a little right to alleviate just that the little bit of muscle strain he was putting on the gun that might throw off this careful shot. Again, Jack breathed in and out deliberately. The rifle cradled in Jack's relaxed arms, its muzzle lined up perfectly with the approaching chopper. Jack waited.

He intended to utterly destroy the chopper, but not the *Corsican Sun*. Like Gordon, he wanted to know who these cutthroats were and why they risked so much to kill people who should have looked like no risk to them. The chopper neared to within about 200 yards of Jack, and 75 yards from shore. Jack took up first stage in the M-1's trigger—its "slack." Jack held his sights on the Agusta 109E Power—for Jack now recognized the Italian-built aircraft's shape— as the chopper closed to about 150 yards range.

Close enough to put 'em all into a paper plate, but wait. Might as well let him come in even closer. Jack cranked down the M-1's rear sight.

At 75 yards, *Close enough*, Jack told himself, and began squeezing off carefully placed, rapid shots. Later, he would reflect that the first shot probably killed the pilot, the second hit the co-pilot, and the others had been superfluous. The chopper, still hovering at about 100 feet, rolled over sickly, stuck its skids out to the side, and dropped at a sharp sideways, yawing angle. Fascinated, Jack knew he should hide behind a tree to avoid getting killed by flying rotor blade fragments, but he just had to watch.

The destruction was a sight to see. The rotor struck the beach first. Wrenching metal screeched then sang overhead. The chopper cabin slammed onto the shallow water just off the beach, erupting in flames. A man on fire popped up from the hatch yelling some unintelligible death-gibberish, and Jack watched him a second before shooting him.

They would not find any information on this chopper; it was burning up as only a flashbulb mixture of fuel, saltwater, and magnesium can. Coming from the 101st, he knew the incendiary characteristic well. For helicopter-borne troops, accidental crashes were the number one cause of death, short of being killed by the enemy. He personally knew young soldiers no longer of this world who had ridden these choppers down to a fiery death during training missions, as well as operations.

Jack remembered the night he had stood with his men, shivering at a PZ (pickup zone), waiting for hours, wondering if his toes were tingling from the battery-powered warmers he was trying out, or from frostbite. They had waited long for the lift returning to pick up his own platoon, only to learn later that the pilot and crew had gone down just after the last chalk had been dropped off at the LZ. Not all died in the crash. Survivors, horribly burned, spent months in rehabilitation, and never fully recovered.

The public did not understand the risk incurred by soldiering, even in peacetime. He loved the ugly choppers and their brave pilots, for they weathered hails of fire and got men in and out of places where nothing else could. The pilots could fly "nap-of-the-earth," frisking treetops, materializing suddenly over enemy who could neither see nor hear them until seconds before their doom.

There was nothing quite like sitting in the door of a Huey or Blackhawk, feet pulled in close to your body, butt puckered tight as if to suction-cup you onto the metal floor, looking almost straight down to the ground as the choppers made tight turns. No matter how many guys assured you that centrifugal force held you in the bird, you still wondered why you did not slide right "out" the door.

He respected the choppers, and revered the gutsy men who flew them, but saw the airships as risky transportation subject to gravity's relentless tug.

This time, these bums bought the farm on their chopper ride to Hell. Too damned bad. C&C bird eliminated; escape from the island eliminated. *Uh, oh.* He vaguely recalled something from Sun Tzu about the desperate determination of men attacked with no way of withdrawal, and turned his attention to the ground battle about to blow up.

14

Antonio Lopez de Santa Ana:
Move this battery forward!
General Castrillon: Excelencia...
With all due respect for your safety...
Davy Crockett is in the Alamo.

—from the motion picture,
"The Alamo," 2004.

All heard Jack's shots, and the chopper's explosion. Revaca, dropped off from the Agusta, had collected his six men, and the first seven to land, and begun to file inland, uphill where he knew the mission to be located. No one had told him about the fate of *Corsican Sun,* only that some civilians had blundered into something they would pay for with their lives and, "Oh yes, they might have some guns." He had observed the two boats in the lagoon, but could not apprehend their tactical significance without more of the puzzle pieces.

The shots and crash transfixed him. Revaca raised his hand in a leader-like way and weighed his next move. Aha! He did not have to decide; El Jefe' would do that for him. If only Revaca could reach the stern Middle-Eastern pilot, the pilot's altitude would permit radio relay to Revaca's chief, who held the satellite phone.

However, the pilot did not answer Revaca's insistent radio calls, each of which advanced in both volume and desperation. What the Hell had happened and what the Hell was he to do? Who was out there? He turned to look at his men, all who were staring back at him. He could read their stupid eyes. Damn them! When halted, they were to get down, face out and be alert, and there they were, standing like stupid chickens waiting for him to throw them cracked corn! He cursed them and ordered them down, but burned with the embarrassment and pressure of not knowing what to do next.

Revaca glanced in the direction of the hilltop, then back to the explosion site. He strained his eyes upward, wishing to see the familiar and comforting speck watching like an angel from above, like his mother had comforted him with years ago. Nothing! Realizing from the carping glances of his men that he was the only one left standing, he dropped to a knee and faced forward, mostly so they could not see the indecision stamped all over his countenance.

Vainly, he tested the radio again. Damn things! They were notorious for quitting the second your feet hit the ground. They were so sensitive to moisture that pissing near one stopped it cold. He bet there were radio problems.

But why did he not *hear* the chopper? The dawning realization connecting the explosion with the scary radio silence welled panic up in his guts, confusing his efforts to think. First, he lost contact with the *Corsican Sun*, now the Agusta! Minutes passed.

Men behind him murmured. Suddenly, what had seemed to be an easy killing, including the promised woman he had been told about, no longer stood framed with perfect clarity. He did not know what had happened, or what the Hell Revaca was to do.

He did know one thing. He had armed men behind him, and a vicious commander, capable of torturing insubordinate lieutenants. This fear propelled Revaca to his feet. Unthinkingly, he beckoned with his hand in the timeless manner of leaders trying to get men to "follow me," turned aside from the uphill azimuth, and headed his column toward the explosion.

Mothers will tell you that boys are drawn to such uproar, and it's true. The mixture of confusion, curiosity, and cacophony called irresistibly to Revaca. The men, un-briefed by their leader, fell in behind him and shuffled down the coastline toward the beach crash site. Revaca would learn the fate of the *Sun* and the Agusta first.

Jack slipped silently away from the beach about 100 meters, and turned toward where he had heard the chopper land, presumably to disgorge field troops. Jack knew the Agusta would carry seven troops, but didn't know how close the sleek Italian had staged from, or if the pilot had already made one trip. That's what worried him. The *Arcturus* crew fought this one on its own. The pirates—that's how Jack had come to label them—obviously had support somewhere in these islands, but he didn't know how close. He needed to see the enemy force's capability.

Perhaps the crash had put them on pause, delaying their attack. If so, then he might not be too late to intercept them and recon the enemy situation. One man moving toward an armed band was risky, and so Jack moved uphill first, avoiding a direct path between the beaches, and assuring that he would not be cut off from the others if he came on the band moving uphill to the attack.

Then a thought struck him. One of those insights. Maybe just a distraction, he questioned. But no, what would *he* do if he had been dropped at an LZ, lost all commo, heard his extraction bird go down, and was not all that far away? The castaway pirates had no way off the island, other than to steal *Arcturus*! Why would the buccaneer squad leader not show some flexible judgment, delay the attack, and investigate? He could always resume the attack later, and the chopper—presumably carrying the pirate Captain—could maybe use some support if anyone still lived. Jack doubted it. The more Jack considered the matter, the more he reasoned that the attacking ground force would move to the chopper explosion site before pressing ahead to the attack.

Jack circled back to his left, back toward the beach, keeping low, moving slowly, carefully avoiding setting vegetation in motion, or, if necessary to move it out of his way, pushing it down first to let it spring back up in more natural movement. He moved from tree to tree, bush to bush. A few minutes of this led him back to a view of the surf rocking the boats. He shifted his weight further down into the soft, white sand, sprinkled some leaf-litter over his arms, and waited.

Revaca nervously drew near the white sand he saw through the low jungle. Now that he had almost completed the movement, the foreboding sound of the explosion played with his fear. He had seen movies. He turned and motioned for one of his men to come forward. They were all looking at him expectantly, instead of covering their sectors as they were supposed to do, but Revaca did not scold them this time; he did not even realize their collective lapse of security. He felt too pleased with the leadership he was poised to exert.

"Ernesto, get up there and take a look and report back to me what you see," Revaca commanded authoritatively. Ernesto gaped back at him.

"Go, fool!"

Ernesto, clearly displeased, eyed his leader and cousin murderously, but stepped into the beach clearing. No cataclysm snatched him from life, so he took another step. Peace and quiet. Emboldened, and mindful of the attention he now garnered from his *compadres*, who, of course, should have been covering their security sectors but were all watching him, he stalked forward like a hunter.

Rounding a copse of trees that had blocked his view of the crash site, Ernesto froze, his brief bravado dissipated, replaced by wonder and fear. He approached the flaming hulk, but the prohibitive heat repelled him. He gazed around and saw nothing but the two boats, one beached, and the other tied up, both about 100 meters from the burning chopper. He removed his hat, wiped his brow and wondered just what he was to say to Revaca.

Little did it matter, for now, recognizing the sound of licking flames, the remainder of the column had ambled onto the beach behind him to see the harbinger of their own doom, not yet realized. They had never seen a chopper burning and the slow recognition of the significance scared their courage. Clearly, no one had survived. The grisly sight of the blackened, shriveled pilot's corpse spurred Revaca to action.

Nothing could be done here until the fire burned out. They would return to their instructions and kill the people in the old mission who, Revaca surmised, were at least somehow responsible for this. He would seize their yacht and get away, back to their own island camp nearby where the rest waited in safety. He was angry.

Revaca grabbed his gawking cousin, turned him toward the forest, and ordered the men back into column. The stunned men slowly responded, shuffled into rude order and each began following Revaca.

Only seventy-five meters away, Jack grinned. Through the palmetto and fern bobbing in his line of sight, he saw men collecting themselves, with only one glancing nervously around on the alert. The rest seemed oblivious, all their common sense suspended in fascination with the death-chopper. They should never have all occupied the beach without reconnoitering the surroundings first, but there they were, all gaggled up, but looking like they were collecting themselves to move out. Instead of down and ready in a 180-degree perimeter facing inland, weapons out, eyes peering, with the leader moving them out once satisfied that all was in order, they appeared to be randomly sorting into column, ready to head uphill.

Jack figured he knew what that meant: the attack was back on. Counting them, he saw they numbered 14—two chopper loads— with no geniuses among them. Three packed the telltale ugly tubes signifying rocket propelled grenades: probably RPG-7's, probably tipped with high explosive (HE) anti-personnel grenades. The 40- millimeter launchers already exhibited the characteristic much larger swelling at the end telling him that the rockets were loaded into the tubes, but, strangely, he saw no one carrying other rounds for reloading. So, they would have to survive three RPG rounds. Others slung short, ubiquitous, Communist carbines with long, curved magazines hanging below, no doubt the AK variants Jack viewed as cursed symbols of world oppression. Bandoleers of more ammunition decorated the men's chests. Only five carried their car- bines at-the-ready. No shotguns. No light machine-guns, thank God.

Jack glanced upward like a rabbit might keep watch for a red- tailed hawk, saw no other choppers, wriggled backward, rising slowly when out of view and began to turn to beat feet to the mis- sion to report, then halted, crouching.

Why not? Yes, the others needed to know, but these fools had gifted him with a chance to reduce the odds. Dropping prone again, he crawled back to his former observation post and discerned the "targets of opportunity," as Jack viewed them, sorting themselves out more purposefully and beginning to shuffle into the jungle's cover. Spreading his feet, and propping someone's dad's M-1 on a fallen tree limb, he prayed it had served that young GI well and would once again prove Patton's brag that the M-1 was the ultimate battle weapon.

Jack chose the man in the gaggle next in line to blunder into the brush. Specifically, he tried to center the front sight of the M-1 on one of the RPG's. However, from low down in the prone, occasional weeds and palm fronds waved at him throughout the trace of his field of fire, and he quickly moved his aim to the larger target, the gunner's back, before he got away. He had hoped to disable one of the RPG launchers. It was even possible to ignite the booster charge on the RPG round with enough impact in the right place. While fully capable of this fairly easy shot, this terrain was not a shooting range, and Jack knew that the natural cover waving in front of him could deflect the bullet just enough to throw it off course. Better to go for the larger man-shape with certainty than to try to hit the bobbing tube, through brush at seventy-five meters, with iron sights. The heavy .30 caliber bullet slamming into the man anywhere was destined to make him a casualty, taking him out of today's action if not sending him to Hell forthwith.

All of these thoughts zoomed around inside his mind like so many homeless electrons. Enough. Jack pressed the M-1's trigger, barely heard the boom, barely felt the rifle kick his shoulder, mind concentrated on killing. He fired the remaining seven rounds into the confused column as fast as he could return the aligned sights to center of mass on more targets, all of whom were moving after at least Jack's third shot. The distinctive "ching" sound of the ejected, empty, metal clip unique to the M-1 signaled Jack to reach for another from the bandoleer tied across his own chest. As he reloaded, he rolled to the left two complete revolutions to where a tree trunk afforded his next move to cover. Glancing to see the first victim sprawled on his face with legs and arms splayed in a dead-thing sort of pattern, Jack stuffed another clip into the M-1's magazine well and heard the bolt slam home.

Jack's first kill stunned and froze the column. Hearing and watching two more shots and seeing three kills kicked even the most untrained man into reflexive action: the remaining men dove, ran, or scrambled in some other manner in a direction away from the M-1's booms.

Jack watched tangentially as he fired, seeking new targets and catching patches of heads, clothing, or boots in his field of view. After the first three kills, his targets were moving, making kills at this range less likely. He was sure he had taken out three men, maybe wounded two. As fast as he could put the front sight on a man's partially hidden figure, Jack repeated firing eight rounds, rolling and re-loading. Hoping for the chance to kill some more, Jack instead scurried off as men cursed and automatic weapons fire sprayed randomly high and into the trees to his right. No one had been covering their rear. Tough. He could do little more here now, the element of surprise gone.

Quickly now, Jack low-crawled through the sandy leaf-litter, willing himself into the ground, if that was truly possible. He scurried on his belly in this manner for about 30 yards, glanced around to check the field of vision, rose to his hands and knees and quickly crawled another 20 yards, rising to a low crouch and running, dodging left and right. In this manner, Jack retreated to the mission, radioing in his approach to avoid being shot "re-entering friendly lines." He had cut the numbers, but the survivors would have a better idea about the direction of the mission and would probably assume that the crew had holed up there. However, they would not enjoy any more sporting advice from the mysterious C&C (command and control) chopper.

15

Jack paused about 100 yards from the mission. Only when he confirmed by radio check that Bobby had announced Jack's return to friendly lines to the forward riflemen in ambush did he get up and approach the hilltop. Jack thumb-upped the rifleman who lay prone, expecting his approach, lying down and ready, forward of the wall, as he passed through to "friendly lines" and reported to Bobby with Gordon listening.

"About nine men left, all armed, three RPG's, some automatic weapons, sounds like Kalashnikovs. Troops untrained," Jack added, breathing fast.

"Plan B then. Best to go Alamo and forget about starting this battle from the low wall?" Bobby asked.

"No, I probably took one of the RPG's out of commission, but they still have two. I think we should hit them first with the skirmishers out front at the low wall just as planned. You'll re-write your beloved *Vom Krieg* with this one. We hit them with the old combined area ambush and fortress defense!"

Bobby stared at him as if he had sprung purple horn-growths from his face. "Yeah, we got those two rifles out there on the flanks to start the whole party, but I don't see the low wall being a good place to socialize when those RPG's come in. We have shotguns inside the building with Elvis, and we need to bring these buccaneers in close to cut down their RPG advantage, and get those shotguns into play," Bobby assessed.

The two shook hands, laughed, and agreed to brief the riflemen behind the low wall to shoot twice—fast—and retreat, hoping to induce the attackers to stop and shoot the RPG's. They exchanged "Let's kill!" looks. Jack consulted with Gordon quickly, filling him in on the plan, which he seemed to grasp instantly, while Bobby briefed the two low-wall riflemen.

Jack ran forward with the remaining two other riflemen, positioning each forward toward the line of attack, which they expected to be from the general direction of the beach, but placing them off to the flanks, in widely separated, concealed positions about 100 meters from the mission. At least this would provide some advance warning and make the attackers deploy, pressuring them from trying to outflank the defenders. After shooting twice from the flanks, these riflemen would then drop back and away, further to the flanks, and circle back into the mission's rear door. Here, they'd pass Donna guarding the rear, and take up positions to cover the two men at the low wall as they, too retreated into the mission's stone protection.

In the meantime, Bobby explained to the two rifle-owners stationed at the low wall their key role: "Let the pirates approach. Catch them as they move in line into that kill zone," Bobby said, pointing to the narrow band of irregular open ground separating the jungle from the mission.

As Jack re-joined Bobby, he heard his friend deliver his final battle speech to the low-wall riflemen in terms the two quickly grasped: "Old Hickory said we could take 'em by surprise, if we held our fire 'til we look 'em in the eyes," Bobby instructed, reminding them of Johnny Horton's classic, rambunctious hit song and General Jackson's tactics simultaneously in what had to be sheer, genius-level, instruction method.

"What a lark!" Bobby exclaimed to them as encouragement. These guys looked at Bobby as if he were crazy (which was pretty much the effect the frightened Bobby wanted to achieve) but the men hunkered down in a way that gave Jack confidence.

Their fear was that the pirates would attack the way the boys would attack. The RPG's lent strength to the pirates. Fight your strength, not your weakness. The weakness for the pirate infantry was that they had to assault the fortified defense quickly. If these pirates did not do their murderous deeds fast, the Coast Guard or some other help would be on the way, or the defenders might survive the initial blast to recover and blast away. The pirates surely would know that the *Arcturus* was radio-equipped and that its captain had broadcast a desperate plea for help.

No, this attack had to come fast and be over fast. That was one of the pirate weaknesses to exploit. So, Jack spoke to his enemy in his mind, as if among them, one of them, convincing their commander that he had the best plan: *Play to your strength by deploying those damned RPG's as massed firepower, firing all three into the mission simultaneously, either killing or stunning the defenders, followed up by an immediate automatic weapons assault from the rear and one side.*

That's what Bobby and Jack agreed they would do. They would certainly not approach straight up the hill to the face of the mission, but they hoped that the terrain and the front, low wall would channel the attackers to a frontal assault. They knew their own plan was hastily put together, not pretty, not elegant, but violent and, Bobby pretentiously sniffed: "Consistent with Clausewitz's classic *On War*, as you should know Jacko, my dear boy."

They gambled that the pirates had not read Clausewitz. One plan had been to scatter out over the island, using the long guns to hunt down and pick off the attackers. The helicopter had made the intended prey the hunter, so the "hunt them down" plan was scrapped. Despite Jack's having taken out the chopper, they stuck with the original plan: drawing the RPG's in had looked like the best option.

As Mr. Grau wrote in a prescient 1998 issue of *Infantry* magazine praising the virtues of the devilish RPG-7, "The chances are, whenever a US soldier is deployed to a trouble spot, the RPG-7 will be part of the local landscape." Really? Even in this subatomic, side-cranny of the world, his prediction rings true!

The RPG-7 is like some persistent foreign pest. It's not that it's better than the American equivalents…well, maybe it is. It is cheap to make, proven to be reliable, easy to load and shoot, and is deadly out to around a thousand meters, depending on the round loaded. It must be good: it seems like half the belligerent Hell-holes in the world manufacture it and sell it to the other half. Maybe it proliferates by breeding.

The boys suspected that their opposition lacked anti-tank rounds, not expecting to encounter tanks, but they just did not know. It did not matter. This fight would not test the limits of the RPG-7's effectiveness against armor or troops at a distance. This would be up close and personal where the RPG-7 excelled.

Yes, bring those high-explosive rocket rounds on in here. *Some plan,* Jack secretly doubted. *Did Varus devise such a plan before commanding his doomed legion into oblivion in the German woods before the time of Christ?* Jack imagined Varus' Sergeant Major warning him about those wily Germans. "That column's getting strung way out through the Teuteberger forest, sir," the Smadge might have cautioned. Varus might have scoffed, "Bring 'em on!" right up until he comprehended that the German ambush was going to massacre his entire legion, together with wives and children. He would not live to answer Caesar's vain, indicting demand for an explanation:

ARCTURUS

"Varus, give me back my legion!" Yes, lure those RPG-7s right on in here. Jack shook his head and dismissed his doubts.

Jack and Bobby hid in the low wall's covering rubble, sprinkling dirt over their clothing, designing to wait for a flanker rifleman to spring the ambush. Donna watched the rear entrances, radio in hand, ready to call foul if need be. Gordon chose a firing position in the mission, and waited, pleased with the preparations and plan.

All were to make their "last stand" hidden out a few meters into the mission itself, prepared to stand their ground, killing as many as they could firing from the darkened interior of the building before retreating ever further into the building's twisting corridors if required. If this worked, it took the two-stage RPG's out of play by depriving them of the distance the shooter needed for the rocket to deploy under its booster power, and then fire its sustaining rocket engine. Besides, the grenadier did not want to be too close when the round exploded. The RPG needed about the distance of a first down on the football field just to get its rocket engine going and really take off. Any pirate directly behind the tube was toast from the back blast.

Jack laughed to himself calculating the good odds that at least one pirate would be blown to smithereens by his own mate unless these boys really knew the weapon. So, the best plan for the enemy was a carefully coordinated assault, but only after first wreaking havoc on the Alamo with those RPG's playing a punctuated, percussion concert.

The good news was that attacking a defended building was not fun. While the *Arcturus* defenders had to be prepared to fight off attack from any direction, they could move quickly within the mission, communicate with each other, and ambush untrained men moving into the building with the sun silhouetting targets from behind. Taking up positions back into the building, not right at its doors, the defenders planned escape, a way to move further away and deeper into the building, and, if possible, away. Choosing to ignore the low wall as their main line of defense, they could use it to channel the enemy. Either the pirates came through the gate openings and breaks already tumbled down and rubble-strewn, or over the wall, presenting their carcasses as targets.

Soon, Jack heard movement forward and began to see shapes through the vegetation. When two men emerged from the growth, approaching the mission carelessly, the posted flank rifles compliantly fired twice, killing them both. These shots signaled to the others to fire at will. Jack wished his flank rifles had waited just a bit longer. Behind the two were more men coming, some carrying the long tubes. Jack had tracked one of the grenadiers and shot him when he jerked in response to Bobby's M-1's report. Two down, and at least one of the rockets. Six left. Not bad.

The fight now quickly progressed. Every time the defenders spotted an attacker prop one of the tubes onto his shoulder to fire, they concentrated rifle and pistol fire on him. Jack did not see any more enemy going down, though. The flanker ambush sprung, the next phase kicked in: time to defend the fort and lure in remaining RPG's before they opted for maneuvering around behind. Jack motioned the two riflemen to his sides to retreat to the mission. Jack and Bobby poured rifle fire into anything that moved to the front to cover them.

"Your turn; go, Bob, go!" Jack shouted.

Bobby crawled, keeping low, sprinting the last 10 feet into the mission, diving through a window while Jack covered him. Bobby immediately took up his own pre-selected firing position and opened fire to cover Jack's pullback.

"Go Jack, Go!" Bobby yelled above the din, signaling his friend to now "leapfrog" back.

The Cuban "pirates" saw the retreat and mistakenly thought they sniffed victory. Popping up to shoot the withdrawing Jack, they quickly ducked back behind the trees to shelter from covering fire coming now from several openings in the mission. Only seconds later, firing abated. Jack wondered if it was too soon to go out and take a body count.

Jack shuffled on hands and knees to confer with Bobby. Bobby raised both arms in the "I don't know." position.

"Bob, what do...?"

Gordon's shouted warning cut Jack off: "Get *down*! Jack, get down! All of you!" Gordon screamed, and gestured wildly, palm down, emphasizing his warning in the universally understood hand-and-arm signal.

Jack heard both of the two-stage RGP launches, the booster and the rocket, did not see the signature gray-blue smoke plumes, and had time only to drop before the world exploded next to him. Apparently, the pirates had held a counsel of war and some bright boy had hit on what was left of the massed-fire approach. Damn. From within his fog, it occurred to Jack that maybe *their* plan had been to get the victims penned up in the Alamo and then pop the RPG's. Jack blacked out.

16

*Atop Perdido Cay
In the Spanish Mission*

Silence reigned. No pain. Something like formless ghosts hovered above him. It seemed that he was about an inch or two off to the side of himself. Weird. Was he dead? The ghosts began to manifest discernable form, but then flitted away. A sharp, jabbing pain in his back proclaimed what was obvious to the lucid, but what required a little time to sink in, given Jack's dulled state. He was alive!

OK. He recalled the double RPG blasts. What remained? Partswise, he meant. Fear gripped Jack, powerful enough to slice through the daze. He tried to roll to his left and get up. Now, the pain in his left side screamed at him the truth that he remained, for now, in this world. This world, for the moment, was the Alamo, and the RPG rounds had announced the final assault. Get up! Get up!

Jack saw Jim Bowie, flat on his back in bed, dying from disease, too weak to fend off attackers, but fighting to the last. Bowie died, of course, bayoneted by the Mexicans, and Jack did not want this Tennessee boy to finish this Alamo fight like the soldier-of-fortune Colonel Bowie. He became aware of action behind him, including the sound of high-powered rifles, mixed with sporadic automatic weapons fire that somehow sounded half-hearted.

Jack eased back down and managed to rotate to his right, straining to see his comrades. Vision returned to focus, dust settled, and he began to comprehend the RPG attack. Just as planned, the *Arcturus* crew fired from positions within the mission, forcing attackers to expose themselves getting in close. Following up on the RPG explosions, charging and entering from bright sunlight, the Cubans must have been almost blinded. Continuing to clear his head, Jack saw a man down and a rifle blown apart, red smears painting it a gaudy, marbled red-walnut. He saw a rifle bolt handle in a hand. It was one of the *Arcturus* riflemen. He groaned and collapsed back.

That renewed the stab in the back and side that had poked him to consciousness in the first place, and he rolled to his right again to relieve the pain, resting there successfully this time. Then he saw it. Blinking grit from his eyes, and spitting more grit out, he peered again, foggily forgetful of the final throws of battle behind him, of which he knew he was no longer a part.

Jack squinted across the room about four feet to a corner of the cloister where a row of low stone blocks were lined up on the floor. He and Bobby had reasoned that these were extra seats along the sides, but, of course, had no idea of the customs of these missionaries and churchgoers of 200 or 300 years ago. The RPG round had struck one of the stone blocks squarely, shattering it, sending fragments around, one of which had stunned Jack with a jackhammer-like blow to the head, now beginning to throb. Jackhammer. Definitely. Exactly like a "Jack hammer," emerged the thought from somewhere in the bewildered back reaches of cognition.

Behind where the mason had laid the block Jack saw a hole. Bathed with sunlight piercing the interior of the mission church, a glimmering brilliance shone back from what should have been just a dark recess. Jack crawled closer, recovering function and thought, shaking himself like a wet dog.

He looked down at his legs. They were there. Stuff was where it was supposed to be. Arms were there. Fingers flexed and extended. No blood but for that running into his eyes. He took off his shirt, wiped his head, felt the bigger-than-golf ball-sized protrusion, and knew he had lived through another close call, wondering how many neurons had given up the cellular ghost this time. Jack's left side ached, but he found no wound. Finding no immediate threat in this self-triage exam, he turned back to the glint.

Rubble from the former stone blocks lay piled around the opening, except, of course, for the piece that had knocked him down. He rose to his knees, nodded at Donna and Gordon, and then Bobby, who all had turned and seen him re-joining the living. Jack braced himself on the nearest stone, sitting back down. He couldn't help it. Nauseated, he got down again on all fours, which put him back into position peering into the hole. Jack swore he saw…No.

Fumbling for his SureFire flashlight, he shot its beam into the hole, revealing a room-sized chamber full of crates, rope handles rotted away, and marked—something, he could not make it out. Besides, Jack was gaping at the spilled contents of a rotted bag.

He heard shouts in Spanish, men encouraging each other, proclaiming victory, and ordering "charge." Jack crawled to the gap, scraped rubble back into the hole, covered it with its original fallen stone slab, and promptly passed out again.

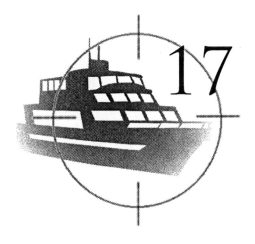

Miami,
Jackson Memorial Hospital
Three days after the attack
on Arcturus

"Jack, Jack!"

"Huh?"

"Wake up!"

"Why?"

"Why not?"

Jack foggily pondered this absurd dialog and willed his eyelids open to see Gordon offering a cup of coffee in his direction. The coffee-cream-sugar molecule clusters wafted his direction and excited a couple of receptors. A few other neurons began to slam like a splitting maul on oak: his head emanated pain and he touched the right side of his skull, finding it gauzed. Glancing down to perform an equipment check with no small degree of apprehension, all else seemed in place. He, shuddered, collected himself and rose successfully, with soreness humming like a Star Trek transporter.

"What happened? Where is everybody else? Who won"? Pause. Then, "Who died?" he ended the rapid fire interrogation on a grim, mumbled note.

"Harry Conacero, the rifleman, died, Jack, but he died well. Donna had a bad cut on her leg, but we stopped the bleeding."

"What day is it?"

"All this happened three days ago, Jack. Chris and his rescuers flew you out. You're at a Jackson Memorial Hospital in Miami."

Jack had no idea where Jackson Memorial Hospital was. He opened his mouth to ask more but Gordon started talking again, quickly.

"Your CT scan of the brain showed swelling, but no bone fragments or fractures. I saw it happen. The RPG blast threw you against the back wall and a rock fragment hit your head, so you took two blows to the skull. We saw you crawling, figured you were all right for the time being, and, well, we had our hands full of pirates. They fired two RPG's at us simultaneously, just like you'd talked about, and then assaulted. Both rocket rounds came in the front door. One of them exited the building, missed Donna by about 20 feet, sailed right over the crumbled down back wall, and went "balooey" behind in the trees. Loud, but no damage to us. No harm, no foul. The other, boy, was another matter."

Jack raised his finger to ask a question, but Gordon kept going.

"They must have decided for one to shoot high and one lower to increase their fragmentation spread. We all spied it coming and hit the dirt. The round ripped right in the front door opening and exploded in the back of the church near where we found you. It killed Harry, who must have hidden right there. I saw you diving for cover right after my warning, but you sure were close." Gordon kept going.

"We were prepped for the assault and were ready for them. Just like we'd planned, we jumped right back up, shook ourselves out and stood to. They charged through the front door, assuming that the RPG work left us either dead or stupefied. We might have been stunned, but we immediately reckoned what was next and were ready for them when the remaining three guys poured in.

"They sprayed as they came through that big arched doorway, but I don't think they could see us, entering from the sunlight into the dark church. They definitely were not ready for living, conscious troops like us and we killed them all. Pretty quick work. That's about it."

He sounded a little distant.

Jack and Bobby had killed men before, some scratching and kicking with blood splashing around and others coolly at a distance. They had reconciled to the horror of taking another's life—for the most part. Jack remained silent to let Gordon reflect and make his finish.

"I can't really tell you, Jack, how long it lasted. They came hey-diddle-diddle, right up the middle, poured through the main door silhouetted against the sun, blasted around on full auto, and we precisely cut them down. The final assault was over in a heartbeat, I think. They just never grasped the force they mistakenly chose to take on. Must not have had good intel about us. That's strange after what we did out there in the water. Anyway, it was the old cliché with time seeming suspended." Gordon returned from his reflection and looked at Jack, shuffling from foot to foot.

"How'd we get back?"

"Chris picked us up about three hours later in an official Coast Guard chopper. You had to be littered. Everyone else ambulated. We left the *Arcturus* beached where it was. The Coast Guard towed it and the *Sun* in. For now, the mission's scrubbed."

Jack wondered why the Coast Guard would be willing to undertake towing the boats, but asked about more pressing concerns.

"Donna?"

"Fine, Jack, she's just fine. She's here in Miami. I'll call her when you and I are finished and I'm sure she will want to come to visit you."

"Bobby, where's Bobby, Gordon?" Jack looked past Gordon, out into the hallway for his friend.

The time Gordon dreaded arrived. No other way to say it. Gordon sighed deeply and just said it.

"Bobby's dead, Jack, killed in the RPG explosion. Sorry," Gordon ended, suddenly tired. His eyes held Jack's in piercing intensity.

The moment necessitated no speech. Gordon had both spoken the lament and heard the bad news before. So had Jack. This would not be the last time for either.

Jack said nothing for a minute, shrugged, and ended the silence with "I'm tired, too, Gordon. I think I need to sleep awhile." "Must be the pills," he added.

"Sure. You'll get out tomorrow, as soon as they are sure that you don't have some latent head injury. Donna will call me when you're released, she'll pick you up and we'll go from there," Gordon added vaguely.

"Go where, Gordon?" Jack asked absently. "Go where?"

Bobby was dead. Jack knew the stages; he skipped *denial* altogether. See enough friends die, and you can't even fool yourself temporarily. Besides, Gordon was too factual to permit denial. Then, you always started blaming someone. Jack blamed Gordon. He'd get over it; Bobby had chosen this mission, and infantry was his way of life—just like his own—Jack pondered. He'd be pissed at Gordon for awhile and get over it. Bobby was dead, killed in battle. No more need be said.

"Go *where*, Gordon?" Jack asked again, this time expecting an answer.

"Recover. Get ready. Make no plans or commitments until you hear what I have to say. I'll call. We'll go from there."

"Go where, Gordon?" Jack hated unanswered questions.

"Deeper into the truth," Gordon replied, and having said that, Gordon left Jack to his "stages" and recovery.

18

Havana
Three days after the attack
on Arcturus

Stale cigarette smoke pervaded fibers of faded curtains, split upholstery, worn carpet, and cheap clothes. Add to that the sweat stench of failure, the burnt offering of thickening, hours-old coffee, and the haze of confused, frustration. The dowdy room positively stank.

Four men stood, facing one seated at an old desk with eyes bulging, body crouched forward, hands clasped together, elbows braced on the cut and stained leather pad, as if posturing to forge answers out of formless lumps of slag by force of will alone.

"Explain to me where they all are!" Casteneda cursed again and glared at his men, as if his laser stare could excise the truth from them. They stupidly looked at each other, at Casteneda, at the ashtray spilling over, at the brown-tinged map tacked to the corkboard, back at Casteneda, and could only shrug. They were not stupid men. Worn down, maybe, but at least of average intelligence and motivation. Their pained ignorance and subordinate position to Casteneda, synergized by the general terror of the totalitarian machine weight above them all, dictated no response other than their subservient silence.

"Why have my men and my helicopter not returned to me?" Casteneda pressed.

All four immediately gulped on the temptation to remind their boss that the lost chopper was not his, but checked.

Showing his men slight relaxation, Casteneda eased his belly back, unclasped his hands, stood up, put hands behind his back—assuming a now reflective posture—rotated to face the map, and resumed.

"Let's go over all of this again," he encouraged, looking not at the men but to the map of the northern Caribbean, including Florida's east coast. "You lost radio contact with the *Corsican Sun* first. Then, the Revaca sent two helicopter lifts of men out, with him in the last lift. He left you to man the headquarters and radios. He landed all the men, and then you never heard from any of them again, not even Revaca. You decided someone needed to be alive to report and so did not go to check out the cove at Perdido Cay. That feeble story is all you have to tell?"

Casteneda shifted his technique from lambasting the four, who obviously knew nothing, to quiet, dangerous, dripping sarcasm designed to foreshadow disappearance, dungeon, and torture, if not death. He perceived the four shifting, sweating, thinking of family and wishing somehow to be somewhere else—probably America, Casteneda fumed.

Enough of this game. Casteneda enjoyed playing but long ago lost his fervor to "disappear" any man who failed the State—which failed all men. He dismissed the men, told them it was not their fault, told them they had probably made the right decision, and heard their audible sighs of relief, locked his door, turned out the light in the hall, and decided to walk to the harbor to think through the disaster's meaning, starting from the beginning.

It looked simple enough. First, Saya-dar offered him a lot of money to "make possible the sale." That was straightforward. How much more was needed to know? Besides, Saya-dar hosted with opulent hospitality, offering pleasures—now. There was no harm in that. Being plied with the entertainments on the Persian's yacht cost Casteneda no commitments, and gave him fodder for reports to write to his chief. Money spoke to Casteneda, promising even more pleasure, with which he doused his pain. A poor Deputy Chief of (Intelligence) Operations found few means of supplementing his income.

When Saya-dar revealed the true purpose of his shopping trip, it took Casteneda aback—momentarily. So what? Nuclear material, polonium, contaminated waste. What did it matter? Since the USSR fizzled out, the stuff traded commonly like sugar futures, Casteneda rationalized. Casteneda had conveniently assumed that the Iranian self-appointed envoy to poor Cuba had his own buyer already lined up. Casteneda did not mind being one of a chain of several middle-men so long as his own profit sufficed, and, without question, it sufficed! However, Saya-dar had begun to hint at sinister "revenge" against America and Casteneda had lingered to listen to him. Maybe he had tarried too long in the presence of evil.

Casteneda ran agents in the United States, mostly to report on the Miami population's conspiratorial fantasies. He also trolled for weird American traitors and sifted through their far-flung bits of bizarre information. Casteneda featured himself as a *spy* on America. All of these DGF Deputy Chief functions exacted some form of mostly innocuous retribution against the *Norteamericanos*, but Casteneda entertained no grand notions about it; he'd forgotten the "Why?" behind the retribution. Yes, he admitted, he indulged in passive-aggressive spy work, but it truly was mostly harmless.

Long ago, Casteneda's youthful Communist ardor against the capitalist-pig-dog-warmonger-imperialist-blah-blah-blah America faded to a more realistic comparison between his beloved Cuba and the United States. Casteneda found his covert travel north not only effortless; he enjoyed his trips! He had loafed in America's street-side café's and marveled at the contrast between the American life he sampled, and the American life reported in Cuban, European, and even American newspapers. If he'd not seen the place for himself, he'd have believed all manner of propaganda horror stories. Casteneda remained keenly suspicious of capitalism, but submitted to the facts unmistakably before him during his travels: it produced.

Return to Cuba pained him each time, not because returning repelled him, but because he wanted for his home what Americans possessed as easily as breath. America's neglectful disdain for Cuba angered him, but somehow, over the years, this bile shifted from sworn (if not precisely identified) enmity to the tight, tense resentment a tired small-claims-court judge might perceive between two ill-natured neighbors who don't remember the inciting event behind their antipathy toward one another—but insist that they hate each other. Plus, maybe Cuba deserved America's disdain; Cuba had not exactly been a good friend, inviting the Russians in like that. Thinking back about it: probably a bad move.

No, Casteneda utterly lacked the lonelier, implosive, inculcated hatred that drove callous men to evil, evil men to destruction, and destroyed men to Hell. Casteneda would probably see Hell, but by some other regression. He lacked the malevolent, maelstrom motive that sucked men down and down and down until their simmering, sickened souls compressed like primordial matter, until poised on the brink of critical mass and consuming holocaust.

1 9

Havana Reflections

ack in his office, refreshed by the harbor breezes, Casteneda
leaned back in his chair and opened his desk drawer. Few
Cubans enjoyed open access to the Internet. His government expected him to prowl for intelligence-gathering opportunities, and to watch everything the North Americans did. If he
failed.... Casteneda made his case for his requirement to read
American newspapers online. The Committee groused but begrudg-
ingly agreed. Casteneda suspected that the mere fact that he read
outside his country's propaganda would be his own undoing, but no
alternative lay before him: his own country *had* no information to
give. *Where else would he go to gather "intelligence?"* he fumed (but did
not say to them).

He had printed the article and circled its last sentence.

Editorial

The Washington Post (www.washingtonpost.com)

Saturday, January 27, 2007; Page A18

Venezuela's Satellites

A year of elections has left democracy and free markets flourishing in
most of Latin America. Pity the exceptions.

A REMARKABLE year of democracy in Latin America has left the
region generally stronger. Presidential elections were held in 11 countries
in the past 13 months, and political moderates won seven of them,

including those in the four largest countries: Brazil, Mexico, Colombia and Peru. Throughout most of the hemisphere, the elections reinforced a consensus that continued growth must depend on free markets and free trade but that governments should concentrate on narrowing the large gap between rich and poor.

The new year nevertheless has begun with attention focused on a handful of countries where democracy is dead, dying or in danger. Venezuelan President Hugo Chávez began his term this month with a flurry of authoritarianism, promising to cancel the license of the largest independent television station and seeking authority to rule by decree. He then rushed to attend the inaugurations of Nicaragua's Daniel Ortega and Ecuador's Rafael Correa, whom he hopes to convert into satellite leaders in a Venezuelan-led "socialist" bloc. Bolivia's Evo Morales and an ailing Fidel Castro are already in Mr. Chávez's orbit; thanks to Venezuela's petrodollars, Cuba's totalitarian system may survive Mr. Castro's demise.

"Thanks to Venezuela's petrodollars...."

Money. It all came down to money. Cuba languished, lacked lucre, and would latch onto the latest dictatorial sugar daddy. All along, Casteneda assumed that his leader would go the way of Lenin and Stalin: he would die. Cuba would turn. Cuba would not throw its socialism out with the trash—outright, but Cuba would— *live* again—in all the color and passion that is Cuba! Its CDR neighborhood surveillance committees would just *quit* and mind their own damned business. Casteneda faltered even to think the word, but he treasured the hope that Cuba—his beloved, lost island, would be *free.*

Raoul put on the friendly face and announced his own version of *glasnost.* He invited discussion and criticism of life under the Communist regime. The most frustrated and the more naïve answered the call, showed up, and filled full the eager ears of the

116

Party agents masquerading as Raoul's friendly listeners. They were listening all right! What better way to build the list for the purge later? Casteneda warned his family and friends not to go and some went anyway! People so cling to hope. Now, with Chavez on the scene, the hope of shedding Communism's chains and moving on seemed to Casteneda even more remote.

This article dashed Casteneda's hopes. Chavez! Where had the fat-faced anachronism come from? How out of place in this century, finally beyond Marxism! Of all the unlikely places and people to keep Cuba's rusting chains in place!

He read the last line again: "…thanks to Venezuela's petrodollars, Cuba's totalitarian system may survive Mr. Castro's demise." *Maddening!* He threw the article on his desk and put his head down on his folded arms.

Looking back, he saw that he had been primed for recruitment by the ordinary-looking man he had met on the fishing docks that day. Casteneda should have spotted the case officer's embryonic pitch immediately. He admired the seamless transition the American CIA officer effected between greeting, introduction, cultivation, relationship, and—finally—recruitment. Paradoxically, Casteneda saw no conflict of interest between his duties as Deputy to Cuba's top intelligence operations boss, and his on-and-off assistance to the CIA. He could not discern if he should attribute that smudged line to the smoothness of the American, or to the realpolitik pushing the two countries into natural friendship. Castro's "in your face" Communism simply made no sense in the post-Soviet world, if it ever did at all.

He was, naturally, only one man: an Intelligence Colonel, yes, but still only one. He speculated at the number of other Cubans— his office friends, passersby, subordinates maybe, and bureaucrats—

who bided their time, poised for reconciliation, reunion, rejuvenation, and fun! Few others seemed to have the fire to devour the capitalists anymore. Certainly, neither did he anymore; he *needed* them. Casteneda laughed. The day the *Norteamericanos* came back, Casteneda would become a wealthy man!

Cuba had things Americans liked. Oh sure, Cuba had beaches and bars, but other Caribbean islands offered those too. Cuba offered Americans something unique, something no other land in the world could supply. This monopolized commodity spelled prosperity for the sharp entrepreneur, if only he could wait out Cuba's rusting, post-Communism malaise. Casteneda had gotten "in on it."

Fifty years ago, when the Americans and prosperous Cubans saw that the self-proclaimed liberator Castro intended to lock the islands down in the iron grip of Soviet-styled Communism, they packed up and fled. However, they could not *drive* off the island, so they abandoned their cars, now frozen in Cold War time along with the rest of Cuba.

Time marched on. During the melancholy decades of protracted Cold War, the teenager *Yanquis* grew up but held onto their fascination with the "antique" cars of their Rock-and-Roll era. These same makes and models abandoned in place in Cuba, the remaining islanders depended on for transportation. The islands would shut down without these old cars! Other than the few rentals available for tourists, these vintage American stalwarts made the island move. Quietly, over the decades, while America filled full of bright, shiny, spiffy, new cars, Cuba's quietly became "antiques."

Some smart car repair shop owner in one of Havana's shabbier suburbs saw the opportunity and started hoarding the better 1950's era General Motors, Chrysler, and Ford cars other Cubans still motored around in. His business had grown over the years. Friends and family asked him if he could store one for them too. No one could keep a secret though! Soon, men and women in slick suits began to call: government and party officials! They, too, had one or two good deals on old cars they'd picked up, and could he store theirs too?

Casteneda knew of several warehouses with rows of "vintage" American cars in storage for their owners. His cousin had gotten him in on the deal. It was like the American stock market: even the little investor could play. Casteneda owned 10 himself; someday, his red '57 Bel-Air, two-door hardtop would finance his own beach cottage. It needed paint, but he would leave that to the future, hobbyist owner. For now, it sat in the air-conditioned, guarded warehouse, together with the largest collection of "classic" cars in the world.

At first, he toured the warehouse often, suspicious of its owner, but finally gained confidence. Actually, he was impressed. The warehouse owner showed him the random storage system, the HVAC equipment, and the backup power equipment. He could point you to your cars in seconds! The fire prevention equipment came from France; the security system came from Germany; the customers came from everywhere from the *barrios* to the Capitol.

Customers could rent space for either cash—dollars, of course—or cars. Most paid in cars. Casteneda came back infused with a new appreciation for capitalism and put the word out that at least the functionaries of the ideal Communist state machine he controlled would enforce the warehouse owner's and investors' security. In a most *Nortamericano* way, the Cuban car speculators adopted the attitude of "Mess with the Chevy and you're dead!"

How Casteneda loved his *Cubanos*, his islands, his nation! Where else could impoverished people turn their gray, drab repression into market opportunity with color and fun and passion!

Casteneda laughed again at the thought. Capitalism! The great bugaboo turned out to be so imaginative and vital! Already, ordinary men on Cuba grew wealthy speculating in the cars, buying low, selling higher, and never even taking possession! They just bought the titles! Some just made a contract to buy the car in the future and sold the contract!

In the early stages of this practice, a few reneged on the deal. They disappeared. This enforcement mechanism proved effective, and never again did any party default.

Others worried that such a glut of Cuban Classics (as they were known) would hit the market after Castro's death that the prices would plummet. Casteneda did not think so; he'd seen the size of America and knew that these cars became rarer with the passage of time. *Never fear, nostalgic Norteamericanos! Cuban Classics will save your hobby! It will be "Happy Days" in Havana for you!* Casteneda just couldn't help himself; the whole scenario was hilarious. Like an American watching his mutual fund, Casteneda found himself longing for the day.

Casteneda frowned. The Day had better come soon. Those '50s and '60s Yanks were growing older. Soon, they would exchange muscle-car wheels for chair wheels. The younger generation had its own fads to connect to. Like baseball cards, and the tulips of the 1500s, car capitalism success depended on market demand and the owners quietly voiced concern that the market allure of their investments was time-dependent. If only.... What? No one dared voice it.

So long as official Cuba stuck with its pre-occupation with its own vociferous expatriates lobbying to liberate the island, peppered with sporadic bellicose rejoinders (without toothy threats) from Castro, the two nations stayed at peace and the United States showed no sign of the much-feared "invasion of Havana." The opposing intelligence and military forces played the game, but exhibited no intent of war at any level more than the equivalent of pranks. Every once in awhile, one of the nations blundered, but even those bumps never led to the brink of war. That Canadian's arrest and escape illustrated just how confrontational the two nations weren't.

MXI monitored the Canadian's phone calls, got it in their heads the tourist worked for the CIA, and tossed him in jail, albeit carelessly. The Canadian escaped! This enterprising outdoorsman found himself transported from his familiar north woods, and dropped into a mixed, urban-rural, Spanish-speaking, Caribbean island.

Over several weeks, the adaptable Canadian worked his way down the north coast, following the vague plan to make it to the American outpost at Guantanamo. "Get to Gitmo," he chanted in his mind, putting one foot in front of the other.

Twenty miles short of Guantanamo, at a resort catering to Europe's incessant holiday seekers, a Dutch couple took him in, befriended him, gave him some money, and admitted him to their holiday resort enclave. Here, he nattered his way onto a wave-runner rental, defrauding the hapless concessionaire into the idea of handing him extra gasoline, usually denied to all renters to dissuade any idea of using the wave-runner to escape the Communist paradise. Why would a Gringo, who for some reason selected Cuba to visit, not return to fly home the way he came? This honest Cuban just trying to make a buck eyed the man, mis-perceived only another eccentric British or perhaps Australian tourist, and failed to ask for identification.

Miles out guarding the Windward Passage, the U.S. Coast Guard's cutter *Mohawk* nervously tracked a fast-approaching small craft as its wave-beaten rider turned directly toward them and raced straight at *Mohawk* in a most non-drug-runner manner. Alert to the danger of terrorist attack, the sharp Deck Watch Officer almost ordered the man blown out of the water.

The 76mm seemed overkill but the .50 caliber machine-gunner stood with thumbs on the butterfly trigger; their chopper's "precision targeting rifle" (politically correct, warmer, fuzzier term for "sniper rifle") marksman pleaded with his eyes to be the one to stop the craft.

All alert, young, hot-blooded guardians stood poised to execute the "Destruction of Hazardous Vessel" drill they had rehearsed to choreography. These Coast Guardsmen grimly determined to avenge and "remember the *Cole*" but not to duplicate her fate. Later, the Lieutenant would marvel by what judgment he had permitted the approach. Perhaps the lack of visible means to pack explosives held back the threat meter. Fortunately for the escapee Canadian, and for all governments concerned, he wisely stayed his finger from the trigger.

The Canadian made it home, the *Mohawk* acquired its own wave-runner—Christened and signed as one of the ship's extra craft—and the soon to be promoted officer avoided an international incident. The Cubans inquired oh-so-innocently about a "stolen" wave runner but lost their prisoner to the *Mohawk's* Captain's pretense of ignorance. That's the way diplomacy was played in the Cuban Caribbean, far from the State Department's suits. That was about as confrontational as it got.

At least, until 9-11. America now kept a different kind of watchful eye on the hostile islands spitting venom from the southern Gulf of Mexico.

Paradoxically, at the time of the Great Reconciliation, Cuba's stature would increase: Cuba would emerge from its Cold War time warp and re-join the world. The Persian utterly failed to comprehend this corner of the globe, and how it had changed from the Cold War. The Persian's own hatred for America must have convinced him that, if handed the prospect, Casteneda would wound the beast, interrupt their glorious party for a time, infuse their bloated, frivolous hearts (if they still had hearts!) with terror, etc. He misread Casteneda's motives, but the conspiratorial host had offered him the chance to make some real money and anonymously at that.

Now, Casteneda cursed himself for his greed. What was it the southern Americans said? "Pigs get fat, but hogs get slaughtered." He foresaw blood, and it was Cuba's.

20

Aboard Babylon
Havana Harbor

The Chief, too preoccupied with his mistresses to bother with the man's plan, introduced Casteneda to Saya-dar. The handoff of this wealthy, obviously important visitor to Casteneda appeared not to insult Saya-dar, who dined Casteneda on his yacht, plied him with young women, and always looked at him appraisingly, with just the hint of a friendly smile. Saya-dar had eventually asked Casteneda to tell him about Florida, idly curious at first, then expressing sharpened interest, and had insisted on paying Casteneda for the information.

After all, who in Cuba could better brief Saya-dar on the out-of-place American peninsula stuck into the Latin Caribbean? In reality, any German tourist could fill him in, but it was true that Casteneda's own data about the peninsula included militarily significant data, while the Germans, like the American tourists, thought sun, sand, seafood, and sights. Casteneda wondered why the Persian did not sail there himself, and suspected that he might not be welcome, but it was true that no one in Cuba knew more about the air bases, air fields, some of the radar installations, declining Naval presence, Coast Guard patrol patterns, and other matters useful to intelligence heads. He would, as the man in charge of all of Cuba's *Nortamericano* agents, again personally sample the Emerald Coast's bright hospitality to Middle America, and the

Gold Coast's cosmopolitan opulence. Casteneda had both smacked mosquitoes while listening to 'gators bellow in the back swamps of the Yellow River, and smelt the dust, gasoline, and beer while cars roared by at the Daytona 500. He had "gone to Disney World."

Yes, he serviced the agents and briefed his own Chief routinely, if blandly. Casteneda gave himself to his topic, studied hard, and kept up with the capitalist giant that his superiors just *knew* would wake up listless one day and manufacture some excuse for a D-Day invasion of his island. Preposterous, but it kept Casteneda in good work.

Casteneda knew better. Unless the Castro boys soiled themselves in stupid and unholy alliance with America's new terrorism plague, America would continue to forget Cuba. No, the capitalists in America had not *forgotten*. They didn't care! They did not *have* to care. Perhaps the Americans exacted their own revenge against Cuba by neglecting Cuba to its chosen fate. For whatever reasons, the CIA tolerated Casteneda's network and turned a blind eye to Casteneda's service calls on his agents. He supposed that to be the price the CIA paid to ask him questions about his homeland. Casteneda had recast himself as the "Deputy Chief of *Intelligent* Operations and laughed at the joke. He would help both his Cuba and America. He was Cuba's unofficial ambassador to the U.S.A. He was the "back channel" between the two. Perhaps there were others.

The wall came down, Europe shed its iron curtain, and all breathed a sigh of relief—but only for a short time. Along came the

Muslim *Jihad*. The Iranians! Their embassy takeover stripped a soft America naked for the entire world to see.

Then, Cuba caught America's renewed attention. Those three Afghans Cuba had helped smuggle into the Caymans made America nervous. Castro's courting known terrorists caught the United States' attention. Fidel's biological weapons lab didn't help assuage matters. America was eyeing Cuba more closely since 9-11. After 9-11, the gadfly *la Red Avista* spy network the FBI had caught—complete with its pictures of American defense installations—took on a more sinister meaning.

"Be careful of the company you keep," America had communicated to Fidel, as a quite-so-clear warning. Cuba's interests and the Islamic *Jihad's* interests did not necessarily coincide. A death-wish demon might possess the Middle East, but the Cubans had no desire to blow themselves up or shoot themselves in the foot. Cuba needed to be more careful. Castro, however, just couldn't resist tweaking the U.S.'s nose.

No, despite Castro's saber-rattling, the Cuban government would not jeopardize the stale stalemate by endorsing the Iranian's plan. The more Casteneda considered what he'd done, the more uncomfortable he grew even to permit Saya-dar's anchorage in the harbor.

When the report on the Middle Easterner's yacht visit floated to the top of the papers on Casteneda's desk, he had stamped it and tossed it aside, then retrieved it. Personal opportunity and a sense of foreboding piqued his interest. The Muslims hated America more than the old-line Communists did. They gathered and struck, surprising America time after time, and without mercy too. America wrung its hands, flung a few missiles, but reeled like a drunk and eventually ran, abandoning her troops symbolically at the front, but, really, twisting in the wind, as the Americans would say. He would see what this Muslim yachter wanted. Perhaps they could "do business."

So, strategically an hour before dinnertime, Casteneda in his best khaki suit, French-blue pressed shirt, and solid red tie, had showed up one day in his official launch, requesting to board the visitor's yacht, *Babylon*. The cold stares from the young gunmen glaring down in killer rebuff elicited only Casteneda's courtly smile and casual cigarette ignition. He laughed when his reaching for the lighter jerked their hands and arms into near weapons-draws and he offered them a smoke instead. Casteneda had faced dangerous young men before and had, indeed, been one himself. He enjoyed rattling them, testing them.

An expensively-outfitted, dignified, swarthy, smiling Arabic-looking man appeared at the rail, greeted him warmly, calmed the Hombres with a casual wave, asked him his business, and invited him up *Babylon's* ramp. Up it was for certain.

Saya-dar knew how to live and to host. They explored the bar, and each other's motives, finally agreeing to attend dinner that night, with Casteneda as guest of course. Casteneda openly declared who he was and the nature of his business, and watched the Iranian's reaction. Saya-dar merely sat back, laughed, and ordered more wine.

Casteneda liked this guy. On the spot, the Cuban determined to recruit this rich visitor, and to enjoy his opulent hospitality in the process. He showed the Muslim Havana's clubs, and noted the suspension of Islamic Law outside the borders and watchful eye of Islamic land.

Their conversations deepened; this Saya-dar, as he was called both by name and title, preached that America merited a comeuppance. Perhaps he could learn from the man some piece of intelligence that the Americans might use. Certainly, he enjoyed the Iranian's fine wine, and bottomless bar.

Frangible, Saya-dar had said of America. America is *frangible*. Casteneda enjoyed the new English word and had flaunted it in his report, impressing his Chief. It became part of the office lexicon to observe that America was frangible. The Chief, ever blasé, approved the contact, patted Casteneda on the back, and left him for his own pursuits. Good.

Then, one late afternoon, with feet propped up on a cushioned Ottoman, lazily watching the red sun slip into the West from the aft deck of the Persian's yacht, Casteneda began wondering just who was recruiting whom.

"I trust you find the payment satisfactory? Your intelligence about the United States certainly is fresh, I am told by others who would know."

"*Gracias*. Yes, the compensation is satisfactory." Casteneda cleared all he told Saya-dar with the Chief, and turned in part of the money to assure the Chief's support. Most of what he told was publicly available, obtainable by tourists or from simply standing around as if on vacation. Some tidbits were harder to come by and had value.

Casteneda had wondered what the man wanted. He discovered this answer while reclining in an overstuffed leather chair in the aft cabin of the Saya-dar's *Babylon* as the red sun fully melted into the dappling harbor waters. Windows surrounded the lounging men on three sides; Saya-dar stood casually behind the bar mixing Casteneda another Scotch and water. Saya-dar swizzled the drink as he walked to Casteneda, smiled and sat down. He held Casteneda's eyes, and scooted forward in his own chair, until he and Casteneda faced each other directly, only three feet separating them.

"Let us talk as two men who are brothers, who share the same enemy, my friend."

"Let us *be* brothers!" Casteneda responded, the Scotch whiskey amplifying his sentiment.

"Then let us strike our enemy," spoken quietly.

"Yes, let us," Casteneda followed up without thinking, raising his glass, but blabbing with less conviction and the sudden, sobering realization that he had better pause to hear what the host had to propose.

Saya-dar's bold ambition stunned him at first, frightened him, even repelled him, but the plan's promise of personal profit seduced him into its conspiratorial arms.

What was that line? Casteneda cursed himself, reflecting on all of this while sitting in his own office later. He'd taken up the habit of checking every Gideon's *Bible* he found in American motels after finding a $50 bill in one. The crisp cash marked a passage in "Proverbs" warning the lonely male traveler, in a way most wise, to "avoid the harlot." Casteneda guessed that Gideon chose that verse knowing the temptations men far from home face, particularly when fueled by the bar downstairs and the selection on TV.

Whiskey mixed with soft, warm skin, deep, drawing eyes, and hints of forbidden pleasure, combined disastrously to make young men fools, old men wise, and then fools again! Now, Casteneda's greed and foolishness threatened the Great Reconciliation—and his Chevy prices!

The would-be Middle Eastern terrorist must know that the Cuban government should never risk being caught directly aiding Islamic terrorists. Why come to Havana, talking up such bold strikes? At the precise moment of the end of that question, but after the sale, it came to Casteneda.

The Son of the Desert, camel-thumping bastard was not lounging in the harbor with aged Scotch whiskey in his glass to co-opt the Cuban government. He breezed into town to bypass the government and buy himself a cooperative Cuban co-conspirator as well as Cuban contraband. Casteneda blanched, felt dizzy, and sat backward into his creaking oak chair, forgetting that its weakened spring always threatened to dump him on his back. He reached for the bottle of Ron Rico in his lower drawer. He watched the tan fluid cover the bottom of his sludge-bottomed coffee mug, and sipped rum.

I am now a Middle Eastern terrorist! He pictured the report Saya-dar might even now be typing out about the "Cuban connection" and wondered if Washington was listening! Casteneda blanched and downed the rum. The rum both burned and comforted as Casteneda evaluated his new role, and he did not like it. Why the Hell had he let himself be lured into the sale?

Casteneda was a man of action. Problems required action, required that he do *something*. More immediate than the mockery of his own vices was the question over what happened to the *Corsican Sun* and its precious cargo? He had specifically charged her crew with the duty of watching over the anchorage site chosen for the two canisters. In reality, Casteneda had his man watching Saya-dar. As he recalled the briefing, Casteneda's orders to Revaca's buc-caneers now seemed defectively vague.

Casteneda wrung his hands and rubbed his face. He had not dispatched them to pillage! They were merely to stand guard over Saya-dar's staging site, that diminutive, abandoned island about 150 kilometers from the American coast. Orders to "watch" implied protective action upon encountering peril he supposed, but he had not foreseen any problem and had not planned for combat contin-gencies. Had Revaca undertaken more than just to observe and report? The cutthroats he had subcontracted to were capable of anything, particularly so far from Casteneda's control. What Casteneda did know was that he was missing a hired crew of scoun-drels and, Saya-dar's fancy Italian-made helicopter with Casteneda's subordinate sent along to monitor.

What evidence had Casteneda's men carelessly left at the scene? What satellite phone conversation had the *Yanquis* intercepted? Casteneda worried over what ramifications would be set in motion by fumbling the nuclear containers' poison, brokered through the guilty Cuba. Where was the awful stuff anyway? What the Hell had he been thinking? He should have sold the fiendish imp in the bottle and washed his hands of its mischief, or foregone the profit this time and just told the Americans. Maybe they would have remembered him on the day of the Great Reconciliation and bought him Cuba's first McDonald's franchise. Instead, Casteneda faced jail and Cuba harbored disaster. What was going on out there at that far-flung wisp of an island at the extreme north end of the Bahamas chain, almost 400 miles from sunny Havana?

J ack smelled her light scent before he opened his eyes and saw
her. Donna sat next to the only window, legs curled up tight,
arms clutching a hospital pillow about to fall off the chair
back, head bobbing as she dozed, sunlight glinting from her shoul-
der-length hair.

"Donna," Jack called gently.

She awoke, stretched, smiled, and came to him. Donna took
Jack's hand.

"Pulse fine," she teased, but held on.

"Stronger now, I think," Jack added. Jack breathed deeply.

His head no longer pounded after four days rest, but he felt the
bed growing and engulfing his body. Got to get out of here.

"Today is checkout day," he told her.

"Yes, I know. I'm here to help you break out," she said.

At 1:00, Jack thanked the nursing staff at the busy desk.

"That's all right, boy," the graying, plump woman in the pink-
flowered smock assured him. "It looks like you've got your own
rehab lined up," she added, eyes twinkling and all but laughing
aloud. Donna looked away. Jack felt his face redden. He pursed his
lips and pretended to glare at his favorite nurse, but winked, hugged
her, and said his "thanks" and "good-byes" all around.

ARCTURUS

Jack carried his plastic bag with his few belongings, and said little. He felt sore still—all over—but far better. Mostly, he needed some movement, some exercise. He needed to run and work it out. Right now, though, Donna had other ideas.

"Well, I'm picking you up, I might as well take you out on a date, huh?" Donna asked, beeping her bright yellow Saturn open.

Jack started to protest, but stopped and stared at the car. Tracking satellites wouldn't miss this machine.

"Yes, I'd like that very much," he said and got in, not missing the color but not in a mood to make any wisecracks today, either.

Donna let Jack sit quietly as she turned out of the parking lot onto 14th Avenue.

"My boat?" Jack asked, re-orienting himself from institutionalized recovery and grief to real life again.

"Tied up where you left it. I hope you don't mind, I've been staying there," Donna said, glancing his way. She explained: "*Arcturus* is in dry dock and I've had nowhere else here in Miami to stay. I didn't think you'd mind me watching over your sailboat." Donna paused. "I've been gathering Bobby's things, too, so you'd have less to do when you got out. The marina finished *Arcturus* yesterday and I'm rooming there now," she added.

He didn't mind at all. Jack was grateful not to have to do the grim job. Never fun, especially when the dead man was your best friend. He thanked Donna and smiled his "OK," granting his permission retroactively.

They drove 10 minutes. Jack thought she was heading out to the beach and marina. Just before crossing the Causeway Bridge onto Harbor Island, Donna turned sharply right, took a side street, and then doubled back under the Causeway, where she parked at a small café, ringed by palm-shaded tables on a stone patio.

The bistro hung out over the Bay, fully 2/3 of it on piers, the other 1/3 claiming just enough of a perch on land to own an address.

"Jack, this place serves the freshest salads and the chef selects his own seafood. The coffee's Brazilian," Donna described, adding "It's porch away from the Causeway is quiet. Perhaps we can talk."

Jack had been warned about women using those words, but the warning flashed like the fortune coming up in the old "8-ball" toy from the '60s, recently back on the shelves in retro-digital form, fortune floating up, warning you, and disappearing again. As always, the warning about women wanting to talk flashed in vain. Jack accompanied her inside, finding a charming café on the other side of the massive, dark oak door.

The perceptive waiter sized them up, smiled, and directed Jack and Donna to a corner table overlooking the Bay, flanked by an aquarium on one side and planters of flowers on the other. Jack held Donna's chair and then eased his weight into a chair, back to the wall, facing her. On impulse, Jack reached forward and held Donna's hand, trying so hard to find the right words. He did not, but he did not need to.

Since the attack, Donna had been on her own. Gordon had disappeared and Jack lay in a hospital bed. Having fulfilled her responsibilities, the terror, the excitement, and the tragedy overtook her. Donna cried softly as she held Jack's gaze. Jack just held her hand and sat. The waiter appeared, perceived again, pirouetted, and permitted the two their privacy.

"Harry and Bobby are dead, Jack," Donna said simply, finally.

What could he say? Briefly, Jack went a thousand miles away. He shook his head and returned. He looked at Donna. Jack realized what a strain the terrible episode had created, and felt even more gratitude for this girl's staying behind to help him recover—and seeing after Bobby's things. She'd seen combat and death with no chance to let it out until now. Jack gripped her hand more firmly.

In this way, and talking it all out, the two passed the afternoon.

22

Havana,
the Castillo de la Puenta
One week after the attack
on Arcturus

The *Castillo de la Puenta*, the old Spanish castle-fort guarding the point, always soothed Casteneda, making it prominent not only strategically in the old days, but also prominent to Casteneda personally as his favorite place to reflect.

Casteneda thought a lot—more lately. He thought about his wife, dead now for 10 years. No children. No hobbies other than fishing split his attentions from work—unless a few women and much good rum counted as hobbies. He thought about Saya-dar's madness and his plan. He thought about Cuba's dilapidation, the lying promises of the Revolution, and—the future. He saw himself as the personification of the *Castillo*: perched vigilantly on the point, oriented toward every threat from the sea, guarding all that was Cuba and preserving all it could become again. Even if others obliviously worked their jobs, and even if his own job and Party sometimes echoed of the absurd, Cuba's future and security demanded steadfast guardianship. Cuba remained distinct from, and bigger than Castro, Communism, and the Party. In the end, his loyalty and love stayed fast to Cuba.

Casteneda feared mounting another expedition to the Cay, or even to lurk in the area out at sea for week "fishing." He burned to know the fate of his men. Some were distant relatives and he owed explanations. His Chief didn't care, but his aunt certainly did. He puzzled over why that particular Cay had suddenly risen to any level of strategic significance. For now, he must put aside the question; the island was too "hot" even to check out.

He would go again into the United States, just as he and Sayadar had planned. He would arrange travel to accomplish a needed meeting with his best agents. It was time and the trip would arouse no particular suspicion, even if detected by the Americans. The travel to America to service his top agents would mask his true secret mission to save his beloved Cuba from destruction—a destruction that he had inadvertently—no, recklessly—spun into motion.

Casteneda turned the key in his car's ignition switch and swung out onto the Avenue Del Puerto, turning south toward the Academy of Sciences. He parked by a nondescript stucco building like many others, and walked up the stone pathway. The old Spanish buildings seemed to close in on the cobblestone path, an impression heightened by the palm fronds that brushed Casteneda's shoulders on his way to the entrance.

Stopping at the path's end, he fumbled for his key to the heavy, wooden, ironbound side door, swung it open, paused, checked, then stepped through the portal into a surprisingly modern, if small, office. He sat down at the computer, powered it up, and e-mailed a simple message, leaving in less than 10 minutes to go home and drink. Scotch had drawn him to this precipice, and rum would anesthetize his lonely anguish and fortify his residual reservoir of resolve to protect his Cuba.

Across the city, another computer alerted its master to the incoming message. Juan del Le Cruz read Casteneda's order and made the arrangements according to the pre-arranged code, filling out the required paperwork, sealing it, and delivering it on his way home. He envied the man who sent the e-mail—a man he would never meet—and wondered what that man would do and see in the United States of America. Perhaps one day, rather than just arranging travel for others, he would go to see America himself. Perhaps he would stay.

A week later, Casteneda departed from Buenos Aires for Montreal, where he answered the customs agent's humorless questions, replying "business and fishing" as his reasons for visiting Canada, showing the agent his "FishVenture" card, proclaiming Casteneda to be a marketing representative for a Buenos Aires-based, world-wide fishing expedition outfitter and agent.

Casteneda celebrated his infiltration method as a particularly brilliant piece of tradecraft. First, the ploy required no faking: he fished regularly, plying the warm waters off the Cuban coast from government boats. Fishing gave Casteneda so much peace. He thought so much more clearly casting his baits here and there. He struck upon the idea of his infiltration method while fishing one day outside of Coxim, Brazil, poised on the edge of the Pantanal's vast swamps, half the size of the Florida peninsula. He had watched the Cayman crocodiles slip in and out of the water and weeds. Their ease of infiltration back and forth from land to water gave him the idea for his own infiltration tactics.

In Argentina, Casteneda made the switch from Cuban "diplomat" to Argentine businessman. Argentina was the country Casteneda chose as ideal to "clean up" his identity. Both countries—Canada and Argentina—hosted world-class fishing expeditions. No Canadian customs agent would be suspicious of a foreigner outfitting himself with outdoor gear, flying from Montevideo, into Buenos Aires, then into Montreal, renting a car, and disappearing into the vast interior for weeks at a time. No one tracked his movements. If Canadian intelligence decided to tail him just as a random curiosity check, he could spot the tail and lose it during the hundreds of miles he would drive into increasingly lost country.

At first, this method of working his way into America through Canada had intimidated him; the vastness of Canada's forested wilderness overwhelmed his isolated island mentality. He forced himself to embrace it, enjoyed acting like a Canadian, and smiled at how easily he penetrated his enemy's border. Once heading west across southern Canada, he could pass for an Indian, or one of the numerous non-Anglo immigrants and Casteneda noted that he attracted little attention. Wear fishing clothes from Cabela's and sport a Bass Pro Shop billed cap, and that's all they see, he decided: just another angler up here for his dream vacation.

Dressed accordingly and picking up his long tubes with a couple of older poles and reels as "props" at the airport, Casteneda worked his way pleasantly westward into Ontario, to Thunder Bay, financing travel with his Citibank credit card, issued in Argentina to "FishVenture." That traceable trail looked normal for any fisherman. From Thunder Bay, across Lake Superior, he could literally see across the U.S.-Canadian border. The numerous islands created a maze and the Apostle Islands on the American side would screen his illegal landing eastward of Duluth-Superior. He had done it before. He just needed some friendly fellow-traveler help.

Casteneda dropped off his rental car and rallied with his boat-owner contact, a Canadian socialist who nonetheless enjoyed the extra cash earned while tweaking the United States' nose. They traversed Lake Superior freely, taking advantage of the joint agreements reached between the two countries giving each other's citizens hassle-free passage back and forth. The Canadian wove through the Apostle Islands creating a path so non-descript by satellite that he felt—invisible. Approaching the American shore, Casteneda donned swim trunks, a river-rafter's jacket, and rubber sandals, bagging the clothing he would wear traveling south through America.

Behind one of the islands, Casteneda slipped over the side into the Canadian's used lake-kayak, waved off the Canadian agent, and felt the clear water's resistance as he dipped the double-bladed paddle into Lake Superior, swiveling the slender craft about, toward Wisconsin's northern shore. Paddling leisurely for 45 minutes brought him to the infiltration site. Bumping the gravelly sand with the bow of the kayak, Casteneda climbed out and peered in every direction, pretending to stretch his muscles. Quickly growing cold in the very non-Caribbean surf, Casteneda simply waded ashore and walked to the nearby fish-camp parking lot, drawing no attention.

The Ford Explorer rented for him by the American agent waited for him, just as arranged. He found the secreted key at their dead drop, stood off, circled, and finally, remotely unlocked it. Casteneda appreciatively sniffed the new-car odor. He reached over and popped open the glove compartment, retrieved his wallet of American paraphernalia including cash, license and credit card, and headed south, not wanting to linger at this critical link-up site. A few miles down the road, Casteneda pulled over into a secluded woods road, and donned khaki pants, a white dress shirt, and a microfiber vest. Resuming his trip, he then celebrated his successful infiltration by stopping for pancakes with bacon and eggs at the first small town restaurant. America must have thousands of little places named "Kountry Kourt" or some variant he reflected over coffee, perusing the region's newspaper. He preferred the American non-franchise restaurants with big, block letters on the sign broadcasting the suggestion "EAT" with no subtlety.

Casteneda needed the meal; the feared link-up with the Canadian agent tightened his nerves, stressing him out over this high-risk rendezvous. The method was sound, and the route safe, but the risk lay in having to rely on the Canadian contact to the north, and the American agent on the southern side of the lake. Had they turned? Had they gotten drunk and bragged? Had they simply decided that the Cuban cause was not worth their own risk or the meager cash they were paid? For that reason, he ordered the Canadian agent watched by another agent who continued to report that the watched agent, a university social sciences professor, remained reliable.

Likewise, it was difficult for Casteneda to recon around the fish camp parking lot without attracting attention, looking like a lost, confused idiot. This forced him to restrict his reconnoitering around the planted vehicle to mere peripheral vision as best as he could, and to walk almost directly to the planted vehicle, departing quickly. Such an approach without reconnaissance violated his every instinct and training, but he had eliminated all other approach tactics. He never met this American agent, but mailed his pay to a post office box in Madison, Wisconsin. Nuisance car thieves threatened the plan's integrity more than betrayal and Casteneda insisted on using the big, red, solid-steel security bar that locked onto the steering wheel.

With the highest link-up risks out of the way, and assured of freedom from being tailed, Casteneda drove south, through Wisconsin's vast, sparsely-settled, marshy, low "up north" woods, but stopping suddenly periodically, exiting the truck to listen for helicopters. Hearing none, and seeing no hint of a tail, he found Interstate Highway 39 and made straight way for Chicago, about seven hours away. The traffic gradually increased as he left the scantly-inhabited rolling forests behind and entered the rich farmlands surrounding Madison, then giving way to the same terrain in northern Illinois.

By early evening, having dutifully tossed in his coins at Illinois' irritating toll booths, he passed the exit for O'Hare Airport and rented a decent motel room close to a commuter train station, ready for his trip into the city in the morning. He would turn in the Explorer in the morning and rent another of a different color but leave it parked for the day. As nerve-wracking as his linkup had been, that paled in comparison to driving into The Loop with morning rush hour traffic. Instead, he'd take the "L" from O'Hare and meet his agent at the Museum of Natural History by bus. In the meantime, a bustling sports bar in Edison Park close by the commuter rail line served pizza that Casteneda found exquisite while he caught up on American television news.

23

Chicago, Illinois
Two weeks after attack
on Arcturus

Early, Casteneda arose, locked the room, grabbed coffee from the "continental breakfast" room downstairs, and hiked the short distance to the train station. He boarded and then watched the station signs indicate the progressive approach to downtown Chicago—The Loop—and alighted within a block of the Sears Tower. It was still early, and a growing crowd hustled with all of the intense industriousness that characterized these urban Americans grabbing their insulated paper coffee cups before reporting to work.

Casteneda spied a small Italian pastry and espresso shop underneath the "L" track and sat down with plenty of time to think. He sipped steaming coffee and munched a cinnamon bun, and looked around at the variety of people shuttling to and fro as the "L" periodically clattered like thunder overhead and away.

Some of the people whisking by looked Cuban. Many looked Latin. Casteneda wondered where they all lived, where they came from, and where they were all going. He wondered why they were here, in America. He felt tired. He wondered if Saya-dar targeted this very elevated train track where commuter trains even now rattled and clashed by over his head and to his front, carrying—Cubans, maybe. He compared the faces striding by with such purpose. Imagining their destruction gave him no joy.

Were they not the enemy? He looked at them more. No, he conceded that they did not *look* like enemy. What was he thinking? Was he going crazy?

Casteneda left a 50¢ tip, threw his disposable cup, plate, and napkin dutifully into the trash bin, and moved toward the nearest bus top, trying to decipher where it would take him.

"Lookin' for somethin'?" a smiling black woman about 50 paused and asked. "Need directions?"

"Uh, yes," he mumbled, momentarily caught off guard. "Will this bus take me to the Museum of Natural History?" he asked. He knew the route but he did need to confirm the right bus.

Her eyes twinkled. She knew the answer, and thought him provincial for requiring an explanation, but she delighted in generously directing him to take this bus to such-and-such street, and then told him which bus to transfer to for the leg taking him to the museums along Lake Michigan. She obviously enjoyed helping him enjoy her city and he watched her briskly move off after he thanked her for her courtesy to visitors. She left satisfied that she had exhibited the city's hospitality.

He had always found Chicago open and friendly, particularly after 9-11 for some odd reason. The week after 9-11, Casteneda returned to the United States with the mission of observing and reporting on the state of America's morale. In truth, he was dying to see the brash Americans running around like chickens with their heads cut off, as his grandmother might have said. He thought it too risky, but found the most material change to be only that airport security had tightened. He had gaped when they told him to remove his shoes. Was this 200 years ago? That's where their hero Nathan Hale had hid his sketches of the British fort. Did they think he would have "the secret code" lining his socks? He had been unaware of the steel shanks in his American-made shoes, as the polite screener advised him.

Casteneda had expected different. Pandemonium, maybe. Maybe the inward writhing to snap and snarl at each other that one might see in a pack of starving dogs. Cowering would have been nice. But, no, the people he watched were anything but cowed.

On the bus, he watched again the throngs of people passing on the sidewalks as the bus lurched its way east toward the lake. Dismounting the bus in the huge turnaround area in front of the museum, he sat down on the low concrete wall adjacent to the sidewalk to watch the passersby and wait for the time to meet his agent.

He sat across from the rendezvous point, by the Museum of Science and Industry, looking across at the Natural History Museum. He pictured the area bloodied, with these same people dying. School buses began arriving and lining up outside the museum. He checked his watch, saw it was about 8:30 a.m., and noted that it must be "field trip" day for some summer class groups. He had thought they would be on summer vacation somewhere. There were so many buses. So many children.

Casteneda lifted his weight slowly and moved across the distance between the two museums, toward the buses, picking a line that passed between two and put him on the steps leading into the Museum of Natural History. As he approached the gap between the buses, a little girl, about eight years old, bounded down the bus steps, lost her balance, and pitched hard forward onto the asphalt right in front of him. Without thinking, he reached down, took her hand, and gently lifted her up.

She started to cry. Her knees were badly scraped and bleeding. He took a wet-wipe from his tourist's fanny pack, tore open the package, and handed it to her just as the shepherding teacher emerged from between the gap in answer to the cries, saw what had transpired, smiled, and thanked him for looking after the little girl. The teacher took the wipe and began comforting the child. He replied lowly, signaled "good-bye" lamely and resumed his course toward the Museum doors. He heard a small voice call, "Mister!" glanced back, found the girl staring after him. She waved and smiled to her rescuer. Flustered, he returned her sign of appreciation, turned away, mounted the steps and paid for a ticket.

Once inside, Casteneda took the first double-doors to the left and began working his way lackadaisically back into the bowels of this maze of exhibits until he saw them: two scruffy stuffed lions—his favorite exhibit in this museum.

He knew the rules. No patterns. He considered the Natural History Museum to be such a perfect rendezvous that he bent the rule in its favor. This public place offered a warren of corridors, passageways, hallways, and nooks for meeting. Thousands passed through and staff were highly unlikely to remember any one person. The particular passageways he took led increasingly deeply into the museum until it seemed to the visitor that he had found a forgotten corner, unknown to all others.

Here, the two formerly fearsome man-eaters of the Tsavo River basin, and of movie fame, stood. Granted, they had dried a bit, and shriveled to a percentage of their former lion-selves (as explained by a somewhat apologetic placard), and they were maneless lions,

146

in a most un-lion-like way. Still, he stared at the two husks and imagined them pouncing on hapless laborers, dragging the terrified victim off to be eaten for real. He did always look around for cameras and microphones, but he knew that experts would conceal those. There could be a camera in Ghost's eye, or embedded in Darkness's nostril, watching him like prey. A woman of about 55 rounded the entry corner, glanced at the lions, and moved toward them, stopping immediately in front of the display and a few feet from Casteneda.

"Did you see the movie?" she addressed Casteneda absently without looking at him.

"Yes. I want to travel back in time and to Africa," he replied, and turned, walking slowly away. She followed.

Outside the museum, they met and walked down one of the winding sidewalks, northward, roughly parallel to Lake Michigan. The next half hour of this walk-in-the-park would consist of routine conversation. He had directed the agent to perform numerous reconnaissance missions and report back. She could not know it, but every mission she had performed to date had been fake, assigned to test her loyalty, to train her, and to disguise the critical mission that Cuba one day would assign. Today was such a day.

Chicago was famous for its winds blowing westward from Lake Michigan. The skyline towered over the lake surface like New York rose from the Atlantic. Immediately east of the park and museum area, jutted the boat slips and Meigs Field (the same of MicroSoft Flight Simulator fame). To the immediate west thrummed Chicago's fast-paced business district.

The harsh practicality of terrorism against a free culture was simple: even diligent defense assures failure. Not every attack must work to achieve terror. Many may get caught. Terrorists win when any attack makes it through the security filter. Al Qaeda achieved spectacular results with its coordinated 9-11 hits, but Casteneda's understanding of America told him that Americans expected all manner of freakish happenings in New York City. They did not necessarily foresee that one, although Tom Clancy had written a hauntingly similar plot scenario a few years earlier. They just did not see New York City as *real.* Larger than life, perhaps, but not real. Until 9-11, that is.

Casteneda, thoroughly Scotched, lounging on the *Babylon,* had spouted off his own theories to Saya-dar, who listened attentively. "The terrorists should have hit Middle America," he'd advised the terrorist mastermind. "Kill real Americans in the real places real Americans go every day." While flying jetliners into strategically significant skyscrapers struck spectacularly, most Americans did not work in the World Trade Center, Casteneda had criticized dryly. About 35% of them disdained their military (a seemingly ubiquitous, self-destructive phenomenon over history and over the world, Casteneda thought), so the deaths of their defenders in the Pentagon just did not hit close enough to home to strike fear like an ice pick into their soft hearts.

Casteneda had droned on, a bit drunkenly, but through the whiskey fog, a worry dogged him: What if the playboy Muslim was not just playing terrorist? What if the Americans connected a plot to Cuba, blamed Castro, and hove a cruise missile down onto his beloved Havana? Casteneda cursed his own stupidity and almost swore off drink.

The urbanites in Havana and government types would go nuts if the Americans took Havana, but the guy out in the sugar cane country would hardly notice a difference. He might even experience a shot of "smug" about it. The Americans' hearts had warmed to New Yorkers, but he did not think the farmer on the other end of his island would so readily rally to the Castro cause. He noted cynically that Washington and the Pentagon did not merit the same outpouring of sympathy as shown to New York City.

The damned Iranian had heard his message, had concurred, and had selected nuclear poisoning as his ideal strike. Casteneda recalled his own boozy voice seconding the plan and it struck him now as surreal. Perhaps he should have foregone that last frozen Daiquiri— or the last several. Damn the fickle bravado of rum!

He completed the contact with his agent, left instructions for the report drop off, and peeled off onto a different path, choosing to shuffle northward along the lake instead of heading directly back into town. No tail. He idled down Navy Pier and bought a ticket for the huge Ferris-wheel ride there, dutifully snapping digital pictures like any other out-of-towner wowed by the big city. He then continued northward to Lincoln Park and sat to rest his feet. He pondered his own unusual behavior; no tradecraft motivated his pensive walk.

What troubled him? He replayed the day. He replayed his many trips to America, mostly to work his way south to contact his Cuban agents in Miami. He had roamed the country, mostly on the eastern side, and no one had ever stopped him. He had bought newspapers, watched television, and snapped pictures in state parks. He recalled the bacon-and-egg breakfasts served by mostly friendly faces along the routes.

The face of the little girl looking up at him for help this morning haunted him. The Deputy Chief of Operations for the Cuban General Directorate of Intelligence (DGI) recalled the dry corpses of the two man-eaters, the Ghost and the Darkness, and wondered which he had become and which was Saya-dar. He assigned the Darkness to the Saya-dar but chose not to become the dry, dead husk of Ghost. Castaneda's operational mind kicked in and generated the inception of a plan. He took the "L" back to the airport and spent the next week busily planning, free of second thoughts, and free from the specters of either the little girl or Ghost.

Miami,
on the road to come what may,
July, two weeks after the attack
on Arcturus

Jack ran three tortured miles, watching the red sun glow through smoke-colored skies at the horizon. Full sunrise sneaked into the day behind the cloud cover. When he heard Miami's traffic noise off to his right simmer, then boil, he stopped and lay in the sand, face up, arms spread out, and worked himself into Jack-shaped depressions, and then inventoried his joints and muscle groups. The combination of body-slam against rock and four days' hospital time stiffened him all over. He'd have to work it out on the soft, sand-strips along the surf.

I have a lot to work out. Out of my Army. Telling Bobby's family. Deep in someone's adventure. In love? That euphoria morphed into visions of responsible citizenship, which called forth the next reminder: *No job!* This thought—and the apprehensive looks from a passing retired couple—brought him back to earth. Jack gathered his strength, rotated to ease the soreness as he stood, and turned around to head back to his sailboat, breaking back into a jog for the three miles back.

The pier where he moored his boat resounded in the way of wood reverberating above water as Jack jumped from the sand to the pier. He jogged in place a few minutes on the springy wood, walked briskly to his sailboat, and stretched to board. *Man that hurts! Good.*

In the galley, Jack poured his promised-reward mug of coffee and returned to the deck. The sun now lit the eastern horizon as if someone had brushed flames across the ocean surface. A light breeze carried off the steam from Jack's coffee, its aroma mingling with sea-smells. As Jack lowered himself—slowly—into the deck chair, his phone rang.

"Jack here, good morning." He was in a good mood.

"Good morning. I trust I'm not getting you up," Gordon greeted him.

"Oh, no, not at all. I've been up," Jack said, a little irritated that Gordon would even think he was lounging around.

"Jack, I'll come to the point. *Good.* There's so much I want to talk with you about—Bobby, and—well, so much, but I believe these matters warrant face-to-face working out. I'm asking you to come to Tampa to meet with me—Friday. Will you?" Gordon asked, knowing he would.

Jack thought. *Tampa?* He almost told Gordon he'd have to consider and call back. *Stuff it, Gordon.* Bobby was dead, and from combat while on Gordon's supposedly-peaceful cruise. Not that Jack thought of Gordon as sinister: he just knew Gordon withheld far more than he had told Jack. Still, something about Gordon told Jack to trust him, made Jack view Gordon as—an ally, a man on the same side as Jack.

Gordon heard the hesitation and added: "We've been through quite an experience. (*Lame,* thought Jack.) I am obligated to give you the full story."

"The *full* story?"

"Yes, Jack, I'll tell you why *Arcturus* in the first place. I know you, Jack, better than you think. You'll understand. You'll feel better about your decision to ship with the *Arcturus* and—you'll feel better about Bobby's death," Gordon ended quietly.

Jack said nothing.

"I want you to get back into shape, work out the injuries, and get over here. After I've answered your questions, I'm going to make you a proposition and introduce you to some people you would like to meet," Gordon ended.

A *proposition.* Jack had accepted one of those already and Bobby lay in the grave. *Stop! Shut up, McDonald!* Get past the blame phase. Who was he blaming, anyway? Who invited Bobby to join *Arcturus?* Not Gordon: *Jack* had called his friend. *Jack* had sold the *Arcturus* gig hard: "Piece of cake" *Jack* had told Bobby. This is the *cream job* you and I never landed in the Army. (They had never sought such a slot.)

No, whatever this Gordon had withheld from the young men, Jack opened this door. Bobby—he had been a big boy—a soldier. Bobby had no longer served as Jack's junior officer. Bobby owned his own reason for signing onto *Arcturus.*

"On the road to come what may," the 200-year-old lyric line piped through Jack's guilty reverie. A man didn't volunteer for Ranger School and choose Infantry to die old. Bobby didn't join Jack on *Arcturus* for a summer vacation; he joined because people needed him to do dangerous work, and he was—had been—a dangerous man. *Do not dishonor Bobby by whining over his corpse. Currahee.*

"I'll be there, Gordon. Time? Place?"

Gordon thanked Jack and supplied the details. "Jack, Donna said she'd give you a ride back this way, since your truck's parked here in Tampa. Her car's in Miami and she's finished seeing after *Arcturus,*" Gordon said.

"Sure."

It was set. He'd left his truck in Tampa at the marina and sailed his own boat to Miami. He'd ride with Donna from Miami to Tampa on Friday. He *wanted* to know what *Arcturus* had been about. What business did *Arcturus* leave unfinished? Was it worthy? Whatever their mission, it hung there, waiting for those who would carry it out. What had been their *cause*? Who needed *Arcturus*? Did they still need *Arcturus* or had they all failed someone? Jack had to know.

Besides, had Gordon told him he'd be traveling with Donna, Jack would have agreed right away. Why didn't he just say so in the first place?

25

America
Three weeks after the attack
on Arcturus

Once freed from indecision, all crystallized remarkably clearly to Casteneda, as he wound around Chicago on I-294. He kept the radio off to think. His head spun at how quickly he had reversed his course.

How could it be? But it was. He knew it. He knew his change, wherever it had arrived from, was—right. Not right in a Marxian dialectic sort of way, fitted crudely into the blather he now finally admitted was mindless propaganda without truth, but—right. His decision *felt* right. For the first time in his life, he felt—free. What did that mean?

Regardless, Casteneda drew from his new source of conviction and steeled himself to his precise new plan. Turning south on Interstate 65, through Indiana's cornfields toward Indianapolis, he mentally rehearsed his moves. Finally satisfied with his approach to the Americans, he rented audiotape books (political action-thriller stuff, of course) from a Cracker Barrel between Indianapolis and Louisville, Kentucky, to pass the time as inconceivably vast cornfields blurred by.

Casteneda craved American fiction. Political censorship dictated the contents of the Cuban drivel; the American literature was so—*wild*. Free-wheeling. He did so wish that Cuba featured more in America's consciousness, but his islands remained largely ignored, even fictionally. The crazy thought that perhaps Cuba could be the 51st state made him laugh out loud.

Two days' relentless driving, sustained by fast food and captivating plots, motored him across the Florida line and into Tampa almost before he realized it. He bought a map, a local newspaper, a few magazines, some dried peanuts, a chocolate candy bar, and an espionage thriller paperback, and rented a motel room. He prepared for the next days not knowing exactly what they might send his way, but he knew one thing. When dealing with the military—anyone's military—he would likely be waiting. Time to clean up and rest first.

The next morning, Casteneda strolled down the hallway to the lobby. He, again, took advantage of the free, light, complimentary, "continental" breakfast of toast and coffee, but glued his eyes to MSNBC which faithfully roasted the current president for "his war."

Years ago, Casteneda had personally brokered a sale of dismantled nuclear weapon isotope acquired through his Russian and African connections. He'd sold to an Iraqi, knowing full well that Saddam was his real buyer. He worried now what the mad dictator had done with it. More to the point, he wondered what caches of paperwork the Americans might even now be sifting through, and what evidence of his own devilish transaction those boxes might hide. For the first time, it occurred to Casteneda that, perhaps, the Iraqi dictator had also been brokering sales as well as collecting. Why not? Saddam had the money and the connections to buy and sell and he could have made millions dealing death. Did he re-sell to the Chinese? Worse, did he supply Hamas? Al Qaeda? Ouch! He suspected that the valuable mineral now lay buried somewhere in Syria, hidden by Saddam during the months before the American invasion, but he could not rest in such speculative assurance. Maybe other death-brokers had packed that same material—sold earlier by Casteneda—into the canisters this smooth-talking Muslim pirate had somehow gotten his hands on and had brought to Cuba!

Casteneda sat on his bed, thumbing through the Yellow Pages. There! He jotted down an address, looked it up on his map, and noted it. He sat for a time with the phone book open in his lap, gazing at its open pages without moving. Then, he breathed deeply, exhaled, and simply did it.

From the room phone, he jabbed the number to MacDill Air Force Base, waited while a real person directed him to the office he requested, and then left his own code name and number with the man who took the call who identified himself as a Sergeant. Casteneda sat back, mounting a reflective vigil by the phone. Lying on the bed, shoes off, cup of coffee made from the room's small electric pot in hand, he flipped on the television and trolled through the news channels—waiting.

The phone rang. The polite, southern, American voice asked him a few verification questions and directed him to the main gate where he was to wait, with a security team of course. He understood and hoped that "security team" meant something different here than it would have meant in Cuba.

Casteneda, already packed, left immediately and drove to the location he had looked up earlier, purchased a new suit at the Joseph A. Bank store located there, together with a blue traveler's dress shirt and a stylish "regimental stripe" tie. He moved to behind the building, clipped the tags, donned the garments without leaving his car, made sure his tie was straight, and drove the short distance to another world and another life.

It was surreal. It was inevitable. He had no better choice. It was the right choice. He stood on the point at *Castillo de la Punta* guarding his country, but in a way he had never expected. He saw his duty so clearly now. He was prepared to see this through and, oddly, he felt relieved. It struck him as bizarre that he could call the American military, turn himself over to its mercy, and drive there, stopping to shop on the way.

Slowing to turn, having already noted the surveillance watching his approach, he spied the austere, boringly military, main gate guardhouse, and stopped just as multiple signs made it quite plain he must. He intentionally exhibited his bemusement at the serious young men and women assembled to assure that he was no danger (and not in any danger). They peered into his vehicle and thoroughly—but not rudely—searched his person, addressing him courteously but earnestly as "Señor," in Spanish. He never saw the four sniper-team members posted at two locations, tracking him in their riflescopes. Later that day, the snipers and spotters would wonder who they had "scoped" and why, but they'd done this routine before, sometimes being ordered to shoot, but mostly not, and then moved onto the next mission. Casteneda obeyed the even more serious security team that had been standing by with M-4s slung, accompanying them to a waiting, nondescript car, which took him to a nondescript building with a nondescript sign by its door, where he met the not-so-nondescript Army liaison to SOCOM (Special Operations Command), General Paul Ortega.

General Ortega (the irony of the Spanish surname did not evade Casteneda's notice) locked eyes with Casteneda, shook his hand genuinely warmly and firmly, and introduced the others in the room as his intelligence officer and an "interrogation" team.

Casteneda gulped and glared, but the General reassured his guest quickly that the men were present to secure the room and to record the conversation only. Only. "Interrogation team" meant something more sinister in Cuba's jails.

Ortega made it even more plain: "Mr. Casteneda, you walked in on your own and you can walk out if you want. We'll drive you to your car when you say the word."

Neither man took that seriously, but the sentiment conveyed by Ortega fortified Casteneda who was tempted to test the General's promise just out of sheer curiosity.

General Ortega drove to the point, "What is your situation, what can we do to help you, and what are you bringing to the table?"

An hour later, the men broke and ordered lunch in. The General phoned out and Casteneda heard him say, "Gordon, you are not going to believe who I have been talking with and what he has to say explains a lot of goin's on. Why don't you come on over? Make that as fast as you can." Next, the General ordered his aide to get Major Hodges, the British Army's liaison officer in for a briefing ASAP as well.

When both men had arrived, General Ortega addressed the newcomers, in Casteneda's presence. Casteneda saw two fit-looking men, one, a hard-looking and very ugly British officer in Army battle dress uniform, sporting a major's rank and the name-tape "Hodges," and the other in khaki trousers and white dress shirt, unbuttoned at the top, and wearing casual, hiking-type low-quartered shoes. Ortega introduced the Major—but not the other man.

Ortega explained that Major Hodges represented Her Majesty's Army's presence in SOCOM as its liaison officer; the General stayed vague about the other man. Casteneda watched as General Ortega addressed Gordon, attempting to assess the relative power held by each.

Ortega spoke for Casteneda and explained succinctly to Hodges and Gordon that Casteneda acted on his own; that he saw the peril to his own nation if Cuba assisted a Middle Eastern terrorist cell, particularly with any form of nuclear attack; that he saw nothing that Cuba had to gain by such an attack on the United States; and that he foresaw better relations after Castro's death. All men agreed that Colonel Casteneda should cooperate to infiltrate his terrorist benefactor from the Middle East into the United States just as Saya-dar requested, and then return to Cuba as normal. They'd work out the means for each to contact the other. Casteneda listened all the while, agog that the torture team hadn't yet arrived.

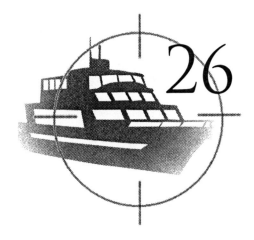

26

With Casteneda introduced to temporary quarters and contacting Saya-dar to let him know of Casteneda's arrival in Florida, Hodges excused himself, telling Ortega that he did not want to know any more. Ortega and Gordon then challenged each other. This was not a fight; the men engaged, as they had for years, to sharpen each other, to reveal the flaws in their analysis, and to metamorphose their separate thinking into an operations plan.

"Paul, you know that using me to tag this terrorist in the U.S. is illegal," Gordon warned. "You can't run around at war in the country. You're Army. This is not Iraq. This is not even Columbia. The Posse Comitatus Act says you have to have the specific authorization of Congress. How about it? Could I see that, please?"

"I'm operating under one of the exceptions: this is a 'sudden emergency,' don't you agree?" General Ortega asked, not seriously, referring to the Congressional Act and the accompanying regulation that at least suggested some legal cover basis for what he had in mind.

"No," Gordon chided.

"I'm protecting federal property then," Ortega offered, citing the other exception.

"You're not even protecting your own hide, which is also federal property. You should at least cover its backside! CYA is about as USA as you can get."

"I'm calling you forth as militia."

"You can't; only Congress has that authority."

"Well, now you know why I'm not calling the lawyers."

The men stopped and reflected on the gravity of their under-taking, measured against the immediate threat.

"I'm afraid if we don't do something, I'll get that legal authoriz-ation to send troops only when some Governor asks the President to exercise his authority to mobilize the Army for 10 days of 'clean up the nuclear debris and body parts' work," General Ortega said, somberly.

"You ever heard of *Bivens vs. Six Unknown Agents*," Gordon asked.

"No."

"Yes you have. You be careful; you can go to jail *and get sued* for unlawful exercise of your authority."

"Then, I'm safe, Gordon; I don't have the authority to exercise unlawfully."

Gordon opened his mouth to argue, but gave up. He could tell his friend had tired of the banter and planned to charge ahead, regardless.

"I hear you, Gordon, and I have an idea. I have to check it with counsel. Are you for hire?" General Ortega inquired, notably before checking with counsel, Gordon mused. Gordon suspected there would never be such a consultation with counsel. Counsel would say "no."

"Yes, of course."

"No, the Army is not supposed to fight here, but, damn it,

Gordon! The country's hands are tied by so many Lilliputian cords staked to the ground that this powerful giant can't even protect herself. Every time I pass on critical intelligence my men have died to get to the CIA, it ends up run through the press blender, then plastered on the front of the newspapers in a form not even recognizable as the truth. Look around, Gordon. Who's not here?" Ortega, gestured around the room.

Gordon understood both his friend's frustration and his question. SOCOM hosted a full-time CIA liaison officer, complete with staff. Bill _____ was a good man. What Bill had sacrificed for his country was beyond recount. Bill had run operations, healed from knife slashes, awakened bound, and endured torture. Bill _____ survived all of that but finally incurred Langley's wrath for his barrage of reports urging Washington to recruit more agents from the natives and mount more direct action operations. This man whose loyalty should have earned him his employer's (and his nation's) respect earned himself, instead, the get-him-out-of-here assignment to SOCOM.

On the surface, the assignment looked pretty glitzy. Bill _____, after all, got to live in Tampa, Florida, enjoying the Gulf of Mexico and Florida sun as opposed to the dingy, dangerous posts he'd worked before. Bill could perhaps reconstruct his family life, devastated by months of isolation, secrecy, and unpredictable disruption. In reality, the assignment was Langley's cheap way of trash-canning Bill _____ out of the field and away, soiled even more by his Chief's parting, finger-wagging order to "report back on what that animal Ortega is up to." Politicians at CIA not only neutralized Bill's effective, aggressive, covert defense of his nation; it lowered him to spying on his own Army.

Bill _____ had reported in to MacDill AFB, drawn his ID card, settled into quarters, fretted through the initial, official introductions and immediately confronted Ortega with the cold truth the first time the men talked alone.

"CIA's demoralized case officers are undercut, often-betrayed, and resigning in droves. I'd ring the FBI but I am not about to sound the hue and cry for so many layers of command to get involved that we trip all over each other. Anyone I call will be afraid of violating some law, worry about the political repercussions, and stop us cold, so, I'm calling the right man: *no one*. Get it, Gordon? "Mr. No one" from Washington will head this operation."

Paul Ortega pointed fiercely at Gordon Noone as he underscored his point. Gordon knew that the General delighted in adapting Ulysses' word-play trick to their own scheme, and rolled his eyes.

"*Very* funny."

"Besides," Ortega relaxed a bit, and continued, "This may not be a specific operation anyway," the General stated absently, offering the half-hearted justification that they might be "legal" after all. "Look at what we know at this point: a Cuban agent has given the Army intel about a suspected terrorist infiltration. I'm treating this like intelligence gathering, not operations. I have authority to gather intelligence so long as I'm not listening in on American citizens. Able Danger, right? I'm keeping this streamlined, tight, and secret. I'm not jeopardizing Casteneda either. I'll want him in place and intact when this is all over. I may turn him over to CIA then. They'll fume, but there will be nothing they can do about it. I need—I don't know what I need and that's why I'm going Black. Look at this!" Paul Ortega said, as he slammed a folded newspaper down on his desk.

"Jealous C.I.A. Accuses Army of Running Amok," by Ebert

Barratson, the circled article proclaimed. Gordon already knew the article and its background. Hell, he was up to his neck in its background. Bush nominated a General to head the C.I.A. and that pissed off the establishment. Hearing his cue, the Pentagon's old-time special operator General Boykin was already sending mysterious troops out to get intelligence before the shooting started. Imagine that! Before!

Boykin had headed up Delta Force. Well, perhaps, Gordon admitted, this did somewhat signal that the Army had set up shop in the intel market with gusto. The Army had the ill-defined lawful authority to "prepare the battlefield"; certain commanders thought they ought to be about that business before the battle! If C.I.A. were too hamstrung, then the Army would get its own intel and worry about whose "realm" was whose later. They were hardly "running amok" as the Congressional staffer-dweeb had whined. Nevertheless, Gordon and General Ortega were trying to decide just where the amok-line ran.

General Paul Ortega, soldier for 34 years, Ranger, friend of Gordon, and patriot, rose to make his point (entirely unnecessary except to permit Paul to vent): "I don't give a shit about the CIA's *'realm.'* The CIA has no *'realm.'* CIA has a *mission*: spy for the United States of America. They forget who they're snooping *for.* Gordon, the *Army* is the biggest customer the CIA has; the Army needs that intelligence and my men are dying out there for lack of it. The Congresswoman wants me to stick to 'preparing the battle-field.' Well, my post-9-11 *battlefield* appears, disappears and shifts all over the world. She can't *show* me the battlefield. I can't just order out patrols to find their 'lines.' They don't have 'lines.' Intelligence doesn't drift into you on the winds. Gathering intelligence can't be done without conducting *operations*. Not just in Paraguay, either," Ortega ended.

Paul Ortega alluded to a publicized shootout in Paraguay between Army covert operators and an erstwhile armed-robber, dead from picking on the wrong victims emerging from a bar. The controversy brought the Army's own overseas covert operations to published forefront.

"Gordon, you aren't government—any longer—and you're deniable. I'm not supposed to be even talking to you. I don't know you. Gordon Noone is "no one." I'm keeping Casteneda "off the books," run personally by you until you figure out what we have here. Understand?"

Gordon understood. The Atlantic and Pacific Oceans had sheltered the United States from its birth. Unlike Europe, with inimical cultures poised across mere gated checkpoints, or just across the Mediterranean, America enjoyed a veritable fortress of sea and land terrain with friendly neighbors north and south.

Freedom and technology changed the defense calculus formula that worked so long.

Using our own freedoms against us, Muslim terrorists adapted technology, erasing the old geographical limits that had held Muslim invasion back for centuries, in effect, creating a "time-space warp" erasing America's precious distance. Technology became "maneuver" in military terms. Technology overcame obstacles, bypassed strongholds, enveloped troop concentrations, and undermined the West's historical defenses.

Terrorists use technology like a "wormhole" through which to emerge from their own country to strike deep within. Technology shredded much of former military thinking. Never forget. Memorize the mantra: *Atta had a visa.* He was here legally. Legally. Atta had a visa.

Those who understood learned to incorporate the new technology dimension into the proven three-dimensional principles of warfare, and to reconstruct these principles according to the changing "battlefield"; those who failed—well, "asymmetric" warfare had a way of naturally selecting out the slow for extinction.

9-11 proved that the festering forces of Islamic *Jihad* had thrown off the limits of supply lines and national boundaries. The *Jihad* had arrived in disguise, and attacked like the alien from the movie of the same name: injected from without, growing from within, to devour and burst forth at its own chosen time. While some from within America's scores of defense-related organizations instantly grasped the new era, and explored creative tactics, a large percentage of the country's population and politicians persisted in their comforting delusions. As always, government changed oh, so slowly.

Gordon respected CIA's case officers. He'd worked with CIA case officers, and fought with them. He'd cried in front of the wall with the anonymous stars—one for each CIA officer killed in the field in the line of duty. He had known some of the men behind the nameless stars. He'd held one's head in his hands as he took his last breath. These "stars" were killed with no glory, no recognition, no reward from the country, other than the gold star. Spying sucked, basically. You traveled to filthy shit-holes, hung out with filthy scum, had no set hours other than "all" and "odd," and came home to a country that treated you like a leper—if it knew about you at all. No, not like a leper. The lepers garnered sympathy and drew disability.

Once home, Washington politicians didn't know what to do with you. You were an embarrassment. Maybe you were even a criminal. Thankless? You bet. Without reward? Never. You didn't run agents for the CIA for the rewards *from* your country. You did it *for* your country in the classic John F. Kennedy speech sense of the words. The peaceniks and anti-Americans hated you for it. They weren't all outside the CIA either. Spies had to watch their back-sides from all quarters. It hurt Gordon to watch CIA gutted, libeled, and scorned. It hurt the United States too, he knew. Until CIA recovered from its pummeling, the military—through its Special Operations Command—had decided to "deploy its own scouts."

Speaking of running foreign agents, a knock sounded. The General's aide announced that Colonel Casteneda was settled in and back. General Ortega invited him in.

"General, I thank you for your courtesy. What now?" Casteneda inquired.

General Ortega addressed Casteneda without guile: "I under-stand that, when this is over, you are returning to Cuba, along your normal route, as if nothing's happened. This is your choice. You have the option of staying here. We, of course, salivate over the prospect of a highly placed intelligence agent in your country, but I am not sure why. I am looking at this as if we owe you a tremen-dous debt of gratitude. I am not looking to run you as an agent until we all die. I'd like to do that, understand, but I can't ask for more than you've already done. You're free to return and resume spying as usual."

The men all looked at each other and laughed, Casteneda with relief, Gordon and Ortega from the craziness of it all. In reality, General Ortega had sifted this man's motivations and saw this promotional offer as the most likely method of recruiting a life-long inside source. Nevertheless, he was sincere in making the offer. He had to be to make it sound sincere.

General Ortega continued, assuming the answer he wanted, "I will leave you with means to contact us. Otherwise, we won't jeopardize your life by contacting you. Say, I have to know something though," Ortega shifted his tone and cocked his head at Casteneda, as if to realize something important for the first time. "How did you get into the US?"

Casteneda knew he would ask and had already decided he would have to explain. "One of your Marxist friends to the north owns a nice boat."

"Huh?"

"A Canadian Communist ferries me across Lake Superior. Getting into Canada is easy. Traveling within Canada is easy. The Lake is huge. I make what you might call an "amphibious insertion." An American sympathetic to Communism's continuing Cuban experiment helps me out on your side of the lake."

Ortega and Gordon exchanged looks. The Department of Defense would not like this at all. For decades, the U.S. and Canada shared mutual defense concerns through their joint operation of NORAD—guarding against Soviet air attack. They even worked side-by-side in uniform at Cheyenne Mountain's air defense nerve center. NORAD worked out well for both sides; the U.S. had to have Canada secure to secure America's North; Canada understood the threat to its own territory—and to its national sovereignty—so both rolled up their sleeves and kept watch, ready to go to war if necessary. Implicit in this partnership was the fact that America would not watch Canada fall to an enemy. This went as far back as the Monroe Doctrine, with Roosevelt underscoring the point that

U.S. defense meant defending the *continent*—not just the borders. Canada's reaction had always been to preserve its own sovereignty by promising to guard the north.

Now, top U.S. commanders questioned Canada's will to take on the new terrorist threats. The U.S. had asked Canada for a re-commitment to the NORAD agreement, but one fitting the new threat. For whatever reasons, Canada had dithered and it sent the angry, post-9-11 U.S. the wrong signal. Further prodding from the United States still got no response. The U.S., therefore, determined to act on her own. The U.S. quietly created Northern Command. NORTHCOM's responsibility included defense of the whole of North America—not just the United States—but included only U.S. forces.

Think about it. In other words, in the wake of the Islamic *Jihad* at home and Canada's equivocal signal about its will to fight back, the U.S. acted unilaterally to fight on the North American continent—outside the U.S. borders if necessary. Weak Canadian commitment to strengthen its own military further eroded U.S. confidence in its former ally. It looked as though America was on its own to defend North America.

Ortega understood; "Hell, 40% of our own country lacked the will to fight back," he'd often complained. Nevertheless, what Casteneda now told him reinforced that Canada stood as a weak partner—if a partner at all. Well, someone else would have to work out the international relations. Here was a Cuban agent telling him how easily he infiltrated the U.S. through Canada. "FishVenture" was going to get some attention. There would be earnest meetings. Department of Defense and its Canadian counterpart would, no doubt, resume talks on Canada's role in combating terrorism. Department of State would sulk over its reduced influence. More would be said than done; Ortega was convinced of that.

"It appears that our neighbors collaborate to work our undoing," Ortega said coldly.

Casteneda blanched. He considered reminding the General that an American traitor met him on the U.S. side of Lake Superior, and another in Chicago, but decided to let that go right now.

The General paused, reddened a little, and continued with a bit less bluster, plainly a bit self-conscious.

"Look, Casteneda, our countries have been facing off as enemies since Castro took over 50 years ago. I see that changing once he dies. The Bay of Pigs was decades ago and you can see we're not gearing up for an invasion. You, in turn, are not pointing Russian missiles at us. You also are not—at least officially—hosting these terrorist scum, and that is a good thing."

The President's threat to countries harboring or helping terrorists hung in the air like a suspended dagger. Casteneda understood that the dagger hung over his head and over his islands. He fought back the urge to cast his eyes up where he suspected he might see the dagger pointed at his skull.

"I am no diplomat," but, by the God who made us all, I thank you for telling us all of this and for seeing it through," the General concluded as he extended his hand to Casteneda. Casteneda shook hands with the American and appreciated that he had not been bought or threatened with prison. He thought of the *Castillo de la Puenta* and appraised that he was honoring it as the fortress's modern manifestation.

"Our law is questionable about the extent of operations I can conduct here," General Ortega went on to explain. Casteneda looked to the other men's expressions, which remained straight-faced. It must be true. What was coming?

Ortega calculated correctly that Casteneda had studied the U.S. Government and understood the country's aversion to large standing armies kicking in doors, and to military rule at home. Ortega agreed with the Constitution's second, third, and fourth amendments and even the principle of civilian authority over the military. These damned terrorists strained the country's laws. Law that worked for moral, peaceable people had no way of accounting for the existence and treachery of merciless traitors. When people got afraid, the government tended to forget its lawful constraints and get heavy-handed. General Ortega had been shocked at how fast the local governments shredded those Constitutional amendments, going door-to-door confiscating citizens' guns in New Orleans after Hurricane Katrina. He did not want to become such an arm of the government. He was repulsed by the very idea of Americans acting Soviet-style with a "knock on the door" to get your guns and search your house. Nonetheless, hiring Gordon to run this domestic counter-terrorism op was pushing the boundaries of the Army's authority to operate. He'd go this far—for now anyway.

"What I want to do is turn the opportunity you brought to us over to my good friend, Gordon. He knows what to do."

Gordon had no idea what to do. He supposed he could put a plan together and act on it, but he did not know how he would go about using the senior Cuban agent to interdict the terrorist and figured it would be highly illegal, anyway. Gordon did not think the cryptic answer, "No one," would amuse congress when they held hearings and asked "Who are you?" despite the enjoyment Paul got out of the word play code name.

The men shook hands and Casteneda returned to quarters.

"Get Major Hodges back in here," Ortega said to no one in particular, facing the maps, but expecting from experience for the big Captain to carry out his command. The aide moved impassively.

"Show in the young man seated in the lobby too, please," Gordon directed.

Miami to Tampa
Three weeks after the attack
on Arcturus

Jack had awakened to Friday with excitement. He shouldered his pack, walked the two blocks to the wharf where *Arcturus* floated, and speed-dialed Donna's cell phone number.

"Ready?"

"Yes. I see you." She waved from the deck. "I'll be right down."

Minutes later, Donna's bags and Jack's backpack filling up the back of the Saturn, the two headed north and then angled northwest, across Florida toward Tampa. Jack chose his time when they were well underway and away from the coastal metropolitan areas.

"Donna, you asked me on *Arcturus* why I was there, remember? Jack asked.

"Yes, I remember."

"I gave you a straight, honest answer, did I not?"

"Yes," she responded, eyeing him.

"Now, please tell me why we were all aboard the *Arcturus*," Jack asked, but really commanded, feeling he'd earned the right.

Donna cleared her throat, sipped some iced tea, and began.

"Jack, I'm from Destin, Florida originally. This is near Eglin Air Force Base where the Ranger School's Florida-phase camp is located, but, of course, you already know that. I attend a church in Fort Walton Beach nearby where some of the camp cadre also

173

attend. I met an Army couple there. The husband side of that pair is a Major whom you know, a Major Cantrell."

Jack gave her all his attention. He trusted Cantrell. That explained how he got this mission, too.

Donna drew a deep breath. "From a Cuban family who also attended, I learned of a blind lawyer in Cuba. The government there arrested, tortured, and threw him into prison—indefinitely—for speaking out against Castro's abuses and for holding secret prayer sessions in his home. They released him all right, but now he is crippled by what they did. The Cuban government, only a short distance south of the United States, represses religious freedom like the old Soviet Union.

Now, the Cuban government threatens to arrest his son, too. Only the fact that the son is a popular, championship soccer player holds them back. The Cuban family worries that the secret police will not hold back much longer."

Jack foresaw where this was headed. Unbelievable!

"The church wanted to help somehow. We talked through what we might do to help, but, as we brainstormed every possibility, nothing short of direct action seemed sufficient. What good would it do to write Congress? Maybe the Ranger camp's nearby location prodded us. They rehearsed the Son Tay POW escape raid there, you know. It still sounds crazy, even to me, but some of us in the church decided to arrange to contact the family, get the son out, and the father too if possible."

Donna paused for breath, looked at Jack, who said nothing, but held her gaze. She decided to finish. "I know this seems like a tall order for ordinary people to undertake, and we did not start out with a mission quite that broad or ambitious. At first, we just wanted to write, to pressure, and to try to influence the Cuban government to leave this family alone or to let them get out. That got nowhere. The son was a 16-year-old Cuban national soccer team prodigy. No way would Castro let him get out. They had already lost one high-profile player when Lazaro Abuin Sanchez grabbed the opportunity to escape to the United States at Miami International Airport in 1997.

"One day, I asked Major Cantrell if he knew anyone who would try to get these men out. He thought I was not serious at first, but my question prompted his own thinking about whether a team could break them out. He came back, asked if I meant what I had asked, and I assured him we were going to try; we just didn't know where to start, and we knew we were out of our league."

The story took Jack aback. She surprised him. Jack opened his mouth to marvel and Donna raised her hand.

"There's more," she said.

"I bet. (*Direct action!*) Please go on," he asked.

"Jack, Gordon is my uncle." She glanced his way to enjoy the surprised look. "I never knew what he did other than some sort of 'sales work,'" Donna continued, watching the road but a bit distracted-seeming as if talking to herself. "I now wonder why my own parents moved to Destin, near Eglin. I mean, my parents are from Pennsylvania, not Florida. Why *there*, just a short drive from Eglin and the Ranger Camp and the headquarters of the 1st Special Operations Wing from the Air Force? I have my own "full story" to get while you are in Tampa, I think," she ended and looked at Jack.

"Anyway," she said returning to the present, "Cantrell put Gordon in touch with me and you know the rest. Gordon understood from the start that we were serious. He eagerly took the mission, and he and I put it together with me acting as his assistant and getting funding."

Jack was speechless, considering the scope of all that Donna had disclosed, wondering what neither of them knew. He was surprised that Gordon agreed to head such as task force, and said so.

Donna explained and Jack just listened: "At first he thought I was crazy. He had no network there. Without telling you more than you need to know and naming names, his old Ranger buddy at SOCOM whom I think you are going to meet put him in touch with a man who runs a network of agents in Cuba. This man could spring the lawyer, and his son, and get them both to a remote place on the lower tip of the island for a pickup. You know, Cuba is over 600 miles from west to east. And, it's not just an island; Cuba is an entire collection of islands, particularly on its northern side along the Caribbean. Gordon checked with the powers-that-be and, while our government would not undertake the mission, it would look the other way while a private team went in, linked up with the defecting Cubans, and got them out."

Here, Donna left her story, and addressed Jack. "That explains to you why the Coast Guard took its time getting to us and why no Coast Guard patrol boat halted us on the way back in. The Coast Guard stayed well away from the area on purpose. They were pulled off the area on the Atlantic side of the Bahamas and told to look innocently the other way. We were on our own, though, except for the Coast Guard help you lined up on *your* own," she explained.

Donna resumed recounting the plan. "We actually considered the whole trip very low risk from the point of view of the *Arcturus's* crew. We would stay in international waters. We would have no direct contact with any Cuban agent. We would press a little bit into Bahamian sovereignty, but Gordon said security demanded that we keep this thing as tight as possible, and we decided to run that risk and ask for forgiveness later if necessary."

Donna stopped. "That's sort of what I'm doing now, I guess," she added a bit sheepishly.

ARCTURUS

Central Florida flew by. The traverse west somehow defied the laws of physics, requiring far less time than Jack would have liked. Jack was behind the wheel when Tampa's outskirts appeared. Soon, the drive ended as Jack turned into the parking lot by Tampa Bay. There sat his truck.

The time had arrived for them to part. Standing at the trunk to help her with her belongings, Jack turned to face Donna as she closed the trunk and turned toward him. He moved toward the young woman, put his arms around her, and pressed her close. He needed to shelter her. He needed to shelter in her warmth. He needed not to need her or anyone else, but yielded to the moment and to her eyes. She did not resist. He felt her arms wrap around his chest and her hands press close, even urgently. She said nothing, but sighed. Jack buried his face in her soft hair. Their embrace reminded Jack that Bobby had died, that he had killed, and that—despite his own determination to *continue the mission* regardless of the mission's toll on him—Jack McDonald was human. Human.

He could train. He could crack jokes. He could deploy and kill. He could drink. He could suspend his soul and body for a time. He could not, however, *stop* being human—fully human—including needing another. A woman. Needing a woman. *Needing Donna is for real right now, but now must pass.*

Then, stepping back, they looked at each other, both wondering if they'd see each other again, both fearful and expectant at the same time.

"What now?" Donna smiled and broke the silence.

"While you're quizzing your parents up the panhandle, I'll see what Gordon has on his mind," Jack said and stopped, lapsing back onto his teasing mechanism to avoid the anguish of needing her but knowing she would leave—maybe forever.

"*That's* not exactly what I mean!" she replied.

"Ha. I know, dear." More seriously and more quietly, Jack added: "I don't know what's next, Donna. I do know that I am reporting to Gordon. I suspect that he will have—work—for me to do. I suspect that I will do it. I know that you are returning home, for now, anyway. I would like very much to call you after a couple of days to see what your situation is." Jack frowned. "I really do not know exactly what the future holds for me. I want us to talk more about all of this."

In her wise way, Donna replied to Jack's expression and confusion.

"We've been through a great deal, Jack. Perhaps some time will make a difference—in the way we each feel about everything, I mean. Look, you go see Gordon, but watch out," she cautioned. "He has a way of getting you 'on board.' I'm going home and I'll wait to hear from you. You call me, though. Soon." Her eyebrows raised, and her finger pointed his direction emphasized "soon."

28

Tampa, Florida

Feeling down, Jack took stock of his surroundings. Donna's yellow Saturn disappeared and he stood alone in the parking lot. The Hillsboro River shimmered to his front, on its way down to the Bay. The truck stood ready at his side.

Jack's cell phone vibrated: Gordon's number.

"Hello, I'm in Tampa," he answered.

"Good. Donna?"

"She just left for home."

"Jack, you can check into the Comfort Inn there on Dale Mabry—on me—and I'll call you at six. OK?"

"Yes, thanks. I'll be ready."

And he was—for pretty much anything.

Gordon called at six. Jack drove following Gordon's directions back toward the Bay and parked near a marina. Gordon, standing at the end of one of the piers, motioned Jack down a walkway flanked by yachts, stopping near a much smaller one.

"Yours?" Jack asked.

"No, but you know what they say," Gordon answered, referencing the so-true adage cautioning against owning a boat when you have access to one.

Gordon sat with Jack, rocking in the suspended rope-and-wood

Pawley's Island chair and finishing the Low Country Shrimp Boil he'd dumped in the middle of the table, as if all were on the beach. The mood ranged fitfully from comradely to somber. Something was up. Jack's intuition could not identify it. Jack avoided more than one beer, as did Gordon, Jack noticed.

They exchanged pleasantries, recounted the details of the battle, finished off corn-on-the-cob, red potatoes, hot sausages, and peeled shrimp, and then wrapped up the scraps in the newspaper. By that time, Jack had enough of it.

"Gordon, what the Hell was that all about?" Jack demanded matter-of-factly, even a bit rudely.

Gordon grew silent and peered at Jack, preparing himself to apologize, to heal new but fire-forged friendship, and to recruit, all simultaneously.

"I will tell you all." Realizing what he had drawled, Gordon lamely teased, "Not 'you all' as in 'ya'll' but all that launched our mission, exactly what our objective was, and where the raid at sea leaves us—leaves *me*—since the pirates caused me to fail to accomplish the mission."

He paused to gauge Jack's reaction and could see that Jack remained unimpressed with the introduction, and that the young ex-officer would not be charmed. Gordon understood. Lighthearted, crude, even trite military humor masked a deep sense of fairness, of justice, and of the need for *someone* to step forward and fight to defend these. Wisecracking did not mean shallow immaturity; it was simply a survival mechanism used by young men to avoid the grimness of their work. Besides, it is characteristically American and soldiers feel such is expected of them, much like the British are expected to be "cheeky" and understate disaster. Time for the full facts. Gordon cleared his throat and began.

"I know people who fight and people who back up the people who fight. Years ago, as a young soldier, I, too, earned my Ranger tab, just like you." He saw that these words resonated and, so, continued. "One young man in my Ranger School training platoon struggled just like the rest of us, but rose in the ranks over three decades, survived Panama, Mogadishu, lots of other close calls, and will soon head Special Operations Command—Central. SOCCENT, in Army jargon. Right now, he's here in Tampa. I'm sure you know what it is." Gordon smiled. "We didn't think he was any more special than the rest of us. No one lacking grit made it through the Mountain Phase of Ranger School, much less finished the Florida Phase and won the tab. By that time, you knew you could do anything, survive anything, kill any enemy, and accomplish any mission and all alone if you had to. Of course, by the end of the Florida Phase, you were so exhausted and skinny that you might need a week's sleep and two steak dinners. Anyway, my old Ranger buddy had a good attitude then, kept it over the years, and has done well."

Quite an understatement. Jack said nothing, but waited for Gordon to resume.

He had him now. Gordon knew this guy. He *was* this guy.

"Donna is my niece. She came to see me a year ago with a request I could not turn down," Gordon stated, turning serious. "She's maybe told you what she contacted me about."

"Yes, she told me why we were all aboard *Arcturus*," Jack answered.

"I apologize, Jack. I did not anticipate what happened out there. I have no idea where the attack came from. That hit was probably one of those improbable coincidences that screw up missions. I believe there is no way those Cubans perked up to gun for us specifically! I hired you because I wanted somebody reliable, trained,

181

and mature to ride shotgun against drug runners or other random weirdoes and—I'll admit it—for some experienced firepower if things did get hot. I couldn't do it all myself and wanted to apply my full attention to the most sensitive facet of the operation—the pickup. I still don't know who the pirates were or why they attacked us. You already know that the quick search of the *Corsican Sun* turned up Cuban food, drinks, cigarettes, and other Cuban stuff. They looked Cuban. They talked like Cubans. If it looks like a duck…. Why would a bunch of Cuban desperados cruise so far north though? I mean, who would expect a Cuban hit squad lurking around on the northern rim of the Caribbean basin, virtually poised to make a run into the U.S. coast? It makes no sense, and yet, people have reasons for what they do and there was some reason those Cubans made war on us hundreds of miles from their own coast."

He stopped for breath and looked at the young man who revealed no emotion, no assessment of his confession. He might as well keep going.

"I fully expected you two to stay on alert, get tanned even more, eat well, flirt with Donna, and it was a chance for me to evaluate mature, already trained-up troops recommended by Cantrell as motivated, smart, alert, trustworthy, and, well, worth getting to know, for the future, I mean." Gordon sprinkled this ambiguous reference into the conversation carefully. Gordon had recruited long enough to know that flattery works even when the flattered know they're being flattered. He meant it, too, anyway.

"I did not conceive that you would be leading a classic hilltop perimeter defense against an armed assault force with air support." Gordon halted again, looking intently and making his face grave. "I do have to say, 'Thank God you came along.'"

Gordon's eyes glistened. "You know your stuff; you fought fear-lessly, and we'd be dead and disappeared without you—and Bobby. You know that, don't you? Tell me you forgive me for not telling you the nature of the mission. I missed the call, assuming what I thought the threat would be. My assumption was like so many other assumptions. You know what I mean." Gordon sat back, relieved to get it off his chest. He relaxed, and waited.

Jack did know what Gordon meant about making bad assump-tions. He'd done the same thing and now Bobby was dead. He gave Gordon the benefit of the doubt and forgave Gordon the oversight.

"I had no idea that our job had a more noble purpose. I wish you had told me; I wouldn't have missed it for the world," Jack toasted simply, raising his beer stein. "We did need to know about the pickup though," Jack admonished, locking eyes with Gordon. "There's more to you than meets the eye and you are still not tell-ing me all; of that, I am sure. I'm with you on this. I would not have taken the mission any more seriously knowing, but I respect what you and Donna tried to do, and I regret only that we didn't succeed," Jack added, intentionally exonerating Gordon.

"Well, that brings me to the next level of our conversation," an obviously relieved Gordon segued. *This is working perfectly. I do so know these young infantry Captains.* Gordon was not tricking Jack; he was merely assisting him in finding his calling, his destiny. Jack was *looking* for someone like him, whether he comprehended it or not. He would be Jack's "Rendezvous with Destiny," Gordon thought, identifying with the line from both Seeger's poem and the 101st's anthem but substituting "destiny" for "death." The "rendezvous with death," Gordon hoped, would come much later—after Jack had accomplished many missions. Time to introduce the willing Jack into the mission.

"While you two prepared the hilltop ambush-defense, I finished searching the *Corsican Sun*. You would not believe what I found there," continued Gordon, all hint of humor gone. "Fastened down to a welded bracket in its hold was a polished stainless steel canister about the size and shape of a grill's propane tank. I stowed it aboard the *Arcturus*. I had it checked out and got the report back. The canister is packed with an unidentified, heat-resistant matrix buffering a core of radiating material including polonium."

Gordon rose, signaling the end of their dinner and conversation for the night, and passed Jack a piece of plain, white paper. "Jack, here's an address and building number at MacDill. My phone number's on back if you need me. Meet me there at 10. That will give you some time to process—well, just read the instructions for getting on the base and to the office address on that paper. See you in the morning," he ended.

The men shook hands. As Jack departed, Gordon stopped him.

"Thank you, Jack, for forgiving me and for fighting for us."

Jack did not minimize either Gordon's deceptive omission, or the gravity of his own—and Bobby's—sacrifice. He could think of nothing short of a long speech commensurate with either, so, instead, he replied: "You're welcome. I'm glad we were there. Thank you for the opportunity, both then and tomorrow," he replied.

29

*Cruising northeastward toward
the Bahamas,
40 miles off the Florida Keys
Four weeks after the attack
on Arcturus*

aya-dar popped open his laptop and started PowerPoint. He created a new presentation and titled it "Failure Analysis: Windy," then chose a two-column slide format. He set his coffee aside and, rapidly, he began keyboard-brainstorming the aborted mission, sorting out those points that remained in place or had gone well from those that collapsed. He had fought down panic at the loss of his sleek, expensive, Italian-made, new Agusta helicopter and both canisters, but panic was a feeling. Panic was pure fear, not thought, not action. The men and the helicopter were expendable and easily replaceable. Gone. Check them off.

The Urns, though, were like fine diamonds, hard in dirty hands, glinting through mud to reveal their sublime nature to the eyes and hearts of men, but afterward strewing a path of broken hearts and murder in their wake, on their journey through history and around the world. The Urns of Judgment were not expendable. But, let's start with what had gone right, he decided.

First, he had acquired the "off the books" polonium. That, alone, ranked as an accomplishment. His shopping trip to Ivory Coast had then pulled him 1,100 miles northeast into Africa's interior, into that band of poor desert representing the southern front of Islamic expansion, to Niger. Niger hosted a busy bazaar of abundant radioactive material, not all officially accounted for. Niger expanded its market horizontally, branching out from mining and selling its own ore, to importing and brokering black market radioactive isotopes of all manner. From the Minna airport in neighboring Nigeria, a Muslim brother contact drove him to the site of the *hajj* camp in Niger where he and his seller hid themselves among the stranded pilgrims trying in vain to achieve Mecca. Here, Saya-dar planned to strike his bargain for polonium and waxed furious to learn that the Niger contact had already brokered the untraceable polonium on hand to the Communist island.

The Cubans, it seemed, craved cash and had discovered that they could speculate in the trade. Chavez has his oil; Cuba—in pathetic contrast—has an economy savaged by Marx, Engels and Castro. Cuba did still have, however, one of the top 10 intelligence services in the world. Put the cash-craving together with the intelligence craft, and….

Saya-dar inferred that Mosadomi, his Niger sales representative, had his own deal with the Cubans. Mosadomi had lured him to Niger only to whet his appetite, drive up the price, and secure Mosadomi's own middleman cut before passing Saya-dar to the Cubans to let the Cubans be the last cutout. That insipid Communist backwater lacked the verve to deploy the weapon, but simply and ironically leached capitalist opportunity from Soviet meltdown! Well, Saya-dar reflected, the Cubans might as well try to salvage something from Castro's decision to "back the wrong horse." He could hardly blame them.

The return trip to his yacht, and then the five-day ocean crossing soothed his anger. A long day out of Havana, Saya-dar sheltered from the Atlantic, bypassing busier Grand Turk Island and putting in at East Harbor on South Caicos Island. Saya-dar peered out over the rail into the sleepy town before him. He had to get off the *Babylon* for awhile. Saya-dar dressed "casual American" wearing the predominant khaki pants and subdued-colored tropical shirt. Sandals completed his yachter's outfit. He strolled down the pier, past the rundown marina office, and found himself on a sand-blown street lined with pastel-colored, colonial era buildings. Few people ambled about.

He located a bar, pushed open the cracked-paint door, and stood in the foyer letting his eyes adjust from the bright sunlight to the darkened interior. When his vision adapted, he saw—not much. Two men sat in a corner arguing why the salt trade just wouldn't come back and bring with it the prosperity these backwater islands had once enjoyed. They took absolutely no notice of the dark-skinned Saya-dar. Good.

Saya-dar caught the eye of the bartender and strode up to the 15-foot long bar. He picked a stool at the end where he could see the door, noted the back door through the pass-through between bar and grill, and rested his body, leaning back into the wall, until feeling its sticky texture through his thin shirt. He'd hoped the wall's finish absorbed the awful humidity and stayed pliable because of the water content, but a quick brush with his fingers told him the wall was simply filthy. He eased up.

He ordered a Margarita and thought for a second that the bartender was going to criticize him for lack of imagination. The man smiled finally, replied "Of course," and pulled a half-empty bottle of Sauza from the wall. By the end of the afternoon, the bartender disposed of the bottle and Saya-dar disposed of every undisciplined trace of fury, which he replaced with fire and polish. He determined to attain more than nuclear trash from the Cuban bandits. Perhaps Allah designed the Niger back-stabbing to bring him to the very rim of the Great Satan. Here he was, perched on a bar stool almost within sight of America.

A much-calmed but slightly sick Saya-dar had thus motored into Havana Harbor and delivered a note to the street address the treacherous Mosadomi had wadded up and thrown at him, laughing. (By now, his team should have already killed Mosadomi.)

With little fanfare, Cuba, through Casteneda, sold Saya-dar the two canisters of polonium mixed with sundry reactor waste-products. Lighter by the costly Agusta chopper, Saya-dar lacked possession of either canister at the moment, and presumed them gone, but could not know if he had permanently lost the Urns of Judgment. "UJs" he listed. He wondered if the Cuban had arranged for the mysterious disappearances: *Probably not*, he concluded. Saya-dar's sources assured him that the Cubans enjoyed their role as confidential, reliable supplier and salivated over repeat business. Double-crossing did little toward new business development. Also, while he was down one helicopter, Cuban men—some related to Casteneda—had died. But, then, what had happened to his beloved Agusta—and Casteneda's men—and the canisters?

Before disappearing as if the Bermuda Triangle had opened up and swallowed the men, their boat, and the chopper, Revaca had reported successfully anchoring one canister. Then, *Arcturus* interrupted Revaca's report.

Saya-dar had listened to both ends of the conversation while Casteneda ordered Revaca to make a pass over the boat to "take a look." Revaca had, perhaps foolishly, flown close enough to read the boat's name and to note its Florida registration numbers on his pass over the craft. Fortunately, Saya-dar had insisted on covering the helicopter's numbers before loaning it and his pilot to the

Cubans. If Revaca and Casteneda acted the whole scene, then they deserved awards.

Why the *Sun* attacked, Revaca either had not known or would not admit. Saya-dar heard Revaca's voice quaver when he reported the *Sun* rocket attack on *Arcturus* to the dumbfounded Casteneda, with Saya-dar listening to it all. Saya-dar recalled his Cuban friend's fuming and admired his restraint recovery over the radio. Saya-dar had not envied the men the retribution their boss would no doubt exact on their return for their folly. Then, a mere minute later, the obviously stunned Revaca had called in shouting the deaths of all on board and the capture of the *Sun!* Casteneda reacted smartly— as Saya-dar bit his tongue and concurred—and ordered Revaca to reinforce and win back the *Corsican Sun*—at all costs. They were in too deep to stop.

Later, Casteneda had confided that the situation—and the lack of complete information about it—compelled him to assume that Revaca's men saw some justification, whether they over-reacted or not, and that the combat was justified. (Privately, Casteneda suspected that these pirates took liberties, succumbing to the stronger temptation to take license now that they were far from Cuba.)

Revaca had returned in the Agusta to their staging cove on a nearby, equally obscure island, picked up the lounging ground troops, returned and landed them in two lifts near the two, now-disabled and beached yachts. He'd reported American voices radio-ing a distress call and then all reporting ominously stopped. No satellite phone calls or short-wave radio hailing raised Revaca's voice ever again. Saya-dar struggled to preserve his composure, as did Casteneda. Had they been caught? If so, by whom? What difference would it make?

Saya-dar assumed, until he had better evidence otherwise, that these *Arcturus* interlopers seized at least the one canister not yet anchored and still stored aboard the *Corsican Sun* when it met its fate—*Allah's* Urn of Judgment. They may have also found the canister Casteneda's men had already successfully anchored for staging before the attack, although, according to Revaca's report to Casteneda, his men had hit the unexpected yacht with a rocket. Perhaps, in the confusion, the thieves had overlooked the anchored canister.

Casteneda assured that his agents on Florida's Gold Coast needed productive work and could almost certainly learn the identity of *Arcturus's* owner, and the time of its return. U.S. Customs agents would record the Ship's Master's reporting in. They would begin with the day of the attack and search forward until the Cuban agents in the U.S. Customs office verified *Arcturus's* return. Casteneda would not rely on only one agent, but would verify the yacht's owner with a second.

The more Saya-dar considered the staggering reversal of fortune, the more he seethed. Saya-dar would visit Allah's vengeance on this thief and recover his treasure-weapon if possible. If possible, he would betray the bungling Cubans into the hands of the Americans to "take the fall" as a gangster might say.

However, that would all take time, and he had no idea how much time. He depended on the Cubans for canister recovery and had they not already partnered with Mosadomi to cheat him? He had acquired the precious poison, had lost it, might regain it, but probably not without *buying* it again, and this time, from within the United States where the Americans now possessed the one Urn. Such an errand hardly seemed possible! The Americans would probably, eventually now dangle this lost canister as bait before its former owner in a trap set to lure him into the United States for arrest.

He would, therefore, abandon any plan to recapture the lost Urn, and, instead, use their trap as a diversion. Yes, the seeming disaster of the lost canister and the American's expectation that he would follow after it would now serve Allah's hand in deception to mask…what? He entered a "?" at the bottom.

"Conclusions," he next began and keyed these points onto the "slide":

--Urn 1 lost

--Urn 2 beyond reach

At least for the practical future, he possessed no nuclear poison for the attack he had so carefully plotted and prepared. With one found by the enemy, and the other peeping up through the clear cove in a "hot" zone, his Plan A stood fatally compromised and, thus, terminated, he conceded.

"--Lost CJ = operation aborted," he finished, expecting to "brainstorm" the problem for awhile, but, really, finding that he had nowhere else to go with it.

The most secure, strategic date Saya-dar had selected for "opening the Urn" and dispersing its judgments approached soon, if the attack were to have been made this year. The mission might proceed but not this year; the American annual occurrence date he had so carefully selected added a unique element of security available only for a week, once a year. That date so perfectly matched the method he had chosen for the attack. Well, he might get his hands on the polonium and work out when to use it later or perhaps even to sell it or transfer it to another of the loose terrorist organizations if they presented a more concrete plan and the means to act on it. For now, forget it.

30

Planning on Babylon
Lurking off the Florida coast

Saya-dar "saved" his work, pushed away from his desk and strode to the bar, mixing himself a vodka sour. Stirring the concoction absently, he could not resist his mind's return to the picture of the Urn of Judgment that might even now await his hands as it rested in shallow water, only feet from the shore, hidden in a paradise-like cove, a scant 100 miles from the Great Satan. So, had the infidel interlopers also caused the *Jihad* to lose the second Urn of Judgment?

He could not *know* without someone returning to the tiny cove where Revaca's men were to have anchored the poison. Perhaps, even though no doubt visible through clear waters, the victorious thieves had missed it, assuming only one such beast. Perhaps Revaca had concealed it by surrounding rock and forced them from the search by his ill-fated excursion. Saya-dar wryly considered all of the action, far out of proportion to the tiny island's importance, and reluctantly affirmed the second canister as also "lost for now" as a practical, security matter, if not lost in fact. What else emerged from the debacle that he could count as positive?

Next, he reckoned that he had successfully recruited a highly positioned Cuban officer, a man poised close to the United States, able to penetrate its borders at will. Along with him, Saya-dar acquired access to Casteneda's network of non-Middle Eastern agents. He weighed Casteneda. Casteneda was pliable, if not reliable. So long as their interests coincided, he could count on the man. Otherwise, he would have to order the Cuban killed. If he needed to subcontract out a non-sensitive portion of whatever other mission he might incite, then he had ready labor. Better yet, he might employ them to *mischief* rather than to mission, to deception rather than to death-dealing. "C-Net" he added to the plus column, for "Cuban agent network" and sat back, taking a sip. His thoughts returned to his original masterpiece plan, unable to surrender its elegance to the trash bin.

Saya-dar had originally dismissed the Meigs Field takeoff-attack almost as soon as the absurd idea surfaced: a gamer's fantasy, spawned of too much Red Bull and too many late nights at the computer, no doubt. There could be only one such breach of their defenses; afterward, the bloodied enemy would rouse, mount the walls, search out her traitors, and lash out at any who even looked like threats. *So much for the Taliban and Saddam—"Gone with the wind," as the Americans say.*

Saya-dar had lurked in the Mediterranean letting 9-11 die down. He watched in disbelief as the Americans seemed to just stop worrying about terrorism and then return to fussing about European-style matters. Jobs! They are worried about jobs? He read about states and regions with 97% employment; they were turning a blind-eye to half of Mexico showing up for work in the U.S. each morning and they were worried that they couldn't find work?

Let them stew in their distraction broth! In 2003, he had returned to the Meigs Takeoff plan and downgraded it from "absurd" and "preposterous" to "audacious." Maybe—just maybe. Then, Mayor Daley had made his midnight raid in March, 2003, bulldozing the Meigs runways. Saya-dar had assumed a traitor in his own midst had handed the Americans his kernel of an idea, and he had begun listing names of men he targeted to purge. He had almost dispatched his assassins to cleanse the *Jihad* from suspected turncoats who must have tipped off the Americans about his plan, when his assistant brought him the Chicago papers he'd requested. The take on the entire matter, according to the reporters, was that Daley had wanted to close the airport for years anyway, seizing on the 9-11 attack to justify his illegal power-play to destroy the air-field and convert it to the park he wanted. Saya-dar took more time, investigated his suspects, and determined that no traitor had leaked the plan, after all. The valuable, downtown, lakeside real estate had just lost its value as an irrelevant airstrip.

Commentators had speculated over whether Flight Simulator's default takeoff-from-Meigs Field scenario had inspired and trained the terrorists. It had not, he knew; blowing up the basement of the World Trade Center tower failed, so Atta looked at a top-down attack. Standing on the Jersey side one day, looking across the Hudson at the towers, an airliner passed high above, its silver-glimmer literally flashing the plan their direction. From there, they quite capably concocted their own hijacking conspiracy, but the connection between 9-11 and the widely popular everyman's flight simulation program made sense.

The terrorist mastermind knew how the 9-11 plan hatched, having arranged the financing behind it. The World Trade Center in New York City was so logical, the target so suggestive. They overcame the obstacle of smuggling in so large a weapon simply by seizing what essentially became an improvised guided missile already in everyday use in the United States. That was why they had selected multiple, high-profile targets; they had one shot, but what a shot!

The hijackers knew they could rely on the U.S. Government to disarm everyone on the plane except perhaps for a few dangerous men pocketing formerly legal-length knives with blades under four inches. The Americans co-operated with the hijackers, assuring the team that crew and passengers would lack firearms, leaving the whole plane vulnerable to the hijackers' takeover with the humble box-cutters! The hijackers slyly seasoned the seizure with the hopeful and deceitful suggestion that this hijacking would terminate in the routine of demand, statement, posture, negotiate, release, such that no passenger would conceive that he would need to attempt heroics. That plan had suggested itself as the "work-around" to the inherent obstacles, and succeeded wildly.

Still, hijacking an airliner and converting it into a guided missile worked reliably only once. After that, its element of surprise blew up along with the jetliners. The U.S. Government disarmed passengers even more now than before, but the "expect-to-live" deception that elicited the necessary, sheep-like response died with the hapless passengers and crews that day. United 93 showed that ordinary people would fight back, once cornered by the dawning truth that they had no other way out.

Saya-dar watched America forget about 9-11. The "Global War on Terror" lost traction faster than a disgraced *American Idol* candidate. The roused sheep sent their own guardian-wolves far away to do their killing and went back to sleep in the pen. Their politicians positively wanted to "protect America." It's just that, to many, "protecting America" didn't seem to mean actually *doing anything*. Saya-dar watched the divide grow between their valiant troops and their dithering population. This crack raised new possibilities as America—once again—viewed the *Jihad* as something happening "over there" that they could end merely by coming home.

So, Saya-dar re-visited the now merely "audacious" Meigs Field takeoff plan. He substituted a blank in place of the mayor's new park, a quiet, rural airfield within striking distance of Chicago. While he savored the Meigs plan's sheer drama, it was a bit theatric. He really didn't need to take off from a field right downtown. Meigs maintained a single runway still, but without its covering busyness, using Meigs posed too great a risk.

What about Midway or O'Hare? Certainly, the theatrical showmanship didn't outweigh the extra security he knew Chicago's remaining airports maintained. Apart from the delicious twist on the flight simulator game, what did those airfields offer that other plans lacked?

He listed the Chicago aerial attack's benefits. A densely packed population lived and worked immediately adjacent to the air strip. Chicago's multiple, bustling transportation routes offered infiltration and exfiltration opportunity if needed. The city contained important subset targets, such as its commodities trading centers and the Great Lakes Naval Training Station, as well as the Argonne National Laboratory.

Saya-dar frowned: all of these offered important targets, to be sure, but, paradoxically "off-target" somehow. He couldn't quite grasp why it was wrong. Saya-dar targeted the American *people* this time, not highly symbolic icons of business and military complexes. Terrorists—*terrified*. They terrified *people*.

The Americans, oddly and disappointingly, had hardly cowered after the devastating-beyond-all-expectation 9-11 victory. Indeed, he considered—wryly noting the "run-out-of-town" status of the former Taliban, and the hung-and-buried Saddam—one could credibly advance the argument that 9-11 had grossly backfired to a degree more than commensurate with the thunderous success of its initial impacts. Yes, the 9-11 shot was still being heard around the world, but with disquieting anti-echoes drowning out the inciting event's drama. One would think the Americans would remain paralyzed or furious, one or the other. Instead, they had returned to their own political infighting as their chief preoccupation, while toppling two enemy governments, 4,000 miles away. Only their own disunity restored hope to the stunned, demoralized Faithful. Astounding!

No, he must strike deeper. He must drive a stake into the *heart* of America.

31 *Planning on Babylon*

Where *beat* the heart of America? Saya-dar pondered the troubling but crucial question as he reclined and propped his feet onto the leather-cushioned ottoman from the 15th century. He absently swizzled his neglected and now diluted vodka sour. The Saya-dar—The Shade—first used the remote to switch on Beethoven's *9th Symphony* to help him work through this profound question, but glanced at the time and also turned the television news on, choosing Matt Christopher's "Big Leagues" political commentary and talk show.

Christopher and his guest immediately seized his attention. Instead of the usual partisan diatribe against Bush, Matt was interviewing an ex-CIA case officer so familiar with the Middle East and so critical of his own country's decades-long intelligence malaise. Saya-dar knew this officer. He had *met* this officer.

They were discussing a recent proclamation from Osama bin Laden! Saya-dar involuntarily stirred from his resting posture, propped hands on knees and stared at the screen. Turn the volume up! *Where is the remote?* He paused Beethoven.

Saya-dar sat spellbound as he saw and heard Osama bin Laden on tape, urging the Faithful to action and promising attacks *in* America, scoffing at the notion that he and al Qaeda froze in inaction due to American security measures. The Persian smiled at bin

Laden's veiled suggestion of a truce—immediately recognizing the feint that seemed to succeed time and again against the deluded West. Bin Laden warned the West of new attacks and promised death *within* America, disclaiming the group's purported inability to hit America again.

Christopher: "What message is he trying to give America? That the war in Iraq leaves America more in danger than it was before?"

Interviewee: "No, he's not saying it so that *you* would understand, but this is a message directed to the *Faithful*, to his followers."

Christopher: "What makes you say that?"

Interviewee: "History. Experience. That's how he has directed the worldwide Islamic conquest in the past. He knows his videotapes will not sway the current administration's strategy, so, while he purports to address America and the United Kingdom, he really is using this tape as his "bully pulpit" if you will; this is his only way of going straight to his people. Our own newspapers tipped him off about his cell-phone calls being traced, so he dares not e-mail or even make a single cell-phone call, knowing that we would kill him before he could say "good-bye." Instead, he speaks directly to the masses.

"This is crucial, Matt: hear me on this.

"He is not *warning* about attacks inside the United States. He is *ordering* attacks within the United States. He has not planned them; rather, he is *calling* for them and he is appealing to his followers to get up, get over to the U.S. and *do it.* 'Kill Americans, wherever you find them,' he is saying—but especially at home. Notice: he extends this command to hit our British allies, and any other nations who dare to defy his Islamic onslaught. Expect to get hit *here.*"

Christopher: "You mean like subways? There are not really all that many of those places in America. New York's been hit already. Chicago has "The L." More cities have commuter rail. Is that where you think he is talking about hitting?"

Interviewee: "Maybe, but not necessarily. Just listen to him: by his own words, he means to hit *inside* America. He's already hit Washington and New York City. Look for him to hit the heartland."

Christopher: "What about the suggestion of a truce?"

Interviewee: "You *can't* be serious."

The interview ended abruptly there; the newscast went to commercial. Saya-dar arose, re-started the *9th,* paced, faced the East, and drank in the words of his leader, and the American CIA officer's analysis. *That* man, he respected. The case officer had spent 20 years collecting intelligence on terrorism and trying to track down

the Beirut embassy bombers. He understood bin Laden to be calling his followers to strike America, and within the country too. The
man's instincts drove to the point; Saya-dar also understood his
leader's call to arms against America, and this time, not on its
periphery.

Atta and others fixated on New York City and Washington,
D.C., collectively, as its heart, its nerve centers really. The target
seemed like top choice at the time, and they believed that they had
driven a stake into America's heart, but 9-11 and the aftermath
upset that notion. The entire country had rallied to New York City
in a surprising way and, most disturbingly, New Yorkers resumed
life and went on. Quickly, too. The impertinent Republicans challenged the *Jihad*, holding their Republican Convention in New
York City only three years after the attack. Hardly shunning the
city in fear, the Americans flocked to New York as if the attack had
not flattened part of lower Manhattan.

"Ground Zero," as they called it, is only a short bus ride from
Madison Square Garden where President Bush only three years
later rallied, cheered and pressed on to victory again. Indeed, the
Great Satan hardly seemed to be in retreat, he sardonically
judged.

Saya-dar had monitored the American election obsessively and
its outcome fascinated him. He had hooted hearing each insult
hurled at Bush and he had reveled in the anti-Bush propaganda that
tricked the wealthy Persian into predicting mass revolt. He dismissed the reports of some of his agents who claimed to be close
to American acquaintances, who warned that election clamor was
internal sport, not pre-revolution workup frenzy. The Bush states
on his colored map taunted him. Regardless of the opposition,
apparently a large percentage in 2004 still supported war in Iraq,
or at least war *somewhere* against the Islamic world. In 2004, any-

way, millions of Americans were willing to face the armies of Allah's jihad.

Saya-dar sat back down in his cushioned leather recliner, looked at his now thoroughly-diluted drink and pushed it aside on the glass table. He kicked back and looked at the ceiling, closing his eyes to think. An image appeared in his mind. He once again leaned forward, took the notebook computer, and opened his web browser, clicking to open one of his "Favorites" that he had bookmarked.

The Iranian master terrorist, follower of bin Laden, and sometimes financier for al Qaeda clicked on the link to the *U.SA Today* image he had saved. Saya-dar puzzled once again over the maps splitting the nation into roughly two camps: blue and red. The colored blotches seemed to suggest "massively urban" and "other" with a few exceptions. What did they mean? What pattern emerged? America, he observed, despite huge cities, remained, in many respects, a rural nation, or at least a small town, small city, *dispersed* nation. Yes, compared to South America, or the Middle East, its people were more dispersed. Perhaps its heart did not beat from its capital, or from New York City. Perhaps, its heart beat out there, somewhere in the red-colored counties. His leader called for him to strike *there.*

But, therein lay the problem: where was there? What a paradox! A few backpack bombs in their beloved Madrid, and the once great bastion against the Moors shivered and ran. What would it require to force America to bow on its knees?

Saya-dar minimized all open folders and files and stared at the digital picture he had designated as his "wallpaper." He had traveled to a place he viewed as the entry-point to the Christian West.

It was an impertinent place, a place jutting out across the Mediterranean glaring at North Africa's shoreline as if to keep the

Muslim armies in their place. Below the stony platform where he stood as a young man with his camera, other westerners—mostly British—vacationed along Spain's "white coast," the *Costa Blanca*. The rail line zipped back and forth. Boats came and went. A gigantic hotel hosted their holidays. From where he had stood, you could see the tourist panorama below while Spain (symbolic of The West in Saya-dar's mind) frivolously ran back and forth, disdaining the Moors as ancient history.

A picture he had taken from the top of the fortress of Santa Barbara constantly reminded him of his purpose, his mission, his own role in the *Jihad*. The fortress of Santa Barbara perched like a hawk atop Alicante', on Spain's southern, white-sand coast. There, years ago, he had dedicated himself to Allah's conquest. The grand old stone fortress appeared to grow from the mountain rock. Its walls soared. Iron cannon testified that Santa Barbara stood guard over Spain throughout centuries. The anomalous array of communications antenna bristling atop the ancient bastion proclaimed Santa Barbara's modern role as coastal defender and stalwart watchman. The Spanish flag flapping in reminiscence of leather-tough empire stood alongside the radio-communications masts, juxtaposed upon the imposing walls and austere guard towers, jutting defiantly into the air. Saya-dar marveled at this Spanish challenge, thrown out across the blue water toward the North African coast.

Ha! His modern "Moorish" invader-terrorists had simply walked around all such fortress sentries so easily—indeed, were invited in!—and sauntered boldly into the very soul of Spain—into its Madrid, unnoticed. Their attack on Madrid's Atocha Station was all that *Jihad* had required to bend the Spanish will into dull submission: a few backpack bombs and the Spaniards were sent packing—with the exception of that obstinate judge and their dangerous, trained, counter-terrorism units. They would not stop the hunt! The masses might blanch, but the Spaniards still fielded warriors.

Like all nations, though, while masses buffeted by the headlines might cower and snap back in fear only at each other, a hardened remnant could be counted on to rally to the country's defense and fight back. All nations needed such men and all nations *had* such men, just some in greater quantity and quality than others.

Well, so long as the West struck *back* they left the *Jihad* to plan *ahead* for the next evolution in tactics. Saya-dar burned to test America's mettle, like Spain's had been tested. The Spanish turned against Aznar, with only days to go before the election, and elected an appeaser instead. They said it had been his quick accusations— later proved hollow—against the Basques. No one wanted to admit that the Spanish people had simply lost the stomach for the fight. Years of anti-American, European press propaganda preparation helped set the people up for their quick reversal. Within only days of his election, the new President of Spain ordered the Spanish troops fighting with the Americans retrieved home. Spain rejoiced. So did the Faithful, all over the world. Victory! A few daypack bombs! Saya-dar considered how much was achieved with so little!

"Terrorism." It worked.

Saya-dar never stopped evaluating. He never permitted himself the indulgence of thinking he had archived the pinnacle. He used pride as the trigger to return to critical thought. This celebration reverie over victory over the ancient enemy, Spain, led him to question the fundamental strategy behind the nuclear poison dispersion attack that he had originally intended. He did not question the tactics, although the attack seemed somewhat banal, given the fact that a similar attack had already "played the Broadway stage."

While adding the atom to the plot certainly heightened the jihad's tension, the disaster Americans seemed so worried about was—if such an attack can truly be anticipated—*expected*. They produced TV shows featuring a nuclear bomb exploding in their country. The British had even made a movie about the so-called "dirty bomb," and had unimaginatively named the movie, literally "Dirty Bomb!" The British were so practical.

The movie played like a training film and had frightened the Persian and his staff with its accurate detail about how Muslim terrorists organized and planned operations, but the West's masses hardly stirred from their sleep; they did not even seem to notice the blatant warning. The Persian supposed that, lacking some popular, Hollywood-approved American actor, the movie simply fizzled. He'd watched it, but had to search around and order it on DVD. The West never heard its accurate lecture on Saya-dar's organization structure.

The dirty-bomb plan's horror and audacity attracted him, along with his expectation of achieving surprise in the face of—no, because of—the publicity surrounding the flight simulator program and its famous default airfield. Almost seven years lapsed between 9-11 and today, and no one could maintain constant vigilance.

Saya-dar thrived on achieving surprise. He had specifically chosen the opening day of the Experimental Aircraft Association annual rally for the attack. A sleeper agent living in the area had described the event, attending hoping to photograph an F-117A stealth fighter on display there. (In truth, the agent, an Iraqi, ex-jet fighter pilot, just wanted to see the show, vacation later in Chicago, and enjoy the presence of thousands of other airmen, even if foreigners.) A keen U.S. Air Force guard armed with an M-4 carbine and a Beretta M-9 as backup permitted no one to approach past the guard rope, and seriously looked as if he would shoot any close-up photographer, but the agent had justified his pleasure jaunt by returning with a descriptive, if little-read, account of the event, including the event's effect on the locale for 100 miles around. The jet was sexy, but the event's far-flung effect on the area caught Saya-dar's interest.

The Experimental Aircraft Association annual air-show is a big, rousing event, in scope far beyond the limits implied by its name. Thousands of aircraft of every possible description and size converge each August at the airport outside of Oshkosh, Wisconsin, about 40 miles west of Lake Michigan and about 100 miles north of Chicago. The EAA holds its giant rally more as a celebration of flying, flyers, and all things aviation than as display of esoteric "experimental" aircraft. Airmen and women swarm the overtaxed airfields of northern Illinois and central Wisconsin farmlands for that entire week. Motels raise rates and fill. Men grounded by their wives make the road trip in party-vans. Motor-home cities coalesce to emanate grilled bratwurst aroma, only to dissipate and disappear overnight at the show's end. A few accidental deaths spice the news reports, adding tragedy to bravado and festival. In other words, the EAA annually hosts a Mecca-like pilot pilgrimage that fills up air-fields for a hundred miles around.

Saya-dar's originally chosen Meigs Field, too, would have been festive as well, with flyers from all over the world landing, avoiding busier O'Hare, seeing the sights in downtown Chicago, and swapping lies. Intelligence bought from Cuba included just such a report during the last rally. Tactically, because the EAA Air Show gave cover, the plan was sound. Stuck on the Lake Michigan side of downtown Chicago with its runways oriented north and south, Meigs Field sent planes up and over the Shedd Aquarium, then past the John Hancock building and the Sears Tower looming just to the left. Meigs Field tantalized Saya-dar and the EAA airshow would hide the plan amid swarms of small planes.

Given the airport's computer-simulator-generated notoriety, Meigs Field had seemed like a most unlikely surprise air-attack launch field. What player had not taken off from Meigs, climbed steeply, banked left and watched the plane smear against the side of the Sears Tower? Before 9-11, crashing into the Sears Tower had seemed like great sport to thousands. Now, the macabre maneuver hauntingly reminded the player of 9-11. The suave Middle Eastern terrorist plotter reveled in the plan's "in your face" component. Just the smallest tweak, and, instead of a repeat of plane-into-building, Saya-dar's Urn of radioactive poison would kill and sicken. While no planes lifted off from Meigs anymore, the countryside offered any number of airstrips. Indeed, the sheer number of airfields frustrated America's efforts to watch them all.

Saya-dar had joked, and later, Casteneda had too, enjoying insulting America's stupidity. They had roared with laughter and had clinked their tumblers over flying the "Urn from Meigs" scenario. The Persian host projected Flight Simulator onto his big screen and they both practiced the takeoff, just for the fun of it.

Yet, now both Urns of Judgment were lost. Almost certainly, the Americans now knew that someone had tried to smuggle in nuclear poison. Perhaps not; the Americans did exhibit glaring gaps in accurate intelligence.

No, despite that glaring security compromise caused by the Cubans' fumbling the canister, what nagged at Saya-dar the most was the misgiving that his previously-planned Chicago strike somehow missed the heart. That was it.

Meigs-Chicago was like NYC II. Atta succeeded in NYC-WTC, but at what? Kicking the beast in its shin? Saya-dar wanted to kill America. He wanted to pierce the hearts of its peoples. He fantasized funerals on cold, rainy afternoons all over its so-called "fruited plains." Perhaps he should switch to "Plan B" as the Americans might say.

32

Sarab

Yes, one must understand the enemy to defeat him. That's how North Vietnam drove out America, Saya-dar knew from studying the campaigns over and over. The North lost its military operations, but won at a deeper level: the Communists defeated America's *will*. Saya-dar thought the entire world missed the greater message: that, despite enveloping South Vietnam into Communism's clutches, Communism stalled in Southeast Asia anyway and stayed, more or less, contained.

"Containment" may have held off the supposedly inevitable advance of Communism, but the West had yet to figure out how to "contain" the Caliphate's renewed raids. Operation Iraqi Freedom (OIF) and Operation Enduring Freedom (OEF) in Afghanistan showed what their military could accomplish when roused but their frayed wills at home held them back.

Saya-dar pictured the West's frayed will as a once-beautiful woman, now fallen on hard times, clothing tattered, hair disheveled, face showing strain, before him on her knees, begging to sell herself to him for the vain promise of peace. The woman was not there yet, though. Shattering her will required something different from shattering their capitol or their icons of greatness.

Saya-dar shuddered, needled for an instant that, just maybe, nothing would bring down enough Americans. Somehow, even absent the unity that they pretended to exhibit, while many of them failed to rise and fight, enough of them felt the anger burn, and rose, fighting and backing those who fought. This truth nagged Saya-dar: when you have almost 400 million people, a small percentage of hardened, courageous warriors, backed by solid support, may save the rest, even while the indulged sheep disdain and betray their guardians and saviors.

Indeed, was not their very *religion* based on impossible strength after crushing treachery? The Muslim pondered the One dying for the many—the undeserving, unloving, unmoved, except to spit on the One who came to rescue them. They celebrated a betrayed Christ *dead*, nailed to a Roman cross, yet returning from the grave to live again, and vanquish the ultimate enemy: death, itself.

Did some lesser echo of such impossible mercy and victory preserve them? Perhaps. Even in a declining country like America, there were noble men who acted from soul motivation far beyond the pusillanimous praise of the pathetic apathetic—and they acted with considerable violence, too. Plainly, if not God himself, warriors of her own ringed America. History proved that, re-affirmed by the US.-U.K. OEF and OIF.

So, of course! If their weakness is their *will*, he must strike at their *will*. He must strike at those dispersed, and as of yet, for the most part, personally unaffected Americans. He would go to their lairs where their families felt safe. It had already been done, but America had missed the clues that pointed to *Jihad* in Oklahoma City. He would go to their hometowns, to their center, and carry the fight to places they had not dreamed Islamic fighters would swoop down on them. Saya-dar savored the imagery of white-robed, turbaned desert warriors, scimitars raised, topping a dune as one, and then plummeting on their snorting horses, downward onto the stricken enemy. As at Atocha: raid! Sweep around the strong points and aim the sword-point straight at the lulled underbelly of America. At the same time, strike even more terror into the worm-hearts of those cowardly dead spirits already too afraid to take up the rifle.

This time, Americans in their "sea-to-shining-sea" hinterlands would not escape the Wrath of Allah's Faithful. The Urns' disappearance was Allah's blessing after all, had Saya-dar only seen it. Allah had revealed this truth, and the next battle plan, and had given him his deception plan to confuse the enemy. Saya-dar returned to planning.

He added "wrong target" to the negative column under Plan A and excitedly opened the file for "Summon the Faithful" operations planning. Bin Laden had called for attacks and now was the time. Saya-dar had not intended to Summon the Faithful, which required the one-time use of such intricate and carefully prepared resources, but bin Laden plainly sounded the war cry for action now. Summon the Faithful stood in place and ready, needing only *activation*. Coordinating Summon the Faithful at this point would require his personal leadership.

Saya-dar reached for the chilled Woodford Reserve and Coke, presented to him by his servant to replace the diluted vodka sour. Condensation dripped onto the glass-topped table to his right as the colorful slide outline for "Plan: Summon the Faithful" brightened his screen. He created a new slide titled "Deception: _____" and copied Plan A so that he could begin its conversion from attack plan to deception plan. He would convert the deception first.

Every good operation incorporated some form of deception plan, a feint. The Saya-dar always crafted a masking or mirage deception plan annexed to any operations plan he wrote: *maskirovka,* the Russians said. He could not overlook the practice of *maskirovka*. He always had made "Deception Plan" bold and red in his outlines because the attack action tended to absorb the intellect. Manipulating the enemy's behavior could even make an attack unnecessary! Deception permitted the attacker to launch other attacks with the forces freed up by the feint. Deception kept the enemy staggering like a drunk. The Soviets mastered it, and Saya-dar still expected the Soviet Communists to re-gather their military and secret police, once the West eroded sufficiently on its own, lulled into complacency by *maskirovka*.

The Saya-dar studied the ongoing war against the West, which had morphed over time but never ended, not since Mohammed's horsemen poured over into Europe's frontiers. To better know the enemy, he studied the West's wars. In Saya-dar's mind, the world was not much different now from its game board setup of 1,000 years ago, but in one respect.

Of all things, *logistics* had stopped the great Islamic conquests from sweeping away the infidels. Geography, distance, speed, all conspired against the Muslim conquerors to trap them in their desert lands, for the most part anyway. Both Europe, and the holy lands they condescendingly called the "Middle East," turned inward during the next 1,000 years and warred internally to consolidate land and power. The two clashing cultures fought to an uneasy standstill in the Balkans, mostly gave up the cause, did business, and eyed each other with suspicion. Given any chance, the Westerners would enslave the Islamic peoples, he knew it. He hated the West. Their filth would seduce and permeate The Faithful if permitted.

The Persian did, however, respect the West. He had studied Operation Overlord and the intricate tricks the British and Americans had played against the Germans to mask the D-Day invasion site and date. In particular, and brilliantly, Saya-dar conceded, the Allies gave the Germans what the Germans expected—preparations for invasion at the *Pas de Calais.* Amazing! Really only a short distance up the coast, Calais offered its shores to the Allies like a Western whore offering her services. Indeed, Calais—a scant 21 miles from England—must have caused the German generals to lose sleep. Defending it obsessed them.

In the same manner, the Americans were so engrossed in their fear of "WMD" that believably suggesting some form of nuclear attack would command their attention. With carefully placed suggestions with "WMD" flagged all over them, the Americans, like the Germans, would follow their predisposition. Saya-dar would arrange for a friendly Saudi Arabian news network to leak the WMD threat to certain correspondents. From print, the "WMD in America" stories would gather steam, ballooning into mass entertainment. Networks would splash cleverly designed logos in the background behind the talking heads. Producers would burn up the phone lines calling "experts" to line up interviews. Threat level colors would go up.

Earnest experts exacerbate expected eradication, played the Saya-dar in his mind, keyboarding in the phrase and laughing aloud. "E to the fifth!" Saya-dar laughed and proclaimed to his servant. His servant cast him a puzzled look, wishing the usually humorless master would share the joke. Once led on the atomic chase, the Americans might even return to a re-hash of the "Where are the WMD?" debate, losing sight of the real threat.

His original plan to open the Urns of Judgment upon the Americans and poison their Chicago from the sky now became his *maskirovka.* He would whip the Americans into a frightened frenzy. They would chase windmills, or wild geese, or—whatever the

American expression was for thirsting after mirages. *A mirage. Yes. That is it! The mere threat of my Urns creates a mirage. Sarab:* he entered the text reverently and stared at the word.

Sarab: a mirage. Saya-dar did a find-replace, trash-canning the humdrum code word "Plan A" for *"Sarab."* Americans would seize his deception and believe it because they were already disposed to believe it. The lost wanderer in the desert followed the *Sarab* impelled by desperation for the watery mirage to be *real.* The Americans, though, would follow *Sarab* from a similar, but perverse obsession: out of blind fear. "Always fighting the last war" he had read in one of their General's critiques. Something in their corrupted psyche crushed their hands aside their heads and twisted their eyes backward, always looking backward, with blinders on.

Perhaps Allah blinded them to the future, blinded them to the pattern of what the Faithful had *done* so that they could not know where the Faithful would *next* strike. Not knowing where or when radiation would sear their urban soul, they would whirl themselves into a desperate frenzy trying to uncover the plot. Instead, while they crawled into the *Sarab,* mockingly beckoning them deeper in, the Faithful would enter their homes and the slaughter would be great. *He* would set the deception plan—*Sarab*—into motion with a simple request of his Cuban ally: *Find my stolen Urn of Judgment.*

33

Summon the Faithful

Now, to "Summon the Faithful" itself. He viewed his outlined operations plan, written long ago. "Summon the Faithful," so simply captioned, exuded manifold elegance. While its cultivation required a lot of money, many men, and so—so much patience—he would trigger the attack inside America so easily.

Saya-dar sent out a few simple e-mail messages to initiate "Summon the Faithful," and then called Casteneda to inform him of the change in plans, and to trigger the deception plan—the *Sarab*. Casteneda would serve as the unwitting mirage-maker. "Others would infiltrate, he would tell his atheist, Cuban, whiskey-aficionado "friend" whom Saya-dar never trusted.

He speed-dialed Casteneda's number. Saya-dar did not care whether the NSA overheard the call. Indeed, he yearned for the Americans to hear and record every word, to replay it looping endlessly as they hunkered down to chase his mirage.

"Good day, Saya-dar," Casteneda answered after three rings.

"Good day to you, *Conquistador amigo*," Saya-dar crooned the flattery he knew the Cuban indulged in. "I must change our meeting plans and ask your generous forgiveness."

215

Casteneda tensed, but forced a calm reply: "I hope all is well with you and that we will still be able to get together."

"Certainly, I have just decided to proceed with establishing my business in the United States as previously planned and to have my representatives meet with you there. I would need you to extend to them the same efficient courtesy you have shown me. Could you do that?"

Casteneda's mind raced. *Still on!* He knew that the NSA would capture every word so that they could examine the exchange later. However, he must respond now! Then, the realization flashed that Saya-dar would already know the stunning effect this message would have on him, and that the Persian would not be surprised at a short delay, while Casteneda collected his wits.

"My, my friend! You are a bold businessman, indeed!" Casteneda stammered, biting his lip at his own clumsiness. "Where and when might I meet your representatives and, I assure you, I will extend them every courtesy as if you, yourself, were before me." He did not expect the wily Persian to blurt out these details, but why not ask?

"The same arrangements as before suffice. Please prepare for four of my colleagues though, instead of for me."

Saya-dar waited for the right moment to sink the hook, straining to hold back the words that would complete his *Sarab*. Every sense heightened; he smelt the sea breeze of salt and fish; the bright sunlight sharpened the edge and detail of every image before him; he perceived every feature of every gull, piling, yacht and cloud before him in panorama, as if Allah had reached down to sweep him into Heaven. He gloried in the victory just before him, and marveled at the calm he felt. *Speak, man! Are you twice the fool I think? Ask the question!*

Casteneda struggled to select just the right words: "Will you need me to arrange for you to purchase replacement—equipment—to replace that which was—found not to be available?"

There! Like the symphony crescendo in the background!

"Why, thank you, that is most kind, but not necessary. I have already made such arrangements. All you must do is greet my representatives, and arrange a location where they might stay and work a few days; outdoors is preferable. I have already provided for their transportation."

Saya-dar considered, and added: "Of course, if you are able to acquire *additional* replacement product where you are, I could, no doubt, employ it in my enterprise as well at some point and would, of course, compensate you for your diligence."

Who knows? Perhaps the Cuban *was* trustworthy and could retrieve the stolen Urn. Either way, he was certain his call to the Cuban had spun into motion the mists of the *Sarab*—and he would sift this Cuban's loyalties. If the Cuban had betrayed him, his four young martyrs might die, but so might these four Faithful add to the numbers of those who would answer the greater Summons.

Casteneda's voice called him back from his celebration.

"Very well, Saya-dar, will that be all?" said Casteneda.

"Yes, thank you, you know how to reach me if need be but, otherwise, please be sure to greet my staff. They will need your introduction," said the Iranian.

"Agreed." Casteneda stayed on the telephone.

"Then, good day, *mi amigo*," and Saya-dar closed his phone. He had recruited this tool wisely.

It was done. From chaos, he created beauty. Out of a grand plan, he orchestrated truly delicious, glorious revenge. It was incomparable! Besides, "Summon the Faithful" offered a feature that was irresistible: he would strike the Jews and these red-state, American, Jew-pawns at the same time—as if from a mist, as if from a *Shade!* Saya-dar had not only determined to summon The Faithful; he had also chosen their targets.

34

Tampa, Florida
Four weeks after the attack
on Arcturus

Jack ran three miles early, hit the weight room at the Comfort Inn, then checked and replenished his "deployment" daypack. He drove downtown, opened a checking account and rented a lockbox.

Inside the lockbox, Jack placed a single sheet of paper with handwritten instructions on it—a short "holographic" will. Next to his Last Will and Testament, Jack placed the letter he had written to his brother, explaining. Jack found little to be said. The letter directed Jack's brother to another bank, in their hometown, where the two jointly kept a box. In that box, Jack stored the few mementos of his father's life: his medals, newspaper clippings, and his Bible. Jack would want his brother to inherit these.

Jack stepped back and took stock: the documents looked to him like precious little tangible evidence of life, he appraised. Well, his life—at least now—charged forward in a different direction. He would leave scant evidence behind on purpose.

Finally, before sliding the box back into the wall and locking it up, Jack removed two maps from his cloth briefcase, looked at the details one more time—satisfied he'd depicted the site well—and slid the hand-drawn map, and the printed map underneath the other documents. Surprise!

Jack drove southward along Highway 92. He pulled off Bayshore Boulevard at the visitor's gate at MacDill Air Force Base and parked, obeying the guard's sharp hand-and-arm motions plainly directing him to pull over and explain his business. The guards watched him climb out of the truck and walk into the guard head-quarters booth there, just as Gordon had instructed. The gate guard booths were always hilarious to Jack. The military shed the "open post" idea in favor of stepping up security. Stern young faces peered at you. This was no "Welcome to MacDill AFB greeting." The guards barely restrained themselves from demanding: "Just what the Hell are you doing here?" Jack understood. They were right to mount a constant "stand to."

Jack produced his driver's license, and waited while the guard checked his clipboard and made a call. The guard handed Jack the phone. Gordon came on, verifying the sound of Jack's voice and told him to hand the phone back to the guard, a wary-looking E-6. The guard listened, closed the phone and retrieved a new ID card from a safe, handing the card over to Jack ceremoniously, adding, to Jack's surprise, "Welcome to MacDill Air Force Base, sir."

"Thanks Airman, and thanks for being on guard." Jack meant it. *Somebody* in this country needed to be on guard.

Now back in the truck, and at the gate checkpoint, Jack flashed his new ID card, grinned at the serious looking soldier at the gate who was not amused, and followed directions around North and South Boundary Boulevard, locating the building with the number Gordon had given him.

Jack idled in front of Building 31, surprised. Gordon had directed him past Central Command Headquarters to SOCOM-Central headquarters. He parked by the Special Operations Command-Central headquarters, only after once again passing through an artificially created, but substantial barricade, and having his ID card and face scrutinized.

Jack halted at the SOCCENT lobby, noted the M-4 armed pair of Air Force Security Force guards on each side of the lobby, and showed ID yet again, asking for the telephone extension Gordon had given him. The guard eyed him oddly, and, without taking his eyes from Jack, called an extension, waving him to sit down at the side. He smiled at the guards, who simply nodded, in the manner of serious guard-duty types the world over.

A door burst open behind Jack. General Ortega's Aide-de-Camp, a huge, linebacker-shaped Captain, greeted him with no warmth whatsoever and whisked him into an austere government-décor inner lobby, where Jack again plopped down on one of the vinyl-and-chrome chairs there and did what soldiers do best: Jack waited.

Twenty minutes later, Gordon barged through the same door and, with no more than a nod and a wink, strode past him and through a door marked most ambiguously "Army." Jack flipped on the TV bracketed to the wall. Good; at least SOCOM rated cable. Jack surfed until he found Fox News. Twenty more minutes lapsed.

Jack grew restless and recalled the kind of "hurry up and wait" life he thought he'd left behind. He was about to start roaming just to see what nervous troops he could stir up when the steel double-doors in the front opened and a camouflage-clad British major marched through. He halted squarely in front of Jack. The two eyed each other. The Major broke the silence.

"Who are you?"

"A civilian."

"Righto! Of course you are, lad! Me too!" the officer boomed, grinned, and stuck his hand out to Jack, gripping hard. Jack liked the energetic, older man immediately. The major plopped down in a matching chair to Jack's side.

"You probably can't say much or *think* you can't, anyway, so I will."

Major Hodges entertained Jack with non-stop, crude, Army-styled humor until the unmarked door through which Gordon had whisked earlier opened and the beefy Captain approached them.

"Sir, please come in," he deadpanned to Major Hodges. The Aide looked at Jack. "You too."

A real charmer.

Jack expected to enter an office like so many other Army offices—colorful plaques hung, tracking the officer's career, with Army-style knickknacks scattered around the generic gray or green steel furniture. These trappings honored past comrades and communicated context to visitors immediately. Jack had hung the humble start of his own wall in his sailboat, at least with those honors he could publicize: just the Ranger School Diploma framed with the "tab" pinned to his uniform, his "jump wings," the 101st "Screaming Eagle" plaque, and the handmade, wood-mounted, recruiting-brochure pictures his Battalion Commander had given him. There was a lot Jack couldn't publicize.

Instead, he was surprised to find comfortable "real" furniture and, on the walls in place of the flags, plaques, and portraits, he saw maps, pinned to corkboard, covering every wall. Behind the desk, hung a single framed document, printed in bold, large letters, a parody on John F. Kennedy's remonstrance to serve instead of being served:

> *Ask not if your country is safer;*
> *that question is unworthy of you.*
> *Ask if your enemy is safer.*
> *The answer had better be, 'NO, sir!'*

Jack knew he was in the right place. Now, there was something he'd never seen before in a non-combat zone: an M-4 carbine—with magazine inserted—hung muzzle-down from a peg by its single-point sling. Jack's eyes swept toward the man at the center of the room who plainly commanded this real estate. He saw a tall man, about 55, hair short—of course—with eyes of steel. A Beretta M-9 waited on his belt, but not in an issue holster.

Gordon greeted him from the standing group of men, and made the introduction: "Jack McDonald, meet General Paul Ortega, Special Operations Command—Central."

"Good morning, McDonald. Thanks for coming. (*Thanks?*) I've heard all about you," Ortega smiled, gripping Jack's hand. "You're the ex-Ranger crazy enough to get mixed up with my old friend, Gordon."

"Yes, sir. That would be me all right," Jack had to agree.

"You met Major Hodges already. He escaped the Norman invasion, deserted, and showed up here. We let him stay—temporarily only—for sheer entertainment value." The older men roared.

"Now, before you get the wrong impression, meet a real soldier, Jack. Here's Sergeant Burnell, the smartest man in this room. He keeps us "Army," Ortega proclaimed, introducing Jack to a sharp, slim, tall Sergeant First Class about Jack's own age. Burnell nodded.

Seeing the introductions were complete, Gordon interrupted. "Gentlemen, General Ortega has asked me to brief you. I'll state the situation, stop for discussion then, and after that I'll get with Jack on the operations plan. I want him here for the strategic brainstorm session so that he knows what's at stake. Besides, he may learn something he needs to know later.

"Stop," ordered Hodges. I do someday expect to return to the Cotswold Hills, nestled midlands in those sainted islands that birthed you rebels, and I don't think I want to know where this particular conspiracy is going. You Yanks keep me constantly debating over what I can hear and what I would *never* want to know. I appreciate the invitation, but I'm out of here on this one. Call me when this attempt at *brainstorming* is over." Major Hodges left his good-natured, mock sarcasm hanging and departed. He knew Ortega would brief him secretly, later. Gordon immediately got to business.

Jack respected Gordon's cogent outline of the situation and the opportunity handed them by the Cuban agent he learned about. The older men argued, the Sergeant displayed some dignified silence, adding some timely comments, and Jack thought through his own circumstances in light of what he was overhearing.

He considered the gravity of a terrorist smuggling in enough radioactive and chemical poison to kill off a medium city, together with the videotape warnings he'd heard played on Fox in the lobby just minutes before. He sized Gordon up as "good leadership." He'd sign onto the fight and work out the "admin" details later. Ortega's shift in the conversation drew him back in.

"Then, let's begin to hammer out a plan. Beginning with what we know, we captured a steel container of polonium 100 miles from Florida and the Muslim terrorist who owns it is on the move to get it back. We don't know his end game. We know that he's backed financially or independently wealthy, and that this "Saya-dar" owned an Agusta. Somebody look that up."

"Look what up, sir? Agusta?" Sergeant Burnell asked.

" 'Saya-dar'," Ortega clarified, "not 'Agusta.' Hell, I know what one of those is. You geniuses are so literal! Goes with the intellect, I guess. Look that up for me. 'Saya-dar'," the General repeated. "Who knows? It may mean something." Ortega nodded to the earnest Sergeant, expecting him to do the research and return with the answer. The Sergeant stood.

"Sir," Sergeant Burnell said.

"What, Sarge?"

"I don't need to look it up."

"What do you mean? Who knows? It might be some key, have some hidden meaning. Besides, don't orders mean anything in this Army any more? I get no respect."

"Quite right, sir—not about anyone's failure to render the proper respect—but it does mean something and it does have a hidden meaning. I speak Farsi—Persian it's sometimes called —fluently."

This particular Sergeant, in the Army for 12 years, had his leg blown off in the Middle East, accounting in part for his assignment to a position assisting a General officer at the SOCOM headquarters, along with his undoubted courage and his fluency in Persian. He was proud of both his record and his language skill, and he saw that his commander needed what he possessed. He let the moment hang just to provoke the older man a bit.

"Well, all right, I can see that you are dying to tell me. Spit it out, please."

"Persian is an old and subtle language."

"Hey, Professor Burnell, can you get to the point and spare us the academic discussion," General Ortega interrupted, provoking back.

"*Sir!* I'm telling you *important* background. This name, *Sayadar* has multiple meanings, and all of them may give you a clue about the demon you're up against, for that's what he is," the Sergeant said, pausing again for drama.

"We're up against Hell itself?"

"Sort of, sir." The Sergeant warmed to his role as educator. "The word refers to *shade*, like the shade created by the spreading, leafy branches of a large tree by a stream. When spoken as *Saya-dar*, it may be a name, even a title; it means "protector" like the shade protects people cooled by it. However, there's a dark side."

"That figures. Very poetic, please continue," General Ortega said, appreciating the man's knowledge and indulging his obvious delight in supplying this information. Ortega knew this man's background and knew that, whatever knowledge he had, he had earned it.

"A shade may also be a ghost, a spirit and, in Persian tradition, the name 'Saya-dar' may also mean a demon or one who is demon-possessed. There's more. A slight variation of the word meaning includes something like 'Protector of The Faithful,' which may be extended to mean that he sees himself as a protector of Islam and Islamic people against false religions. Then, twist that into the word 'Saya-shikan,' and the meaning refers to 'breaking a shade' which, in Persian tradition, means 'Destroyer of False Religions.' While the name's literal meaning doesn't quite include all of these various 'shades' of meaning, I can see this Saya-dar adopting these titles. I can see him assuming his roles as 'Protector of the Faithful' and 'Destroyer of False Religions.' In other words, sir, Farsi scholars may argue with me, but—in these crazy times—extending 'Saya-dar' to interpret the name as a warrior-title like I've talked about is not far-fetched. I think that is exactly who this Shade is. At least that's who he fancies himself to be: the 'Destroyer of False Religions'—that would be you, sir."

"Me? Why me and not you, Sarge?"

"Me too, sir. All of us. America. Europe. The West. Not just the Christian West, but the agnostics and atheists, too. That's how this Saya-dar and the Jihadists see us."

"Hmm. Let me ask you this one, Sergeant Burnell—Oh

Great Ghost Buster in Green—who is this guy? I mean, where does he fit on the Totem Pole? Is this 'shady character' in middle management? What does it mean that this Shade is hovering around? Anything?"

Burnell looked his commander in the eye, and thought about this.

Burnell thought about a lot. He thought about things at night that kept him awake.

Ortega could not see it, but Burnell's own nightmare flashed through his mind's eye. He'd infiltrated Iran to meet with an Iranian family from Tabriz. Burnell shuddered. He'd met his friend, his friend's wife, and their two youngsters when the kids were still very young—in America, where they came to study, while Burnell was an ROTC instructor. He'd seen them off from the airport when they had to go back.

Later, back on shooting duty, he'd obeyed his orders and made contact with them. He'd infiltrated deep into Iran, working his way south through the old Soviet Union, to the mountainous northern region of Iran, far from Teheran. That distance did not keep any of them safe. Someone had betrayed them. He'd cost them their lives. His too, almost.

He knew that many Iranians still loved America, despite the orchestrated newscasts. He knew so many Iranians who yearned to be free—but who were still good Muslims. Muslims, but not hating Muslims. People who felt sorry for America, but did not hate America. So many of them. Why couldn't they be free, too? That's what his friends had wanted and that's what he had wanted to help them achieve. Instead, he brought Death to their house. All of them. All of them. Their ghosts….

"Sergeant Burnell?" General Ortega whispered.

Burnell returned—for now.

"Sir, this man is probably very high up in whatever movement he's part of. He may be the chief of it or he may be a senior commander, like a Vice President, but if this man is hovering around our shores, something big is up."

Jack smiled as Ortega strode up, slapped the Sergeant on the back, and thanked him for the discourse. He watched as the two men chatted briefly and Sergeant Burnell left, apparently dispatched to follow up on the revelation he had just pronounced.

Gordon asked, "How did that man know all of that?"

Ortega looked down in distant thought. He looked up, swept his eyes at them all, and simply said: "That man spent years living in Iran and on its borders. He lived with one of our agents when inside Iran, a brave man, educated in America, and a man with a wife and children. He spent a lot of time with them and knew the children well. He probably heard their dad telling them Iranian traditions, or fairy tales, and that must have been one of them, like "The goblins will get you if you don't watch out!" or something like that.

"Someone saw him coming and going and, while meeting with them one night, all were blown up. Only this Sergeant survived. He played dead in the rubble, among the bodies of his friends, and crawled out at night. Another Iranian risked his life to get the good Sergeant over the border. That's why he limps and that's why he's here. I'm told he sees shades of his own when he tries to sleep."

A knock sounded. The door pushed opened before the General could respond.

"Enter," General Ortega jibed, feigning irascibility, "since you already have."

228

General Ortega's intelligence officer appeared. Casteneda followed him in worriedly. Obviously, something was up.

"Sir, the Iranian called Saya-dar has changed everything. Whatever schemes you two have been cooking up, scrap them. Colonel Casteneda was about to make his call to coordinate infiltrating the Iranian when Saya-dar called the Colonel. Colonel Casteneda does not know why, but he is now to forget about infiltrating Saya-dar. He is instead to meet an infiltrating team of four men in place of the Iranian, and pick out a staging area for them. Here's the real eye-opener. As a secondary mission, he's to attempt to identify who in America might be offering the canister of polonium for sale. Those are his only requests at this point; just get the men in and ask around about where the canister the Cubans sold to this Saya-dar got to, now presumed lost in the Perdido Cay attack."

The men looked at each other, trying to absorb the shift in meaning. The Islamic pirate, this Saya-dar, knew that the canister Gordon found when he searched aboard the *Corsican Sun* was gone, but apparently was not willing to give up an attack, or—worse—possessed other means to press ahead!

Ortega began, "Well, this changes things. We've gone from running an agent and interdicting a single terrorist chieftain to a team landing on our shores. This is as serious a challenge as we have ever faced since the damned British sailed up the Chesapeake and torched the White House."

Major Hodges, who had joined Jack in front of the television a few minutes before The Linebacker summoned them, returned with a steaming mug of coffee in his hand just in time to hear Ortega's comparison, and raised his eyebrows.

"No offense, Hodges. You Redcoats surprised us on that one, though."

Hodges took in the group but did not respond to the joke, and said, "Well, my boys, I'm sure you're up to no good. You're not alone. Have you seen the news? Someone else is plotting surprises." Hodges could tell from their blank looks that they had missed the newscast.

"Best to fire up the telly, my American bully boys. There's a show on about you!" Hodges kept up the British cheek that he supposed the Americans expected of him, but he felt anything but at ease. "Some guy living in a hole in the mountains has a few words for you here in the Colonies. He has a new tape out threatening—well you just need to hear it."

When the men finished watching, Gordon tied the loose ends together: "Well, bin Laden warns "Operations are under preparation, and you will see them *on your own ground*," and we learn of a team coming in. This may signal some major operation here is in the offing. We already know this Saya-dar had his hands on polonium within spitting distance of our own coast; we have no idea what is next, other than he has cancelled his own infiltration and put into motion a team of four of his soldiers to infiltrate into our country. Jack?"

"Gordon, someone has to stop that team—and kill them," Jack said.

"Correct. Might we interrogate them first?"

"Whatever," Jack conceded.

General Ortega interrupted, "Gentlemen, I appreciate your vicious enthusiasm, but I'm going to have to coordinate with Homeland Security and the FBI's Counter-terrorism Center on this one. We've gone from running an agent to identifying a specific, terrorist, infiltration team." He paused, reluctant to relinquish control. "I can't monopolize this one. The Army can't run this op by itself. Stand down. I'll call you later, Gordon."

Thus, the Saya-dar turned their attention to his decoy team of four Faithful, his *Sarab*.

35

Tampa, Florida
Outside SOCCENT Headquarters,
MacDill Air Force Base
Late July

Boat noise from the Bay off Catfish Point a mile away hinted at people going places with purpose. The sounds depressed Jack as Gordon and he shuffled down the SOCCENT HQ steps toward the parking lot. So much had happened—was happening. No sooner was he back in than he was sidelined. The shifting plans and orders reminded Jack of the military, whimsically blown back and forth by whole hosts of variables: Congress, political-correctness pressures, a single Spec-4 taking obscene snapshots of a prisoner, not to mention the leadership personalities and prejudices up and down the entire chain of command from the Corporal fire team leader to the Commander-in-Chief.

For the action-man—the soldier with the M-4 in his hands—it was like standing on a tiny island in a bubbling cauldron of ever-changing forces. It was like the Heisenberg Uncertainty Principle applied to combat operations: no sooner did you receive your mission and start your Operations Order, than it changed: the mere act of *looking* at the situation seemed to alter it. You just thought you knew what the Army wanted you to do. *The Objective*: the first principle of war. Define it, identify it, refine it to its essential elements: know exactly what your superiors required of you. Right.

"Jack?"

Gordon's voice brought Jack back. They stood on the sidewalk.

A<small>RCTURUS</small>

The American flag flapped high atop its pole in the round garden decorating the grounds in front of the building. "Retreat" sounded. Both men stopped, turned to the flag, and stood to attention, honoring the long tradition as the color-guard lowered Old Glory for the day.

"Jack?" Gordon asked, again, as the last bugle note faded and the stopped traffic resumed.

"Yes, what?"

"These things happen."

"I know."

"We're sidelined right now while they all take stock of the threats. We'll be back in the action, I have no doubt," Gordon assured.

"No doubt?" Jack looked at him.

"No doubt, this unexpected interruption affords you and me the chance to further define our own arrangements—and to prepare. I have an idea," Gordon said.

Gordon was right. They'd barely struck a deal for Jack to do— God knows what. As a former combat leader, Jack knew that variables flurried about every operation, whether a basic patrol or a strategic invasion. Good commanders watched for every piece of new intelligence, for every change, every shift in the sound of firing, every nuance of battlefield noise, and adapted accordingly. Jack—at this point—was a tactical weapon. Command would have to wait to see if it should deploy him. That's all there was to it.

"What's your idea, Gordon? I might just be available," Jack replied.

"What else do you have going on? Oh, that's right! You'll be starting up classes soon, I suppose!" Gordon teased, knowing full well Jack would not be starting his Master's degree at UT in the fall.

Jack smiled. He really had no choice except—once again—to wait. "What's your plan?"

"You might be surprised, but I actually have a home. I occupy a hilltop on some forested acreage—all hills, valleys, and woods—with a clearing for the house and a narrow valley below just right to accommodate a 300-yard range. You come up and stay with me for a few days and we'll talk about your future. Bring your weapons too and we'll do some shooting."

Then, Gordon sank the hook. "I need you to give my niece a ride up too, if you don't mind. She has to be there to do a complete de-briefing on the Perdido Cay operation," Gordon lied.

He's lying. He's not calling up the other Alamo survivors. His maneuvers always seem to work though. "Well, I'm unemployed and skipping school. I'll join you. We do need to talk more about this whole matter of being on your payroll," Jack agreed.

"Good, it's settled then. You'll enjoy the break, Jack. My lodge sits between the Tennessee River and the Appalachians on a 1,000-foot-high ridge. I've lots of privacy, although the city is growing out toward me and I'll be overtaken someday."

"Where is it?"

"Even a wretched Ranger can find the way. Simple. Follow the yellow brick road. Start "there." Gordon pointed back the way Jack had entered MacDill and laughed. "Seriously, drive straight north out of MacDill on the Dale Mabry Highway. Hit Interstate 275 and head east. You'll intersect with I-75 as you get downtown. Get on it and stay on it—just get going north from Tampa and keep going. The same highway gets you to Knoxville. Weird, isn't it? Get off downtown, go through the tunnel there, pass the Sunsphere on your right—you can't miss it—looks like a big golden golf ball on a 100'-high tee. Check your e-mail; I'll send you the detailed directions. I'm about an hour west of Gatlinburg, just a few miles outside of Knoxville, on the French Broad River. You'll like it, and Jack?"

"Yeah," Jack replied, but thinking of spending more time in Donna's company.

"I do not think we are out of the action. I suspect we will hear more from General Ortega about this Saya-dar. Come prepared to deploy without returning to either Tampa or to your boat in Miami, OK?"

"Do you already know something that causes you to tell me that?"

"No, these situations change fast; that's what I know. Expect the unexpected."

36

The Saya-dar hated the man who stole the Urn of Judgment. He lounged on the deck of *Babylon,* now weaving in and out of the eastern Bahamas Cays, working his way northward, drawn to the Urn, but avoiding the more traveled Caribbean side. He could not tolerate the impudence.

Arcturus. He looked it up. *Oh. They named the boat after the star.*

Saya-dar leaned back and sipped, pondering the name—the *sign,* for that is how he viewed the yacht's name.

That's not unusual, since sailors ply the seas canopied under the night sky seen only by those escaping civilization's ambient light. Nothing on the web about a *boat* of that name, though. He closed the search windows about the star, viewing research on the star, *Arcturus,* as pointless, and sat back even more puzzled. It bothered Saya-dar that he seemed—obsessed—with the name. Swizzling his Margarita, he returned to his notebook computer and idly resumed his reading: *"Arcturus."* He searched yacht names again.

What was his enemy trying to tell him with this name? Names meant something to the Iranian; names signified *something.* Finding nothing about the yacht, he returned to researching the star: *Arcturus.*

Then, he saw it: "Bear Guard." *Arcturus* stood *guard.*

Guard over what: the *bear,* for Russia? That made no sense to

236

ARCTURUS

Saya-dar. Guard over its constellation? Is the constellation guarded by *Arcturus* the field of stars in America's flag, her states? Dissatisfied, Saya-dar continued opening and perusing pages that looked most promising, until he found a page listing the star's names in other languages. *Worth a try. There it is in Arabic.*

Saya-dar stiffened. The Arabic name was not just a translation of "bear guard." "Keeper of Heaven," he spoke in hushed tone. *Keeper of Heaven.*

Saya-dar rose, stunned, and stumbled to the bar. He mixed a drink—forgetting the one at his work station. *Impossible! I am the Saya-dar, the Protector of the Faith. I am the Keeper of Heaven!*

Saya-dar's hands shook. His mind could not focus.

He stood, drink before him on the bar, leaning on the solid granite surface for support. Time passed. Rage and fear obscured all.

The name spoke an omen. The name accused him and all of Islam of being false. The name challenged Islam—challenged Allah!

Saya-dar saw what he must do to counter the omen. The boat Captain must die. Someone *must* pay for what *Arcturus* had done to his—to Allah's—plan and the Captain of the *Arcturus* would pay the price. The Christians could look to their crucified Savior to welcome their sorry shades into Heaven, and the Jews could hope in Moses and Abraham, but Saya-dar would prove whose Heaven waited for the Faithful and whose Hell lurked with jaws open wide for the infidels. Saya-dar would earn his place in Heaven by confirming his destiny as the Keeper of Heaven as well as the Destroyer of False Faith. He would earn Heaven by adding to his names The Instrument of Allah's Vengeance.

Saya-dar's hand tensed with fury as he reached for his cell phone and dialed a number retrieved from a coded contacts list. Only a short conversation set the inquiry into motion.

Saya-dar expected now to be able to relax—he could not. With the task done to its current, possible point of completion, he should be planning the next action. He could not; he burned for vengeance and nothing else mattered—not even vengeance on the United States—until "Allah" saw this false Keeper of Heaven—this *Arcturus*—punished. Allah. *Arcturus.* Allah *demanded* vengeance on *Arcturus.* Allah might punish him if Saya-dar wavered, or delayed action! This fear spawned urgency.

Saya-dar reached for the phone again, flipped open its cover and watched it light up. He thumbed through his contact list, scrolling to another of his U.S.A. infiltrators.

Saya-dar controlled many sources he could call on for information. Several lived in Florida, along the coast, easily mixing among the cosmopolitan population and travelers. He intended to dispatch more than one to inquire about the man behind the *Arcturus,* but stopped cold. Saya-dar frowned, put the phone down, closed its clamshell cover and took stock of what mistake he had almost committed.

One inquiry into the *Arcturus's* origin and ownership should go unnoticed, but the question did establish some sign of interest in the boat. Why would someone be asking? Oh, the agent would be smart enough to craft a pretext, but a second inquiry could flatly alert like a siren going off. An alert enemy, perceiving multiple inquiries, would spot some sinister force surfacing and watching *Arcturus.*

No, Saya-dar would wait. He would wait for Allah and the lawyer in Florida to hand him the *Arcturus,* for that was how Saya-dar now personified his enemy. *Arcturus* enraged him and he would destroy it by destroying the soul of the ship, the man at its wheel, the man who directed the attack on his helicopter and lost him the Urn of Judgment so carefully gained. He would destroy this usurper Keeper of Heaven.

The cell phone vibrated. Saya-dar glanced at its number, automatically transmitted and logged by his cruiser's main computer. The agent.

Opening the phone, Saya-dar answered and listened for about a minute. He closed the phone cover without saying any "good-bye" and glowed inside. The agent made the preparations and Saya-dar would be inside the United States of America within the week.

37

Donna slept. Jack watched the trees, signs and exits flash by in turmoil: he was in turmoil, that is—not Interstate 75. Jack's mind raced and reeled, as it raged against his country's enemies, and at his own frustration. Had he gotten out too soon? Been too self-important?

No, really, he'd done the right thing. He'd done right. In an Army that huge, the system could not prevent a few jackasses from running wild and he'd crossed paths with one of the granddaddies. That's all there was to it. Not the Army's fault; not his fault. He'd done right by his duty, his own superiors, and his subordinates.

But, he was out of the war.

Gordon. Enigma. Mystery. More to him than at first it seemed. Jack was grateful to Gordon for the chance to get back in, whatever that might look like. They would meet at Gordon's lodge and make a plan. Jack could hardly stand the constraints of engine, speed limits, time and space. He was willing to relax and recuperate some more at the lodge, but only for a short time, as preparation. He knew the mission; he just didn't know *his* mission yet.

Jack stole a glance to his right where Donna reclined.

38

At Gordon's lodge
Southeast of Knoxville, Tennessee
Late July

Jack followed Gordon's directions and wound their way straight north, through Georgia, crossing the line outside Chattanooga. Two hours more brought them past Lookout Mountain, over the Hiwassee River, past "The Lost Sea," and to the junction of I-75 with I-40 where traffic picked up measurably. They checked Gordon's more detailed local instructions, noted the warning about perpetual construction, worked their way through the cones, and exited downtown, through the tunnel. You couldn't miss the Sunsphere landmark Gordon told them to watch for: it stood like a huge, golden golf-ball high atop a steel-structure tee, left over from the 1982 World's Fair.

Ten more minutes' driving brought them to John Sevier Highway, named after "Nolichucky Jack," the area's famous frontiersman and Revolutionary War General. Whimsically mentally comparing adventurous Nolichucky Jack with Gordon amused Jack McDonald: he thought it apt. The two had much in common.

They stopped at the local Biz-R-Market and picked up a few things. Following Nolichucky Jack's highway led them to the French Broad River. They found the entrance to Gordon's nondescript road not far from the river, marked just as he described, and turned off the highway.

The more modest hills here rippled generally northeastward

through broad river valleys. The Appalachians framed the valley to the east in the form of the Great Smoky Mountains National Park. Miles to the west, the collection of high ridges called "Walden's Mountain" rose up forming the Cumberland Plateau, and ran almost completely through the state from Alabama to Kentucky. Far from placid and flat though, the valley between where Donna and Jack now drove rippled with its own, more modest sub-ridges and hills, all folded and oriented the same as the Smokies, as all marched northeastward together toward the Mountains' terminus in Maine. They found Gordon's gate, marked as he had said by the red mailbox. Jack confirmed the gate by GPS as well as the map.

"It doesn't look like much," Jack observed, and searched Donna's face for her own reaction. The rusting farm gate would have looked abandoned but for the stout six-by-six treated posts at each end and the combination lock.

"This is exactly where Gordon told us to find him and the location matches the description," she announced, looking at the printed message, "Right down to the hens."

A rooster crowed. Several hens of varying colors perched and clucked in the farmhouse yard across the road. Donna got out, spun the combination lock as per the directions, swung the gate open, and held it as she motioned Jack through. Jack turned on the four-wheel-drive axle and entered Gordon's private preserve.

"I'm sure there's more to Gordon's place then we've spotted so far," Donna said, re-seated and bouncing as the two slowly climbed the grass-and-gravel road cut close into the hillside. Honeysuckle vines and low branches brushed Jack's truck as they passed.

A dilapidated but stubborn barn loomed uphill, through the trees on their right. The road curved and Jack saw that it passed through the barn. The timber-framed barn cued Jack to call. Jack stopped just outside the barn, got out and stretched his legs. He fished out his cell phone and hit Gordon's speed-dial number. A familiar voice answered.

"Glad you could make it. I see you're tired and in need of stretching your legs. Come on up."

I didn't see any camera! Jack glanced back into the barn, but in vain.

Gordon sounded tired. They were all tired. Not really tired. Something else, something not temporary, not remedied by a few solid nights of sleep.

"Thanks, we're glad to have arrived. You gave flawless directions. I assume you've got security here," Jack asked more than stated.

"Yes. Somewhat. *(I bet.)* See the road continuing to your front?" Gordon kept going, knowing the view before them. "Just drive forward—you'll need 4WD if you've not switched over already—go up the hill to the next ridge, then curve to the left and follow the road along the ridge top for about 100 yards. You'll see it angle up sharply and split. Take the right split. It'll curve up the side of the slope and you'll pop out onto a meadow on the next ridge top. You should see my place and I'll be outside waving at you."

Gordon had considered a warmer greeting. He'd hoped the two enjoyed their time during the drive, but these were grim times and he'd learned that Jack transformed to a grim young man during such occasions. Gordon closed the phone and sat down on his deck steps. He'd hear their truck shortly. These next few days would be important.

"Your uncle sure lives out in the boonies, does he not?" Jack asked, and eyed Donna as he wound along a narrow, serpentine ridge top. "Hey, look!" Jack pointed as he scattered a flock of wild turkeys, loath at first to leave the forage they had scratched from the thin, stony soil barely covering the folded rock beneath, but finally rising to fly through the trees and down into a deep draw.

Jack and Donna saw the road split and rise. They bore right, clinging to the hillside on a rude road barely wide enough for the truck.

"There," Donna spied the house.

Before them rose a three-story, stone-and-log lodge, facing south, out from the side of the ridge. The house seemed part of the woods that grew close in beside it. Gordon stood from his seat on the steps of a deck that wound around to what must be considered the front of the home, Jack reasoned, seeing no door on the side facing him. The lodge front faced southeast, toward the Great Smoky Mountains. The deck fronted massive, high windows. To the left, Jack saw a five-bay garage, separated from the house by a covered walkway. A room probably topped the garage, but Jack could not tell for sure; he saw dormers and windows above the garage bays, though. Maybe these were his quarters for the next—what? Week or so? Couple of days?

The whole setting exuded isolation and secrecy. The secluded lodge grandly commanded a hill and view, although absolutely nothing about the entrance or approach heralded the jewel on the hill where Gordon lived. The lodge was casual, but so—alone. Jack pondered Gordon's invitation.

Odd. Gordon had assumed he would come and he assumed correctly. After all, Jack had no job, no place to be. Jack still marveled at the attack on the *Arcturus*, resting now in her berth in Tampa. Yes, a thorough, mutual, de-briefing was in order and Gordon had the place for it. The disruption in mission planning and operations afforded them the time, and Jack had learned never to miss an opportunity to take on water, eat, and rest: a soldier never knew what terror the next five minutes might bring, nor how long the mayhem might last.

Jack parked outside a garage bay, turned his truck off, and swung the door open. The Titan had seemed to revel at the chance to show off its muscle.

"Welcome to the lodge," Gordon smiled, hugged his niece, and shook Jack's hand. For an uncomfortable second, Jack suspected that Gordon was about to hug him, too, but the older man ushered them up the deck steps, extending his arm to Donna while Jack shouldered his pack and lifted her baggage. Gordon exuded relief—and even apparent joy—at their arrival.

"Let me show you the lodge first. I'll show you the whole place later—the terrain here, too—and we'll take a walk. You can relax walking the woods here. I've cut trails. Tonight, we'll talk it all over: the attack; what's going on right now as a result, and—well, we'll talk."

The three mounted the stone steps, wound around to the right and front on the deck walkway, and onto the broader deck, facing the mountains. Far in the distance, maybe 30 miles away, Jack spied what must be the tips of the Smokies and appreciated how Gordon had sited the lodge. While the approach up the ridge had wound through the forest, the house turned aside from the driveway and faced across the valley below, looking out to the lines of lesser ridges in the distance. Finally, Jack could see the far-off mountains. It was as if the lodge invited visitors both to delight in them and to honor the old hills at the same time. Jack saw that the house entrance, or "front door," really was not a front door at all but opened directly into a stone-floored greatroom from the broad deck. The deck, thus, served as both entrance and platform for savoring the landscape stretching out to the mountains.

Gordon showed them to their respective rooms, leading them up a wide staircase and overlooking the main, open room below. A stone fireplace and ceiling-height chimney rose upward from the greatroom.

Jack dropped his belongings, ran a cold, wet cloth across his face, and returned to the lodge greatroom below, where he found glasses of iced tea waiting to refresh them. Gordon was elsewhere. Jack chose one of Gordon's overstuffed, leather chairs, stirred his tea, and relaxed.

Donna emerged from her room above, and Jack rose as she descended the staircase. The two smiled as she approached Jack, stepping right up to embrace him. Jack pressed her close, treasuring both Donna and the moment. Donna warmed in his arms; the two lingered in their embrace.

Gordon walked in, coughed, smiled at the two, and said, again: "Welcome, welcome. Is everything OK? About your accommodations, I mean?" He asked them.

"Yes, thanks," they both answered.

"Then, let's go out and I'll show you the entire layout so you know what's around—and, then, I'd like to talk with Jack for a few minutes."

39

Late July,
four weeks after the attack
on Arcturus

Saya-dar told himself over and over that he should simply get on with it. That much he *knew*. Would he? No, he would not. He hated. He hated the man who had sailed into his plan, his masterpiece plan, and spoiled it. He feared, too. He felt Allah's disapproving scowl for every minute Saya-dar delayed vengeance on the pretender Keeper of Heaven.

Still, Saya-dar was a student, a strategist and a tactician.

Perhaps the Americans learned something that compromised his anonymity during the attack by the Cubans. Saya-dar had spent his lifetime methodically painting a false portrait of a rich playboy, a frivolous but mysterious man, so tied to western ways and customs that it would be absurd to suspect him of first growing, and then commanding a far-flung, deeply covert Army.

The Japanese defenses in the South Pacific, and later the NVA operating around and so close to Saigon, had inspired Saya-dar. These soldiers embraced deception and illusion as a first principle, and disappeared. Indeed, they "embraced the mist" as he had thought of their ways. The Japanese dug in, not into some European-style trench system just to deflect rifle fire. They looked *into* the earth and saw another world, a world unseen by the landing Marines. The Japanese saw, and then carved out a secret world, operating beneath the feet, but above the experiences of the American youths charging island shores.

Of course, Saya-dar had recalled, the Marines wiped the Japanese out. Somehow, even the Japanese, steeped in and drawing from Ninja lore, had overlooked the deeper way, the more profound and elegant magic they had begun to weave but failed to finish. Their defenses failed like a bad magician's stage trick, only the audience slaughtered the wizard instead of laughing him off the stage.

The Chinese, and more so, the North Vietnamese, had learned from their fellow Orientals (but their despised enemies). They, too, saw the West's truncated vision as an advantage to exploit. They moved out of the way of the power wave by simply fading into the earth, and fading away further when finally confronted by military power they could not prevail against. By this means, they survived, using time to wear the Americans down. *Time* and America's own *moral* rot cooperated. America vacillated over the cost of resisting Communism's evil, and, one day, the Americans simply left. The world watched as America boarded the last Huey and lifted off from a decade-long war. Something profound exuded from this lesson and, just as America strove to forget it, Saya-dar yearned to absorb and even *become* the lesson's every instruction.

Saya-dar had succeeded, he was sure. He had taken the kernel of infiltrators left to him by his own mentor, and grown them like carefully-tended flowers. He, too, lay in wait for the West in an unseen world, but one parallel to theirs, a world *among* them, almost like a science fiction parallel universe.

After decades, Saya-dar controlled access to over 2,000 Faithful in America alone, and three times that number in Europe, with fluid numbers who might be swept along. The summertime French riots had proven his thesis that his cadre there could tap into even greater hordes, mentally and spiritually prepared for someone to incite them to violence. That was Europe.

America was *different*. America had an acid-like character: it corroded everything that touched it. The Great Satan must have infected the souls of its young Muslims. America did not teem with disaffected, young, fire-eating Muslims. There, he must launch his attacks either by inserting new soldiers from outside as in 9-11— always a risky operation in itself—or by calling up his covert Faithful. Calling those Faithful to duty probably meant a one-time deployment. He'd firewalled their knowledge and they could not give each other away, but even the most diligent planner lacked the omniscience of Allah. Mistakes lay in wait and America sifted the world looking for his mistakes—looking for *him* although they did not yet know his identity.

He should simply retrieve the Urn from the cove and lie in wait for the right time to loose the Urn of Judgment, but he could not shake the need—even the *command*—to destroy the *Arcturus's* Captain. Saya-dar gave in. Destroying this false Keeper of Heaven must be the will of Allah or, otherwise, Allah would grant him rest.

Allah granted Saya-dar no rest from his lust for vengeance. He resolved to block the greater attack from his mind until he had sated Allah's thirst for revenge. Saya-dar sent two e-mail messages, one activating Kadir, and the other ordering Saya-dar's infiltration, and then he shut his computer down.

40

Saya-dar's Poachers

The untrained moviegoer thinks that tough Harrison Ford types conceive operations and plan the details, hot, younger people carry them out, win, and they all list the credits before two hours pass. The average citizen thinks that infantry merely walk around with rifles waiting for someone to shoot. They do—like orthopedic surgeons just cut and sew. Enemy there. Jump on helicopters. Land, jump off and begin shooting. Get on radios and yell. Hope planes come with bombs.

Reality: unless you have done it, you would not believe the degree of detail and training required to choreograph military operations, at the "tactical" level as well as at the strategic.

Terrorist operations are military attack operations. More precisely, they fit under the category of raids or ambushes. The raid is an attack on a fixed location; the ambush is an attack from a fixed position on an enemy moving to the attacker. Terrorists use both, and include kidnapping or "snatches" as well as robberies. The IED attack is a "mechanical" ambush. The 9-11 attack was a raid. Bigtime. Spain's imaginative Atocha station bombing combined elements of both, ambushing people on their way to work but cleverly bringing the ambush to them. Both attacker and attacked were mobile. The well-planned military operation foresees contingencies and includes rehearsals and detailed sub-plans or "annexes."

The ordinary western citizen thinks that the terrorist cell is just a group of hyped-up suicidal idiots, set in motion like demonic wind-up toys. This prejudiced ignorance blinds the West to the deep danger of intelligent Islamic terrorism.

The Control Team is the terrorist headquarters element: the boss and his staff. Management. None of the other team members will ever see these players, or know their identity. The Control Team will orchestrate the attack far from the battlefield unless the particular mission absolutely requires a closer presence. The Control Team collects its target information from its Recon Team.

The Recon Team members may know each other, but have no need to know members of other teams. The Recon Team deploys to the target, but may also call on resident agents for information. The Recon Team remains ignorant of the purpose behind its information collecting and picture taking, although its members may infer the operation from the target.

When needed, the Control Team will dispatch a Logistics Team to the battlefield, using information from the Recon Team to equip and outfit the Attack Team and the Recon Team's further reconnaissance, if any. Logistics includes readying safe houses, arranging for cars, trucks or other transportation, credit cards, cash, and identification, as well as setting up cell phone accounts and Internet connections.

The Attack Team deploys only when necessary and executes the attack, using the support already in place from the Logistics Team and guided by intelligence from the Recon Team provided to the Control Team. Thus, the entire operation is "firewalled" in that there will never be a mass meeting of the entire force; they will not know members of other teams, and will never know who dispatched and supported them. Recon and Logistics will carry out their specific missions, but may never know the overall mission undertaken by the Control Team, although the eventual attack probably will disclose it in dramatic fashion. Logistics and Recon will leave the battlefield as soon as their tasks are accomplished, whether before the attack or after. Attack Team members may leave, but are often scraped up in pieces.

All of this requires money. Part of the Logistics Team is not forward-deployed, but supports the Control Team from afar also, and arranges finances. The bankers. Long after the smoke, dust, and body parts settle, the financing tracks left by the Logistics Team provide clues leading to the guilty, clues that could have tipped off alert or lucky investigators before the attack.

The clues that could make terrorist preparations stand out are always there. Clues are manifestations of actions already taken, changes to the environment you might say. Cause and effect. Do anything in this world, and you change its contents in some way, whether catastrophic or miniscule. Ordinary people do not arrange mass bombings, or shop for surface-to-air, shoulder-fired anti-aircraft missiles. The trick is to make the clues look like ordinary background cause-and-effect noise.

For example, if the planner cannot conceal preparatory steps, then he may lie about their meaning. The Ayatollah may insist that Iranian nuclear research and development strictly aims to produce electricity, not weapons to fling at The Great Satan. People struggle to see objectively against the lie offered up to them that comforts them.

Another more subtle technique obscures the clues by accomplishing overt logistical steps far in advance, but spread over time so that an intelligence analyst fails to see malevolent patterns emerge from the far-flung, murky data in front of him. People think in terms of the next meal, not the next decade. A flurry of activity, acquisitions, purchases, charges, and travel may signal an operation launching. The same transactions, spread over 20 years, pass unnoticed because these individual clues cast no appearance of connection to any pattern of telltale other transactions.

Saya-dar, the Persian terrorist, the wealthy Iranian, would draw on operations planning from years ago, plans set into motion without knowing the precise conclusion, plans made even before his time. Visionaries foresaw the time when the Faithful would strike inside America and laid the groundwork.

"Students" earned degrees all over the United States, forming communities, making contacts, all while these agents recruited other inflamed young radicals. When they grew too old to maintain the student cover, younger members, sometimes even younger brothers or cousins, took over the university cell leadership, and the older agents "graduated" to their choice of jobs, academic positions, or self-employed businesses. Those in media seized every opportunity to slander the Jews, garner sympathy for the Palestinian cause, and later expand those propaganda campaigns to greater sympathy for Muslim "insurgents" or rebels, or the "poor, disenfranchised youth."

The post-USSR, pro-socialist West identified readily with this fakery, undermining the West's resolve to combat Islamic onslaught even before the attacks escalated into *Jihad*. Thus, the initial news reports mentioning widespread rioting in Paris failed utterly even to allude to the crucial fact that the rioters were Islamic; they were merely disenchanted "youth." The truth crept out, but the emphasis remained on the social unrest of poverty, immobility, lack of education and opportunity, as if the Islamic French had inherited the simmering resentment of peasant French from a previous revolutionary era. This was not some mere reporting oversight.

Motels and rental properties acquired throughout America structured an arrangement of safe houses. Convenience gasoline stations stockpiled diesel fuel, tanked as part of ordinary business, for the time when Allah required incendiaries, and made the agent-owners self-supporting as a plus. Retail came naturally to men and women comfortable with the bazaar, and the mix of people moving in and out of stores created cover for the time when those few who waited as Allah's martyrs and agents would activate and need logistical support. All of these people imagined that they were the only such agents, or part of a very few. Over time, their numbers accumulated hiding among the mass of honest merchants.

Land purchases in the United States made good investments. Land ownership means nothing without the confidence that you will still have the right to use the land years later, and your children after you. In unstable countries, land is cheap because the secret police may drag you from it next week, never to be seen again. In stable countries, owning the exclusive right to use the property, sell it or leave it to your children is taken for granted it is so firmly established.

Saya-dar took advantage of America.

With his rise to the head of a collection of al Qaeda-like groups, the terrorist mastermind known only as "The Saya-dar" or, simply, "Saya-dar," inherited the secret inventory of rural parcels bought throughout the United States (and the world) and perused it like a catalog. Logistics teams had bought small U.S. farms tucked away far enough to remain out of sight from expanding cities and towns, and purchased them in the name of obscure Anglo-sounding corporations. Prior commanders had even sold parcels as development approached, made money, and spent it acquiring more strategically-sited land.

Think about it. You do not know when or where you will need a secret storage building, a training area, a camp, or a landing zone, or a place to hide a car, or bury a body, but you have faith that the day will come when you will need facilities. In the meantime, the properties gain value like a deadly but slow-acting parasite. *Jihad* invested well. What irony! They practiced careful building for destruction.

Managers deeply embedded over decades receive property tax bills, pay the taxes, and, periodically, check the site to assure that nothing has occurred to draw it to anyone's unwelcome attention, such as impermissible overgrowth of weeds and trash-dumping that might spur a complaint and ordinance violation citation. You can't plan to use the property, as a training site, for example, only to find some deer hunter poaching from his tree stand on the big day.

41

In the 20 years Samir had performed such site checks, he had seen it all. Sometimes, it amazed him how much work there was in managing his tenant-less properties. He had busted marijuana growing. He had hunted dove, and chased out poachers. He had buried dead stray cows and once, a dead person. He never learned the identity, never knew the body's sad story, never saw a reference in a newspaper, and never quit worrying about it. Sometimes, he wondered how many other men there were like him in America, and in Europe too, for that matter, fully employed by invisible masters, and tasked with so simple a service to Allah.

Samir sat dumbfounded when he opened Outlook Express and read the subject header on the e-mail message. He panicked that he would mistakenly delete the message and wondered what would happen to him and to his family if he did. Then, he was tempted to delete the message on purpose but fought back the impulse. Samir was finally tasked to perform his duty and he would obey.

Obedience was simple; at this point, all he had to do was reply using an innocuous code word indicating "site ready and secure" and then stay away from it until further notified. He could handle that. He briefly wondered why the cryptic message appeared in his life now, but dismissed the thought, checking his watch. Almost time for his son's soccer game.

AYSO also called him to duty and, despite the simple but staggering e-mail alert, Samir was scheduled to referee. He donned the garish black and yellow uniform and called to his son to bring the keys to the Altima. Samir's mind reeled and he wondered how he would spot off-sides violations. Would the parents whisper that his meticulous, reliable calls suffered? He would call this game accurately for Allah, he chuckled nervously. Then, he would buy the land as directed.

The unmistakable red, yellow and black colors of the Pilot sign rose from the horizon and Ismael was glad to see it. The sight of the sign evoked a learned response like Pavlov's dogs: it meant good truck stop coffee and food, as well as a cleanup and some rest. The Pilot stations sprinkled along the Midwest and South interstate highways uniformly offered clean showers, a huge selection of trucker paraphernalia, and even some of the new IdleAire units catching on with truckers. The cell phone and laptop had changed trucking forever. Men gone from home a week at a time could now instantly, if distantly, touch base with home.

Ismael signaled, geared down, and veered onto the exit ramp that would dump him off at Columbus, Indiana. First things first, and he topped off the tanks before edging his rig into a slot between two other truckers. He exchanged a friendly wave with one passing him on the way into the store, a big black man sporting an "America Love it or Leave It" tee shirt. The slogan's challenge did not provoke Ismael in the least, its significance to him lost in time and the promise of lemon icebox pie, a specialty here that lured truckers in from all over, he supposed. He'd gone out of route for it before; it was worth the price.

New girl on the cash register. He guessed they still called them cash registers. No more "ca-CHING" sound unless it was programmed in. They exchanged some good-natured banter. Ismael next hit the buffet. You could always count on this place.

He allowed himself only decaffeinated coffee at the end of the day, knowing from experience that "high test" would keep him up at night. He signed his check as he downed the last sip. Ismael unlimbered his laptop, powered it up, and connected to the facility's "Wi-Fi" network, bringing him to this far-flung Midwestern United States portal on the World Wide Web.

The trucker glanced at the news on his home page and saw nothing of particular import other than the usual stuff. Democrats criticizing Bush. Republicans dithering. One side had no strategy; one had pulled their punches. Flood somewhere ran people out of their homes. Kid missing from some burg in Nebraska. His self-directed IRA stock recovered a little today, signaling better times. Good. He might place a "buy stop" order before it went up too much.

Ismael munched on a cracker as he absently clicked on "Inbox" to check his webmail and then blanched. He blinked, shook his head, and peered again. Then he caught himself looking left and right and then back at the screen. He sat back, stunned.

As Ismael reeled, the pleasant waitress brought his prized pie. Ismael stared at her as she said something. He heard, but he did not perceive her good-natured banter. Ismael forced a thin smile. She glared at him, first with amusement, transitioning to some concern, and then, after a brief pause, she coaxed him to "enjoy" and returned to her own duty. The fluffed meringue reached out and lured Ismael partially back to reality. He spooned a taste into his mouth. The tangy lemon taste revived his reasoning. Allah called him to so simple a task.

OK. He would do it tomorrow. Easy enough. Right on the way pretty much. He was already filled up. He would, indeed, as instructed long ago, pick up and drop off a load of diesel fuel. Not much of a sacrifice. No problem.

What was it for?

No, don't even ask! Don't even wonder. Couldn't be for much. Just 1,000 gallons of diesel out of his tanker. Anyone could buy that. There were big tanks underground right outside.

Then why didn't they? Not his business why. Just a delivery, really like any other. He e-mailed his wife to let her know he'd be home tomorrow and to buy some steaks to grill out Saturday night since the neighbors were coming over. He closed the browser, powered down and shut the screen.

Damn! He looked around. Everything looked the same. Two burly drivers chatted up the young, would-be-blonde cashier. A trucker at the next booth guffawed at the Packers' faltering season, while his companion steadfastly declared the Packers' eternal glory and inevitable return. But all had changed like the face of the earth after a volcano. It wasn't the same. Not inside, it wasn't. Not ever again.

Ismael could not know it, but only an hour later, another driver, an independent truck driver and tractor owner who was really not so independent after all, slid into a cushioned bench seat in another restaurant, received a similar message, and after exactly one week, would roll his tractor up to the same secluded barn, hook it up to the tank trailer there, and drive away to deliver it to another secluded location, where he would be knifed while dropping the trailer. A small sacrifice for Allah—perhaps too small to enjoy the fruits of martyrdom, the Mullahs had debated when discussing the long-term plans.

42

Syracuse, New York
At the Forks of the River
Late July,
four weeks after the attack
on Arcturus

K az turned the key to his office and swung the door open for the student to enter behind him. He kicked aside yesterday's now-empty box from UPS to clear the way for his visitor and cordially waved the fidgety, young man past the clutter to an oak side-chair. Habitually, Kaz glanced at the flashing, red voicemail-indicator before settling himself into his own chair and relaxing. Voicemail could wait. Between voicemail, e-mail, and "the" mail, there was hardly time for this male to answer it all. Mehdi Kazem was a busy man, whose world was about to shatter.

The student, a bright (but distracted) young man, had not fared well on the last test, and wanted to assure his professor that he could and would do better. Kazem smiled inwardly, and outwardly, and returned the fatherly assurance that he understood that we all have bad days. If some portion of the material gives particular trouble, the professor would be glad to answer questions about it. Next test in a week. No doubt, better then. This dance had predictable moves: the student prepared the way to make his pitch for raising his grade at the end of the term, hedging his bets in case the numbers did not match the aspirations. The teacher encouraged, but declined to commit to the easy way out. The student thanked his teacher earnestly and left.

Dr. Mehdi Kazem, Professor of Chemical Engineering at

Syracuse University, New York, next glanced at his stack of mail as he powered up his desktop computer. Quickly sorting today's mail entirely into the "unremarkable" category, he absently touched the telephone controls for voicemail as Windows came to life in its various stages before presenting the computer ready and eager for work. He fished out his wire-bound pad from underneath the layers to jot down the phone numbers, names, times, and notes.

Mehdi had perfected hiding in the open. He arrived from Iran in 1977. After achieving his master's degree in chemical engineering, he applied for employment with an explosives manufacturing firm and hired on as a process engineer. Good job, good pay, and he picked up his Ph.D. along the way, and on the company tab, too.

A contractor threatened with bankruptcy by a lawsuit had called his firm asking for technical support and courtroom testimony. No one in management wanted even to touch any project that might lead to the witness stand, but Mehdi's curiosity about the application of the product in the field drew him irresistibly. He embraced the opportunity, knowing it would further hone his cover and his skills. Not only did he travel to the construction site with the contractor and consult confidentially over the contractor's use of the explosives, but he also held 12 jurors' fascination at trial on the contractor's behalf. Mehdi had delivered his opinions, but with the energized qualities of enthusiasm and common sense language that the client would call "salesmanship" as he slapped Mehdi on the back and hugged him in spontaneous gratitude. Certainly, the other expert witnesses had contributed to the victory as well, but the grateful contractor had praised Mehdi openly when they celebrated and had written his boss thanking him for providing such a man to help during a time of dire need.

The trial launched Mehdi's career as a diving board springs the diver. Lawyers are always prowling for experts who not only prove their technical proficiency, but who also speak to the public in a way that people can understand, and who possess the will to face the crucible of cross-examination from an obnoxious barrister. Mehdi, the recognized demolitions expert and respected academic, found himself in demand. His career blossomed, he delivered advanced seminar lectures, and he joined the International Demolitions Institute, serving on various committees and eventually rising to President. His alma mater noticed and invited him back to speak. The delightful trip garnered Mehdi more than just a chicken lunch and accolades. He had suspected—correctly—that the invitation doubled as a job interview, and was not surprised at all when the department head called him, played coy for a short bit, and then asked Mehdi to join the faculty.

Mehdi Kazem, a handsome, engaging, Iranian of 6 feet height and athletic build was smart, technically at the top of his game, and motivated. Very motivated. Before long, he made full Professor. The Professor had, indeed, grown in his profession, but his mission—and, therefore, motivation—remained always the same.

A potpourri of voicemail began. A Standards Committee meeting tomorrow cancelled. His friend, John Blackwell, down the hall, offered two spare football tickets, if Kaz and his son wanted to catch the game with John. A reply from the river-rafting outfitter in the Catskills announced apologetically that water levels still dwindled away too low to both excite and cushion the rafters from repeated beatings on the rocks.

Then, over the speaker came four innocuous words, spoken in a pleasant voice. Just four. Slightly accented Middle Eastern, but from what country, even he could not determine. The message was so brief. He touched the key that played it again. And again. And again. It was for real.

Dr. Kazem's head spun. He felt faint. It occurred to him how the world could turn in a flash. An auto accident. A telephone call. A doctor announcing a diagnosis. Life never the same again. This moment had arrived for Mehdi.

He knew his job. Unlike the men who would drive the component delivery trucks though, who could only speculate later at the degree of their own complicity, Mehdi's task foretold the broader mission unmistakably. Mehdi would not awaken on future mornings, continuing life in the luxury of ignorance about his contribution to the cause. Combining a large quantity of diesel fuel with nitrogen-based solid fertilizer in the right proportions, with the most effective ignition-accelerators added, then coupled with the correctly specified detonating device, all tamped according to Mehdi's design left no room to rationalize.

My God! No! It could not be for real.

But it was. All this time! He felt sick. He opened the plastic bottle of water always at the right corner of his desk and drank deeply. He looked dully at it, this ordinary object in his hand, as if only it and he existed. He envied its soulless, material, innocence.

"Rio Vida" its brand name proclaimed: "River of Life" he understood the simple Spanish phrase to mean.

Ironic. Paradoxical. A message? A sign? A scathing rebuke?

His wife picked it up for him by the case at Sam's. He had not selected this life-sustaining water, nor had he seen this brand before. Perhaps he had seen it but not *perceived* it, not having arrived at the ford over the River of Death, or at least not having been ordered to unleash its floodgates, before today. Such cold waters they were, too.

"Rio Muerte," he counter-pointed out loud, *"Rio Muerte—River of Death—Death River."* The sound of his voice, naming the grim river mocked him. (Mehdi had learned the language and visited

south of the border as a tourist to prepare himself for any mission requiring him to pass himself off as Latin.) Did Allah truly fate him to unleash a river of death? So proclaimed the four-word message.

Again, Mehdi stared down at the water bottle in his hand, avoiding the grim directive just delivered on his voicemail. Water: just a simple compound, but so vital to life, so common, so universal—so neutral, like the ocean, neither good nor evil, but simply a vast collection of molecules.

Evil. Was there such a thing? Some said not. He envied these American and European moral relativists. The dulled masses at least pretended that evil did not exist. No right, no wrong, just do what you think is right for you. Don't judge anything or anyone— until someone else's grotesquely evil deed butchered the people you hold dear. Where was the comfort of clinging to the belief that evil was mere superstition then? Evil is so to be feared that the West hid behind the construct that *it* did not exist; it was mere fable, they confidently asserted, and made up by men. The word should be archaic, dropped from use, the culture having moved on.

He envisioned the death—the *evil.*

Kazem's mind tottered. My God! My God!

Get yourself together!

Why the shock? Islam—Allah supposedly—had always required this of him. It's just that so much time had passed and, well, life had become so—ordinary. He felt a wave of guilt, thinking about the martyrs and the oppressed for whom life was not ordinary at all.

He looked around at the American things in his American office. The wave of indicting guilt reversed, a *tsunami* backwash sweeping over him like a combination one-two punch as he pondered his friend's generous offer of football tickets and his own impending betrayal of that friendship. Dr. Kazem stood slowly and steadied himself at his window, hoping for solace there. He always found peace there.

Below his window, the sidewalk streaming toward his building split and continued to wind around both sides of the mulched flowerbed directly below his second-story office. He so appreciated its seasonal, changing beauty. He could not name the flowers but recognized the lush fig that anchored the center of this particular landscape feature. Squirrels flicked their tails and darted across the walkway; students strolled along the sidewalk both directions, as always. He recognized one of them approaching, an American girl who excelled in one of his research statistics classes. "Sadistics," the students joked.

Was he sadistic? Was he evil? Were these young students evil? Yes, they were infidels, but were they *evil*? This tortured reverie rocketed to crescendo, and then veered to panic. He scanned the entire park-like quadrangle below for uniformed men who might be coming, even now, to arrest him. He briefly prayed they would.

Prayed? To Allah? Could he pray to Allah that the mission, supposedly Allah's own, would abort, or that the Americans would thwart their plan? He looked again for the American agents; none appeared. Students joked with each other and the girls flirted with the boys, obviously flaunting their subtle power to *charm* (another word almost antique).

My God!

Another drink of the water with its mocking message. His throat felt so parched but the amoral water failed to quench his thirst.

His thirst for what? What did he thirst for? Blood? The blood of these Americans? The blood of these students? The blood of John Blackwell and his sons?

Why was he fated for such killing? Why could he not question his fate? He rebelled against the fate he had been taught to accept. What if his controller was wrong? A mistake! My God, let this be a mistake!

He keyboarded in the web site address he knew he was to check. There they were: GPS waypoints. He printed the screen, stared at the numbers and letters, and closed the web site, deleting the site address from his history.

Waypoints! Indeed!

Death lurked theoretical until it materialized at time and place, snatching a real, breathing human being. People could deal with death that way, much like these Westerners dealt with evil, sealing their minds from the future horror by concentrating on the now. Life, death, fate, power, planning, and the physics of pyrotechnic chemistry would all intersect at these waypoints, where Death would strike like a lightning bolt, suddenly, as if to crack from ghostly nothingness in the void of the sky, to burn into a selected, precise point in the real world.

A "waypoint." A point where the way changed from life to death. A point where the River of Life forks and the River of Death begins.

Like Death and Evil, all of Mehdi's skill stayed safely theoretical unless pinned to time and place. For certain people, fated by Allah, Mehdi's know-how and ability to instruct would rip the time-space continuum, snatching these men, women, (and children) from their green America to Hell. Waypoints into which these people would wander would be portals into eternally-fixed damnation for these infidels, and Mehdi would prepare the portal for them! No comforting shade awaited them.

The *Saya-dar* gave Mehdi the waypoints.

The Saya-dar. Who was this man—or woman, Mehdi mused— who directed such fabric-of-time ripping power? The word, the name, fascinated Mehdi.

Saya-dar. Mehdi felt the cool shade implied by the name. Somewhere, though, the word got lost in the depths of Persian history or folklore. Like so much of his Persian home and history, Islam subsumed the coveted title. The simple, agrarian phrase, twisted a bit, now proclaimed a recognized Guardian of The Faith, a Protector of Islam. This *Saya-dar* spread his strong limbs and protective blessing over Islam, killing its enemies and mere faithless straphangers. Mehdi did not aspire to be known as a *Saya-dar* but saw himself as such, even without the acclaim.

Always, though, lurked a different and sinister "shade" of meaning behind this title. "Shade" also whispered of the underworld where disembodied but eternally tortured souls wisped about, lost. Ghosts. Not "friendly" either. *Saya-dar* had an alternative meaning, oddly, just as *shade* in English could mean either cooling relief from harsh sun, or a haunt. Mehdi wondered if *shade* came from Farsi's *saya-dar*. Why was he thinking about this now?

Mehdi's instant messenger interrupted his anguished, stunned meditation with a pleasant "ping." John Blackwell was "I-imming" Mehdi. The ethereal, shade-like, message preview coalesced and called for "RMTMB" to get back with John fast. Those tickets were "hot" and John would offer them to other friends if his favored friend declined.

Blackwell joked with his friend, calling him "Kaz" or "Rimtimb," taking off on the acronym "RMTMB." Blackwell usually seized any opportunity to introduce his friend as "Ready Meddy the Master Blaster" or at least he would dramatize this humorous introduction at less formal party circles. His friend was a "real blast." He had a "short fuse" though. Blackwell's good-natured jokes about Mehdi's intriguing field had no end. The two friends played off each other at social gatherings, relaxing the guests while, at the same time, promoting Mehdi's status. John devised new ones when it seemed that surely he had exhausted all possible puns.

The vaporous football ticket reminder-message preview in the lower right corner of the screen faded—like a "shade."

Indeed, Saya-dar was as shade. Mehdi had never met Saya-dar. He assumed Saya-dar was a devout Muslim, a *Jihadist*, a *fadayeen* in Arabic. Mehdi assumed that Saya-dar hated the Americans, all things Western, and all things Jewish and Christian for certain. Mehdi's own hatred, the same hatred that propelled him from his beloved Iran 30 years ago, had somehow quelled, fading like a shade.

At first, Mehdi had lived up to his name, *Kazem: a man who hides his anger.* Mehdi had succeeded in hiding his anger. Saya-dar sent him periodic messages, mostly updating the plan to take advantage of commercial technology advances, but Saya-dar never propagandized Mehdi, never preached, never railed on and on about the decadent West. Perhaps Saya-dar saw no need to sway or motivate the younger Mehdi who hid his hatred so well. The Shade was all business while the Mullahs were all hate. Hate.

What was hate? How could any man, Muslim or Christian or atheist, hold onto hate for so many years? Saya-dar's hate seemed to pervade his shady soul so deeply that The Shade had no need to manifest it; he manifested his hate as The Plan, in its continuing evolutions and improvements. Recipients of the updates simply assumed the hate, perhaps like they assumed their own.

Hate. If not palpable, hate certainly was real. Every day, the

U.S. newspapers featured headlines about this Muslim or that Muslim blowing himself up for Allah. Hate *existed*. Hate moved. Hate drove. Hate—the kind of hate Mehdi read about and knew must be out there—escaped The Professor who had lived among the Americans for 30 years. He had imperceptibly come to see some of the Americans as *people* and not just *infidels*. If *infidel*, then they were de-humanized, then they were inanimate almost and, thus, could be disposed of like garbage. Only abject hatred could incite such a conclusion that people were garbage.

However, Mehdi could not see his friend, John Blackwell, as garbage. Could such warping hatred come only from Satan? Mehdi considered the ramifications for his own people, and for his mission. What if he were working for Satan? Hatred—Satan. They seemed to go together.

Mehdi reminded himself why he had come to America. One simple reason moved him then: position himself for the day he would be given a mission—a mission for Allah. Mehdi had lived in America, at this point, most of his life. *Most* of his life, for God's sake! Had The Great Satan infected his own soul, his faithfulness? Yes, certainly. Mehdi looked out his window again.

The girls on the concrete walkway swayed their hips alluringly. They were gorgeous. Their every movement, their just slightly-naked bellies, their curved shapes, their taunting-laughing mouths and eyes hinted at pleasures beyond a man's imagination. Their seduction not only drew weak men to the women; they drew the weak men away from Allah. The West was overrun with seduction. The West was seduced. The West, by now, was *willingly* seduced.

Mehdi's Mullah told him that America was The Great Satan. No higher calling wooed a man than to seek mortal combat with

The Great Satan. How better to challenge The Great Satan than to fearlessly plunge into its belly, and eat it alive from the inside out?

That had been Mehdi's calling and he strove to recall the fervor that had accompanied his calling—but Mehdi could not summon up that kind of hatred for the West any more. Hiding his anger became less difficult over the years, merely because Mehdi grew less possessed of it.

Regardless, here Mehdi was, a devout Muslim, living within The Great Satan, and now called on to take the sword to wound and kill citizens, residents, and, perhaps, his own friends too.

"Of course!" Mehdi concluded that America had insidiously seduced him too! This open land tricked him into believing that the infidel actually *mattered* other than to serve as an example to show the world Allah's chastisement. Mehdi stirred from his daze and decided to *do something* (even though his next action would not quite complete his mission).

This next step required some time. Mehdi opened 20 other sites, each of them from all appearances just another travel site where a family might post its pictures and captions to describe their holiday to friends, and to read others' similar posts. He could have used only one site for all 20, but, why compromise all operations by using a common site? He chafed at The Saya-dar's use of only one web site to get update data messages to Mehdi. He had always wished that The Saya-dar had e-mailed the others directly. Instead, Mehdi served not only to provide the recipe for 20 efficient truck bombs, but also as the communications link to pass on any changes to the weapons' composition, construction and delivery. Why could he not have merely e-mailed the Saya-dar who could then have posted changes to the 20? Mehdi suspected that Saya-dar had made him the link to avoid the personal risk involved in so much electronic communication but he had burned with shame at his own accusatory thoughts.

To each apparently innocuous site, he uploaded a GPS waypoint. One step remained—only one—and his mission was accomplished, regardless of what he set in motion. Others—his message recipients—would then accomplish their own missions, about which he would probably read in the news. Mehdi poised, slumped at his keyboard, unaware that his friend worried that he had not heard from Mehdi about the tickets. Mehdi thirsted.

John's emoticon-with-sound urgently chimed "last chance." Mehdi keyed out "cant thanx."

Enough! Before his western-infected will faltered again, he e-mailed 20 recipients a simple message devoid of any suspect trigger-words that might alert a data-mining sentinel. Other industrial or academic chemists would routinely check their own e-mail, as he had done, and their lives would forever change too, although he could not know who they were. He assumed they lived and worked close to the respective chosen bomb target waypoints. He sat back blankly, reaching unconsciously for the water bottle.

He drank deep from the cooling, life-sustaining fluid. Mehdi lowered the bottle, stared again at the jeering label, and imagined the bottle full of blood—the River of Death in his hands. The Saya-dar noted the log onto the website by "The Professor" and relaxed at his own terminal, grinning.

43

*All the rest of us—you and me and
even the thousands of soldiers behind
the lines in Africa—we want
terribly yet only academically for the
war to get over.—Ernie Pyle*

"Jack, I am recruiting you."

"I know."

"I know you know."

The two turned down a steep, leaf-strewn trail.

"They are among us. They are "inside the wire." The public remains willfully ignorant. The terrorists have learned—probably to their own surprise—that they can surface, kill us in the most dramatic way, disappear and—given time—our furor will subside and we'll forget. It helped that the 19 died in the 9-11 attacks. Their martyrdom created the illusion that the killers had also died, that this was one, single plan, horrible in its extent, but now over. A mere few years later, Americans are more bothered by the price of a gallon of gas than of their sworn, intractable enemies." Gordon rested, having vented his philosophy and frustration.

"OK, Gordon, I see all of that. What is going on here, with you, I mean?"

"After the first WTC bombing, and after America did not go to war, a group of Army officers met. I was one of them. Our question was how to go to war against this sub-surface, unseen enemy even though the rest of the country slumbered. We determined that we needed to fight them in a like manner."

"What do you mean?"

"We identified our weakness and determined to turn this weakness into strength, into a strategy. This is not lip service to Zen; we saw this conclusion as imperative. America, as a whole—as a people—sat and simply declined the challenge; given that, we asked if we could use that very act of collective cowardice to mask America's true intent."

"And just what was—is—America's true intent?" Jack came to the point.

"To hunt down and kill every Islamic terrorist who sticks his head out of his hole, whether in Beirut or Boston," Gordon stated flatly. "Put more accurately, the True in America could not stand by and let this great country wither in the face of determined killers. I suppose it's this way the world over; a country can count on a small, determined few; the rest are strap-hangers. The few suffice, though. Think about it: Why would you crawl around in Philippine and Columbian jungle Hell when other young men are sipping wine at sidewalk cafes on the upper west side?"

The men laughed at Gordon's pointed, yet poignant question. Jack understood several things about Gordon in that instant.

First, Gordon somehow knew about the classified patrols Jack had run in Columbia. That revelation did not surprise Jack, given Gordon's running-buddies, but the information remained classified. Gordon had access. Assassination dirtied politicians' hands and put careers of military men issuing the orders on the line. Columbia was covert and classified, but Gordon knew what he and his team had done in Columbia. The men pulling the triggers coped with it well enough but today's political absurdities, moral vacillation, and just plain moral bankruptcy permitted no such clarity.

Jack McDonald possessed clarity. His country had enemies and would always have enemies. His country needed men with the will to kill them. This hard will resulted naturally from—clarity. Those lacking clarity hesitate, founder, and debate. The cocaine dealers weren't out to infect the U.S.; they just didn't mind seeing the United States stink and sink from the rot of drug-destroyed lives. They did not at all mind inflicting violence, even torture, to seize and keep their clutches on the money and power the drug sales lavished on them. Thus was the source and power of their "clarity." They did not hesitate, founder or debate. The Abu Sayyaf in the Philippines shared that quality: clarity. The times and the enemy required extreme measures. Jack saw himself as one of the extreme measures.

Clarity gave Jack McDonald the will to kill. Understanding the times gave Jack conviction; the violent world tested Jack's convictions; the tests proved his hypotheses: protect yourself and those you love; kill your enemies. If you don't, those enemies with clarity about their own evil convictions will enslave you.

Jack's missions in the Philippines and Columbia guarded the United States; his shots and demolitions stopped evil men cold. That sufficed. Jack did not ask for the public's understanding or acknowledgement. He had not killed for glory or his country's gratitude, which he understood he'd never have. He'd killed to protect. Plain and simple. Let others debate the nuances.

So, Gordon knew of the classified patrols. *What else did Gordon know?*

Second, Jack understood plainly that Gordon intended for him to "continue the mission" albeit in some other arrangement that Gordon was about to define.

Third, Gordon already *knew* that Jack was on board. That third realization surprised Jack. That meant that Gordon held even a deeper understanding of the soldier's mindset than Jack perceived.

Jack needed that level of understanding and knew only one way to it: live the life he'd been created for and trained for, and pursue the soldier's way. After all, how could he not?

Jack returned to the hanging question, and answered Gordon: "You already damned-well know why I'm here, don't you?"

"Yes, I suppose I do. I'd like to hear you say it, though. I'd like to learn from you what makes up the hearts of young officers. I *need* to hear you tell me. In this day of so many of my own countrymen turning their backs on America, I *need* you to remind me why it's worth it."

This took Jack aback. He'd not seen Gordon as a man who craved encouragement. Jack had worked out his own motivations long ago. He decided to answer with more than his usual clipped responses.

"Well, I'll tell you, then. I fight because I love this grand experiment. The America of Washington, Jefferson and Madison permits no would-be kings or committees of kings. America is gutsy that way.

"At least, America was gutsy. As much a threat as the newest wave of Muslim invasion is, the real question for America is different. The real question is whether we will give up our natural freedoms in return for the vain promise that the in-vogue crop of "intelligentsia," playing to our fear, will take care of us. Any experiment in people governing themselves is fragile enough. Add to that the dictator *de jour* from the outside and it's a wonder we've survived for 200 years. I want the grand experiment in freedom to live.

"I believe that people are too corrupt to be trusted with power over others, and that God made people to be free. America's founders manifested those truths. They fought to create such a country;

I fight to preserve it. Otherwise, the experiment in liberty known as the United States of America will fade into oblivion. More accurately put, tyrants—from within and without—will destroy the grand experiment and erase every trace that it ever existed. Freedom is anathema to tyrants. They can't tolerate free citizens. America affronts their tyrannical, evil souls. I, in turn, confront them."

Jack stopped, satisfied with his summary and grateful for Gordon's providing him the opportunity to review his own purpose.

44

*At last we are in it
up to our necks,
and everything is changed,
even your outlook on life.*
—Ernie Pyle

"Jack, do you remember the names, 'Martin and Gracia Burnham?'"

"Yes, I patrolled in the Philippines, you know. I not only know *of* them. I deployed there shortly after the Abu Sayyaf kidnapped them and held them for a year. Gordon, I spent nine months out of that year with Bobby, working with the Philippine Army patrols tracking Abu Sayyaf trying to set them free—and trying to kill their kidnappers. We did kill them, but Martin was killed during the fight."

"Do you remember what that young Muslim kidnapper told Gracia Burnham when she asked him *why* they had kidnapped the Burnhams and held them for a year?"

"Yes, I remember very well. I had that conversation with her, and read it later in her book. She wanted to know what all hostages want to know. 'What do you *want*? Will you stop fighting if you take back your island? Will you let me go and stop fighting if you take Manila and the entire Philippines? Will you stop fighting if you drive all infidels out of the South Pacific?' She asked one of her captors those questions. What he told her is a real message to the West. In a nutshell, he said they'd never stop fighting until all infidels are vanquished because 'Allah is for the world.' 'Allah is for the world.'

"I was back here on leave when the news came out that Martin had been killed. Few back here in the States even knew; none understood that Abu Sayyaf just started with Martin; they intended to finish only when the last non-Muslim was dead or converted. I knew she must be terribly hurt that her husband was killed on the front lines and no one back here even took notice. If he'd been a journalist instead of a missionary pilot, his demise would have featured on the news for a week.

"I made it a point to go talk to her. I had to. I told her what I had done, what sacrifice those young Philippine warriors had made, how I had spent the year not too far behind them, tracking the Abu Sayyaf dragging them around in the jungle.

"That young *Jihadist's* answer warns all of us: 'Allah is for the world.' Passive people of the world: they are coming to get you. Today the Philippines, tomorrow Israel, Europe next and then the United States.' They've made it real damned plain."

The men strolled along a ridge top, narrowing ahead to no more than a car's width. Jack admired the plunging valleys below, filled with branches fallen from the hardwoods casting canopy over the forest. Beautiful, it was. He heard a disturbed squirrel scold the passersby. He surprised the wild turkeys again, scattering them from their scratching in the earth. Jack loved the solitude, the grandeur, and the peace the woods offered.

Jack sighed as he looked into the trees. Like the rest of the world, evil men had bent the woods, too, to do their black deeds. The woods might also hide his country's enemies. For that reason, regardless of how groggy other men were in their frivolous pursuits, the country needed men like Jack to remain alert—and to act when required.

"Let's talk specifics," Jack said.

"OK, here's the deal," Gordon began talking about pay.

"Gordon, if you don't mind, we can skip pay and vacation days-off. What do you propose is to be my legal status?"

"You're a civilian, but paid by the Army. That's all I can offer you now. At some point, we might get you back into the Army or into the Department of Defense as a "contractor." Between then and now, you're off the books. Ortega and others have given up on Washington's ability right now to face up to our enemies. For better or for worse, you've fallen in with a band on a path of direct, covert, unofficial and maybe illegal action. That's where you come in."

"That's not good enough."

"Why not?" Gordon knew why not.

"You know why not. I'm willing to be the covert soldier. I'm not willing to be assigned to a cell at Fort Leavenworth for the rest of my life if all of this blows up and the top guys are looking to make me the scapegoat. What do you do for legal cover?"

"I'd like to show you that we've been promised pardons, in advance."

"OK, then show me."

"I can't."

"Why not?"

"Because, while I'd like to show you the guarantee, we have no guarantee. I'm in the same spot as you. Here's how I handle it. I go case-by-case. I take orders only from Ortega. I trust him and he's never tasked me with a mission I disagreed with. If that changes, I'll have to turn the mission down or get more detail. You will be well-paid, and you will need an 'escape clause.' Ortega's integrity and your 'escape clause' are your protections."

"What is this 'escape clause' you are talking about? What contingency contract can we strike when we have no contract?"

"Your escape clause is cash. You will be well-paid. Put money aside. Make a plan. Be ready to bug out."

"Gordon, we're here at your lodge sitting on lots of acres. You have a mailbox. You are 'established.' You don't look too prepared to give it all up and run to me."

Gordon sighed. "I got tired of running and living like a vagabond. If necessary, I could probably still pull it off, but, sooner or later, you want to put down roots and 'have a life.'"

Gordon stopped, took Jack by the shoulder and turned to face him, locking eyes. "That's the catch, Jack. You're *human*. I 'retired' but here I am in the middle of your being hired. I'm out of operations, but I'm not out. It could all come crashing down. Ultimately, our legitimate authority comes from the fact that Ortega gave us our orders. If he's not legal, then neither are we. You know the Code of Conduct too."

Gordon referred to the soldier's Code of Conduct, revised after the Korean War and Vietnam to accommodate the reality of soldiers being held and tortured. After Mi Lai, the Army took a hard look at the historical military approach that soldiers are to obey orders instantly, without question. The American soldier's duty to obey now is to obey "lawful orders." Orders the reasonable soldier would understand to be illegal should be disobeyed.

That's quite a burden for a 19-year-old to take on as he rounds a doorway in a darkened room, but it could be no other way; otherwise, men under orders get a pass for anything they do. That's what Nurnberg was about. "I was following orders." didn't excuse them and Jack knew that it didn't excuse Americans either. The German officers convicted knew what they were doing was immoral. The PFC with an M-4 in his hand watching a small car approach his barricade at high speed, driver ignoring commands and signs to stop, faced a far less clear dilemma. He still might find himself the victim of international politics, facing arrest warrants from some foreign government for killing occupants who turned out not to be suicide bombers. The soldier who expected his own country to come to his defense found out that he was easy to write off in the rush to appease the complaining diplomats. Military justice happened fast, too. Soldiers were like cops these days; soldiers needed their lawyer's phone number on speed-dial. Think fighter pilots hitting gondola cables here. Think friendly fire accidents. Soldiers guilty of atrocities during war should be hung, according to Jack's standards. Short of that criminal intent, soldiers deserved the mercy of a grateful nation, mediated by understanding commanders. Instead, these same soldiers often found themselves splashed in the headlines as the poster-soldiers for an "Army out of control." *Politics!*

"In that sense, Gordon, we're no different these days from the field commanders and troops with their guns in the fight, making snap decisions while the world dissects their every action afterward with the video looped endlessly on the nightly news. There may come a time when I would decline without written orders and assurances about the target."

"I've done that. Bear in mind that you and I are off the roster, unofficial, covert, and lower-than-low profile. Paul Ortega, on the other hand, is high profile, in the forefront, and stands to lose all. I've not committed him to writing unless I had serious questions about the mission. Jack, there's another aspect to all of this that you will have to consider and plan for," Gordon added ominously.

"Yes?" Jack suspected what was coming.

"Just like Ortega might decide someone has to go for the good of the country, someone, some day may decide that you have to go "for the good of the country" when it's really to salvage their own political position—their own ass."

Well, Gordon had certainly made it plain. It appeared to Jack that his alternative was to walk away, take his own gun out of the fight, and pretend that his nation was not under attack. That simplified the decision.

"I understand, Gordon. Just where do I come in, now?" Jack asked, ready to move this conversation toward the immediate.

"I don't know yet. I'm awaiting my orders, too," Gordon admitted, fretting just as much as Jack but not showing it.

The men climbed a hill leading back to the lodge, saying nothing.

"Gordon, I'm not happy with that answer, but I've been there before. I could use some recuperation time, anyway. In the meantime, I saw your range setup there in the valley. I assume I've got visitor's range rights in the meantime."

"Of course: help yourself to the targets in the bin. You'll find what you need, except for your own personal hearing protection and eye protection," Gordon answered, and Jack left.

45

Someday when peace has returned to this odd world I want to come to London again and stand on a certain balcony on a moonlit night and look down upon the peaceful silver curve of the Thames with its dark bridges.—Ernie Pyle

Jack's mind spun. So much happened so fast. First, he was out of the Army, then back in—sort of. In between, he'd begun a cruise, met a wonderful young woman he wanted to know better, fought off pirates and defended the "mission" literally in two ways! He'd lost his best friend.

Donna. Jack slung his range bag over his shoulder, strode down the trail to the range, and threw a twig into the woods in the direction of a fat gray squirrel. The squirrel chattered back—from the safety of the leafy heights. Jack continued down the trail, switching back sharply to "contour" the hillside, and emerged at the top of a narrow, grassy draw. Working his way down the draw, Jack emerged into a long, green, mowed valley, running perpendicular to the draw.

This valley, about 30 yards wide, stretched about 400 yards. Perfect. Gordon had stands for targets, posted against a ridgeline. From the far end of the valley, a shooter had a 400-yard shot—perfect for working with the M-4 carbine. More tricked-out carbines and rifles in 5.56mm could hit at greater ranges, but the 1 in 9" rifling twist in the barrel, combined with the standard issue, 55-grain, full metal jacket bullets fired by the 5.56mm round maxed out in practical effectiveness at just over 400 meters, giving the weapon its "maximum effective range."

The debate stewed, of course. Many argued for the military to return to the heavier .30 caliber rounds of earlier generations—World War I even into Vietnam. Some soldiers still preferred the M-14, firing its 7.65mm (or .308 caliber) round. The Army had just completed a detailed study on "lethality," the Army's frigid word for a hot, bloody potential. Jack read it, picked and chose what he wanted, and latched onto his own summary from one terse quote from Majors Dean and LaFontaine's study: "For the Soldier in combat, effectiveness equals death." Jack had always found the 5.56 a sufficient cause for morbid effect.

Jack stayed out of the debate. The M-4 carbine, and its parent, the M-16, had stood by him in jungle, desert, Europe, and in weather that ran the gamut. Always, it had worked for him and he saw no reason to change. Complainers just needed more training—and lube. It's a machine; got to have lube. Oil the damned thing.

Gordon's 400-yard range was fine and Jack would wring out his M-4 tomorrow. He laid the M-4 on Gordon's shooting bench. Today, Jack would work out with his 9mm Glock model 17, another reliable tool.

Jack thought of the steel and composite-plastic pistol as a tool as he whipped it from the Kydex holster and levered out the 17-round magazine. He worked the slide to eject the 18th round, always keeping his finger out of the trigger guard to avoid the "ND" (negligent discharge). Jack retrieved two other magazines charged with cheaper "target" ammunition, inserted one in the carrier on his belt (bullets facing forward and down in the carrier) and swiftly palmed the other into the waiting magazine well. He thumbed the slide release down, hearing and feeling the solid slide spring forward, chambering a round and making the gun ready.

He'd already oiled the Glock. Jack never enjoyed cleaning the things and swabbed it all out only about every 500 rounds—heresy to some. Jack did, however, slake the gun's thirst for oil routinely. Not that the Glock required it to function; he'd fired it when he had no oil and the result was the same: deadly, sustained fire with zero malfunctions. Jack loved his Glock. Oil improved the pistol's chances of staying in the fight and that's what Jack was all about: staying in the fight.

Hawks circled overhead, hoping the human would scare up a rabbit below. The sun began to dip toward the treetops on the ridge. Soon shadow would start to blanket the valley, secluded by ridges on three sides. Jack stapled up a pair of the brown, cardboard, "IDPA" silhouette targets he found in the bin and dressed them up with two, shot-up T-shirts piled in the bin with them. Two hundred rounds later and a lot of walking back and forth to check and patch, and Jack sat down on the log bench Gordon had placed nearby.

Donna. What could Jack do? He would not be around. He would never be around if he stayed on board with Gordon's crew. He could be killed and no one would ever know. He could be captured and disappear forever.

Jack had read about CIA officers John T. Downey and Richard G. Fecteau, the CIA agents shot down trying to get an agent out of Communist China. The Chinese threw them into prison and demanded their confession. They refused, and our Government would not acknowledge them as agents. This went on 20 years. That could be Jack's career.

Was it worth the risk?

"Why the Hell do I want to risk that?" Jack spoke aloud, to the squirrels.

While he walked "the road to come what may," the people he would be risking all for would be unaware. Many, if they knew, would oppose him. His nations' laws might declare him a criminal.

So, why would he even consider such a life? It seemed absurd, considered in this light.

Yet, Jack somehow *knew* that choosing this lonely soldier's life was far from absurd or immoral. He just couldn't quite reconcile the calling with his country's official rejection—and the scorn of many of his own fellow-Americans.

Donna. Even if Jack dedicated only a decade to his country's covert operations, he—and she—would be forever changed. She would, no doubt, find someone else. He would return different, altered by the tension, isolation, and carnage, justified or not. This thought of sacrificing a life with Donna plagued Jack's sense of duty more than any of the other doubts he had.

Jack looked at his M-4 resting there on the bench as he worked the pistol action to spread the oil. *If there is any symbol that deserves to be called the symbol of world peace, this is it.*

While the UN dithered and attended conferences, what the people in Darfur needed was the thousands of America's surplus M-14s and M1s to defend themselves. And, these poor people needed defenders: the starving oppressed of the world needed someone to stand up for them, fight for them, kill for them, and give them hope. If starving, diseased, and confronted by a band of AK-47-armed *Janjaweed*, topping the sand dune above your village on horseback, gathering for the attack, what would you rather see: a white truck from the U.N there to interview and take pictures, or a platoon of Jack McDonalds, all armed with M-4s and an unquestioning will to kill or be killed on your behalf?

The answer to this question had always been easy for Jack. Always. If people were fundamentally *different*, less *sinful*, then appeals to kinder nature might banish evil and stir the good. If wishes were horses, beggars might ride.

To Jack, history proved that being weak and unarmed only invited the evil to pillage. Strength and weapons kept them skulking at your borders, unchanged in nature, but modified in behavior: afraid to incur your wrath. Those without strength needed leadership and training; those without weapons needed arms. Training and equipping them took time; in the meantime, the weak and vulnerable needed men willing to protect them. They needed someone to step forth and fight for them. In Jack's mind, this is what American soldiers did.

Ah, there is the dilemma, thought Jack. *I'm not a soldier anymore.* Jack had pursued his violent calling legally. The Army is the unique, official, legal, "We will kill you if we need to," arm of the U.S. Government. It could go places and do things not permitted of private citizens. The 007-like license to kill distinguished homicide from murder and protected the soldiers. Congress and the Constitution justified the Army. Not so with Jack if he operated outside the law.

If that dilemma were not enough, this led Jack to the even greater dilemma. He was falling in love with Donna, and he believed she was falling in love with him. Choosing a life of outlaw service hardly struck Jack as congruent with growing a marriage—and a family. How could he possibly pursue both?

46

Early August

The Saya-dar noted the log onto the website by "The Professor." Date, time, location. Once the other "activate" messages went out, his was the only other message the operation required from the Control Team. The Saya-dar kept a log, a checklist, to assure that he had dispatched all. What counted was action. He was not worried about escape for the actors, or about failure of any particular attacker. It almost did not matter that some targeted community might escape judgment. The terror would reverberate anyway.

That was the cold beauty of terror. Terror's aftershocks plagued even those who had not experienced the terrorists. Terrorism would be like the old soldier's trick of slipping into the enemy camp, slitting the throat of one sleeping man, leaving his buddy untouched, but shaken by the morning's macabre discovery.

Public trials, if any of the men were discovered and captured, would cause continued reverberation, increasing the terror impact as the Faithful proclaimed America's evil and Islam's victory. Almost anything America did in reaction or response worked in Allah's favor. Success had many faces.

The sheer number of attackers—20—assured the desired result. Saya-dar raised the probability of success by using Faithful embedded long ago to assemble and stage fresh explosives. Saya-dar laughed at his employment of "just-in-time" manufacturing and inventory efficiency. That spate of activity in close conjunction to the attacks also increased the risk; however, the widely dispersed attack sites, and the lack of communication between the attacking cells, assured the inevitability of his victory.

The Islamic terrorist master-controller sat back, checked his log, and chafed, imagining the chaos soon to erupt in the news. He ordered his Captain to return to Havana Harbor. He would order his steward to stockpile food and then he would settle in, knowing that he would be unable to tear himself away from the television news programs on the big day. He expected to spend the day in celebration on his boat while he waited for his Florida-based agents to tell him who captained this *Arcturus*.

The 20 men already living in the United States likewise opened their e-mail to find their missions inaugurated. Kafele, one of the 20 chosen, and an Egyptian by birth, opened a free, publicly downloadable, peer-to-peer file-sharing program, and searched, keying in the memorized combination of random-appearing numbers and letters that no other user would enter either intentionally or by accident. The program displayed a single PowerPoint file as its only search result called "Uncle." He downloaded and saved the file to his desktop, checked it for viruses as was his careful practice, made a backup copy just for good measure, and double-clicked the file to start PowerPoint and open the file.

The opening slide displayed a deep blue background with the text: "Family Vacation Pictures." Kafele paged through the pictures quickly until a slide with a photograph of two, smiling, German-appearing tourists standing outside the Roman Coliseum appeared. Kafele thought about exactly what to do next, remembering the steps.

First, he clicked on the picture to make it active, and then deleted it, leaving a blank screen before him. Next, Kafele moused to the "View" menu on the menu bar and chose "Grids and Guides" from the selections. At that dialog box, he checked "Display grid on screen," approved the selection and returned to the blank slide, now overlain with grid lines. The Egyptian industrial chemist located the key grid like he would locate a map grid coordinate, reading first to the right, and then up, and found grid 3-A. He began clicking in the grid until the miniaturized text box appeared. Next, he used the mouse to enlarge the text box. He right-clicked on its frame and selected "Copy" from the drop-down menu. He opened a new Word document, pasted in the text box, and further enlarged it to almost page size. Selecting almost the entire page revealed the text box, which appeared empty, as blank as the slide had been. The seemingly innocuous PowerPoint family picture presentation concealed the digital equivalent of the World War II microdot, now enlarged before him, but still blank.

Kafele moved the mouse to select the entire contents of the box and then changed the text font setting to black. As if by magic, text formerly formatted as "white" now appeared written in English in the box and Kafele began to read his pages of instructions. The box could contain volumes. The device was virtually undetectable. All that the enemy agent living among us had to remember was the random sequence to search for, the grid designation and the picture that would overlay the "microdot."

Aside from the Koran passages, included, evidently to further inspire the reading terrorist, several pages of neat Times New Roman text chillingly detailed the device he was to improvise, and designated the place he was to use to manufacture it. He could do that. It was really a low technology task. His position gave him access to the conventional explosives he would use. He saved the recipe and encrypted it using PGP.

Kafele carefully picked his way past overhanging branches, worrying about getting stuck at the same time. The winding road, really a scraped flat on the hillside, was graveled with "crusher run" so that the crushed limestone gravel pieces locked together, packed down by rain and travel. The gravel hardened the road into a surface sufficient to carry a tractor-trailer load. He continued climbing the West Virginia hills, rounding a bend, then catching sight of the hilltop barn.

There was the parked trailer full of fuel. He did not know it, but a nervous truck driver had been already mission-tasked to pick the trailer up and get it back into circulation. He parked the car under an oak, opened the combination-locked barn door, and immediately spied the drums inside, with other components stacked next to them, sheltered by the barn's roof.

The old barn had an incongruous floor of poured, smoothly-finished concrete, a repaired, maintained steel roof, solid, lapped side boarding, and a reinforced but appropriate wooden door. Its humble, weathered exterior belied its strength. It was functional, solid, secured, and dry. The location certainly hid the barn out of the way. No one came to greet him. No one was around for at least a quarter mile. Birds peeped. Traffic sounds wafted upward from Interstate Highway 81 below and in the distance. A dog barked far away. He donned the rubber gloves, took his utility knife, and began opening bags. This was labor more than chemistry.

47

J ack emerged between the two shagbark hickories marking the top end of the road, and faced Gordon's lodge entrance, about 75 yards away. There was Donna, resting in the Adirondack chair, feet on the railing, reading. She saw him and waved. Jack waved back and walked toward her, climbing the wooden stairs to the deck in a mélange of emotions, spiced with ardor and confusion.

"Hi, wandering the woods?"

"Yes. I like Gordon's place. I've been doing some—target practice," Jack added.

Donna smiled at him understandingly. "Yes, I heard. Let's see, I heard a pattern: boom-boom—pause—boom. Is that right? Two right together, then a third?"

He was caught and it made Jack uncomfortable.

"Yes," he admitted, "You heard right. Two shots fired quickly, and then a third following up close behind," he only partially explained.

"Would that have been a 'controlled pair' fired to the vital area of the chest on those man-simulating cardboard targets, followed by a head-shot to make sure you've stopped him?" she asked, smirking, but oh, so gorgeously!

Well, I should have known. She is Gordon's niece.

293

"Good shot," Jack joked, pulling up a chair beside her. "Can we talk about something serious?" Jack asked, facing Donna and looking full at her, right into her eyes. She reddened a bit, he noticed.

"Yes, of course, Jack. I'm listening. Please begin."

Well, here it goes. "We've not known each other long, but what we've been through has maybe—sped along our getting to know one another. Would you agree?"

"Yes, I'd agree." *Could this be THE conversation?*

"Donna, so much is happening—has happened—and so much more remains to be done out there." (Jack swept his hand in an arc, pointing to the wooded ridges beyond, but, she comprehended, knowing he meant the world out there.) "And, I mean specifically, the kinds of things we've been caught up in." Here, Jack shifted uncomfortably. Donna saw him and understood his reluctance to refer to the violence, but she could not resist the tease.

"Well, Jack, I'm not sure what you mean. I've been caught up in a sea cruise gone bad, an innocent effort to get a fine young man out of a Communist dictatorship, and, finally, a pirate adventure. What, exactly, have *you* been caught up in?"

Jack opened his mouth to begin some variation on an elusive answer, and then realized she was pulling his leg. He laughed, and relaxed.

"Gordon and I have been talking…"

"That usually leads to some interesting places. Perhaps you'd best not say too much more," she admonished, but not in a way meant to end the discourse.

Nevertheless, as it is with young lovers the world over, fate and kin intervened. Gordon approached as if on cue: "Steaks are ready you two, come on in!" Gordon called from the open doorway, platter in hand.

The two stared at each other. Donna reached for Jack's hand, feeling his strength. She moved slightly closer.

"Jack, we'll talk more, OK?"

"Yes, Donna. I want to *return* to this conversation."

They lingered. The moment passed. The two rose and stepped into the lodge. The prepared table invited them, but Gordon stood silent, plates in hand, staring at the television.

"Again. They've done it again," Gordon murmured.

48

The Attack Team: Infiltration

Yasir had welcomed his selection. He did not know what all it would mean, but he knew the glorious end. They slipped him into Iran for training, which was simple enough. He already knew how to drive. The training village showed wood not old enough to be weathered, and was decorated with road signs and traffic signals, including the characteristic red, green, and yellow electric signals, some with arrows, found in America. Before coming to Iran, they had all driven the busier highways to help prepare for the American interstate highways.

Somali pirates ferried them from beaches to a waiting oil tanker. Yasir disliked these men, suspecting that they acted only for pay, and wondered if they would fall upon him and kill him, but they helped him up onto the larger ship and were gone. He could not have known that they briefly plotted his death, but feared the follow-up from whomever dispatched this young Palestinian to their shores. "Take the pay and do their job," the consensus directed, so they did not slit his throat. Instead, they had delivered him as ordered, and Yasir stood agape outside the orange and white facade that stretched about 40 yards to either side of him. He compared it with the photographs he was handed and agreed that the rehearsal site was well-prepared. Praise Allah!

ARCTURUS

A world away, just outside Washington, D.C., Carmine Riccolo hoisted his fourth cup of coffee for the day. He moused through the images once again. Routine satellite overflights had produced the photographs, and these had been printed and brought to him by the first tier analyst. Comparison done by computer-matching with earlier images showed what appeared to be a new village, about 140 miles northwest of Mogadishu.

Why? Construction of anything new in that part of the world always generated curiosity. Construction of anything looking like a town or village raised the question of whether or not the improvements were a training camp. If so, this was a most unusual training camp. He saw no rifle ranges, no obstacle courses, no trenches for the face-wrapped Jihadist to leap into and out of, "as seen on TV." Nothing he saw indicated barracks, tents, classrooms, ranges or any other sign of anything other than a small town.

The streets perplexed him. He returned to gazing at the streets. They just did not look *right*. Well, they did look right, but somehow they did not look right for this place, for this country. He could not identify what kept commanding his examining eye to return to the streets. They seemed too—complicated—for a village of this size. They had tried to match them to streets already mapped in some real town or city thinking that this might be a rehearsal area built to prepare for a major military operation, but the imagery program tasked with the job ginned out no match. The computer operator had run the matching program twice. Once took considerable time.

Carmine, the great-grandson of proud, depression-era immigrants from Genoa, loved his family, his country and his job with the NSA. His grandfather had returned to Italy with the U.S. Army, only landing well south of Genoa at Anzio, fighting northward until losing his left leg and half his face to the German guns at Monte Cassino—guns that were not supposed to be at Monte Cassino. "Bad intelligence, bad planning!" his grandfather had admonished many times.

Carmine had often marveled at the family history's relation to his own career, and felt the mysterious wonder of blood ties that demanded better intelligence for better planning. Sure enough, here he was, trying to give his country's soldiers the best intelligence in the world.

Yet, he was stumped. He wished he could get better images, but that was always the case. He wondered where the traffic for this road network was, but noted few tracks emerging from warehouses. It did not appear that the roads were used for anything. And what were those roughly rectangular open spaces with what appeared to be medians? They almost looked like—parking lots. Carmine laughed. What were they going to do, park 500 horses out there? Helluva flea market that would be. He leaned back, grasping his coffee mug reflectively, and puzzled.

All driver training was conducted at night. They had been told about the American satellite photography capability and, although the descriptions surely were exaggerated fears, they obeyed the lights-out orders and drove by moonlight only. Before parking the trucks in the warehouse garages at the end each night, one truck received an attachment that looked like a bundle of stiff brush, and then traversed all of the routes, sweeping away telltale truck tracks. By dawn, the streets appeared ready for business, but deserted.

Carmine slid the photographs away onto his desk and rubbed his eyes. He flagged the village's location for comparison photography. He would follow through with this instinct. There was something about the streets that was different from the usual Iranian village layout. It looked more western.

Yasir's training included worship sessions attended by other faithful, other martyrs, and the teachers steeped them further in the Koran's heart-warming messages. He knew they were being reinforced for the task before them and he felt he needed it.

Training included rudimentary Spanish lessons and English lessons. They memorized American traffic signs and drove a course with signals they would encounter in the belly of the Great Satan. They fired a variety of pistols, being told that they would each be armed once in America, but no one knew yet which kind of pistol he would be supplied with. So, they fired Glocks, Berettas, Smith and Wesson semi-automatics, Sigs, and Taurus revolvers, among others. This was familiarization firing without emphasis on marksmanship. They had all already been trained to shoot, attaining proficiency with the AKM and with pistols, so this training would equip them to be able to operate a variety of weapons, shortening the time needed to learn the new gun, regardless of its make.

Besides, any shooting they would do would almost certainly be at point-blank range. Their instructions were to obey the laws, stay within the speed limits, but to shoot to kill a law enforcement officer if stopped, verify his death by a head shot, and drive calmly away.

Yasir and 21 other men kept to crude quarters across the Atlantic, landing on foreign soil they knew to be Venezuela, but never saw the country during daylight. Instead, their single Venezuelan liaison ushered them at night into and out of a warehouse where they then changed ships and boarded an oil tanker bound for the United States.

Kept secluded from the crew, they were each furnished a leather wallet already loaded with the kinds of papers that would be found in an American's: in addition to the driver's license with his likeness, the wallet included a credit card, a bank ATM card, two video rental store cards, pictures of two children, and even a library card issued in the locale where their respective attacks were to take place, all documents counterfeit but realistic. A few business cards advertising them as handymen and a pink card making a dental appointment added the clever finishing touches, designed to diminish any unease that might be plaguing a law enforcement officer.

Plainly, the Logistics Team members responsible for this cover were familiar with American life. Yasir could not know, but in order to mask the attack locations, agents from all over had obtained the cards over years, mailing them to a single location where they were either stored for use as they were, or where they served as templates for forgeries. The driver's licenses, while counterfeit, displayed numbers identical to those held by other Middle Eastern men whose countenances closely matched the infiltrators'.

It had really been so easy. The Americans focused on their Radiation Portal Monitors, looking for the much-feared nuclear bomb. No Mobile Gamma Scanning Device would detect Yasir and the others. Saya-dar's brilliance shone through; if the Americans were looking for nuclear weapons of mass destruction, then smuggle in human weapons of mass destruction. Just as in Spain, bypass the stronghold and laugh at it. Strike how the enemy least suspects you.

The Venezuelan oil tanker entered Mobile Bay early in the evening, cruised the 40 miles from the bay's entrance, by Fort Morgan, to the wharf district, where it docked, and began unloading its cargo as usual. Its Captain had already submitted the required Passenger/Crew list 24 hours in advance, indicating the crew who would go ashore. Crewmen's Landing Permits waited.

The 22 were not on the list. It was simple enough for the men to emerge from their compartment deep in the hull and slip over the side at 3:15 a.m., out a low hatch disguised as a crudely bolted-on hull patch. They boarded a small craft, rode up the bay to an obscure boat-ramp away from the heightened scrutiny of the Port Police, and then filed into the back of the truck driven there by their liaison. This liaison's instructions had been to drive the truck to the ramp, park close by, unlock the back of the truck, and sit in the cab until a man knocked on his door and greeted him with "God send you on your way." The men quickly clamored into the back where all sat quietly, praying and swaying as it left the dock, headed for a nearby warehouse.

The warehouse was empty but for a stack of old wooden pallets of no apparent connection to the mission and some used couches, chairs, and blankets. The men slept. Shortly after daylight, a woman brought bread and cheese and delivered cases of plastic bottles of water. Her face remained covered and she spoke no word to the men. The 22 men studied the Koran during the day until, one by one, a man appeared at the door, called their number, and guided them into a car.

49

Mid-August
The American South

Yasir dozed, prayed, and rode northward from Mobile along I-65, across lower Alabama to Montgomery, changing to I-85 and on to Opelika and West Point, where the men crossed the Chattahoochee River into Georgia, bypassing Fort Benning, Georgia, the Army's Infantry Center. Yasir passed by, unaware.

"Some other time…," Saya-dar had thought during route planning, passing up the inviting target. Besides, the Americans did not care enough about their military to get too upset if he confined his attacks to armed forces. They hardly noticed when the *Cole* was bombed and their sailors killed. Saya-dar had viewed the attack on the Pentagon on September 11, 2001, as the greater success, proving that the Faithful could rain death even on the headquarters of The Beast. He marveled that the Americans hardly noticed the fiery deaths of their military defenders, obsessing on the civilian casualties at the World Trade Center. That successful attack caused dramatic physical results, proving that dedicated Muslim terrorists could terrorize even the symbols of American power, but the attack caused disappointing psychological results, making this Islamic terrorist re-think the American character. Plainly, target selection required more subtle analysis.

The two men continued northeasterly to the outskirts of

Atlanta, where they skirted the busy core of the city on its also busy I-285 wide bypass, exiting onto I-20, driving east for about 15 miles, taking a two-lane highway in Conyers, Georgia, past the South River Gun Club, and into a driveway between pines that masked the land behind the trees.

The driver stopped at a barn hidden in the pines and wasted no time when Yasir stepped out. Nodding to Yasir, he left immediately, as he had been instructed. Yasir stretched his sore muscles. He longed for his journey to paradise, but the travel so far had been less than comfortable. He keyed in the combination, opened the door and beheld his chariot to Allah. The driver had pointed out the target location on their way. Yasir timed the drive as taking only 15 minutes. Easy. Yasir watched his driver speed away. The man was eager to disassociate himself from the martyr.

Yasir looked around at the tall pine trees and red earth. Strange land. It was quiet by the barn, although he could hear traffic on the two-lane highway. He looked at his watch. All attacks were set for 3:00 p.m., Eastern Time, the next day to give the more far-flung men time to reach their destinations, and to assure just the right time of day even though scattered across the time zones. In the truck cab, he found, as he expected, a Tarik 7.62mm pistol of the kind favored by the Iraqis. He also found the food and water, a pillow, two blankets, and a Koran his instructor had told him would await his arrival. He slaked his thirst and stuck the pistol in his waistband, checking chamber first and finding it made ready.

Yasir flipped open his cell phone and confirmed sufficient signal. He sent one text message to the number already on the dial pad: "RD." Then he thumbed the phone off. He was to sit in the cab, with the barn door closed until attack time.

He obeyed for two hours. Growing hot, bored, and curious, Yasir looked around, walked past a small, elevated water tank, into

the relatively open woods, and located a secluded patch of pine needles that looked inviting. He returned to the barn, retrieved a bottle
of water and a blanket, and walked back to the pine needles, where
he kneeled down, prayed, and then slept.

The 22-man *Jihad* could not know, but their drivers were
nervous, long-time residents of America. The compartmentalized
mission of these drivers was simply to pick the men up at a precise
time (times were staggered), drive them to their respective staging
areas and drop them off. That was all. Some drove only for the
morning. Others needed two days to reach deep into America.

Most targets were located in the Midwest and South, in keeping with Saya-dar's goal to strike the heartland and to keep driving
times abbreviated; longer drives meant greater risk of discovery
either during the drive or while those with shorter drives waited.
Each staging area was another piece of farm property with a small
barn or storage building, such as might be seen anywhere in the
country. A graveled driveway snaked through woods or around
rocks, depending on the terrain, working the trucks to garage doors
locked with a pushbutton, combination lock. The men had either
memorized the number, or simply kept the door code in their wal-
lets. Pushing the buttons in the correct order, they opened the door
and found a delivery van styled truck.

The trucks were of various makes, all American, with blocky
cargo vans bolted to their frames, painted in different nondescript
colors. None exhibited any lettering or logo. Each bore license
plates from a different state. The men had learned pertinent
American state automobile law and procedures, and knew that each
state charged a tax—a license fee—and licensed operation of the
vehicle. They were to check the metal plate screwed to one end of
the vehicle or both, depending on the state, to assure that its expi-

ration date had not yet arrived. Agents already inside the United States would have the trucks ready, licensed, serviced, and filled with fuel and they would not have to worry about making these arrangements; a logistics team had that responsibility.

Each checked the cell phone's clock, noted the time, made his check-in call, and settled into the truck cab to wait, finding a pistol, a sack of food and several bottles of water—and a Koran. If anything went wrong during these stages, the Attack Team members were to use their cell phones to make a single telephone call in the clear and either abort the mission, or receive alternate instructions from the Control Team. Otherwise, they would power the phones up 30 minutes before departure time to check for any message conveying instructions.

Their times to move came at staggered intervals and hours, but they were all to converge on their respective assigned parking lots 10 minutes before attack time. The 10 minutes was a buffer allowed for travel-time error, and increased the probability that each chosen man would attack simultaneously. Saya-dar knew that exact surprise was not necessary; strategic surprise was an almost certainty. Even if half an hour separated two attacks, by the time a stunned public grasped that it needed mass reaction, it would be too late. In practicality, as much as 45 minutes to an hour might separate attacks and still achieve surprise. However, Saya-dar liked the idea of simultaneous attacks and had carefully pre-positioned the men to achieve that effect. For that reason, each of their respective targets had been chosen, in part, because it was a short drive from the local barn staging area.

Yasir awoke as the Day of His Death dawned. He faced east, and prayed. He felt at peace. The day dragged by. At noon, he opened the barn door and started the truck. It started immediately, of course. He shut the engine off and sat in the cab, reading the Koran. At precisely 20 minutes until 3:00, he started the truck, drove it forward clearing the door, parked it still warming up, climbed out, shut the barn door, and got back into the cab.

Yasir drove out onto Klondike Road, eyed the South River Gun Club warily as he passed it again, halfway suspecting an ambush or sniper shot, and arrived at the Biz-R-Market parking lot within minutes. He selected the parking lot lane that led straight into the Garden Center entrance, which stood just where he had been told it was, and parked the truck.

Minutes dragged by. At 2:57, Yasir retrieved the hand-held electrical switch wired to the truck's van contents. At 2:59 p.m., Yasir turned the key, started the truck engine, and drove forward slowly. Pedestrian shoppers on their way to and from the store strolled maddeningly slowly across his lane of travel. A driver backed out in front of him, causing him to stop. She waved in apology and he waved back.

Another driver to his side appeared irritated, impatient at being blocked temporarily from leaving the lot. Yasir smiled at her. As soon as the backing driver was gone, Yasir floored the gas pedal, shifted into second as the truck jumped the curb by the lawn mowers on display, and ran down the bewildered, elderly greeter frozen at the door in disbelief. He plowed forward, deeper into the store, scattering merchandise just as planned.

Yasir held his last breath in exhilaration. He turned the wheel a quarter turn to the left. The front bumper bulldozed plants and bags of soil. He cleared the goods stacked in the center of the floor, glanced at the shocked cashier in the corner of his visual field, his attention caught by the clerk's leaping over the counter. Yasir ran down a mother with a small boy strapped into the shopping cart as the mother stood where she had been trying to decide whether to buy a gas or a charcoal grill. The truck slowed to a halt as it stalled on stiff shelves and piles of merchandise piling up between the truck's grill and the target concrete-block corner, beyond which lay the core of the store.

Yasir made eye contact with a woman staring straight at him as she still held her cart. As he looked at Janice Harbison, whom he believed he was about to dispatch to Hell, he shouted *"Allahu Ahkbar!"* and pressed the red button switch.

"Between Halloween and Thanksgiving," the landscaper had advised: "That's the only time to plant shrubs." Odd. Nurseries obviously did big business in the early spring, when homeowners began to stir, picturing a magazine-cover yard in their minds. By mid-fall and early winter, who cared? Grass was browning, leaves falling, and holidays beckoned.

This year, though, Janice Harbison would do it right. The azaleas would live, planted during dormancy and ready to root when warming spring sun first stirred its life. She hooked the borrowed utility trailer to her van and puzzled over why the lights didn't all work. No matter; she'd buy all of the tools, fertilizer, and bags of topsoil and ready herself to pounce on the planting season when just the right day arrived.

Janice swung the trailer onto Highway 20 outside of Conyers, Georgia, and, minutes later, turned into the Biz-R-Market parking lot. She continued toward the Garden Center, ubiquitously on the end of the store as she approached. Janice watched other drivers hover around the parking spaces closest to the storefront and shook her head. People who plainly need the exercise will stop traffic, delay others, and sit just to park 15 feet closer to the building. *Good grief!*

The parking lot to the front of the Garden Center lacked the supplies and goods present outdoors there during the busier spring season and there were ample spaces. She chose two vacant spaces, further from the building, end to end, so that she could pull her trailer through the one, leaving the van in one with the trailer occupying the space behind. She would need room to load some bags of soil and also for some bales of straw to mulch.

A short walk took her past the greeter, into the store's outer area with some plants and gardening supplies stocked on shelves. These were stocked with insect spray, fertilizer, hoses, sprayers and all manner of outdoor lawn care supplies. Janice needed a new sprinkler and now was the time to get it; she might yet save those bushes she'd planted a bit too late in the spring. The weather had been so dry lately. She'd rescue the wilting ones and be ready for the optimum planting season this time. One of those reciprocating adjustable sprinklers would work.

Janice Harbison searched the aisles and located the item she was looking for. Turning toward the checkout area, she began thinking about what to prepare for supper, when her plans were interrupted by a crash, followed immediately by a commotion at the Garden Center entrance. Shelves toppled and merchandise flew. Rounding the aisle, Janice, a nurse, saw the front end of a delivery van-sized truck and instantly reasoned that someone had lost control of the truck and run it into the store! She fleetingly thought about the greeter and the cashiers toward the front, and figured they would need emergency treatment. Then, she heard what sounded like a triumphant shout that she did not understand, and looked up into the eyes of a young man perched behind the steering wheel above her in the truck cab. Yasir's already faraway expression framed her last perception on earth, as a roiling shock wave of flame and debris tore her body apart.

The truck bomb detonated. Some of its components ignited as they sprayed outward. The truck's full tanks of gasoline ruptured as the shock wave caused a roiling inferno of igniting gasoline to roll across the floor. Garden equipment made of plastic melted, baring its metal components as flying, shattered shards. Shelves bent, broke, and flew like spears. Fragments shredded everyone nearby the blast.

To the truck's front, the concrete block walls broke, propelled by the blast behind. The former wall fragments flew like massive, jagged cannon balls. Later, the FBI's crime scene analysts would find concrete chunks 100 yards from the explosion site. Yasir had turned the store's aisles into a killing zone, blasting away the store's interior sections, and wounding people on the far side of the building. Finally, the blast and heat warped or melted the supporting structure in the explosion's vicinity, and the roof collapsed, dropping beams and heat-and-air units on patrons.

Biz-R-Market success is beyond arguable. Outside the largest cities, Americans would have to try pretty hard to locate themselves more than 30 minutes from a Biz-R-Market. Many live only 5 or 10 minutes from the stores. No doubt, management-science types consult with the property buyers to pinpoint the precise population epicenter for a particular area.

Given the dispersed locations of the staging areas, but almost identical, identifiable, orange and white facades, the stores had suggested themselves to Saya-dar as he pondered which targets to select. Brilliant! Rather than having to issue customized instructions for each bombing, he added a degree of uniformity to the attack plans that reduced error. The stores were always easy to find and always obvious.

Almost everyone shopped there at one time or the other, many several times per week. The stores added groceries and gasoline, drawing in even more customers. Biz-R-Market had become iconic, thought the Muslim, symbolic of America. Striking the Jewish family-owned stores hit America in a way far more powerful than hitting the World Trade Center, a place most Americans had never seen and could not identify with. Who could not identify with Biz-R-Market? Even its sullen, jealous detractors shopped there.

A single delivery truck parking in the lot for a brief time would go unnoticed until attack time. Each bomber could start his engine and complete the attack within 2 minutes, achieving with as much certainty as possible the simultaneous truck bombings of stores in 20 locations spread among American states.

Thus, Saya-dar would seek out Americans where they live, where they felt safe. He would kill them deep within their territory, and they would never again know from where Allah's faithful would fall upon them. In the bloody process, he would punish the impudent Jews of America who thought they might escape the eventual Islamic massacre when the Faithful drove the Jews from Palestine forever.

The bomber very simply aimed his truck at the Garden Center entrance, a structure with wide doors and an open floor leading deeper into the store, then gained speed down the parking lot lane, crashed through the entrance, jerked the wheel to the left and continued to veer into the corner of this section. Ordered to keep driving until the truck either ground to a halt, or made it to the corner, he would then detonate the explosive charge wired both to the truck battery and to a spare battery (for good measure). The conventional explosives in turn, ignited the explosive mixture of diesel fuel and fertilizer, firing a massive explosion that, in turn, converted merchandise into fragments. Mehdi's creative water-jacket tamping covered and surrounded the barrels of fuel-fertilizer explosive, forming closely around the sides of the truck, over the barrels, and at the back door, concentrating and directing the explosive force forward, toward the store's inner aisles. Other agents had wondered why Allah would demand 10, readily commercially available, waterbed mattresses delivered to each staging barn. The Professor's innovations turned the trucks into aimed cannon.

The Garden Center typically sold insecticide, herbicide, and fertilizer, all which Saya-dar had hoped (but had not tested) would enhance the fearful impact of the attack. The powerful improvised explosives should collapse at least portions of the store roof, killing many of the store's customers. When they tested this plan on the concrete block, steel-truss, roofed structure they had built as the sole experiment, they celebrated the success: the truck had burst through the outer doors, veered left by accident, and detonated in the corner, to the driver's front and left. This corner, built of stacked concreted blocks, jutted into the store near the checkout counters. The corner, with the exploding truck behind it, broke and flew forward in an arc like a Claymore mine, like cannons set in a crescent. This swath of jagged concrete block smashed everything in its path, well into the structure. After walking through the rubble and conferring, they modified the original plan, which had been to crash through the inner doors by the cash registers, impressed with the destruction caused by detonating in the corner of the concrete block structure.

Multiply that impact across America at the modest sized cities and towns Saya-dar had chosen. All 20 truck bombs detonated. The two spare bombers died along with their fellows, superfluous since all 20 made the journey without illness, injury, or detection.

ARCTURUS

From Gettysburg, Pennsylvania to Castle Rock, Colorado; from Corvalis, Oregon to Warsaw, Indiana, and at towns interspersed in between, full stores became cauldrons of death, and all at once, with no more than five minutes separating the attacks. Saya-dar, the Iranian, the Jihadist, the Muslim Caliphate's own "Tip of the Spear," had expected at least five attacks to abort for various reasons. All Attack Team martyrs succeeded as planned, with one exception, and that one had still carried out his mission.

51

War makes strange giant creatures out of us little routine men who inhabit the earth.
—*Ernie Pyle*

A t the Warsaw, Indiana location, Carson Huskey had driven to the store to buy some padlocks. Huskey built log homes, so popular in the northeast Indiana lake district area as vacation getaway cabins, but he had lately been plagued by construction site theft. He was not amused by the Sheriff's Department's laconic observation that such thefts had reached epidemic proportions, and he determined to act on his own. He'd like to stake out the site with his shotgun; only the prospect of spending his life in jail and losing everything he'd ever worked for in the perp's family's wrongful death suit moved him to more passive security measures. No doubt the worthless trash stealing him blind would be trumpeted as a model citizen, father, son, and pillar of the community to justify a judgment of millions. Carson, on the other hand, would be portrayed in closing argument as a madman. He could hear the ambulance-chaser now, making his final argument at the trial. Carson would end up like that British farmer who got tired of being robbed and—at the seventh burglary—shotgunned the professional thieves: Tony Martin went to jail—and was denied parole. It appeared that a man's home was no longer his castle.

So, instead, Huskey simply pulled off the highway for chore-stop number 1. He'd swing into Biz-R-Market, park at the less busy

Garden Center end, dash in, buy some locks to secure the new gates he had put up, and get back to work.

Huskey had parked his Ford F-250 truck, gotten out, and begun walking down the asphalt lane toward the Garden Center end of the store, which was not far from the hardware anyway, when a bike like his grandson might like caught his eye. He stepped over the curb, and stood admiring the racy bicycle, marveling at the modest price, when he heard a big engine "gunned" behind him somewhere in the parking lot.

Turning automatically, he spied a yellow delivery truck, front bumper raised up as if it was a dragster just off the line, gaining speed, roaring straight at him from about 50 yards away.

Stunned into momentary inactivity, he stared at the wild-eyed young man behind the wheel. *Guy looks foreign.* Near the front of the lot, about 35 yards from Huskey, someone in an old Oldsmobile coupe backed out without looking and the truck screeched to a halt. What the Hell?

Then, he caught the young man's eye. The truck driver's face contorted in hate and rage as the Olds driver lolled into forward and drove off, taking her time and completely oblivious to the near crash.

Huskey did not like this one bit. Something was bad wrong. That inference was confirmed when, with the car out of the way, and Huskey gaping down the middle of the traffic aisle, the young man waved a pistol stuck out through the door where he had the window rolled down, and started firing at Huskey, lurching the truck forward, racing the engine, all at the same time. Huskey reacted as he had trained.

Carson Huskey carried a Springfield Armory, American-made, "XD Compact" in .45 caliber, loaded with 10 in the magazine and 1 in the chamber. Huskey toted the gun legally, authorized by his handgun carry permit issued by the state of Indiana. He had been one of the first to apply for the permit. He had sworn that, when the state got its head screwed on straight and respected its citizens enough to let them choose to go armed, he was not going to miss the opportunity to carry legally. He pictured himself as a good, solid, Hoosier, from a good, solid state, and both were true. However, the more complete truth was that he had kept a pistol handy for years anyway, but now was no longer made into a criminal. Most of the time, he carried a Smith & Wesson "J-frame" .38 caliber "snub-nosed" revolver, but he had staked out one of his construction sites the night before and had holstered the bigger weapon onto his belt beneath his loose fitting work coat rather than storing it in his glove compartment. The XD was new, but he'd fired 1,000 flawless rounds through it to put it through its paces.

Better training would have prompted him to move aside to available cover while drawing to fire. Too much range time, firing at motionless, non-threatening, cardboard silhouette targets, had taught him to firmly plant his feet, square off against the target, draw, complete a solid two-handed grip, right arm locked, left hand pulling the gun back toward his body, eyes both open with the sights lined up. Huskey's marksmanship was good—very good; his tactics just somewhat lacked the edge of practical realism.

Time froze in slowly advancing frames. Huskey was unable to acquire the priority high-center of the driver's chest for the dashboard that partially hid the driver; he instantly adjusted to head-shots as the truck built speed and charged him like an elephant. He fired the customary pair of shots and then continued firing as the truck bore down on him, pressing the trigger as soon as the sights re-aligned, firing a total of 11 rounds as what shooters call a "non-standard response" or NSR. While his form of practice pre-determined that he would stand in the path of the charging truck, his range time served him well where his accuracy was concerned. His last thoughts as the truck plowed into him were satisfaction over lethal head-shots well-made and "Is this ever gonna hurt!"

Carson Huskey tensed and jumped up as the truck slammed into him, intending to roll off the hood, but his broken-rib pain was short-lived; as the young martyr died from the well-placed multiple bullets to his head, his slumping body weight pressed the switch anyway and the truck erupted.

Later, witnesses close enough to see but far away enough to survive the explosion, whose attention had been commanded by the engine noise and gunshots, would verify Huskey's heroism. Lives were saved they all agreed, after learning how the other attackers fared. Huskey became local legend, particularly at the range.

Saya-dar later read the account, but did not care. He had achieved his terror anyway. Even America's prepared, armed men could not completely stop Allah's rain of death. He liked it. Saya-dar's only regret was that he could not watch all news accounts simultaneously from all of the different locales.

Citizens with cell phones immediately called 911, which, in turn, dispatched fire trucks, ambulances, police, and pretty much every first responder available. As officer reports filtered back, emergency coordinators across the country began to send in what they assumed were isolated reports to their respective state emergency management organizations.

It took time to begin to correlate that identical attacks had wreaked havoc all across the country. It was hours later that night when the nation finally comprehended the number, locations, and scope of all of the attacks, and concluded that Muslim terrorists had once again launched an all out assault on the United States of America, and from inside our own country.

Reactions varied widely. Government went into near-panic mode at all levels. No official wanted the ineptitude exhibited at the municipal and state level after Katrina to be his own legacy. No one knew where bombers might strike next. Phone lines jammed as the chatty sought release in conversation with loved ones.

Then, streets went silent as all sat by their television sets as people excluded all outside action and chained themselves to the TV news programs. Some cleaned rifles and checked ammunition. Some cried. Some were paralyzed with fear. Some were so damned angry that they stone-cold wanted to kill. Young men went to their rooms, rifled through the debris in their dresser drawers, or cardboard boxes, looking for that recruiting brochure they had picked up and dismissed. Bewilderment fogged most; much of America did not know what to do.

The President spoke briefly and reassuringly, and even eloquently, Saya-dar assessed, but the day belonged to Allah. America belonged to Allah. The world belonged to Allah. "Allah is for the world," Saya-dar declared aloud.

For the first time, Saya-dar saw himself as Allah's man, Allah's emissary heralding a message of judgment on the degenerate West (forgetting about his own sins). He had been raised to wealth and learning for this purpose. The Iranian known only as The *Saya-dar*—Farsi for the *Shade*, the *Protector*, but also, in a double *entendre* manner, bearing the more sinister meaning, The *Demon-Possessed*—sat back, swirled his iced Margarita, and foresaw America's destruction at his own hands. For America, he loomed as the Shade of Death reaching far over its homes, not the comforting shade of a green tree, lovingly spreading its limbs over the Protected Faithful.

The harbor visits stopped. He let his fishing gear lie. The ward brought his meals. He ordered no more rum and tequila drinks. He thumbed through the long-neglected Koran retrieved from his shelves and majored on the verses written early: the ones about infidels and what believers should do to infidels. The options included enslaving them or taxing them. He was in no mood to tax them. We were far beyond that.

52

Early August
After the coordinated attack
against Americans

Dark rage descended over Jack. Once again, a conspiracy of Muslim men had butchered Americans, in their own country! The outwardly isolated and ineffective bin Laden had warned them and now it had happened. This attack was not what they had looked for. Between the most recent tape, the discovery of the polonium canister, and Saya-dar's call to Casteneda, the Islamic devils had gotten them all watching for the attack that did not come. Instead of some dirty bomb detonation at the Mall in Washington, or in Los Angeles, the bastards had waited a few weeks after losing the canister and then blind-sided America on a Saturday afternoon where it least expected terrorists to show up. *Brilliantly diabolical*, Jack grudgingly conceded.

Donna, Gordon, and Jack absorbed the cable news commentary, and surfed the Internet for all facts available, but, in the early hours of one morning, Jack stood up, shook off lack of sleep, shut down the computer, turned off the television, and went to bed.

Waking to the music of the morning, playing as before as if his America had not been treasonously attacked, Jack retrieved his 9mm, spread newspaper, and disassembled it on the coffee table. He checked its parts, and lubricated the bearing surfaces. He bagged up 300 rounds of ball ammunition—"hardball" for range practice, not the optimum for killing enemies—and returned to Gordon's pistol range. Jack renewed his pistol training with sharpened purpose, switching hands to exercise the "support hand" as well as practicing his familiar draw-and-shoot sequences, moving back and forth as he shot. Besides feeling good, it prepared him for whatever role he was about to play in killing the men responsible for this.

Jack removed his earplugs and set them on Gordon's self-built shooting bench. He scanned the trees, appreciating the wrist-thick wild grapevines draped from the oak limbs. He heard squirrel-rustling sounds, and peered for their lumps of leaves high in the trees, revealing their nests. Serene, but surreal.

There is no peace. The peacemakers may be blessed, but they are so few. Jack threw his range bag into the back of his pickup truck, pushed the buttons to start some New Orleans style blues on one of his favorite CDs, and left the range, knowing that once he left Gordon's he would not return for awhile—maybe never.

When the first responders began to learn of the other attacks, someone had finally realized that this was a major terrorist attack and had alerted all to test for radiation. No one anticipated a dirty bomb in mid-America and no initial teams had checked for radiation except for a team at the Oswego, New York attack site. The New York emergency responders had been practicing with their equipment and a sharp young woman powered up her Geiger-counter as the ambulances removed the wounded. Nothing. She reported that to her supervisor who, in turn, reported to New York Emergency Management. The coordinator at NYEM grasped how remiss they had all been and reported to FEMA, where the word was then put out to all state EMAs to check for radiation. None. Anywhere. The entire grieving nation breathed relief.

While the various government jurisdictions (and some agencies like SOCOM with no authority at all to investigate) thought more about what mayhem loomed next, the rest of America inverted its entire attention to the truck bombings. By now, the stages were predictable. Party leaders would make speeches while they tried to figure out which way the political winds would blow. Appeasers reluctantly muted their message for the time, letting the national angst blow over. Even rants against Halliburton subsided for the time, with the exception of a few kooks who blamed Halliburton for the attacks. Halliburton had trucks. The bombers used trucks. Bingo. Ergo: Halliburton did it.

Soon, voices would demand congressional hearings. Senators would pose questions to witnesses in long-winded, demeaning speeches. The national anger that should have united all Americans against the nation's sworn enemies would implode into an internal turmoil, something like the incubating creature in *Alien*, eating away at the guts of the being in which it lived until it destroyed the host. It would be hilarious to a detached observer.

The Iranian secluded himself in his lounge and watched them all, fascinated, in celebration of what he had wrought: terror; confusion; infighting. The Americans majored in murky language and vague concepts. Things like "standing in solidarity" with the grieving families. What did that mean? What good was that? What action was taken? What enemy was killed? None. He would have thought that Americans would be angry—righteously angry, more war-like, and would focus this collective anger to get revenge, and to eradicate its enemies. The 9-11 attacks proved otherwise. Oh, sure, some more young men showed up at the recruiting offices; the entire country should have joined up en masse. Flags flew, but not at all houses. Leaders called the nation to rally, but others produced and marketed movies denigrating Washington.

Some insisted on all out war, but others cautioned the need for international consensus. While that reliable percentage steeled their hearts with cold resolve and set to the ruthless business of war, the rest of the country got on with its frivolous ways and picked through the enemy's havoc looking for methods to advance their own selfish political agenda.

Predominantly, instead of spurring on endeavor to carry the battle to America's enemies, the news programs grasped for any information about the truck bombings that had already occurred. *Fools!* thought Saya-dar. They could do *nothing* about the destruction across America at its stores. Among the experts appearing on news programs giving interviews, only a few voices warned that this attack revealed America's lack of resolve, leaving it open to future attack. The country fixated on what *had* happened, not on securing its perimeter, you might say.

Biz-R-Market instituted new security procedures. Too late. Like the 9-11 aircraft guided missiles, that assault on its retail centers would not happen again. The news about the company's new security procedures did, however, produce one constructive result for Saya-dar.

Saya-dar logged onto his trading account site, and clicked on his "Watch" list. Biz-R-Market's stock price had already plummeted as if Saya-dar openly threatened to chase after the retailer in some sort of blind frenzy. Biz-R-Market was safe now. It served its purpose. Surviving family members filed lawsuits against the retailer, causing its stock to crumble even more. It seems that, while no one foresaw coordinated attacks against the retailer, trial lawyers complained that its management should have emanated with superhuman prescience, foreseen itself as a target of Islamic terror, at all of its many locations (worldwide) and patrolled with MP-5-armed platoons of orange and white-vested Biz-R-Market Security Corps.

Absurd! Saya-dar chose the popular retailer precisely because it would have seemed to the Americans to be a most unlikely target. He reveled in the reaction.

Saya-dar chose a strike price and keyed in a substantial limit order. He would buy when it bottomed out and make another killing when it recovered. He should have foreseen this and placed a put order—not too large; he'd not want to appear to have been "insider" trading.

Gradually, a picture formed. The Attack Team members were publicly identified by their own proud family members, not by American investigative technique. Forensics teams recovered pieces of all of the trucks but were unable to trace them. They looked for rental records, and canvassed all rental agencies to report, and all agencies scoured their records, but no rentals came to light. No one discovered the Venezuelan tanker insertion.

The guilty bomb engineers and sleeper agents lived in their own terror, fearing reprisal from both their unaware host and their masters. They fulminated over all possible ways of identifying them with the attacks, and could not find the link. They thanked Allah for giving wisdom to their leaders for limiting their knowledge so tightly. Their pieces of the operation were all so infinitesimal, so limited. Each various team member was unable to identify other team members and, if their own position was so firewalled, so was everyone else's. Gradually, they breathed easier.

The FBI showed visible frustration. Now able under The Patriot Act to lawfully share information among themselves, the too-many intelligence agencies conferred, competed and sought inspiration from each other and gradually began to understand that they faced a much deeper conspiracy than the 9-11 airliner hijackings.

A growing number of Americans pressed for revenge and

offensive combat, killing off would-be future terrorists until none dared even to give America the finger. These voices did not much care whether the exact persons responsible were located or not. They openly advocated destroying Syria as an object lesson. The Syrians foresaw their role as target and vociferously insisted they had no part in it.

The Left mostly subdued its voices, cautioning "justice," and speculating on the causes of "terrorism." Some politicians interviewed proclaimed their determination to bring "those responsible" to trial.

Out of sight and hearing from Americans, a South American law professor strode onto the auditorium stage to begin his lecture, but led with the staggering announcement. His celebratory tone caught on and students expressed their jealousy by standing and cheering. Few in the United States ever learned of their sick delight. International blogs exhibited some smug satisfaction over the United States' "comeuppance."

A nervous Europe eyed its own major retailer stores and other heretofore-unforeseen targets and began to wonder widely how far this new Caliphate invasion would go. "Peace" graffiti bloomed in Rome.

53

Early August

The news programs provided some screen for Saya-dar by keeping the emphasis on the ongoing effort to try to discover the details behind what had happened. They should have all been mentally going hunting to kill the predator before the next attack. As dramatic and successful as the simultaneous, dispersed, truck bomb attacks had been, there was no reason for the *Jihad* to stop. In that way, the truck bombings could be both victory and deception.

All of the reaction furor pricked the Persian's thinking. Yes, he held the Americans in his grip. The day belonged to him. Their fear literally smelt. They suspected sleeper agents amongst their people, but turned up little as hard evidence. The dispersed truck bombings shifted the spotlight from the dramatic, urban concentration catastrophe to terrorism in the towns.

Huskey had almost stopped one of the trucks, but only one and that was a fluke. The truck-bomber lost his composure and disobeyed his instructions. Saya-dar had provided handguns to the bombers only for two purposes: to kill law enforcement officers who might as happenstance interdict them for some reason, like a burned-out tail light, and for the bombers to use to commit suicide if necessary. The guns were not offensive weapons and Saya-dar cursed the idiot for his foolishness. He should have simply run

Huskey over instead of shooting at him. No doubt, the pistol shots fired at Huskey mobilized him vital seconds sooner. Huskey came close to stopping that attack altogether.

Nevertheless, the bombings succeeded, wildly. America focused on the martyred drivers and failed to look for the other, supporting teams.

And so the idea hovered. The second Urn of Judgment waited, perhaps. The Urn waited for a courageous man to retrieve it and open its lid, releasing its Judgment on the infidels. Saya-dar's psyche swam in a lurid pool of glee over America's grief, mixed with the combined fantasies of vengeance against *Arcturus*, and releasing the Urn's Judgment on America. His hatred seized a tighter grip on his emotions and affected his ordinary sense of precaution.

Saya-dar's computer "pinged" its "New Message" alert. He hoped this would be it. It was. While he had asked the Cuban to mobilize his own agents to discover the identity of the *Arcturus's* owner, Saya-dar had numerous agents of his own and these had already, and easily, named this Gordon as the registration holder. Oddly, the *Arcturus* was foreign-flagged, requiring this Captain Gordon to report to Customs. Saya-dar's agent knew who to call.

An automation software specialist in Toledo, Ohio easily hacked into the Customs server and stole the video check-in image showing Gordon and his crew, complete with their identity documents. So easy. Gordon had called from one of the Customs Service's telephone check-ins taking up the slack in the busier Florida ports. Under the new system, this convenient check-in required the Captain and passengers to produce themselves and their documents before the camera. Saya-dar knew his quarry's face and lair.

Saya-dar called Casteneda, now back in Havana. If the Cuban were a loyal Communist and friend, then he would express his sorrow at his friend's departure and that would end it. If the Cuban were disloyal, greedy, or just stupid, he might assist the *Jihad* in planting the suggestion that Saya-dar had gone home.

Casteneda strode up the ramp to *Babylon* and hugged his ostensible colleague. The Persian smiled and seemed perfectly at ease. Casteneda hoped he seemed equally relaxed, but doubted it.

"Casteneda, my friend, welcome, drink!" the Sheik crooned.

"Gracias, my friend, gracias," Casteneda replied sincerely, taking the Margarita and drinking deeply. "What is the occasion?"

"I am returning to my homeland after enjoying your Caribbean warmth and hospitality, and want to see my friend once again."

Casteneda was speechless.

"You look so sad! Cheer up, as the Americans would say!"

"I think you are wise to give up the plan and return. Someone has stirred up quite a hornet's nest to the north." Casteneda grinned knowingly, throwing out one of his fishing lines to see if The Shade would bite.

"Yes, indeed, someone has. It seems that I would have a difficult time adding to their misery. I am needed at home, and am returning there." Saya-dar did not take the bait.

"When do you sail?" Casteneda asked.

"In the morning. Enjoy my hospitality one more time and I would be honored," Saya-dar said.

The two sat and talked about Cuba, fishing, drinks, and the Perdido Cay incident. Casteneda tried to insert conversation about the Urns, but Saya-dar avoided any mention of the "lost" canisters. It was a simple sale: Saya-dar bought; Casteneda delivered, someone else spoiled the transaction and that was all there was to it. The Iranian had lost an expensive Italian-made helicopter, and Casteneda had lost men, but Saya-dar deemed Casteneda's obligations performed. It was not the Cuban's fault that the customer lost the goods. They shook hands. Casteneda watched as Saya-dar cruised serenely out of the Harbor and northward into the Caribbean.

To Casteneda, relieved that Saya-dar was leaving, the smooth Sheik seemed so—*philosophical* about the loss. That night, Casteneda e-mailed a friend. A call to his surveillance chief arranged for a chain of watchers to keep an eye on the slick desert trader.

The next day, Colonel Casteneda, guardian of the Castle on the Point, friend of Cuba, and American agent, strolled to the coffee shop a block from his office, bought steaming hot coffee—Cuba did have such good coffee. Stan Kenton's orchestra played "The Peanut Vendor" in the background. Holding his coffee, he walked south along Cardenas, turned right on Arsenal, where he bought a newspaper, and leaned up against the building at the corner.

No one could see, but while leaning there perusing the paper, he palmed a small piece of white chalk and marked the corner. Casteneda turned the page, checked the sports section, and continued to the train station only a block away, where he took the train to the end of the line. Few took the train to the end of the line at *Castillo de Atares.* He stepped off the train, strolled to a street merchant and bought a pastry. Genuinely enjoying the baked delight, Casteneda continued strolling around the block, doubled back, cut through a short alley, circled again, doubled back again, and entered the park near the Castillo.

Glancing around as if enjoying the wind in the trees, he ambled on, rounding a corner stepping over to a place prepared for people to sit, feed pigeons and rest. He sat on the concrete formed bench, opened his newspaper, leaned forward as if intent on the news, and slipped a note into a crevice between the right side formed-concrete leg and the horizontal seat. He relaxed and finished reading the paper and his pastry. No one followed him.

Later that day, a man in his thirties bought a paper too, from the same vendor, and paused at the corner to adjust his coat. He flipped open the sports section. When he left, the mark was gone. He spent the two hours walking, taking busses and trains, changing directions, and saw no surveillance. Finally, he arrived at the park at *Castillo de Atares*, but not by train, and sauntered through the gardens, resting on the same concrete bench. He was alone. Opening his newspaper, he leaned forward as if stretching an aching low back and slipped his hand beneath the bench, retrieving the note. He would decode it later.

54

The Urn of Judgment
The Bahamas
Mid August

Saya-dar truly enjoyed his Bahamas vacation. Who would not? He motored his yacht away from its anchorage in Havana harbor, snapped pictures as he cruised between the two ancient castles occupying the points at the harbor entrance, and turned south-southeast, rounding the point below the castle fort called *Castillo del Morro*. Well under way later, he waved at the American Coast Guard cutter *Diligence* patrolling the Windward Passage, scanning for drug runners, no doubt, and made like a tourist for the Turks Islands.

Reaching Grand Turk, Saya-dar changed course generally north and northwest and cruised among the many islands. The Persian feasted on fresh seafood and listened politely to yachtsmen brag until he reached Snake Cay just off Great Abaco Island at the northern end of the chain of Bahamas, anchoring at Marsh Harbor.

Here he made his final preparations. First, his crew would harbor in Nassau, ready to pick Saya-dar up on his return. Allah willing, he would be back on board his yacht soon enough, and bound for Greece, but, first, he would penetrate the beast personally.

He had raped America already, all of its fresh faces, the oblivious ones, the impudent pig Americans whose very existence affronted Allah. His own Persia would beat America to the ground.

America thought of Iran as history, or as peopled by maniacs, one or the other. America would lick its wounds at the feet of his Persia, and The Shade would be the one Allah would honor to bring their shame about.

Next, only four e-mail messages set into motion the preparations he needed accomplished in America. He had sought to craft a plan with one less message, but could not reduce the number below four.

The first alerted an infiltration agent in Florida to deliver a message there to an American traitor about when Saya-dar would insert. He had permitted his agent to arrange the method, and to select the traitor and the site, long ago. If conditions changed over time, then the agent would accommodate the change, adjusting the method and location if need be. Those were the agent's decisions. His sole mission was to stand by for the single sentence from Saya-dar that ordered him into action. Saya-dar withheld instructions identifying where the agent would pick him up at sea; this information stayed secret, with Saya-dar alone, until the last minute. For now, it sufficed that Saya-dar designate where the agent and traitor would set sail from.

The second message, Saya-dar e-mailed to a deep-cover, deployed Logistics Team member. This message triggered the instruction to leave forged identity documents, cash, and credit cards ready for pickup so that Saya-dar could function independently in the states. Even if Saya-dar discovered his insertion site to be compromised, forcing him to abandon it, the distinct logistics support remained intact.

Likewise compartmentalized for security, the third ordered a wealthy Iranian lobbyist to have his corporate-owned Beechcraft Baron flown to an obscure rural airport, have it hangar-parked there, and left. That was all. Just deliver it, park it, refuel, and leave it.

The fourth told The Engineer that his time had come.

Saya-dar sent all four apocalyptic messages and sat back. Now, all that lacked was to retrieve the polonium he had lost. He would return to the site where Casteneda's men had anchored the second canister, posing as a yachter trolling the Caribbean's Out Islands. He could innocently-enough survey the cove first. If Americans swarmed over the cove, he could merely cruise on. If not, and if satisfied that the cove had returned to serenity, and remained unwatched, then he could retrieve it if it remained.

Why not hit America again, as she reeled from his first attack? Arrangements for his weapon, his transportation, his cover, and his poison—all would be in place. Osama bin Laden had called out to the Faithful to attack. Saya-dar had responded, summoning up men emplaced long ago. However, this time, he would not just work in the background.

Saya-dar pretended to be quite the French fisherman on Walker's Cay. Cruising in and out of the small Cays, dodging the treacherous shoals that had wreaked such havoc on so many craft, revealed no activity at all other than stray shark-divers done watching the sharks nearby and now idly checking out these remote, quiet Cays. Gossip overheard while drinking at Rosie's on Grand Cay, and hanging around the Marina on Walker's was completely devoid of any mention of government types poking around at Perdido Cay; Saya-dar knew that the bars would have been abuzz had the Coast Guard, or the BDF been on-site, watching the cove. Saya-dar concluded that the lost Urn taken from the *Corsican Sun* led the Americans off-trail; they had missed the second, anchored Urn!

While lounging at the hotel and charter-fishing to support his alibi—just in case anything went wrong—four of his crew operated the yacht's launch, worked their way to Perdido Cay's cove, waited for dark, and then found the Urn quietly waiting for its Master. They were back before morning was out. No one saw and the cloudy night Saya-dar had waited for cloaked the men in invisibility from any satellite that the Americans might have been able to shift. They chained it below the yacht for cooling and concealment, ready for its journey to America.

55

Atlantic Ocean,
forty miles north of West End,
Grand Bahama Island
Mid August
Eight weeks after the attack
on Arcturus

At 1:30 in the morning, Saya-dar's phone rang. Two minutes out. He strolled to the rail to the north side and heard the thrum of a powerful engine. The "go-fast," running without lights, loomed from the darkness under the star-dotted sky and pulled alongside. A man climbed the ladder and bowed before Saya-dar. The agent and the traitor had arrived. Without ceremony, Saya-dar nodded "Good-bye" to his Captain—his brother—and descended the ladder into the go-fast.

As the fast boat pulled away, Saya-dar admired it, or at least the portions visible to him in the night. The starlight and low moon showed him a deep-hulled, slender boat, built for speed. Its appointments nonetheless afforded comfort, needed for the kind of fast runs over rough seas that drug-runners might endure. Its décor and contents varied from the typical drug-runner shell of a boat, making this cruiser more like any other pleasure boat. Fishing equipment serving as props on this trip lay about, neatly stacked behind the coolers. The Agent handed him a Thermos of coffee. Another man sat at the pilot wheel. Saya-dar saw his back and knew him to be the wealthy Florida lawyer who owned the go-fast. Saya-dar thanked Allah and the man silently, in his thoughts, and knew that the man would sacrifice his life before the night was done.

At a signal from the agent, the go-fast turned, nosed toward the cove's mouth, and headed out to sea slowly. Running without lights, the pilot-owner picked his way carefully back out, mindful of any reefs or rocks and the need for quick reaction to avoid sticking the boat on some unseen sandbar.

Brandon Barabian IV trembled. Every muscle and nerve in his body quivered with fear. He so regretted each step he'd taken leading to this night.

At first, he prided himself on offering some service for the cause. Brandon rejected his family's Catholicism and converted to Islam in law school. They collected around this one particular table in the student center, drinking coffee during breaks. There, he had met young, hotheaded, Palestinian students. He found he shared their anger at America, although theirs had a unique Arab flavor. He first visited, then regularly attended their Mosque. Even after graduation, and once working, Brandon continued. Eventually, the Imam asked him to donate to "charities." He had known that the money went to support brother-Muslims taking action against Zionists. He suspected that these Brothers were "terrorists" as America labeled the charities' beneficiaries. Nothing had been said about it, but it was the demeanor of the men at the Mosque that gave away their purpose.

They *hated*, these men did. They hated Israel—as did he—and they hated America. As did he.

He hated America too, but his own hatred for his country differed from theirs. They did not *know* America. He did. He knew America as only one born in America could. He hated America's aloofness from the world's problems. He hated America's willingness to act "unilaterally" in the world—to project its force without submission to international consensus. He hated America's stubborn resistance to treaties permitting international agencies to regulate the world's fisheries, forests, and farms. He saw that it was time for America to decline, and for his country to submit to world authority.

Brandon sublimated his hatred; he grew wealthy, targeting America's businesses—these despised icons of despised capitalism. (He never perceived the irony that he, Brandon Barabian IV, Attorney at Law, profited from his own small business.) He wielded statutes to carve out a niche practice, suing businesses across the land for all manner of discrimination. Why, in the arena of the Americans with Disabilities Act violations alone, the fields were ripe! Who would ever have dreamed that toilet paper holders mounted a few inches this way or that could cause such mischief— or such *profits?*

Brandon had succeeded wildly, but now the call from his mentor at the mosque jeopardized all. Underneath the courteous request, he had understood that no choice presented before him. He must accede to the "request." He understood that there would be this-world "consequences" if he declined to give Allah this meager service, and those consequences hung over him here and now, in this life, as well as in the next.

Oh, the man had uttered nothing even remotely like a threat. All words were gentle, humble, and the leader asked for Barabian's most generous help in this one small way: a man needed to travel inside the U.S., but needed to make his way into the country quietly. Barabian wondered who he was and trembled that his thoughts even asked. No! He did *not* want to know. He did not want even to see the man who sat as his passenger, relaxing back into the cushioned bench where, just the day before, his bikini-clad wife had stretched, teasing Brandon Barabian IV with her body.

The man sat calmly, hands folded, with the steel thermal coffee mug close at hand. Barabian held the wheel tightly and felt as if a ghost stared into the back of his head, and not just any ghost, but a spirit of power and purpose, a spirit who could read his thoughts and feel his fear. An *evil* spirit!

Well, he was in now. He steered his custom-built go-fast on a due westerly course and gunned the engine hard. The boat leapt in response, the bow rising and then lowering level with the plane of the Atlantic surface as Barabian started his run to the coast, less than two hours away. They would enter the harbor at Sailfish Point during the quiet, dark hours of the morning, and he would be done with this chore, this *man*. At least, he hoped he would be done.

An hour and forty minutes later, the GPS showed him they were approaching the coast. Radar revealed nothing. No cutter or launch sped toward on intercept. This was so easy. The diligent lawyer had rehearsed this before, just from curiosity, and had never been checked. America just owned too much coastline to watch. The fast cruiser he owned and had customized—like the fiberglass shell-and-engine go-fasts built for drug-runners, only luxurious— shot across the Atlantic from the shallow northwestern side of the Bahamas to the Florida coast so fast, exposing him to the Coast Guard for so little time, their guardians had little time to detect and react. Besides, the waters off Florida's Gold Coast were teeming with yachts, wave runners, and other fast cruisers, at all hours. His was just one more boat, and a registered, "legitimate" craft at that.

Brandon Barabian IV, suave, moneyed, and misguided, at age 42, adjusted his course for the inlet between the jetties and throttled back as he passed between North and South Points, heading upstream into the St. Lucie River mouth. Now, he sighed with relief and loosened his taut muscles. He was essentially, home free. If he'd not been interdicted at open sea as he approached the coast, he almost certainly had escaped interdiction altogether. Now, he threaded under the bridges, and wound up the North Fork of the St. Lucie, passing a maze of channels and coves where his fellow-citizens slept in their homes by the channel. Still, only when docked by his house, and inside would he rest.

Barabian's Imam had told him that the passenger would depart directly from his dock, by car. Barabian, the barrister-betrayer, assumed that even now, a car with patient driver waited down the block from the Barabian mansion. That thought shot a bolt of enhanced fear through the man. The driver poised outside his home—his family sleeping away inside—would be more than a driver. He would be part of this network of men—and women he supposed—who lived inside America and who—like him—did the bidding of others "asking" for services for Allah.

That relaxed him a bit, again. The driver would, of course, be a man like him, just an ordinary American, with a job or a profession, recruited from his own mosque somewhere into a specific, limited task. The man probably right now shivered from the same fears plaguing Barabian. Ha! The man probably feared *him!* The driver wondered who would arrive and how he would arrive and probably had inferred that his passenger would arrive by sea, or else why these arrangements, skulking around a neighborhood by the canal? He would imagine that Barabian belonged to some secretive organization and that only he—the car owner and driver—held such a limited, low-level rank. He would wonder what would happen when his passenger finished the ride. He would wonder who waited for him at the end.

Enough! Barabian would dock his boat in 10 minutes now, after slipping slowly and quietly up his own cove, turning into his own canal and tying up. His passenger would thank him for the ride, step up to the gunwale, onto the pier, and disappear forever into the black night. Brandon Barabian IV would go inside, slip into bed next to his lover, put his arm around her warm, smooth waist, and hear her moan softly as she stirred. Then, he would either drift off for a few hours' sleep, or make love to her in celebration of being alive—and rich—which depended, of course, on her signals. He hoped she would join him in the act that would confirm for him that he'd made it, in every way.

The traitor at the boat's wheel could not know that, already, his wife and their child lay dead, their throats cut, their bled-out bodies being prepared for the short trip that would "disappear" them from their home and forever. Swift hands cleaned up his house and loaded the bodies. Just west lay the trackless wastes of Florida's swamps. Circling the sophisticated coastal developments like wolves around a sheep-pen, the primeval swamps lurked, hungry to swallow corpse evidence of crime. It would not be the first time the alligators, crabs, raccoons, and the swamp itself would assist: Brandon Barabian IV and his family would simply vanish.

Saya-dar eyed the man at the wheel. He loathed him, although he had never met him.

For now, though, the go-fast owner and litigator crept up the canal fronting his luxurious, single-story home, oblivious to the destruction visited on him already and unconcerned about the devastation the passenger planned for his countrymen.

There was the Francisco house, reading lamp on in the sunroom as usual. Did the man never sleep? The Northcutts' dog gave its customary, half-hearted three yaps. Having satisfied itself that it had herded, or guarded, or annoyed the neighbors—or whatever its motivation—it returned to its doggy bliss. There was his dock and his house.

Lights off. All quiet. Car nowhere to be seen on the street in front, but probably masked from view by the Live Oaks and moss or by the garage on the end of the house. Patience. Passengers would off-load, pad softly up the pier, past the grinning pirate statue whose leer and cutlass stood sentinel between pier and patio. Brandon would give old Captain Kidd his customary pat on the head and get some rest so he could resume hassling hapless entrepreneurs in the morning. His wife knew not to ask about the night and the event would fade from memory. It never happened. *What trip? What passenger? What pick-up?*

He tied the boat to its cleats. Turning to retrieve his Nalgene bottle, he froze—not voluntarily. In a flash, a strong arm encircled his head from behind, a heavy body pressed his own down, down, and a hand muffled his mouth. He felt white heat press into his back, above the belt-line, below the rib cage. Shock carried Brandon Barabian IV away, and he entertained no further treacherous or greedy thoughts, the dagger first piercing his right kidney, carving organ damage on the outward draw, and then slashing spine-deep across his throat.

The killer supported the bleeding corpse, as life said "adjourned" and the lawyer answered the summons call from whatever grim bailiff would greet him in the courtroom of the afterlife.

Saya-dar did not deign to stop and watch. Already, he sat back in a Mercedes and marveled and how easily he had slipped into the belly of the Great Satan—while they slept! Twenty minutes later, the car ramped onto I-10 and in another two hours, Saya-dar rested with strong coffee in a rented warehouse, preparing to make his final plans, part of which he had *not* set into motion years before: these were *new* plans, *new* developments, to account for the *Arcturus.*

For these, he e-mailed his cousin in Detroit. His four Calls to Judgment (as he named his earlier e-mail messages) sufficed to re-start the Urn of Judgment plan. He would poison America with the one Urn recovered from Perdido Cay. While the four Calls to Judgment played out, he had ample time first to rendezvous, to acquire the equipment, to reconnoiter, and to exact his revenge on *Arcturus.*

Why had The Engineer not acknowledged receipt of his message?

56

"The Engineer's" office,
University of Chicago
Mid August,
eight weeks after the attack
on Arcturus

University of Chicago Professor Damir Asmir sat back, gaping at the message and marveling at its import. He stood shakily, poured a cup of coffee from his thermos, mechanically tore the tops simultaneously from a creamer packet and a sweetener packet, and absently swirled them into the coffee with the spoon he kept in his drawer, wiping it on a Kleenex and replacing it for its next use. Sitting back down, he thought of his daughter, a student at this same University, and his son, a software troubleshooter for a small consumer electronics firm out in Des Plains. He thought about Des Plains, still in the country when he moved to Chicago 25 years earlier, now part of the megalopolis of Chicago despite maintaining its distinct small town name. The younger Asmir lived out on the northwest side too, close to his work, proud of having his own apartment.

It was unusual for Turks to enter the violent world of Islamic terrorism. Not all Middle Eastern nations bred and supported terrorists. The paradoxically secular, Muslim state rose from the ashes of the Ottoman Empire, then rose above its disastrous alliances during two world wars, and somehow thrived, with the reputation of being a good nation to have on your side. Indeed, the Turks had proved their resiliency. Truly, the Turks lived between Europe and the Arabic-Persian Middle East, in every sense. They lived uneasily

343

over the roiling violence south of Turkey, and leaned toward the Europeans.

Asmir's decision more than two decades ago that he would perform a covert mission as part of an attack on America sprang from his Marxist philosophy, not from a desire to conquer the world for Allah. Damir, the youth, listened to hotheaded haters in the square and believed that America stood in the way of all common man's success.

Now, it did not seem so clear. An adult life among the capitalists showed him a different picture. Work, study, learn, don't commit crimes, pay your bills and you would succeed in America. He had added to that list, advising his son "Don't have a baby out of wedlock," but the gist of the guidance was the same; opportunity was for real, for all, and only you could mess it up.

Twenty-five years is a long time. Damir enjoyed his work and the freedom he found in America to pursue it. He settled into Chicago, became comfortable there, and grew into the job.

Damir delighted in learning his field of electronics engineering, but always bore in mind the inciting event, the motive, the reason for his being in America. Somehow, though, over time, the motivation changed while the goal-directed behavior did not. He honed his expertise, occupied the forefront of his field, but lost the ache for the destruction of America and all things western. A more mature Dr. Amir had watched Communist utopias stripped naked for the fat whores they really were while the free West prospered even despite its moral degradation.

His youthful disdain for America transformed imperceptibly to grief for its deterioration, as one would feel for a friend whose wife left him, who sloshed in alcohol, who lost his job, and who was "on the rocks" in general. The United States was such a land of liberty and promise, but constantly wallowing in the license it permitted its unworthy until—Damir surmised sadly—America became unworthy of itself!

He had finally decided that it was man's plight that both the profane and the sublime must exist together. Was that not the nature of man? There would be no Heaven on Earth. Surely, if history proved any truth, it proved that human accomplishment utterly failed to perfect the human condition.

A couple of decades of exposure to human nature disaffected Damir of the notion of forcibly imposing some political party's notion of perfection on any population. Perfection was not among us. Odd. People would confiscate property from and kill others in the name of "the Party," or holiness or "social justice," or equality. The flawed presumed to perfect manipulation of ideal outcome for the rest of the flawed. Really?

Damir had decided that the holy were profane in their wrong belief that their zeal equated them to God. Their zeal was not virtue; their zeal was stubborn pride blinding them to their own depraved nature and desperate need for the very mercy they denied to others.

He scoffed at the people who acted as if the *State* were God, making law upon law in vain effort to fix their condition. Somewhere, along the way, in America, Damir Asmir got over Marxism, but what to do about his Islamic Revolution, Jihadist, radical, terrorist controllers? Long ago, at no discrete decision point, he had quietly revolted against his controller and had determined that, if the day ever arrived, he would refuse to execute his orders. Now the Islamic terrorist brothers required of him the task he had come to dread.

It was simple. He would not do it.

Would not do *what*?

It was not so simple. Now, the question became: "How was he to refuse and avoid the murders of his entire family?" If Damir implanted himself so long ago in America, he assumed others also hid out in the States, awaiting their savage destiny.

A corollary emerged from his reasoning: Damir wanted to know how he could take his position, his knowledge, compartmentalized as it was, and help his country. His country. America. Odd that it didn't sound odd.

Damir Asmir locked his door and took a walk. Damir made two decisions: first, he would return to his office and confirm receipt of the horrendous message, visiting the site and opening the file he knew waited on the Web for him to learn the nature of the task he would not do. Secondly, though, he would call a man whom he had seen on television during the aftermath of the 9-11 attack. This man, living right here in Chicago, a former Army General, had been instrumental in re-organizing the Army's special operations units in the late '70s and '80s, and had now retired to promote some military-related benevolent foundation. He returned since 9-11 to lend his expert commentary on television from time to time.

He would know where Damir should turn next. Damir had no idea how to plug into the myriad labyrinth of U.S. Government intelligence-law enforcement-military-counter terrorism etc. organizations. "Homeland insecurity," thought Damir, cynically. He needed a practical, action-oriented point of contact, not a 10-digit phone number swimming in a universe of bureaucracy. The sharp-eyed, retired General living in town was just the man, or at least he was a place to start. Damir pictured himself, sitting meekly in a chair with the congressional committee for this or that investigating what would follow. They would subpoena him to Washington! No, indeed, he must remain discrete—secret. He would avoid the FBI and CIA which seemed constantly under scrutiny in the news.

Damir completed his circuit on the winding walks through the park and returned to his office. One thing about Damir: always calm, never flustered. Not as a young parent, not as a teacher, not as a secret, sleeper-cell terrorist about to flout his orders. He opened Outlook, clicked "Send/Receive" and sat back again.

Damir re-read the message from his mastermind commander, known only as the Saya-dar. The Saya-dar addressed him as Karsten and, in matter-of-fact German, directed him to pray for a sick uncle in Hanover, and to view the family pictures posted there. Damir had worried more about how much concern these martyrs might show for radioactive shielding; with their minds on the virgins, they could easily overlook the putrefying effect of radiation cooking cells from the inside out. Probably, to assure that the material did not trigger some detector, which the Americans continually labored to improve, they would carefully shield the lump and, in turn, keep Damir from later burning his guts to death by radiation. This message dismissively informed him that he was not to concern himself with when the polonium would be added.

Right. So much for the first message. *No way.*

Did these men not know that they would bring down on themselves the wrath of the U.S. Military? Did they read history? No, he decided, the handlers who dispatched the martyrs might read history, but their prejudice blinded them to history and to their own evil. They lived their own false vision of history.

History indicated that the Americans would be highly pissed off, would rally, would attack overwhelmingly, and would depose some dictators. Then, the Americans would fund the conquered people's new blessing of liberty and then quickly fall out among themselves. The recently-freed people might make it, or might once again collapse under the thumb of the dictator's henchmen, only now they would be clamoring for revenge on the "collaborators." In the meantime, the former government would be gone, blown away in the American onslaught, and by that government's own refusal to learn the lessons of the *Lusitania*, Pearl Harbor, and Afghanistan.

Damir followed the news. Perhaps the Iranian religious leaders who aspired to command all of Islam would reach the same conclusion as he, even if for different reasons. He wondered if he would next receive a message countermanding the last. If he took another walk and returned, would he find the Luciferian mission cancelled? Absurdly, he wanted to shoot Outlook, to shoot his computer monitor.

Professor Damir Asmir, Turkish by birth, American by citizenship and loyalty, arrived at the conclusion that his call to the retired General Officer was a sound next move. He had noted the name of the man's charitable organization, looked it up in the telephone directory. (Unlike an Internet lookup, that left no traces.) He jotted the number down on a stick-note, which he jammed into his pocket for reference later at a phone booth, and then destruction. Damir made the call and the man listened courteously, asking only a few questions, aware that Damir had called him as a contact point, not looking for final answers.

General Grainger had been out of that business—mostly—for several years now but knew who to refer the good Professor to. At the end, the man thanked Damir, asked him to stay on the line, and linked him by conference call to that man's former military organization: Special Operations Command (SOCOM) headquarters in Tampa. Grainger insisted that they talk only with his old friend Paul Ortega, and no one else. Once he introduced Ortega to Damir, Grainger signed off with "Thank you" and then, after a pause, "May God bless you, sir."

57

*French Broad River valley,
foothills of the
Appalachian Mountains, Tennessee
Late August*

Saya-dar surveyed the equipment, and his location. He was pleased with his cousin's preparations. From the ridge top, he commanded a view, blocked to the south by a higher ridge, but open to the north. Rippled forest—broken by meadows, a power line easement cut, and a few structures—lay before him in this northern view. The sparse windows flickered as lights switched on where the people lived. These houses spread out loosely, as if the landowners shunned human company for the solitude of the rural hills and hollows.

Saya-dar's cousin had chosen the perfect command post during his reconnaissance and purchased it immediately, through a local realtor and in the name of an American land holding company. Saya-dar had personally surveyed the site before occupying it and complimented him on his tactical eye. The cousin proudly showed Saya-dar the collected maps, satellite photography, and radio equipment. Saya-dar thought his purchasing a used camper-trailer to be especially clever.

A nearby smaller airport—not one with commercial air passenger traffic but one used by private pilots mostly for recreational flying—provided an ideal beginning point for lower altitude reconnaissance. This advantage, Saya-dar had spotted early in his own reconnaissance.

The lodge owned by this Gordon lay near the Island Home Airport takeoff and approach path. Pilots using the airfield worked their way back to and from this island in the French Broad River nearby, using the river as an easy-to-spot navigation reference. The river led them back to the airfield, literally on an elliptical island, where they circled to line up for landing, but only after cruising over the target property. Saya-dar reasoned that the man must see so many single-engine airplanes passing overhead that one more low-flyer would garner none of his attention. Saya-dar's advance-planning cousin had even chartered a flight on the pretext of flying to the nearby national park and back, probably a common enough destination. He'd dutifully exclaimed his wonder at the scenic Appalachian beauty while snapping numerous pictures, making sure to get aerial photographs of Gordon's home and grounds. That's how Saya-dar had discovered details about the lodge.

He had yet to work out his attack plan but he had already decided when he would kill Gordon Noone. The moon would wane fully in three nights. Saya-dar wanted the job done, fretting about remaining in one spot so long.

Saya-dar's greater question was whether to forego the pleasure of personally killing the man who claimed to usurp his own title of Protector, of Keeper. Saya-dar's greater mission should dictate just getting past this revenge and letting his team do the chore, but Saya-dar had never been one to forego pleasure. He wanted this pretender killed, wanted to know the job was done, and wanted in on it. However, his team, led by Kadir could accomplish the job without him, if need be.

Saya-dar frowned. He'd had other men too, and somehow this Gordon and his crew killed them all and destroyed his Agusta heli-copter, making off with the *Corsican Sun* and the Urn of Judgment at the same time.

The team arrived early. Saya-dar was livid at their off-plan arrival. After recovering, he seized the opportunity offered by both the aerial reconnaissance and the team's too-soon arrival. They could rehearse in the secluded hollows, and the unexpected gift of the close-in aerial photographs permitted more detailed rehearsal mock up.

Saya-dar conferred with his Captain, a Chechen, experienced from war in the Balkans, and masquerading as a Russian immigrant. Together, they worked out their plan and readied for the dark night soon coming. He'd liked to have had a sketch or floor plan, but, really, that was "overkill" as the Americans said.

58

Gordon's Lodge
Late August
Night Recon

The night came on, inky black. Low cloud cover swept the stars away. No moon glowed through. A coyote yapped. Jack checked his watch: 1:18 a.m., certainly a dead hour for sentries; this is the time of night when it catches up to you and you want to be in bed like everyone else. Jack had been there before and loved it. Night, not bed. He thrived on the primal sense of prowling, of *owning* the night, of being the only person on alert while all else slept so peacefully.

Besides, he had reason to be on alert. Gordon has flown his own private plane yesterday and checked his pictures. He always took digital pictures, downloaded them, matched them to the last set taken, and performed a software and visual comparison. One thing about taking the risk to settle down in one place: you sure could get to know the terrain. Gordon's routine—and fun—air reconnaissance not only kept his pilot hours up; the flights also displayed to his practiced eye the slightest change in his surroundings.

Flying his "patrol," Gordon spotted one anomaly. Why would anyone move a camper into the middle of the forest, perching on the higher hilltop to Gordon's south where the camper looked out over Gordon's own domain? Had the property sold? He'd find out.

"Got a question for you," Gordon addressed Bob Beamer. Bob operated the airport. Bob sported the ever-present, stained, pilot cap, khaki pants, white long-sleeved shirt, with oil spots on the sleeves from checking vital aircraft fluids—religiously.

"Shoot." Bob was always brief.

"Noticed anything odd or different out to the southeast, on a line with Mount LeConte?"

"Why? No, never mind the 'why'." Without asking, Bob had somehow sensed more to Gordon than Gordon publicized. Bob had flown for Air America in the late 1960's and had his own secrets to keep. He had long ago perceived that Gordon built that secluded lodge in the woods for good reason, and Bob respected his privacy. The men had grown to become friends without ever breaching their shared respect for privacy.

"Noticed anything?"

"No, not out there, but now that you ask, there's something I should mention to you. Feller showed up here about a week ago wanting to charter a flight. Wanted to see the mountains. Wanted to scout for real estate. Loved it here, wanted to develop some resort property.

"Nothing unusual about that. Happens all the time," Bob continued.

"Would I take him out, due on a line toward Gatlinburg, and also circle some nice property he might also be interested in just wherever he spotted it? Sure, I would. So, we get in the Cessna we use for people who just want to go up in a plane and head out. Clear day. I take off toward east and circle south. He's snapping pictures almost immediately before we're out of Knox County, holding that camera close in, body turned away from me, like he didn't want me to see him. Way back, same thing. Gets on the approach heading going right about over your lodge, at it again: scrunched over, hiding that camera. Tells me to circle. He 'might be interested in land along the river.' I circle. Course, it brings us back over your place one more time. More pictures as we circle, him on the inside of the turn where he's looking more down. Get back, he thanks me, pays me cash, takes off. Real estate scout or investor might have wanted evidence of payment for the tax deduction. Didn't even want a receipt. Odd."

"What did he look like?"

"Dark. Dark hair cut short. Stood about 5'8". Accent, but more like British and Indian. Could have been Pakistani. I couldn't place him, and I'm not bad at figuring out where a guy came from."

"Anything else?"

"No."

"Thanks, Bob."

"Anytime. I'll holler if anything else out-of-place crops up and I'll keep my eyes peeled."

Almost certainly, the lone camper housed some Boy Scouts, or others granted permission and grabbing a quick, outdoor getaway. This was not the right time of the year for that group of old blue-grass band-member friends who liked to gather annually to jam. Besides, Donna, Gordon and Jack had heard no stringed-instrument music reverberating over the valley to the lodge. Gordon assured them that, despite the distance, they'd have heard the snap of the banjo showering out rapid-fire notes at night, when sounds seem to amplify and carry. Probably a bunch of poker-players taking a few nights to get away. Hunting seasons for deer, rabbit and turkey bracketed these months, so he doubted the trailer headquartered a hunting expedition. Like so many probably innocuous anomalies, to the alert, the sudden appearance of the humble camper had to be checked out, but almost certainly represented no menace.

The aerial photo-reconnaissance bothered Gordon more. Were it not for that, he'd probably have just forgotten about the camper's sudden appearance. A quick check of ownership records showed a recent sale to TranSun Holdings Group, LLC. The camper might even have hosted a survey crew, or might have been the initial deployment of a construction company's crew. That overflight though.

Gordon's paramount security measure was retirement from black operator status. Given a little tincture of time, wounds he'd left behind on the enemy healed over as the tyranny of the moment demanded their attention: they moved on and so did he. Gordon hoped.

He had operated—as Jack would—off the books: only a handful of old Army comrades knew his exploits. As far as Gordon knew, he'd remained covert, hidden from the enemy as well. Always the chance hovered that some cold bastard from either side—his or *theirs*—had discovered him, ruling that he must "go away." Gordon knew that risk when he started, knew that he'd never completely rest at his retreat in the hills until dead of natural causes. Of course, neither had there been any reason to RPG the *Arcturus*, but….

The three agreed to post guard at least until Gordon could discover who might be camped on the hill. He wanted the camper to go away, but there it remained, with line of sight and approximately 80 feet of elevation higher than his own hilltop. Gordon did not like their vantage point at all and shared his worry with Jack.

So, here Jack sat, Generation-4 night vision scope in hand, M-4 slung, hand on the carbine's "pistol grip," thumb on the safety. He was not dozing, but the black silence hardly brought the nerves to edge.

The camper lay a full kilometer away; they knew this from the "topo," displayed earlier on Gordon's computer, and measured. Gordon had been to the hilltop hosting this odd residence, and knew the route to it. The route would be more like a mile or more, winding up ridges from the main road. Jack did not want simply to amble in blindly.

He had considered just hiking in during broad daylight on the pretense of being a guy just out for a walk. Rejected. They really wanted to remain covert. They wanted to know more about whomever had established an overwatch-recon position than the watcher would know about them.

Besides, simply walking up bore its own risks—like getting shot. In the end, the Ranger way won out: a lonesome, silent patrol in the dead of night. Given that they numbered only three, the patrol would be small—just Jack. Donna would sleep first; Gordon would stay up to monitor the radio and surveillance system he'd installed to watch his own grounds.

Problem, thought Jack during planning.

"I've got to cover a couple of miles. I'll have to move very slowly during at least the last quarter mile to remain quiet. You know what stealth requires?" Jack asked, really commenting.

"Yes—time and patience," Gordon nodded.

Movies and TV create a false picture of this basic military challenge. Have you ever tried to sneak up on someone in the woods? It's not that easy. Reality: stealth is not magic—stealth is trained application of human biomechanics and simple physics. Stealth requires more; stealth requires patience. Patience does not come naturally to the West. Patience means ever-so-slow movement, taking the time required to avoid the slightest leaf-rustle, the smallest twig-snap, as well as perceptible movement.

Jack needed the full night. However, he wanted the darkest night and the deadest hours. Thus, Jack chose 1:30 a.m. departure. Yet, how could he leave at 1:30, travel toward the site, and inch his way in, close enough to lie quietly enough, long enough to learn what they needed, and then exfiltrate the same way, still during the optimum hours?

Gordon solved the problem easily, and with a simple, low technology device: a bicycle. Lacking lights and engine noise, Jack could quickly cover the initial approach. He would ride Gordon's mountain bike, dismount about 300 yards away from the camper, secrete the bike off the trail, and patrol the rest of the way in on foot. The bike also aided with swift escape if need be. Certainly, the bike was silent.

At 1:30 a.m., in the quiet that seemed to retard the fabric of time, Jack pushed off. Gordon watched him go from the lodge's safe-room on the main floor. While Jack pedaled downhill and out of sight of the house, Gordon checked each of his cameras and monitors, and finished the cup of coffee he knew would at least help during this long night. For now, Donna slept in the guest room on the main floor, but she'd set her alarm to join Gordon later to watch for Jack's return.

While Gordon had officially retired, his brain had not "checked out." He had designed his lodge, incorporating his own experiences and instincts. He'd not built himself into a death-lair. Gordon had enjoyed orienting the two younger people to his home and its "features." At least, most of its features.

First, Gordon showed them the passive pathways. These passages—a combination of secret and normal doors linking con-

nected rooms around the house's perimeter walls—permitted anyone who knew the layout to move the full perimeter inside and out
of view of anyone in the greatroom and kitchen area, and to work
his way to the escape portal in the basement. Thus, once out of the
great room, no room became a death-box, trapping its occupant.
Every room included some door or passage permitting escape to
the next. The next passage might also be an ordinary walk-through
closet, leading to the next room, which might incorporate a moveable bookcase leading through the attic space, and so forth. By connecting all of the rooms that had at least one outside wall, Gordon
created his perimeter within the walls, within which someone under
siege could move from one to the other, completely circling the
inner core of the house, without stepping outside, with the exception of the glassed-in great room.

One access on the back side of the great room was a normal
door connecting bathroom to laundry, but the exit from the laundry was a supply shelf that unlatched and rolled leftward, revealing a narrow secret room full of surveillance electronics, plumbed
with water and a dry toilet, and stocked with food. This room
opened into the closet of an adjacent bedroom. If under duress,
and if Gordon had time—and if he could just get away into any
one of the hidden passages—he could work his way to the basement. A tunnel from the basement led north and downhill, and
emerged 40 yards from the house into dense brush.

Gordon could not help beaming as he escorted the two through
the system. Donna had never seen this aspect of her uncle's home
before and Jack was chagrined he'd not spotted it on his own.
Gordon didn't show his "real" home to many and they'd been
impressed.

"I spent less than you'd think," Gordon had boasted. "Building
the escape tunnel presented the greatest challenge. I excavated it,

vaguely referring to the possibility of installing one of those remote, wood-burning furnace systems—you know, the ones you see up north with the furnace removed from the house, using forced air and a heat exchanger to send heat to the house." He could tell from their blank looks that they had not yet gotten into designing their own homes. "Once the trench was back-hoed out, I called a retired Navy Chief I know who now operates a construction company. He came up and poured the concrete walls. Voila! The classic escape tunnel! I actually added the wood-burner later for economy. The furnace gives you a good marker from which to find the opening."

Plainly, Gordon was proud. He had a right to be. Ingenious. They'd been impressed.

Gordon stored weapons variously throughout: nothing exotic. A few revolvers waited—solid reliable Colts and older Smith-and-Wessons without springs in magazines to deteriorate. Two pump shotguns stood guard, out of sight. Caches of 5.56mm rounds for Gordon's own M-4 supplied Gordon with ample ammo.

For now, though, Donna got a few hours sleep and Gordon watched Jack's image disappear from his surveillance limits and property.

Commercial cell phones provided commo, chosen over military radios for several reasons: digitally encrypted; quiet, once set on "vibrate"; reliable; clear. A microwave cell phone tower strobed the night sky from a nearby ridge and bathed Gordon's domain with strong signal. Jack had established points at which he'd check in: if he failed to reach Gordon at any point—well, that wouldn't be good at all.

Gordon munched on some peanuts.

Jack turned from the pavement, onto the logging trail piercing the forest and marking the beginning of his approach to the recon objective, still almost a mile away. This trail, like so many mountain paths, used "switchbacks" to climb steep hillsides. These sharply elbowed, zigzagged roads acknowledge a simple fact of mountain movement. Straight up might be the least distance, but, if you actually wanted to achieve the pinnacle, then "contour" your way up, angling ever upward while traveling either right or left of your objective, and then "switching back" sharply, re-tracing your path but at the next contour line or so upward.

Jack biked on just such a jagged road now. He'd rather abandon the road and approach the target through the woods, but terrain and time dictated otherwise. He had to take the calculated risk of movement on a trail: one of the most prominent Ranger "no-no's."

Feet and blood pumping, Jack thought now about the rule: "avoid roads and trails." Like all principles of combat, sometimes you had to override them. They were good principles, always worth considering and starting from, but the tactician in the woods had to adapt, as Jack had done.

Completing an almost 360-degree switchback, Jack slowed, stopped, straddling the bike, and listened, performing a "security halt." No unexpected sound reached out to threaten or warn through the darkness. Tree limbs would always creak, acorns might give it up and tumble but not every sound signaled an enemy sentry checking you out. Jack fought the inevitable, always-pressing urge to *imagine*.

Now, continuing to about 400 yards from the pinnacle, Jack

360

walked the bike off the road about 50 feet, lay it ever so gently down, and removed the cover strapped under its seat. The combination net and multi-colored green strips would cover the bike. Jack altered the apparent shape of the bike with the camouflage net and scattered leaves over its mass. No chrome on this bike: all surfaces hid beneath their own matte finish, custom spray-painted on by Gordon. Jack hoped he could find it on his way back down, guided by the rock he'd placed at the roadside to mark where he'd departed into the woods. Who knows? He might need to recover his wheels quickly.

Jack could not resist checking the cloth daypack again. Surefire—with the tailcap unscrewed two turns to assure it did not—on its own, pressed by something else in the pack—fire up at the wrong time. A friend forgot that once and put his entire patrol on display for a waiting ambush. The ambushers probably would have failed to spot the silent patrol, but for the brief flash-glow of the man's Surefire. By the time the light was covered and out, all Hell broke loose. This ambush—in the Philippines—cost five men. Two Americans and three of the Philippine Army patrollers, all out looking for Islamic hostage-holders, lost their lives because of the simple, almost absurd mistake.

Well, those mistakes are the worst.

Jack's Glock held its place in the holster Jack had sewn into his pack so that the pistol always waited from exactly the same position instead of shifting around in the pack. He didn't want to lose precious seconds groping for his weapon when he needed it. A simple, off-the-shelf, nylon, belt-clip case held the cell phone at ready access. Jack's Emerson HD-7 folding combat knife clipped into his right-side jeans pocket completed the accoutrements. (The cotton denim brushed past limbs and thorns more silently than artificial fabrics and "looked civilian.") Jack wished for his M-4, but had chosen to leave it at the house. The M-4 looked decidedly not *civilian.*

He had to try to blend in and look ordinary. If discovered by some random intersection of his own foray with someone else's middle-of-the-night ramblings, Jack would look more or less civilian. He eschewed the better "tactical" garb and equipment that police might wear, sporting cargo pockets and a pseudo-military SWAT look. That's exactly how Jack did *not* want to appear if spotted crossing the highway by the late-night deputy on his way home. He'd chosen the darkest-dyed denim blue jeans he could find at the store. For tonight, Jack made the scene in Wranglers and a navy-colored, long-sleeved T-shirt. Almost black.

Avoiding combat or "tactical" boots available from the police supply store only a few miles down the highway, Jack picked up instead some cheap, black, running shoes from the local discount store, and peeled off the reflective strips on the sides. No battery-powered flashing lights on these either. His usual hiking boots stayed behind this time; they were sturdy, but just a bit heavy and he needed all the "feel" he could get in his feet, so as to pick his way over the forest floor litter that carpeted his approach path.

Jack did not chintz on the gloves, though. His black, leather gloves with Kevlar sewn in had saved his hands before. Jack's hands were his first-defense tools and he had learned to take care of them. The "tactical" gloves' dulled leather cut the sheen of his skin.

These days, guys wearing headgear year-round was commonplace. A dark-green fleece cap looked more civilian and less burglar-like than some commando watch cap, and Jack put one on to alter his head's shape.

That left Jack's face. "Shape-shadow-shine." Biz-R-Market's hunting section supplied the easy-to-remove camo grease in tubes, along with a pullover net hood for the final approach. Jack had also thrown into his cart some cheap, camouflage print burlap used by duck hunters to fashion instant blinds. Cutting a neck hole in the middle and shredding it a bit around the edges created a shape-changing poncho on the order of a poor-man's Ghillie suit. He'd need that—maybe—and so had thrown in the odd, not quite civilian-looking piece of gear.

The dark-of-the-moon allied with him. The infantry operator always viewed the night as his friend. You got used to it, though operations took a bit longer for the soldier operating alone at night. It's one thing to wander the night in a patrol of seven other tough men; it's quite another to be out there in the woods on your own. Jack had long ago acclimated to the phase where he viewed the night as his mythical, not-yet-invented, "cloaking device."

Shine: that was another matter. No matter how otherwise benign Jack made his appearance, let's face it: black streaks and smudges of camouflage grease all over one's face would telegraph the wrong message to the Knox County Sheriff's Department instantly. Instead of putting the camouflage grease on in an imaginative pattern, Jack spread the grease lightly underneath the net hood just to dim the shine and pocketed a packaged, moist, wipe in case he needed to get the stuff off quickly.

He'd be virtually invisible—unless watched with infra-red or night vision scopes.

Jack said a short prayer and moved out. At first, the young soldier moved at a pace approaching ordinary, but he slowed as he counted his paces, numbering his path toward the camper. At about 300 yards, Jack stopped, checked all straps on his pack, and slowed his approach more. His watch showed 1:48. Perfect. He'd spend the next hour approaching and listening. Maybe it would take longer, depending on the leaf cover, deadfall, and, of course, any security measures he might find around the place.

The night woods peacefully enveloped him. Jack always enjoyed this part. The whole deal could explode in his face—literally, if mined or ambushed—but, for now, he owned the night. He and the night teamed up. He had spent so many hours enveloped in its protective cape. Jack had learned to become part of the night.

Jack read his 2nd Brigade's history when he took over command of Charlie Company in his old battalion. Back in the 70's, the Brigade Commander, Colonel Menetrey, had nicknamed his unit "The Night Brigade." Jack thought that a bit presumptive, to deem yourself to have *the* night brigade, but the Colonel emphasized the undisputed fact that so much infantry training and operating takes place after the sun goes down. That bit of history explained the oil painting still hanging in the brigade headquarters building, showing a staggered-trail formation of fanciful, bat-winged, Huey troop-carrying helicopters swooping down on an LZ. He'd inquired and discovered that one of the soldiers at the time was also an artist. He'd painted the scene, inspired by his Brigade Commander's vision for the unit. These soldiers had spent many, many nights training. Lots of marriages fell by the wayside. Lots of kids missed their daddies, but, these soldiers learned the night.

Every step he takes, though, reminds the night-stalking soldier that he is a foreign object, an interloper. Every footfall requires weight where weight has not pressed before. Those footfalls evidence the passer's visit. The moment of the movement means the chance to stumble, catching cotton on a briar that would drag across the knit texture like a needle across an old, plastic, phonograph record, sounding out the soldier's passage, even if faintly. A hickory nut could roll and bump. The disturbed nut then might raise the owl perched within thick cedar branches above. The owl's hoots then might first capture the attention of the other wildlife, and then incite a virtual cacophony to the attuned ear. Some skittish bird might beat wings from a thicket, sending out the warning cry. Next thing you knew, the dog you thought was just being a nuisance started really barking, recognizing the shift and change happening out there and knowing in his doggy way that the noise *meant* something. To the alert ear, the whole place could come alive. And why? Why would the night forest now rumble with the rippling after-effects of Jack's toe-kick into a single hickory nut? Because, the forest creatures *lived* there, were born there, with their lives pivoting on their knowledge of the forest's at-peace feel and sound. Jack, in contrast, did *not* live in their world and oh-so little had to shift for them to awaken to his presence.

So, Jack moved excruciatingly slowly forward. He felt for other disturbances on the forest floor, for tripwires, for prongs of anti-personnel mines. (He did not expect mines, but he also did not disdain sound habits.) Jack had cut off a thin, yard-long twig and now felt his way forward, lightly grasping the heavier end of the twig between thumb and forefinger, and manipulating the far tip out, up, down, away and back. If the twig stopped at a taut wire, Jack would feel the "hit" but the low mass of the light twig wouldn't trip the wire. The technique was old, it was low-tech, truly "ana-*log*" Jack liked to joke, but it worked, so long as the patroller proceeded slowly, slowly. Wouldn't help much if the bobby-trap detector twig operator had built too much impatient forward momentum to stop.

In this manner, Jack picked his way toward the hilltop, achieving it after about an hour's stalking. Much of that hour passed with Jack inside the final 30 yards from the camper.

Odd. Jack had heard no sound at all. If rolled into place by lovers, and occupied by the couple resting against each other, Jack should hear shifting bodies and maybe even a drowsy murmur. If occupied by enemy, then Jack expected a sentry. If some sentry watched back, he was a pro: Jack saw and heard nothing from the trailer. His IR detector showed zip infra-red light emanating from the site.

At 100 yards out, Jack had removed the IR detector scope from his pack. Scanning for the enemy's own IR system returned no "hit" as Jack had closed the distance. While the enemy might deploy all sorts of passive detection tech, Jack's insidious approach, his patience, and his IR detector served as his own counter-measures. He expected to detect the human presence behind any deployed technology without being spotted—and, he was confident, no one was here.

That realization struck Jack suddenly. He'd so anticipated *someone* to be at the camper, he was both surprised and—oddly—disappointed. 3:10, the cell phone display told him.

Jack thought the matter over. Sometimes, you just had to get out of tactical-ninja character and take some chances. This was one of those times. No need to get up and start making a racket, but Jack began circling the camper, closing in, keeping a tree between his body and it whenever possible. Finally, he was there. Why not?

Jack tried the door. The handle-latch easily gave way and the door scraped as it opened outward. No sound. No rustle. No explosion of panicked violence from inside. No "Huh? Is that you?"

Jack snapped the red lens over the Surefire's bulb and shone the partly covered beam around. Empty. Jack hardly had time to begin pondering the possibilities when the vibrating cell phone surprised him.

*Outside
Gordon's Lodge*

"Jack here, go ahead."

"Gordon. Anything?"

Not waiting for the answer Jack was about to send, Gordon tensely continued: "I don't think you're likely to find anyone there because, it seems, they are all here. Copy?" Gordon paused.

"Roger, I copy, and you are right. Camper still here, but abandoned. How many do you detect and what's your situation?" Jack was worried.

"Five, I think, and trained too, judging from their approach and the way they move. Here's the plan. You get back here ASAP—watch for an ambush along your most likely approach (You really don't have to tell me that, Gordon.) but get back here! You know my layout in the lodge, but I can't expect to remain hidden here in my surveillance closet forever. These guys are good. They'll figure out my "around the outer wall" passage system eventually and find the monitor room. We'll escape first, but I want to stay by the monitors as long as possible. Agreed?" Gordon paused, breathless.

"Agreed, but what...." Gordon cut him off.

"Get back here, Jack. I want a POW. I want you to get me one, maybe two if you can. The rest—we don't need. Think about it."

Jack heard something different in Gordon's tone—a blend of bitter anger and—fear.

"This is no home-invasion robbery. I'm found out—*somehow.* Somehow, after all this time, I've moved up on the target list and now merit this very delicate operation. This is *America.* Whoever these guys are, someone's force of will compels this operation forward even though the chance of detection is high and the investigative aftermath is catastrophic. They shouldn't be doing this, yet here are these shapes maneuvering around my house and watching, just like you must have been approaching the camper. I want you back here."

"Right. What then?"

"Get to the escape tunnel hole behind the lodge so I can assure it's not been compromised, and then let me know you're in position. Way I figure it, they've got numbers on their side, but we have advantages too. They *think* they have achieved surprise. I have them under watch and have a mobile killer out there in their midst. That would be you, Jack. You will have eyes on and you and I have commo. They're dead," Gordon pronounced.

Jack thought Gordon's eulogy a bit premature, delivered perhaps more as cheerleading than as prophecy, but he said nothing, except to reply: "Wilco, I'm moving. Out."

Speed is a form of security. The adage played hopefully in Jack's thoughts as he raced back over his return steps. He violated tactical movement security, but, sometimes, the situation demanded such desperate, creative flourishes and knowing how to recognize those times sifted the operators from the inexperienced. Wooden soldiers simply reverted to the book regardless.

That would work: after all, explosive, gut-wrenching stress caused men to revert to their lowest level of proficient training. Reverting to the tried-and-true wasn't the worst response.

However, grander principles guided the professional warrior, if only he would listen. First, he had to drill to proficiency in the basics and beyond. Then, drawing from both training and experience, he had to learn to understand his changing situation; otherwise, his training became his own trap, his own self-inflicted ambush. History illustrated this principle over and over. Combat threw so many variables into the cauldron of spastic violence that no one could choreograph the outcome. The experienced—and open-minded soldier—spotted the aberrations and called them "opportunities." He saw the plan evolve, evaluated the demands and openings of the moment, and even abandoned his doctrine when required. Sometimes, he threw caution to the wind.

Jack ran full out down the approach trail, racing pall-mall away from the camper. He held back just enough speed to account for the uneven woodland path. He re-traced his approach trail, violating that principle too, which, if he had followed the rules, put him on some other more random, less-expected and different return trail. Once back on the bike, he pedaled furiously.

"Speed is a form of security," he muttered aloud, hoping somehow that uttering the lesson learned from the tough-looking Ranger Staff Sergeant long ago would make it come true. The increased risks of pounding down the trail with no flankers, no noise discipline and in full violation of the other movement tactics that were stock-in-trade for the Infantryman—the need-for-speed overrode them all and Jack biked all-out back toward the lodge. He did not know how well Gordon's defenses would hold, and, even now, black shapes could be forcing an entry and closing in on Gordon's and Donna's sanctuary.

Fighting back the horror that the enemy were all gathered for a slaughter party up above, Jack braked at the farm gate and dragged his bike into the weeds. He tore into the equipment pack for the tools he'd need.

First, he slid the Glock's Kydex paddle holster onto his belt, pulling the pistol out to feel it's "round-in-the-chamber" indicator knob sticking up like a little friend. He replaced the gun gently to reduce the faint, plastic-to-steel "snap" which told the shooter the gun was again secure in the form-fitting "retention" holster.

Next, he retrieved his Surefire, dropped to his knees, stuck his face and the lamp-end of the light down to the earth, and twisted the tail-cap just until the bulb lit, then backed it off a quarter turn. This readied the light. Holding it between his left index and middle fingers, with the tail-cap switch pressed against the fleshy base of the thumb, pulling backward slightly with the two fingers fired up the brilliant light. Mating the left hand holding the light in this way, with the right hand wrapped around the Glock, Jack combined the two into one unit: gun and weapon-light. It's hard to hit what you can't see. The amazingly bright Surefire is a weapon in its own right. A hunter had scared off a charging bull moose by blinding the beast with his Surefire. At least, that was the legend.

Jack confirmed the presence of his blackened steel combat folding knife, clipped in place in his right front pocket.

POW's. Gordon wanted POW's. Jack pulled from his pack four, foot-long, plastic, electrical wire-ties, bought from the local hardware store on the way up to the lodge.

Finally, Jack checked his cell phone for battery and signal. He'd like to text Gordon that he had achieved the old farm boundary, marking the edge of Gordon's acreage, but Jack's desperation to get back and fight for his friends impelled him to hold that call.

He'd obey orders, find, and secure the escape tunnel opening, and check in then. Gordon was right. With Gordon on the inside, covertly watching the enemy, and Jack freely moving on the outside, the enemy were in trouble.

Jack was in a mood to kill. He thought of Donna, huddled in the surveillance control-center room. He figured Gordon was good protection, but wanted ever so much to make it to her side. Jack would do that, but by carving his way first through the evil men who would kill her.

Jack turned into the woods, and began picking his way uphill. He'd gone no more than 10 yards when he stumbled into the guard.

The guard may have chosen his hiding place because of the woodchuck hole Jack had "found." The watcher sprang on Jack. Jack turned to his left, avoiding all but a slash across his skull. Blood ran like a hydrant. Damn! Any cut on the face or head bleeds like a stuck pig. The blood loss would not impair Jack—it was not enough volume even to notice—but blood dripping into the eyes would, and of course, once you introduced blood into the fight, everything became slippery.

The man fought for Jack's throat with his left hand, seeking to plunge the right-held blade into Jack's mid-section vitals. The men rolled, struggling for the advantage. Jack steeled his mind for more cuts, gripping the man's right cuff tightly to control the knife. He had to control the knife! He thrashed the man's right arm hard back and forth, trying to shake the knife loose.

Only grunts pierced the night as the men grappled in silence, neither knowing whether the other had reinforcements close by and both knowing that they fought this combat alone. Jack bit into the man's left wrist as the man tried to lock his arm around Jack's throat to begin strangling the lifeblood from Jack's brain, his hands unprotected by gloves. This omission—and Jack's teeth—cost the attacker his life.

Jack felt the arm loosen from his throat just a bit. Instantly, Jack thrust his own left arm upward and close in to his own chest, guarding his throat now with his own gloved wrist. Jack also swiveled his body to the right, carrying the man with him and—just for a second—putting the man off-balance. Jack rolled him over onto the man's right side, temporarily smothering the flicking, searching knife blade. That's all Jack needed.

Jack's right hand knew the path: he grasped the combat folder, waiting loyally for its own frantic, fateful moment, pulled it upward and flipped his wrist outward. Jack heard and felt the blade lock into place. Completing the natural arc, Jack's knife-holding right hand picked up strength and speed, arcing clockwise downward, rounding the six-o'clock position, to return upward, completing the circle but, now, finding the man's groin first, then his bowels. Jack felt the knife slow as tendon and bone resisted it; he urged more force from his shoulder and back muscles and felt the knife jerk through the tough tissue and into the soft lower belly.

Immediately, Jack was free. He smashed his gloved left hand into the man's mouth, stifling the stirring scream. The man—probably instinctively, if men had instincts—bit down hard, but the Kevlar armored Jack's hand and he sensed only bite pressure, not pain. Jack shoved his body weight behind his arm and hand, stuffed into the man's mouth. The sentry's lungs and throat tried so hard to howl with terror and pain, but to no avail. Jack finished the job now, completing the circle by slashing deep across the front and side of the man's throat, to catch the jugular vein. Jack collapsed on top of the man's now lifeless body and lay prostrate atop him, exhausted.

Get up! Check around for others! Forcing his own recovery, Jack checked the man's weapons and pockets. No papers, nothing to ID the dead man, but Jack had not expected to learn who this man had been. Jack searched for something on the man that he might use up the hill. He could search for intel later; right now, he aimed to resume the attack and needed whatever this corpse might now offer.

The man's fixed-blade dagger was gone, lost in the struggle, but Jack pulled an Uzi Mini from his back. "Upgrading" weapons made Jack nervous; the Mini Uzi is a fine weapon, but this one belonged to someone else. Jack had no idea how it had been maintained or tested. The former owner could have been a shooter or he could have last fired the Uzi three years ago. Jack had no way of knowing and no way to test-fire the weapon himself. Odd that the Uzi, a fine weapon, rarely made the international scene in black operations, carried mostly by the Israelis who revered it.

Jack searched for and pocketed the extra magazine he figured the man carried, and checked chamber: one 9mm round, ready to go. He thought the man should have had a silencer and, if he had, he'd still be alive and Jack would be dead. He slung the Uzi, stock folded up, tightening the sling across his back. His Glock with 18 rounds ought to suffice, though.

The man's other pockets yielded nothing of use: a now-squashed Butterfinger bar, a flashlight of lesser quality. There! He almost missed it: the man's cell phone. It might provide a wealth of clues later, but might also provide him an opportunity to deceive the enemy during the attack Jack was about to inflict on these bastards. He couldn't find its "silent" mode; Jack powered it down and thrust it into his pack.

Jack dropped into the thick brush just off the track, and moved about ten feet into the thickets. He dropped to one knee, forced regular breathing, and listened. He heard nothing. Maybe the man had made a cell phone call. Jack retrieved the phone, powered it up, cursed when it played some cheesy tune, and checked its "dialed" registry. No, the last call dialed from the phone was yesterday afternoon. Maybe he still had surprise on his side. He must have caught the guard off-guard and left him no time to report in. The guard should have had a text message ready to go. Jack padded 20 feet deeper into the woods, still breathing heavily, and got onto his own cell phone, pressing "Send" and praying Gordon was still alive to answer.

"Gordon."

"Jack here. Came across an ambush at the gate—one man jumped me—he's dead now."

"OK. Think there are others nearby?"

"Not here, and I hear no one. He had a phone, but he did not use it to report me."

"Jumped you?" Gordon sounded surprised and a bit absent at the same time.

"Yes—he paid the price, though." Hell, Jack wasn't some kind of Crouching Tiger, or Hidden Dragon, or Crouching Dragon, or—whatever—superman. He'd raced back, sacrificing his own safety to get back to Donna and Gordon. No need to get critical of his techniques.

"Of course. Call again when you achieve the tunnel entrance. We're OK for now, Jack. They're circling, looking for their entry, but they are not close to the hole. I'll tell you if one of them gets too close to the hole as you approach. I'll see you once you're about 50 yards from the lodge."

"Roger."

"Out." Jack's phone went silent; Jack was already moving again.

This time, he moved away from the trail altogether. He was just too close to the objective to risk it, he'd already been ambushed once as punishment for using the roads, and Donna and Gordon were safe for the time being.

Jack recalled the terrain he now stalked over from the drive onto Gordon's property and from the earlier recon walks. Before him, and inclining upward, spread a mostly open meadow, dotted by low trees, branches trimmed up to about a man's height. The meadow stretched up about 80 yards and fanned out to as much as 100 yards wide. At the top of the meadow, the same farm track Jack had just left behind him doubled back around on its way further uphill and to the lodge, looping to Jack's front and passing through the old timber-framed barn that adorned the hilltop.

The barn commanded the meadow, looking like it had its chest puffed out, silhouetted against the night sky. Jack skirted to the right, keeping inside the tree line, out of sight from the barn to his left. The barn was an obvious danger area—too obvious. Only the untrained would choose it as an LP/OP (listening post-observation post) but only the untrained would assume it to be vacant and waltz right up. Jack saw no reason to check the barn out so long as he avoided it. He had another objective.

Jack worked further up the hillside through its cover of scruffy cedars, moving quickly through their midst, coming out on another cleared ridge where the farm road continued its winding way to the lodge.

Jack crouched and tiptoed easily just inside the tree line along what was now a ridge, the road to his side, until the ridge narrowed to the point that he was forced either off the ridge or back on the exposed road surface. The lodge now lay only about 100 yards away, through the trees. Between Jack and Donna, only steeply rising ground and thickened brush—and killers—blocked the way. Jack gritted his teeth and ducked into the brush.

Jack slowed. Now he chose his footfalls deliberately, working with each twig and briar that reached out to grab him. He had to work his way along the ridge contour, lodge ahead and toward his left, farm road and driveway immediately to his left, steep valley below to the right. Jack spent the next 20 minutes fighting the impulse to plunge ahead to get to his friends. No urgent call vibrated to speed him forward. He'd thought Gordon might be one of those antsy controllers, calling every 10 minutes to urge him on, but the phone behaved and stayed quiet. Gordon must have realized how long Jack would spend stalking. If desperate, he'd call Jack. They would change the plan and Jack would have to hey-diddle-diddle-up-the-middle in full, suicidal, Hollywood, frontal-assault, he supposed—the frontal assault dreaded by all infantry. For now, both men accepted the greater need for stealth to maintain secrecy and surprise.

Jack picked his way upward, spying another lighter shade of gray ahead, signaling another opening in the trees ahead.

Here, Jack stopped. Gordon hadn't called to announce some

desperate charge by the shadowy enemy; he'd have told Jack if the lodge had been penetrated. Jack took his time. A hasty crossing here would blow the element of surprise Jack counted on to outbalance the enemy firepower. He might even carelessly lead the enemy to the tunnel entrance, if not cautious.

Jack recalled some recount of the Persians taking Babylon. They'd discovered an unused old tunnel into the city and, while the Babylonians reveled in some huge party, interrupted by God's handwritten pronouncement of doom, that same night the Persians slipped in and—well, Jack knew that no sterilized account of some ancient storming of a city could clean away the bloody cruelty of those ancient conquerors. He didn't want those—whoever they were up there outside the lodge—replicating that surprise breach. Now was not the time for him to go blundering up to the escape tunnel entrance.

Jack listened. Hearing not a sound, Jack crept to the edge of the woods, dropping first to all fours, and then to his belly for the final 10-foot approach to the clearing. He had to cross this strip to get into the woods on the other side that would then mask his approach to the tunnel entrance on the back side of the lodge. Leaf litter and twigs worked their way underneath his belt and into his underwear. Same damned thing happened every time. He should use some duct tape or something to seal his crotch off from the earthy, surface detritus. Here he was again; begging the ground for protection, low-crawling in the night, pants scooping up God-knows-what. He'd learn someday.

Shadows moved like slow-motion lava lamps; then they didn't seem to have moved at all. Night: his friend, but no tame friend. A mysterious friend. Maybe not a friend at all. An ally? An ally only if you knew how to use it, and only if you didn't let it freak you out.

Long ago, Jack, the child, had feared the dark. His father died when Jack was only three and no man had stepped in to introduce the young boy to the wondrous, wild, ways of the woods. Jack did it himself. Shamed by his fear of the dark, 8-year-old Jack stepped outside one night without telling anyone, and spent the next two hours probing the night, crawling through the hedges, clinging to the shadows and, at the end, just resting beneath the rosebushes, listening to the sounds of the night. When the last light in his house switched off, Jack slipped back in, shimmying up the old television antenna mast, across the roof, and into his room through the open window. Never, again, had the boy feared what might lurk in the night. *He* lurked in the night and his enemies and the enemies of those he loved should fear the night.

Jack gathered his leg and arm muscles to spring forward. He crossed this "danger area" using a modified method taught in Ranger School, a method he and his men learned to deploy naturally, like a dance step. Keeping his time exposed to the low level of ambient light to a minimum, Jack would suddenly dash across. If he'd been leading a patrol, one man would have crossed first to recon and—if all were clear—would signal the patrol leader to cross. The rest would have lined up along the edge of the danger area, and, on signal, would all dart over simultaneously. If some machine-gunner was set up with finger on the trigger to ambush the patrol shooting down the road or clearing to "enfilade" the discovered patrol, he'd have to react fast. They'd be exposed to fire in the "kill zone" less than a second.

Jack sprang up and out and, on toes, darted across the 20-foot expanse of grass, ducking into the opposite trees. He immediately worked his way inward and toward the lodge about 20 more feet and went prone to listen.

Nothing. If he'd been seen, they were real good. He didn't think they were that good. The odds of spotting his dark figure during the second-long rush were poor, indeed. Jack's heart pounded and he heard every course of blood through the veins in his temples. Breathe! Breathe.

Now, Jack started his approach to the tunnel entrance hole, on all fours, hands and feet picking a silent path forward. He began circling the portal, wary as a cat for any sign that the escape was compromised. There was the furnace. The hole lay 30 feet away.

Jack crawled close enough to be sure he could keep the tunnel observed and pulled out his cell phone. He text-messaged Gordon: "N psiton all clear."

Donna's eyes smarted. She'd monitored the six small TV's now for what seemed like hours. For the hundredth time, her eyes swept over the cramped space she and Gordon—and Gordon's security equipment—occupied. She had stationed herself in a room only 6 feet wide and 12 feet long, shelves all along one wall, with moveable panels at each end. This room hid behind two bedrooms connected by a closet that opened into the main room. From the greatroom, people saw louvered doors concealing visitors' coats and a stack of board games.

Behind the innocuous coat closet, the framers had reserved the six-foot passage, assuming the owner would next install heat-and-air equipment, or the hot, new, entertainment equipment so many customers with money wanted. A bit odd, they'd thought, leaving this sized chamber, but maybe this owner planned some exotic system they'd not even heard of. They didn't care. They framed it in and left.

Likewise, the drywallers hadn't given the corridor much thought either, only bothered by the number of electrical outlets they had to work around. Everyone was putting in these big-time "control the whole house" remote systems and entertainment media centers and it appeared like this one would be a doozy. Maybe someday *they'd* have a sound system like this one.

Gordon peered at a screen next to Donna. Wires ran along the shelves, exposed but bundled neatly. Her chair was comfortable enough but hours in this room got on her nerves.

Donna's uncle had awakened her softly at about 1:45 a.m., signaling her with his hand motion only. She'd noted his M-4 carbine slung across his chest and the night vision goggles. Donna didn't have to wonder what was going on: they'd rehearsed the drill. She did not know the "Who or why?" but someone sought entry. Gordon had detected them. Gordon was setting up in the watch room. She'd marveled at Gordon's preparations and romanticized about what it would be like to remain aloof from a siege and in control, but now, mostly she felt irritated, her sleep interrupted. Now, several hours later, she felt the cage closing around her.

That sensation faded quickly. They'd coop up unseen here and watching for awhile, but Gordon's house incorporated movement, maneuver and escape, too. Those who knew the passages could pass from one room to another around the entire house, unobserved by invaders keeping to the greatroom and kitchen area. You'd have to be quiet and you'd have to make sure one of the perimeter passage rooms didn't become suddenly shared with the enemy, but you could literally move all around the inside of the house and work your way toward one of three escape portals. To plan the escape—

or your own attack—you could station yourself in the watch room, settle in, and monitor the video.

That's how they'd tallied the five men moving in on the assault. The outside IR camera first picked up the shapes, triggering the soft alarm that, in turn, called Gordon's cell phone as he'd programmed it.

"Five men south at 100 yards," the dispassionate voice advised Gordon.

Donna watched the sixth shape appear on the monitor and smiled at Jack's approach. She'd have called to alert him if his path were set with ambush, but all was clear on his side of the lodge, for the time. She'd seen his form work slowly to the escape opening and hadn't been at all surprised when Jack had called in.

The invaders gathered on the south side of the lodge while Jack stationed himself north. Donna assumed that the invading team had selected their place and method for breaking in, and she was right. She watched in increasing fright as two shapes approached a smaller window, some distance from the large panes facing the mountains, and heard the glass shatter through her headphones. Two other men rushed up behind the first two and were in. The two who had breached the house poured through the broken window opening after them and now only one remained outside, on guard, outside the basement.

"A good idea," Gordon said, as if talking to the men he watched. "A good idea to leave one man out to guard and also to maneuver, if need be," Gordon finished his thought, glancing at Donna.

"Thanks for the lessons," Donna replied. "What next?"

"I don't know except that I assume they will begin clearing the house room-by-room. Eventually, they will probably find an entrance to our passageways. Then, they'll figure out we're probably still here and watching them. It'll happen fast then."

Donna shuddered involuntarily.

"Call Jack, Donna, and post him with the guard's position outside. If guard-boy moves Jack's way, then call him again."

Donna hit "Send." Jack answered with a whisper, forced from deeper in the throat to soften and reduce the "whoosh" effect to make even his whisper quieter. "I see you still north, near the furnace, right?"

"Roger," Jack whispered, keeping it to a minimum.

"One man stationed opposite you on south side of lodge, apparently as a sentry. Men inside."

"Any movement by sentry?"

"No, he's staying put. I'll call you if he begins to move toward you, and if I still know where you are. Jack, *four* breached near the fireplace and are in the lodge," she finished, trying to banish the fear from her voice.

Gordon motioned Donna to hand him the phone. "Jack?"

"Yes, Gordon, go ahead."

"Take the sentry out."

"Roger, wilco."

No more need be said. Jack understood the mission and the reason it was imperative to take out the one man remaining behind to maneuver. He could call them again for a SITREP and they'd call him to report if the situation changed—and if they could.

Jack listened. He moved backward, retreating from the tunnel opening, back into the forest perimeter brush, and began circling back the way that he'd come in—to the east. He'd have to re-cross the open meadow danger area. The grounds to his west lay even more open, mowed routinely, and the driveway approach crossed these grounds. The western approach lacked concealment along that route. This time, Jack repeated the crossing technique, but hurried the whole process more. He wasn't being careless; he now had less time with the invaders in the lodge and needed to kill the guard fast. He relied on Donna's reporting their locations accurately.

"Donna, these guys are now in the kitchen," announced Gordon.

"Getting a midnight snack?"

Gordon loved his niece and appreciated her brave humor. "They don't like what we stocked in the fridge so they're moving on into the laundry room," Gordon ended and looked at her. Their eyes met, sharing the concern. The laundry included a bi-fold door closet and this closet concealed a slide-away shelf unit. This shelf unit opened into the surveillance room—where they sat.

"When they open the closet in the laundry room and then touch the secret entrance, we'll move to the exit and prepare to make our run," Gordon stated the plan.

"OK. I understand. In the meantime, I'll keep Jack posted and then let him know when we have to bug out."

Donna checked the monitors. The IR still showed only one man plus Jack, already back across the open ridge top and circling toward the guard. Donna knew that the IR camera swept only about 35 feet of range on a pitch-black night like this and it was possible that others were stationed in the woods, but she couldn't see them if off the screen and, so, couldn't do anything about them. Gordon had delivered the same briefing to Jack as to her so Jack knew the system's limitations too.

She watched in fascinated horror as Jack's shape closed on the guard. The guard remained in place. She could not tell which direction he faced but Jack would soon close within such a short distance that he'd see the guard. She pressed "Send." Jack's phone vibrated. Jack answered, saying nothing.

"You're within 40 feet of him. Copy?"

Jack tapped the phone three times near the microphone hole to signal "Roger." He thanked Donna inwardly, but had the man under watch, too close to speak.

Jack worked out his plan. This would be simple. Easy? Probably not, but simple, straightforward and lacking in fine tactical graces. Jack saw little choice. He could slither a few feet closer but saw no way other than to take the man in a sudden rush. He'd toss a stick to the man's front and side as a last-second attention-shifter and use his knife, but he planned to run full-out at the man and cut his throat quickly. Jack would either succeed and maintain their surprise, or he would kill the man but make so much racket that the other four inside would know.

Jack, on his belly and making himself as much a part of the earth as possible again, clawed his way forward like a tiger preparing to spring. He'd read that man-eaters in India always crept up on their man-meals from behind and covered the last feet in a sudden, quiet run, taking the prey before the man could turn to confront. Supposedly, you could ward the man-eaters off wearing a mask with a man's face and eyes, but on the back of your head. Absurdly, Jack thought of this now as he gathered his own muscles to rush.

Jack raised the broken limb piece he carried, preparing to throw his cellulose distraction-device during the first fraction of a second into his rush. The guard—short carbine of some kind in hand—turned southeast and then rotated on around, facing the entry hole his comrades had breached only minutes before.

Now!

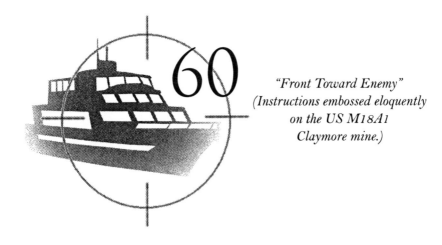

60

"Front Toward Enemy"
(Instructions embossed eloquently
on the US M18A1
Claymore mine.)

Gordon's low voice shook Donna. Why now, with Jack only five yards from the guard?

"Time to pack up," Gordon stated, as if announcing departure for returning home from a beach vacation.

Donna left the monitor with Jack where it was and glanced at Gordon's view. The screen showed three forms, one facing rearward for security and the other two beginning to tentatively explore the laundry room walls. They'd come to the bi-fold door and signaled each other. It looked like one would follow the other on some version of "the stack." In just moments, they would, signal each other, and fling back one of the bi-fold sections and stare at—the washer-dryer. They'd probe the room and—as Gordon had warned earlier when showing the two the lodge's secrets—they would almost certainly, eventually, detect the latch to the hidden passageway door at the closet's end, under the shelf. The men flashed light beams from pencil flashlights. The beams played on the laundry walls.

Donna looked to Gordon for guidance. Gordon took one last look at the other monitors and began switching them off.

Donna panicked. How could she "leave" Jack now? Yet she had to get out. Gordon came to the monitor showing Jack so, so close to danger, glanced over at the only remaining screen showing the men touching the panel entrance, and switched both off. Gordon reached up with both hands and simultaneously pressed two, large, red buttons, placed about a foot apart and bearing no label.

"Time to go, girl," Gordon said, smiling grimly." We have 20 seconds to exit."

Donna's heart sank. She felt like she was abandoning Jack. She'd call as soon as they distanced themselves from the invaders who were now poised to discover them.

Jack gathered both thighs and launched himself up and forward, rising to his toes to sprint the short gap between killer and prey. No stray thoughts played in his mind. Knife open and gripped in right hand. Chunk of wood already leaving his left fingertips to arc toward the lodge.

As Jack closed the last few feet the chunk collided with the lodge siding, and the guard's head snapped around, the chunk doing its job. Jack's timing was perfect. The man did not have time to perceive the trick *and* react before Jack's left arm encircled his throat and Jack's body slammed into him. As soon as the chunk flew, Jack launched his body into another form of missile. Ideally, Jack's chest would slam into the man at the same time Jack's left arm would trap the throat. The weight of Jack's now-dropping body would crumple the victim, whose own very-soon-to-be corpse would reel backward and down under the weight, head levered sharply forward by his attacker's chest, air cut off by the throttling arm. Jack's enhanced version of the brutal "rear strangle takedown" added the knife, readied for the finishing throat-slash if the takedown failed to snap the man's neck as designed.

Jack felt the cervical spine grind and give way at about the C5 vertebra, heard the muffled "snap," and knew the knife's throat-cutting finale was not required. The man went limp. Jack lowered his body the rest of the way down, vise-gripping the throat still with his flexed left arm, but heard no sound force past the arm. The man died instantly. Good.

Jack sprang back, disengaging from the kill and crouching low, snapping his head back and forth to check 360-degrees around. The chunk had collided noisily as planned and, while the takedown had broken the night's silence with only muffled thumps, the chunk hitting the concrete lapped siding, and then bouncing off the concrete pad patio had made what sounded to Jack like a horrendous din.

Jack spied the open, sliding-glass, basement door, already knew that the patio offered no concealment, and stepped through the breach.

Donna watched Gordon's back disappear, the man appearing to her to vanish into thin air. Gordon's passage entry and exit points were clever and the mind still did not see portals, even though the eyes passed on the information. She followed Gordon closely, glancing back at the monitor as if it wanted to tell her Jack was OK. What had happened? The tapping, thumping sounds on the portal panel at the other end of the narrow corridor commanded her attention and she pulled her own panel back into place, leaving the invaders to puzzle over the equipment. She wondered at their most likely reaction. It almost wouldn't matter. Switching the monitors back on would delay them. Turning to run would stymie their search. Pausing to figure it out would likewise buy Donna and Gordon time.

Donna worked herself through the bedroom and followed Gordon into the closet, where the next portal leading to the office waited. From the office, they would step onto a spiral staircase to the basement, tread their way through the basement to the storeroom, into the corner housing HVAC equipment and water heaters, and then vanish into the tunnel. She could touch Gordon's shoulder. She followed her silent uncle out of the closet. Gordon emerged ahead of her, into the office. They were alone; the room was not compromised. In the corner, the spiral staircase wound down, beckoning them to the next escape leg and they began padding their way carefully down its carpeted treads.

61

Nothing. Good.

Jack had seen entering the house as risky but also as the most secure tactic at the time. He couldn't stay outside where he'd just raised cane and killed a man. If anyone else lurked in the woods and off-monitor, he might have heard the chunk hit. Besides, Jack *wanted* in. He'd not heard from Donna and worried that the two might have gotten trapped inside somehow. He listened.

Shit!

The explosion tore his nerves, briefly making a shambles of his carefully incubated cool, maintained up to now. He knew the flash-bang would explode after Donna and Gordon abandoned the surveillance room but that knowledge couldn't prevent his natural response to the deafening blast. Jack wanted to use the bathroom. A half-bath with toilet was right over there. Jack's nerves returned to something akin to normal and Jack smiled at the thought of taking a bathroom break.

Again, he listened for the aftermath of the grenade going off. The men who had just been flash-banged would make excellent targets just now and the plan formed almost as if it was alive and independent of Jack. He scanned left and right trying to recall the exact basement layout.

Gordon's basement was finished—not left rough—and housed an open expanse of concrete floor, unbroken by vertical supports. Gordon had pointed to the ceiling truss system and, with obvious pride, had explained that he wanted floor space for entertainment, ping-pong, exercise equipment and parties in general. A bar waited at Jack's left, at the end of the open "rumpus room" space. Storage shelves—concealing the tunnel portal—faced him from the opposite wall at the back of the basement, and Jack turned to the right to look at the landing for the spiral staircase to the office. This was a bit tricky.

He needed to get upstairs fast to catch the rat-bastards before they began to recover from the shock of the flash-bang. Depending on where they were when the grenade exploded, they could begin to cut through their daze and re-emerge into the situation in as little as a minute. Adrenalin would assist them. Their brains would fight to remind them they were in battle and neurons would be screaming warnings now that the men were both detected and disabled, while the enemy hunted freely. If right by it at detonation, they'd be out of the fight, but any variable could reduce that time so that they might come out of it enough to fight in five minutes. Jack needed to be on them before that. He planned to get his POW upstairs.

Yet, somewhere in the house, Donna and Gordon sheltered in the escape passages and prowled. Jack saw this as a dangerous time and the three had not worked out a plan for this. How would they "link up? He had assumed (bad word, that one) that they would get out and he would rejoin them outside, on the north side of the lodge, at the escape tunnel exit.

Donna kept one hand on Gordon's shoulder as they began twisting their way down the staircase, and, with her right, prepared to press "Send" again. Gordon halted, and they both listened as they heard something weighty hit the side of the lodge below and to their right, from where the guard had waited the last time they'd seen him on the screen. They heard muffled thumps and then—nothing. Donna's mind spun and she fought the panic down. Jack!

Gordon stood stock-still. Donna's heart raced, but she moved not one muscle. After what seemed forever (but could not have been more than two minutes), the explosion rocked the lodge. She stifled a scream when the flash-bang grenade erupted behind her, leaving her shaken and breathless, but still hanging onto Gordon. Jack would probably find that man, still dazed, and ready to be—finished off. Maybe Jack would keep him for questioning. She'd forgotten the flash-bang—even knowing about its timer in advance. Even Gordon had jumped, although he must have timed their escape and must have known the grenade would explode any second. She thought he'd stopped because of the unknown noise below. He must have, and then stayed stationary because of the grenade set to go off any time. My God! Donna's frayed emotions began to loose their grip on her, having done their job and somehow perceiving that she was still alive.

Donna's left hand felt the pressure between her and Gordon's shoulder lessen slightly and Donna knew Gordon was on the move again.

62

Saya-dar listened sharply at the explosion breaking the early hour peace, and frowned. No part of his plan included any such device or noise. Success demanded silent throat-slitting, or silenced shots, and, then, a covert exit. He would not only work his revenge; if anyone controlled this Gordon, the Shade's vengeance should cause him to quake with fear at the invisible reach of The Shade. This underworld-like, death-in-the-night terror wreaked its spine-jellying effect only if his men slipped out undetected, leaving Gordon dead.

Yet, muffled, early morning, dark carried to his ears the distinct shatter of an explosion, from exactly the direction of the enemy's lodge.

Saya-dar always was so careful. That's how he'd remained undetected by the West despite casting his shadow on so many kidnappings and bombings, beginning with Leon Klinghoffer. That one had led the Americans all over the Mediterranean and had chopped a rift between America and Italy, exposing the greater split between the ways the Western countries eyed the Muslim Middle East.

Saya-dar delighted when Italy let the attackers go. He understood what this meant, not just as a fleeting headline victory, but also at the *soul* level. The soul of Europe feared the Muslims. They would squabble among themselves but they had finally warred themselves out, spending their blood and youth on too many causes, unable to call to arms now that the Caliphate rode its borders and raided, once again.

Saya-dar reminded himself that the Americans had captured Abu Abbas in Baghdad in 2004. Abbas was his Captain in the Klinghoffer kidnapping and murder 20 years earlier. The Americans had their own patient timing and seemed not to just forget. Raiding terrorist houses in Baghdad, they'd netted Abbas, after all this time! (Do you recall that fighting in Iraq is not supposed to have anything to do with fighting terrorism?) The PLO lawyers argued that time had expired on the Abbas prosecution pursuant to our own peace accords. Once again—Saya-dar remained the shadow in the background. Saya-dar recalled, uncomfortably, that Abbas had "died" after 11 months in captivity, in the hands of the Americans. Saya-dar did not want to meet the same fate. He wondered what Abbas had told his captors who were there when he "died."

Saya-dar's signature was that he left no signature. He frowned. Why, again, was he here, 400 yards from this American's lodge?

Saya-dar wanted close-in on this one. He'd instructed a capture, if possible, so that he could personally kill his enemy. Saya-dar directed so much death, and had come to take less pleasure in the numbers maimed by others. He, too, could send Americans to Hell. The camper had perched atop its observation hill for five days and Saya-dar sensed the time-lag exposed it to curious eyes—not that anything happened to draw anyone's attention, but, shifting position just in case was a good tactic. Besides, Saya-dar had wanted in on this one. He'd wanted closer to the action, which—he reasoned—would all take place inside the lodge anyway.

393

So, he'd abandoned the camper and its line-of-sight vantage point for a position closer to the action. Saya-dar and his driver, Hussein, pulled off the road and behind a stand of scrubby trees, and waited down in the valley where even the moonlight—had any beamed through the night—failed to penetrate. Hussein had set up the ground-surveillance radar while Saya-dar donned a headset to control the operation by radio. The two sat in folding chairs at the back of their Ford Excursion, hatch open.

Now what? Would the explosion, muffled as it was by the lodge, awaken others in their own homes? He must assume so.

"Hussein, what did you hear?" Saya-dar asked, wanting to know the sound's intensity to a man with nothing on his ears.

"To me, the explosion sounded very loud, although deadened somewhat as if inside, oh Sheik." Hussein trained in Afghanistan where various captured explosives—set off during training—gave the terrorists a frame of reference and some comfort around the bombs they would assemble as their stock in trade. "Grenade, per-haps, maybe one of their flash-bangs."

Saya-dar tried again to raise his Captain. Nothing. He shifted in his chair and stood. Saya-dar sipped a drink of water and felt his guts tighten. For the first time in his life, he swayed before the ris-ing panic. His Captain was also his man, his personal bodyguard and servant. Saya-dar had honored the Chechen Captain by renam-ing him *Kadir*—The Powerful—because Captain Kadir possessed the strength of four ordinary men and two soldiers. Kadir also *knew* Saya-dar: who he was, his habits, his movements—and where Saya-dar had secreted the Urn of Judgment. The realization hit Saya-dar hard. He had been foolish to risk the Urn of Judgment attack for revenge. He'd risked not only the operation, but also his own stealth, his future, and his Urn of Judgment. Saya-dar forgot about Allah's wishes.

How could he yet salvage this mess? He apprised Hussein. Hussein returned the stare, dully wondering what the Sheik would do next. In no way was Hussein soldier-enough to go into the blown operation and salvage it. Saya-dar cursed, ordered Hussein back into the Excursion and flicked his hand, motioning "away."

63

*But to the fighting soldier
that phase of the war is behind.
It was left behind after his first
battle. His blood is up. He is
fighting for his life, and killing now
for him is as much a profession as
writing is for me.*
—Ernie Pyle

ack heard movement ahead toward the spiral steps. He side-stepped out of the doorway's backlit background—erasing his silhouette—crouched, and drew his pistol. Jack's hand found the practiced grip, swiftly pulled the gun from its holster, mated his support-hand to the grip, and went to "high ready." For now, the Surefire would wait, Jack checking for any sign that his covert entry hadn't been so covert. Muffled steps on his right. Donna? Gordon? Why hadn't they coordinated?

From Jack's right and ahead, and from around the corner where the staircase landed, action erupted. Even as Jack watched forms leap, and heard the chilling *"Allahu Ahkbar!"* he sprang to intercept. Now, he knew who was who in the black room, and feared he would intercept micro-seconds too late. Jack heard the sickening thud of some heavy weapon landing on bone, but had no time to ponder. Reaching the closest of whom Jack now saw were two black-clad men, Jack leveled his Glock at the man's back and fired four times. The dead man, his spine severed, pitched to the floor in between Jack and his remaining adversary, a scant 10 feet from Jack.

The remaining man, the lead attacker who had sounded the Islamic battle cry, had checked himself immediately upon charging. He'd seen the Americans on the stairwell landing, illuminated just enough by the starlight glowing through the windows all along the front of the basement exercise room. He'd wasted no time. This Syrian's nerves torqued to the breaking point already, he'd charged, screamed his battle cry, and heard Jack's movement, all at the same instant. Aluminum bat already arcing, he'd found Gordon's head even as his arms shifted course. Jack's own, distracting charge swayed the club's path just enough to veer the bat from crushing Gordon's eyes and nose, but the off-arc bat swung into Gordon's skull solidly enough that Gordon crumpled on the landing.

The man kept swinging, now twisting to take on Jack. The barrage of shots fired behind him swelled his fear and rage to frenzy. Strange. He'd heard the shots, felt no pain, and had perceived the shots as muffled, not as the sharp booms four 9mm +P rounds fired in rapid succession within a concrete block enclosure made. The Syrian assassin swung wildly and blindly at the reports, glimpsing the last muzzle flash. Throwing his body into twisting spasm, abandoning any effort to position himself and hold onto precarious balance, the Syrian lashed out with his club toward the flashes. Metallic ring and grip-shock told him he'd swung true enough.

The blow tore Jack's Glock from his grasp and knocked it to the floor, its steel slide un-deformed from the blow. The bat had arced straight down as Jack had begun to shift his aim from the now dead man closest to him to the shouting maniac at the foot of the steps. The bat's tip glanced off Jack's forearm as the bat's mid-section slammed the gun from his now-loosened fingers.

Shit! That hurt!

The man gave Jack no time to dwell on the pain shocking his right arm. The Syrian toppled into Jack as the aftermath of his wild, twisting smashes with the club. Both men rolled over against the wall, away from the doors, fighting to re-gain balance and dominance.

The Syrian's weight pressed Jack's face into the 90-degree, angled corner of the wall. Jack drew his arms in close to his chest, gathered his knees beneath him, and kicked hard with the power of both legs. His feet found traction against the last stairwell tread riser. The thrust propelled Jack forward along the floor just enough to slide from under the Syrian's press. The Syrian thrashed his arms and hands, clawing crazily at Jack to re-grasp the enemy and keep this American under his control. The Syrian panicked, realizing it was too late and that the American had slipped from beneath him enough to get back into the fight.

Strong hands jerked Donna backward. She fell, pulled off balance, and caught her fall on a carpeted stair tread. A boot! Donna seized the leg she'd crumpled against and held. Her scalp fired in pain as the assailant filled his hand with her hair and threw his weight into hauling her up. She screamed, at first reflexively, but prolonging the shriek intentionally, sounding the call for help. A heavy blow from the side to her temple stunned her. She did not know if she kept up the scream or not, awareness punctuated, body reeling drunkenly, thoughts disjointed. She felt more than knew that Jack was down the stairs but somehow she rose up and away. *Jack!* She wanted so to run to him, to cling to him, to help him, yet she drifted upward, limbs immobile, body rising ever upward.

Consciousness coalesced. Donna's wrists chafed and bled. She was handcuffed! A strong man hauled her upward, up the steps, away from Jack, away from the thuds and grunts she heard receding from below. Gordon! Was he alive? This man—whoever he was—had captured her and was taking her away.

"Jack," she shouted, "Jack, Jack...."

Kadir palm-struck her temple again. Donna's shins dragged over the top steps. Her arms strained at the shoulders. She struggled to stand to relieve the strain.

Kadir knew this mission was over but he could not yet know whether he had at least partially succeeded. He'd followed his Syrian assassin as they left the two men downstairs, searched the basement perimeter and found another staircase leading upstairs. This, they had taken, emerging in the kitchen and laundry area. Kadir had stood just inside the kitchen, back turned to the laundry, on guard and providing rear security when the flash bang went off in the room behind him. He'd been temporarily stunned, but had not faced the brilliant flash. The walls buffered the explosion somewhat; he regained composure and senses quickly.

Not so, though, for his Syrian assassin. He'd born the full brunt and was out of the action for all practical purposes. Kadir's quick look-around told him all he needed to know. They were not alone in the house; they'd been watched. No doubt, the occupants even now were working their way out, counting on the grenade to stop their pursuers. Kadir had stepped carefully back away from the surveillance room, suspecting more booby traps, and begun working his way through the great room to try to cut off anyone trying to escape. Leaving the great room and entering the office, he'd seen movement! The shape disappeared as if into a hole.

The battle cry below masked his own movement noise as he had followed down the first spiral stair-treads. He'd heard his other Syrian assassin cry out, just before all manner of commotion below. He stepped down and around, counting on the racket below to distract and conceal his own approach. He smelled perfume and knew a woman was close.

Two more steps. He could see shapes and movement. Then, he saw his assassin, armed with his favorite hollow, aluminum bat-club, charge someone on the lower steps.

Descending, one of the shapes below materialized sufficiently for him to identify her as the female shape, even as he heard the bat knock Gordon out. He froze his reach for the woman, jolted again by the four ear-ringing shots, amplified in the confines of the con-crete-floored basement, but he recovered his composure fast, real-izing that he'd not been the target. Two more steps brought him just behind her. Men grappled below. A dark shape lay to the wom-an's front, at the landing at the bottom of the stairwell. The shots foretold disaster and Kadir knew the enemy had somehow joined him and his men. They were found out!

Saya-dar's orders were to kill all men found other than Gordon—him too if necessary—and to take no prisoners unless Gordon were killed. If Gordon died in the assault, they would still need a pris-oner to persuade to tell them just who this Gordon had been and why his *Arcturus* had sailed into Perdido Cay. He assumed that the skull bashed in by the Syrian had belonged to Gordon, and that Gordon was now dead. He would capture the woman.

Kadir braced himself, reached out, filled his left hand with her soft hair, and pulled up hard. She yelped in pain but yielded instinc-tively, trying to relieve the pain by taking the weight off; her body rose next to his. Kadir struck her a stunning blow, and felt her resistance melt. With his right hand, Kadir expertly flipped the stainless-steel cuffs onto the woman's thin wrists and jerked the cuff-chain hard to make certain they had locked fast. The woman groaned from this new, cutting pain, and began to shout a name. Kadir balled his fist and back-handed a hard strike sideways, intend-ing to smash the woman's mouth but missing in the dark, stum-bling encounter, and landing instead knuckle-to-skull. His own hand erupted in pain. Better be careful until he gets this situation under complete control, he reminded himself as he hauled Donna's 110 pounds upward, bumping the stunned girl against each step. His phone vibrated, but he had to ignore the call.

Kadir had cuffed Donna's arms tightly behind her back. He knew his upward pulls on the cuff-chain controlled his prey, tearing at her shoulder joints and cutting her wrists. The pain guaranteed cooperation so long as the victim stayed conscious and the pressure continuous. His temple blow had almost forfeited that advantage. He did not want to have to carry her as dead weight. Kadir, now at least out of immediate danger from the fighter below, determined to hit no more, at least until he'd gotten his prisoner down the hill and away from the lodge. The woman's lungs heaved in great gasps but she cried out no more. He allowed her stumbling attempts to recover her balance and to stand, using her efforts to reduce his own load, but jerking the cuff-chain as needed to keep her just off-balance.

Reaching the door to the outside, Kadir elbowed the latch, butted the door open, and glanced fearfully behind and around. Seeing no one, he dragged Donna off her feet, outside, and down the short entry steps, across a slim garden space and into the woods.

Here, beside a large metal box with a chimney on it, he stopped, gulping air. Kadir's heavy gasps slowed as he recovered from the exertion. Twisting the cuff-chain, he retrieved his phone and called Saya-dar.

"Coffee, Coffee," he called for Saya-dar in English.

Donna's frayed wrists, bruised shins, and pounding headache could not stop her from marveling at the man asking for coffee at a time like this. What a caffeine addict! Strangely, she wanted a cup, too.

64

At Gordon's Gate

aya-dar's head jerked toward the phone. He'd set it to auto-answer. The phone rested in its cradle, speakerphone on. There, again, Kadir's call sign!

"Stop!" Saya-dar snapped. As the Excursion slid to an abrupt halt, Saya-dar retrieved the phone from its cradle and spoke.

"Cream. Go."

"I have a package and need pickup."

"What has *happened to*—?" Saya-dar stopped. That would have to wait. He could not better the situation now and was transmitting in the clear. "No, never mind. Where can I pick you up?"

"I can be at the barn in five minutes. Can you pick me up there?" Kadir asked, desperate to escape but not even suspecting that his Sheik had been abandoning him.

Silence.

"Can you?" Kadir urged.

Saya-dar weighed the risks. This mission was blown. Shots were fired. Yet, he heard no sounds carrying through the night indicating any general alert. Sound carried so far and clearly in the night—a fact Saya-dar had never fully understood—that he felt sure he'd have heard if anyone around was aroused and checking out the noise. Saya-dar had noted the ambient sounds in the area:

trucks passing on the highway, shattering the still mornings with their "Jake brakes," intermittent other traffic, and even, every once in awhile, some inexplicable gunfire. Raccoon hunters? Saya-dar never had found out, but he'd noted that the area's inhabitants took no special notice. He could not know that, in the rural south, such sounds seemed to just occur as part of the backdrop. A few shots in the night—people learned—did not necessarily mean murder except, perhaps, of some basement-invading possum or raccoon.

Five minutes, Kadir wanted. Amazing how life required a man to make momentous judgment calls on so little information! Kadir was his man, his friend, if Saya-dar had a friend. Besides, in addition to gaining a prisoner, if Saya-dar stayed and waited, he'd extract the man who knew too much about him. He frowned at that thought and, somewhat sadly, knew that, someday, the best team leader and friend he'd ever had must die.

But not tonight. Saya-dar addressed Hussein who was gripping at the wheel and staring at him.

"Keep your lights off. Turn around. Roll the windows down. Drive slowly to the barn-road gate," Saya-dar ordered Hussein.

"Coffee, Coffee?"

"Cream. Negative at the barn. Yes, to pickup at barn-road *gate* as fast as you can get there. Ten minutes at most. Call on close approach for clearance to link up."

"Roger, out," Kadir replied, relieved, and remembering to use the English radio pro-words as agreed, to confuse any intercepting enemy. Kadir now looked at Donna, recovering her breath, and he tugged her hard to her feet. He hissed a vile death-threat in her ear and began circling from the back of the lodge to its winding driveway, past the barn, and to his salvation.

Jack felt the moment he'd slipped the Syrian's grasp. By now, he'd heard the man's curses and prayers in Arabic and had placed the accent. No time to figure out why a Syrian killer attacked Gordon's home outside Knoxville, Tennessee, U.S.A.

There! A voice upstairs! Donna! Calling his name!

Jack flexed his legs backward again, searching for a toe-hold, as he clawed his way forward. He balled his body up and rolled to the side. The Syrian sprang back onto him, but this time, Jack's movement and mechanics evaded the Syrian's grappling moves and Jack rolled to his feet. With the Syrian still trying to get on top of him, Jack gathered his legs for another lunge and aimed his own body at the weight-point he perceived would lever the Syrian up and back.

It worked; Jack tossed the assassin rearward, into a bookcase, sending trophies and books scattering. This freed Jack to dive for his pistol. His right hand still numbed, Jack dove, grabbed, rolled again, transferred the pistol to his "support" hand, and then he fired. Four times? Five times? Later, Jack was not sure, though he discovered that the Syrian caught four bullets in the body cavity, one of which sufficed to stop him immediately.

Jack lay aching and gasping for breath. Donna! Pistol still held in the left hand, he twisted right, then left, then listened. Nothing.

Jack holstered the Glock to free his left hand, breathed deeply and lunged up each step. His head hurt and his right hand throbbed as he flexed it repeatedly, pumping blood to reinstate function and feeling. Jack picked up speed, pulling himself upward with his left hand, bounded up the last steps, and screamed inwardly. *No one! Donna is gone! Think! Think! My God! Think! Please God, please, what do I do? Where is she?* His head throbbed.

Training. Tactics. Revert. Think. Break the problem down into little pieces and handle the first one. Act. *Secure this area, now!*

Jack drew, transferred to the left hand, and secured the landing properly, going to high ready and scanning left and right for targets. He spied the open back door, which he knew led to the woods behind the house. Jack breathed in and out, forcing the rhythm and inducing some oxygenated calm. Moans from the next room drew him. *Make sure the prisoner is no threat.* He raced over, pistol raised, ready to fire. A body—no he was alive—groped and groaned. The flash-bang!

Jack had his prisoner, but he'd lost his remaining wire-ties; he was losing Donna. *Get to Donna. Save Donna.* Jack shot the groaning man once in each kneecap and ran out the back door. Roughly eight rounds left.

Downhill to the barn-road gate! They were heading for the gate. It must be so. The attackers needed a fast escape and he heard no helicopter. They *must* be escaping by some vehicle. A vehicle needed a road. They would not risk entering the property and waiting at the barn. The gate stood out as a natural rally point. The gate!

They had a head-start. Surely, Donna would resist and slow the escape, but they were already gone. He *had* to reach the barn road gate first, or.... Jack refused to think further about Donna's being lost forever.

Yes! Jack saw clearly what he had to do and plunged into the woods on the downhill and front of the lodge, setting course on a beeline—as best as he could figure—to intersect the gate. Branches poked and slapped his face. He'd get there first.

65

*Swinging first and
swinging to kill
is all that matters now.*
—*Ernie Pyle*

Every time Donna held her weight back, Kadir jerked upward on the cuff chain, shooting searing pain through her shoulders and wrists. Only by staying afoot and keeping up could she alleviate the torture.

Donna knew the path. The man was hauling her down the graveled approach-driveway, along the ridge, toward the barn. She did not know that her kidnapper aimed for the lower, barn-road gate, but she reasoned that he intended escape, with her as hostage. She'd *not* be taken! She *must* not be taken! Wrenched shoulder socket aside, a plan crystallized. When the man slowed, she'd lash out with her feet and try to knock him from his own.

What then? She didn't know, but she must get into the woods somehow and run. She stumbled, knees pummeled and now bleeding through her jeans, as they and the road left the ridge for its final descent to the more open and mowed meadow adjacent to the barn. She gathered her courage, for the moment would arrive very soon and she *must* act.

406

Branches flailed at Jack's eyes. He slid, fell, and rammed his face into the shallow dirt, feeling the underlying rock's stony blow to his cheek. Jack arose, dazed, but plunged downslope again, not hearing any movement off to his right side where he thought Donna and the terrorist must be. He could not be too late!

Ahead, Jack saw a lighter tone of purple-dark gray. The barn lot! It must be.

Jack, now fully alert and adrenaline-charged, almost ran full speed into the clearing. Stop! Think! Jack threw himself down prone in the high grass at the meadow's edge and listened. There!

The barn stood old and gaunt, backlit by a steel-gray, mottled sky. Jack smelled coming rain. The barn's central opening, large enough for the old farmers to have pulled a wagon or tractor through and out, stood wide open at both ends. Dim ambient light framed the opening. Through this opening, the barn-road threaded in and out, on its way downhill to the gate. Silhouetted in the opening's far port, shapes jerked spasmodically and disappeared behind the barn.

One hundred yards! He *must* close the gap. Jack scanned left, down the hill the barn sat atop, and ran down this meadow, keeping along the tree line, ducking and dodging low-hanging branches. He reserved just enough speed to avoid tripping in some woodchuck hole, or losing balance and tumbling over his own feet. At the bottom of the cleared hillside, a small apple orchard divided the cleared hillside from the barn-road's lower and final coil, and then—the gate! He'd cut them off. The well-tended orchard afforded fast passage without the usual breaking-brush noise. Someone had cleared stones from the earth's surface beneath the apple trees. Jack felt apples squash beneath his feet and scented a vinegar-like sourness.

Jack spied a dark pile lumped ahead and paused long enough to stoop and grab an old fence post. Breaking it free from the debris,

Jack hefted it, felt its still solid weight, and noted the barbed wire strand wound around its top. Perfect!

Jack kept his Glock holstered and the Uzi slung tightly on his back. Dark of night. Breathless. Running. Donna held hostage and being kidnapped. Target moving and shielded by the woman he— loved. If her captor erred by separating himself from her, Jack would draw and shoot but, otherwise, he could not risk the shot. The knife required Jack to give up distance and get in real close, but the club was ideal.

Jack gripped the cedar post like a rifle and charged into the orchard, this time governing his speed enough only to stay stealthy. He was sure he had intersected their arc and would reach the gate before them. He adjusted course to burst out onto the road yards above the gate, calculating that this terrorist's confederates most likely waited for him on the paved road just outside the gate. Ahead, through the trees, he could make out the lighter-shaded band of pavement. Jack set his mind to kill.

Donna steeled her resolve. Leaving the barn, she knew, left her with only minutes before her captor would reach the gate and, presumably, his extraction. She'd seen the scenes on TV and in the movies: absurdly, she pictured herself tossed into a dark-windowed, plain van with something like "Package Delivery Express" lettered on the side. The image terrified her. The terror fired every response it was designed to, both in her mind and body. Think!

He'd see the van and his men, think himself home free, and his attention would leave her just fractionally. Donna compelled herself to relax just a bit—willed herself to cooperate with his brutal grip on the cuff chain—to feel more submissive in his grip. She strove now to walk upright and more normally.

It worked! As they rounded the last bend before the gate, she sensed his lessening pull on the chain. Eyes wide, she watched for her moment. Ahead, she saw the dark, dimmed form of a truck. *Now! Oh God, help me do this! Now!*

Donna powered both legs, in an instant squatting, then bursting upward and sideways, propelling her body into the man whose hot, sweaty body had parted from her minutely as he caught the truck's form down the road, no more than 100 feet away. Headfirst, she slammed the Chechen into a solid tree trunk adjacent to the trail. The man somehow still held the chain!

Donna thrust, twisted and tugged violently, uncaring of the tearing, cutting pain in her wrists, but the man held, cursed, and began rising to his feet. Spitting invective and reaching into his back pocket, he grabbed another pair of cuffs, glared at her as he shoved them in front of her eyes, and then deftly snapped one to his own wrist and one to the cuff-chain holding hers!

Through the trimmed trees, Jack spied the margin of the orchard—its border with the lower reach of the barn road. Frantically, he scanned through the sparse, remaining trees left and right. Left, he made out the blurred form of some vehicle, attended by two shapes—about only 40 yards away. Right movement cued him to the approach by one—no two more figures, also 40 yards, but to his right. Donna!

Jack adjusted course to intercept and adjusted again, then burst from the apple trees just in time to see Donna slam the man aside. As he closed to 20 yards, the man rose, recovering, and faced Donna.

The Chechen, collecting himself, further gathered his rage to bash Donna's face in. He squared his body, facing her, raised his fist, and froze.

Stunned by the impact of her own attack, Donna had fought with the recovering Chechen, watching him rise like some immortal demon, shrugging off death to resume his foul assault, to escort her into Hell. Donna never saw Jack fly from the orchard, but she froze at his mighty war cry.

Sprinting the last seven yards to her aid, Jack raised his barbed, cedar-post shillelagh and roared. Jack's downward, "wood-splitting" chop-swing picked up power. The barbed end of Jack's heavy fence-post club caved in the left side of the man's head, just above his ear. Kadir crumpled.

Momentarily, Donna could not tell what was happening, but the Chechen's upward pull reversed, weighting her arm back down, shooting pain through her now thoroughly lacerated wrists. The pain threw her perception back into focus. The man lay at her feet! Jack!

Jack crouched before her, wild, searching her eyes. Donna managed a wan smile.

"Squat down on your hands and knees and hold your hands apart on the ground! Now! Do it, Donna, now! Yes. Hold your arms still. Still! Look away, too," he added.

Stooping to give her right arm relief from the Chechen's body-tugging dead weight, she turned her head aside. Multiple shots exploded next to her. The shots stopped. A snap. A rubbing noise. What could he be doing? Donna threw up, watching Jack saw madly at the remaining joint connecting the Chechen's now almost shot-off hand. Over the sound of her own heaves, she heard the final gristle part and felt the weight fall away, freeing her from Kadir, The Powerful.

Stunned, Saya-dar watched his escape fall apart. While Kadir had not yet called to signal his approach, Saya-dar casually opened the Excursion's hatch, then the passenger door, and then climbed in to be driven away. The empty interior-light sockets kept the truck darkened. He shut his own door softly. Hussein stood by the driver's side front fender, first leaning, then standing, when Kadir appeared around the bend with his prisoner. Saya-dar motioned Hussein to assist when the scene erupted ahead. Shots! And then it was over. Whatever exactly had just played out, Saya-dar and Hussein never knew. Bewildered, Hussein hesitated, the roar confusing him. Time ran out for Hussein to figure it all out.

Jack dropped his war club and drew the Glock again. Ahead of him, two targets presented: one immobile, but through a windshield, the other in the open, frozen in inaction, but facing him. Without even having to think, Jack's training perceived the more immediate threat: he closed the distance to about 25 yards and stood, forming a solid, front-facing stance, Glock locked in a stiff, right-arm, tight grip, left hand pairing the Surefire to the gunstock, pulling back in hard, both elbows tucked in tight and firm. The bright beam burned through the pre-dawn dark, painting the man's figure. Jack centered the front sight on the illuminated mass—just a bit high to catch the vitals—and began firing. Not a "pair to the chest" situation this time, Jack filled Hussein full of copper and lead. A bullet burst the heart causing the immediate kill Jack sought, while the hail of hollow-point bullets ripped at Hussein's chest and bowels, except for the stray shot tearing his right ear off.

Thunderclaps boomed to Saya-dar's front, jolting him and propelling him to throw his body into an awkward sideways scoot from passenger side to driver's side. He heaved himself over the console, clinging to the wheel and pulling wildly at it to achieve the driver's seat. Out the open driver's side door, he saw Hussein stumble backward into the truck door, closing it, but not fully. Saya-dar gaped again through the windshield to where only moments before, Kadir, The Powerful, and revenge strode his way. Now, the monster to the front turned to him!

Saya-dar wanted to run, to spring free from the confines of this truck-cage, now trapping him. Cage? Saya-dar recovered enough composure to remember he was in the front seat of a now-idling truck. Saya-dar grabbed for the gearshift, but unable to resist turning to glance at the terrified Hussein. Blood streamed down Hussein's eyes and nose. The sheen of liquid could not mask the horror and death written all over the man's face. Hussein's eyes caught Saya-dar's and implored his Sheik for salvation. Instead, Saya-dar levered into reverse and slammed the accelerator down.

66

Daybreak
The barn-road gate

"Run, run, Donna, run!" Jack was screaming at her. She rose, ran, and fell, the combination of downhill slope and thick brush overcoming her. *Jack lived!* was her last thought before stunned semi-consciousness.

Don't believe what you see in the theater. If you've never shot a pistol before, add that to your list of life experiences. Handgun shooting is hard—particularly when you're shooting at someone who's fighting back. Think through the physics. You're moving and maybe breathing in great gasps. Maybe you're wounded, or wracked with pain emanating from wounds. Your target is moving too, and not at a constant velocity.

The short-barreled pistol in your hand moves its muzzle dramatically with any flick of your wrist. Work the approximate plane geometry: wavering your wrist an inch sweeps the muzzle where the bullet exits the gun even more. Your wrist flick shifts the bullet's impact 30 yards away about eight feet off your intended target. You've missed—by a "country mile." Get the picture?

There are fantastic pistol marksmen in the world, but add combat to an already difficult skill and those running-rolling head shots you see just hardly happen.

413

The Glock's blocky slide locked back, reliably signaling Jack that he had sent the last round from that magazine downrange. Damn! Jack had not reloaded earlier, choosing to forego a "tactical" reload in favor of keeping the partially-full magazine *and* his spare, and choosing to get going. Jack watched the remaining target scoot to the steering wheel as he mechanically thumbed out the empty magazine, pulled another from the holder at his belt, and mated it in smooth motion to the now-empty magazine well in the Glock's handle. He slammed it home, thumbing down the slide-release. Forget the Uzi; Jack could reload the Glock in about a second. The SUV shot backward as Jack resumed his solid grip around the Glock and ran forward after the retreating truck.

Stop! Stop! Saya-dar slammed on the brakes just in time to avoid careening backward into the ditch alongside the paved road. He jerked the gearshift into drive and slammed his foot to the gas pedal again. Saya-dar was away!

Jack lined up the Glock, leading the truck slightly, but checked as lights flickering on in his line of sight signaled the farmhouse and family behind it waking up to the din. He held his fire, running now forward, through the narrow band of trees and brush between the barn road and the pavement to close the gap. Now, the SUV lurched to a gravelly, skidding stop and took off! Jack searched for a shot through the brush separating the barn-road where he stood from the pavement where the truck now accelerated, and fingered the trigger as the SUV left line of sight with the farmhouse. Impossible!

The brush screened his field of fire and Jack heard the Ford speed out of sight. Jack dropped to one knee, then scanned left, right, then behind for threats. Quiet. Lights on in the farmhouse.

ARCTURUS

Siren somewhere in the distance. Sky beginning to glow orange in the East. Left! Right! Behind! Nothing. Perceiving all threats dispatched, he ran back to where he had left Donna. *Donna!*

67

Aboard the Arcturus
Atlantic Ocean,
125 miles northeast of
Miami, Florida
Approaching the Abacos chain,
the Bahamas "Out Islands"
Mid October, five weeks after the
attack on the lodge

"So, man of mystery, where are we going?" Donna asked Jack, knowing he'd smile and not answer.

Gordon, Margarita in hand, eyed Jack with his own smile and didn't care if Jack answered or not. Gordon knew where they were going, and the journey had nothing to do with this or any other destination. *You are on "The Great Adventure" in more ways than one,* Gordon thought, and continued to soak in the breezy Bahamas sunshine.

Jack lounged with feet propped up on the *Arcturus's* forward deck rail, his own Margarita ice-cold in his hand.

"Why, to *the* island, of course!"

"Oh, I *know* that, but *whyyyy?* Donna picked up the tease.

"We shall see. We shall see," was all that Jack would disclose, and that, proclaimed with mock gravity.

The three laughed at the drama.

As sunset closed, they dropped anchor in the cove off the island where Jack had downed the chopper. Jack radioed Chris, confirming their arrival.

"Hey, I want to thank you again for arranging to back us up just in case some *other* unexpected adventure erupts out here," Jack said to his friend in genuine gratitude.

"No problem. You're wise to do so. Besides, I think I'll just follow you around. The most interesting things happen when you're out and about," Chris joked. "We have a chopper standing by and I'm on patrol along the coast only 20 miles from you. We're real interested in seeing what you might troll up. Uncle Sam should be thanking you for serving as bait!"

"We'll call you back when we pull up anchor and leave. Thanks, again, Chris. *Arcturus*, out."

Gordon had spent a week in the hospital at MacDill recovering from his fractured skull. No sooner had the swelling subsided and the doctor released him, than Gordon called Jack. He was eager to talk out what had transpired in the hills at the lodge, eager to see how Donna and Jack were recovering from their own wounds, and eager to "close the deal" with his new recruit.

Jack perplexed him, though. Jack had been oddly non-committal and even a bit eccentric, Gordon thought. Jack insisted that Gordon and Donna accompany him on a return trip to the cove at Perdido Cay, utterly refusing to explain why, except to laugh and tell them he had his own "missions" to accomplish there. Gordon owed Jack. He gave in to Jack's request, and to his own curiosity, and decided to play it out and see what this capable young Ranger had on his mind. Jack had certainly earned his trust.

Thus, unwilling to wait for a more decent hour, the three climbed down the *Arcturus's* hull shortly after sunrise on a glorious Sunday, and climbed the hill to the mission. They passed silently where Harry had been killed, reflecting on his passage. They stood in the opening in the low wall, looking into the now-again peaceful mission. Jack motioned them into the mission doorway. They stood in the cool, shaded interior. Jack wasted no time.

"I was here when the RPG round came flying through the window, and hit here, blowing me over there," Jack pointed to the damaged corner where he'd been deposited and knocked unconscious.

"Before I passed out," he continued, "lying flat on the floor, I turned to try to get up, and saw a hole—an opening not there before. I crawled over, thinking I'd maybe found a tunnel out and we might need it in case this op went Dien-Bien-Phu." Jack grew more excited and started re-enacting his movements.

"I moved aside some rubble and, sure enough, saw stone steps leading down, but that's not all I saw." Jack paused. Gordon and Donna waited for him to continue, knowing he would without prompting.

"Well, I couldn't believe it at first. I'll get to the point."

Jack led the two to the corner, donned thick, leather, work-gloves, and began pulling away pieces of stone knocked loose when the RPG round hit and replaced by Jack to cover the hole. Soon, Jack's work revealed an opening. Using the short pickaxe brought along, Jack widened the opening and scraped more rubble back.

"See, this must have been covered over with just a thin mortar-and-stone layer. This withstood time, but not the RPG going off so close. I used the rubble to cover it back up before I blacked out."

"Why?" Donna asked him, curiosity getting the better of her.

"I'll show you. Let's go," Jack motioned, ducking and squeezing through the opening, leading them down a short, stone, staircase, with carved stone arching so closely overhead that they had to stoop the entire way. The stairs opened into a chamber hewn out of rock, barely lit by the scant sunshine rays finding their way through the chapel and into the hole. Gordon and Donna saw nothing, other than that they stood in a stone chamber.

"Behold!" Jack announced, dazzling them when he lit the room's floor with his Surefire flashlight.

418

ARCTURUS

Later that night, the three sat, spellbound and exhausted in *Arcturus's* luxury lounge, reading the ship journals and notes they found among the trove. McBan's journal, compiled no doubt to celebrate and document his fame later, instead, chronicled the man's treachery and betrayal. Lucy Rand's diary-written hopes and joys brought tears to Donna's eyes, as she imagined this woman—about her own age—on her way to join her lover, John. Instead, Lucy met the cold hand of lonely death, far from either the yearning arms of her fiancée, or the warm wishes and embraces of her kinsmen and friends back in Sussex.

McBan's accounts inventoried the following, entrusted to him by the King:

> 2,282 Charleville muskets, condition good, serviceable
>
> 827 cavalry carbines, condition good, serviceable
>
> 2 crates spare parts for above
>
> 6 cases flints (no powder, no ball)
>
> 10 bags and casks Spanish 8 escudos gold pieces (pieces of 8), counted and numbered at total of 8,248

The letter from the King, stored flat in the bottom of one cask, wrapped in several layers of cotton, and then oilcloth, read clearly and astounded them. The letter authorized McBan to give the muskets in treaty with Pontiac or "…other representative of Indian nations willing to take up these arms against the rebel Americans." The King directed McBan to

> "…spend from this allotment of Spanish gold any sums necessary to secure the good graces and cooperation of the Government of Mexico, strictly conditioned on its pledge to forthwith undertake to drive Americans from its northern territory called Texas, and to occupy so

419

much of that territory further north as it may. You may advise the Mexican government that it may expect to enjoy the benefits of alliance with His Majesty's Kingdom of England, together with all appurtenant to the same."

In short, King George's commission to McBan stated the highest conspiracy by England to re-conquer the United States.

Plainly added later, McBan had supplemented his inventory with a list of furniture, also found stored below, deeper into the chamber. Jack reasoned that the furniture represented the *Queen Indiaman's* passengers' household valuables, selected by them to accompany them in their new life in India to provide some of England's finery in a more harsh land. McBan must have eyed this cargo, appreciated their discerning tastes, and been unable to resist seizing this store as well.

The muskets and carbines remained in surprisingly original condition. All had been stacked horizontally, raised a foot off the floor on wood beams, separated by oilcloth. All were uniformly stacked 8 guns high, 8 guns wide, in 36 separate stacks. Gordon had examined cloth bags holding what had been several pounds of iron filings spread out underneath the stacks, which were all covered by layers of oilcloth, weighted down at the floor. While the iron filings underneath combined with the scant invading oxygen, and rusted away, the oiled barrels and lockwork on the weapons remained dark brown and un-rusted, the filings apparently presenting the easier oxidation target. The cool chamber, sheltered above by the chapel kept the water off.

"My friends, were it not for you and your generous spirit, inviting me along on your placid cruise, I'd be in the classroom right now and never would have been shown this wealth. We'll share," Jack stated as fact.

ARCTURUS

"Chris? Jack."

"Hi, maniac. What's up?"

"Could you do a little gunboat diplomacy and move from 20 miles out to a station just off this cove?" Jack presented his profound request for personal support from the U.S. Coast Guard, probably asking them to insult Bahaman sovereignty—such as it was—and held his breath for the response. Chris surprised him.

"Of course! I'm tired of fishing and slapping drug-runners around! I don't care what my orders are, I'm coming in!" Chris paused for effect, and then added seriously. "Jack, I'm not asking any questions, but I have been ordered to stand by to give you any assistance you request. Seriously. I don't know what you're up to out there, but you have friends." Mi cutta, su cutta, mi amigo."

Jack didn't know what to say. Gordon! This had to do with Gordon. OK.

"In that case, I request that you join us on the *Arcturus*, piped over with full honors due your station, of course, possibly for the next three or so days—and bring two hearty crewmen with you, strong backs and willing hearts. Roger?"

Chris stammered, but quickly ran this unexpected request through the broad scope of his orders. "Aye, aye, sir! Are you in trouble? Is there some enemy situation you need to brief me on? Give me a warning order so that I know what mission to brief my crew on for the next few days."

"No enemy in sight, and I'm sure *Mohawk's* presence here will keep it that way. It's peaceful. Just tell your men three or four days and they'll be back home and get on down here. Please. Oh, uniform for them is dungarees and leather work gloves."

421

"Here I come to save the day. Mighty *Mohawk* is on the way."

"One more thing, Chris."

"What's that?"

"Did you bring whites."

"Huh?"

"Whites."

"Whites?"

"Whites."

"I always have a dress uniform on board. Why a dress-up uniform? You throwing a party? We meeting some native chieftain who needs to be impressed by the U.S Government? Why the whites?"

"Whites. I have a reason, my friend."

"Well, I won't do it."

"Won't do it?" Jack was caught off-guard. "Why not, Chris?"

"Because I'm not in the *Navy*, you simpleton trigger-puller. I'm in the *Coast Guard*, and our dress uniform is *blue*."

Jack just shook his head.

Even with the strong sailors, it took two days to load. At the end, the three paused to rest and celebrate while Chris and his men returned to *Mohawk*, and then they set out again—*Mohawk* following at a distance—linking up with the agent off the coast of Cuba, and bringing the young soccer star back to Miami—this time, without further incident.

Casteneda read in his American newspaper of the defection of the Cuban football prodigy and groaned for his islands. He longed for the day when his people would be free—like the Cubanos and other Americans he'd met. In the meantime, he'd serve *Cuba* and stand, like its *Castello*, not just to guard over Havana's harbor, but to introduce Cuba back into the world—and into the friendship Cuba *should* enjoy with its neighbor lying—massively—only a few miles, yet so, so far, north. Unless Raoul messed it up, Cuba would soon be free of its dictator. Until then, Casteneda would wait, patiently, but not passively.

Ortega and Gordon shook hands. Jack was in; he'd proven himself. For all the drama, though, they'd not found the missing canister. America's enemies were relentless enemies, adaptable, clever, cruel and rich. They had already penetrated "inside the wire" in a way most of America still remained unprepared to deal with. In short, Americans needed Jack whether they knew it or not.

Mohawk stood 12 miles out from the cove, crew on board resting from hard work.

"Two days, Chris, and then, really, we're done."

"We'll be out here. Call me if needed." Chris started to add, "You *will* fill me in on all of this when you're back!" but he assumed the call to be monitored and held his curiosity for cross-examination over champagne later.

"One more thing, Jack."

"Yes?"

"Congratulations to you and your bride. Out."

In the cove, *Arcturus* bobbed at anchor. Jack held Donna's hand as she kicked barefoot at the dancing surf-line.

The End

For many answers to your questions, and for much more information about *Arcturus*,

visit

www.mjmollenhour.com

and click on "About *Arcturus*"

or

e-mail the author from the website.

Printed in the United States
100321LV00002B/109-243/A